Dying
for
Chocolate

ALSO BY DIANE MOTT DAVIDSON

Catering to Nobody

Dying

for

Chocolate

Diane
Mott
Davidson

Bantam Books

New York   Toronto   London   Sydney   Auckland

Book design by Claire Vaccaro
Interior illustrations by Aher/Donnell Studios

ISBN 0-553-08576-X

Published simultaneously in the United States and Canada

Bantam Books are published by Bantam Books, a division of Bantam Doubleday Dell Publishing Group, Inc. Its trademark, consisting of the words "Bantam Books" and the portrayal of a rooster, is Registered in U.S. Patent and Trademark Office and in other countries. Marca Registrada. Bantam Books, 666 Fifth Avenue, New York, New York 10103.

PRINTED IN THE UNITED STATES OF AMERICA

To my parents,
Admiral and Mrs. William Mott

"I wouldn't ask too much of her," I ventured. "You can't repeat the past."

"Can't repeat the past?" he cried incredulously. "Why of course you can!"

—F. Scott Fitzgerald, *The Great Gatsby*

Acknowledgments

The author wishes to acknowledge the assistance of the following people: Jim Davidson; Jeffrey Davidson; J. Z. Davidson; Joey Davidson; Sandra Dijkstra; Katherine Goodwin; Kate Miciak; Karen Johnson and John William Schenk, J. William's Catering, Bergen Park, Colorado; Rob Esterbrook, Respond Security, Denver; the staff of the Evergreen branch of the Jefferson County Public Library; Ted Ning, M.D.; Thomas P. Campbell, M.D.; John Alston, Ph.D.; Heather Pashley; Melinda Thompson; Emerson Harvey, M.D.; Richard Drake, Ph.D., Department of History, University of Montana, Missoula, Montana; Deidre Elliott, Karen Sbrockey, and Elizabeth Green; the Reverend Connie Delzell; Lee Karr and the group that assembled at her home; Triena Harper, assistant deputy coroner, Jefferson County, and Investigator Richard Millsapps, Jefferson County Sheriff's Department, Golden, Colorado.

Prayer book quotations are from The Book of Common Prayer, published by the Church Pension Fund.

Dying
for
Chocolate

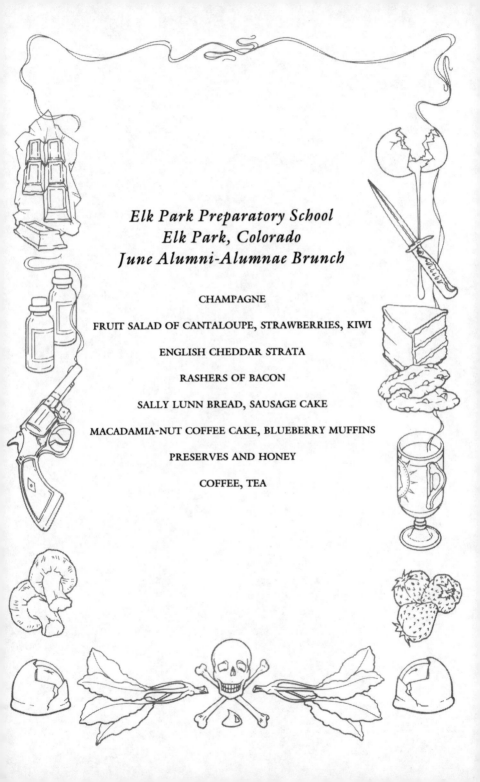

Elk Park Preparatory School
Elk Park, Colorado
June Alumni-Alumnae Brunch

CHAMPAGNE

FRUIT SALAD OF CANTALOUPE, STRAWBERRIES, KIWI

ENGLISH CHEDDAR STRATA

RASHERS OF BACON

SALLY LUNN BREAD, SAUSAGE CAKE

MACADAMIA-NUT COFFEE CAKE, BLUEBERRY MUFFINS

PRESERVES AND HONEY

COFFEE, TEA

1.

Brunch is a killer. I hate it, and among food people I'm in good company. James Beard found the idea of a heavy meal between meals idiotic. He said, "You don't have something called lunny-dinny, do you?"

Actually, the reason professional caterers dislike brunch is that it means getting up at an ungodly hour. As I lay in bed at 4:45 the morning of June 3, I realized that in a little over four hours I had sixty people to feed. There were mountains of fruit to slice. Muffins and breads to bake fresh. Thick-sliced bacon to bring to sizzling. Egg strata to cook slowly until layers of hot cheddar melted over warm custard. And finally, there was coffee to grind and brew. In this case, lots and lots of coffee that I would have preferred to have been drowning in.

With eyes closed, I imagined floating in a warm lake of cappuccino. The cocoon of pima cotton sheets and down comforter begged me to stay, to ignore the upcoming meal.

But no. The lake of predawn consciousness yielded a few troublesome bubbles. The Elk Park Prep brunch was a popular annual gathering to which my ex-husband, Dr. John Richard Korman, might wangle a ticket. This would not be fun for anyone.

Without thinking I touched my right thumb, the one he had broken in three places with a hammer a month before we finally divorced, four years ago. Anyone else would have said, Four years without abuse? You must feel safe now.

But I never felt safe. Especially now.

Here's why. In the last month John Richard had started acting strange. Or rather, stranger than usual. In the evenings he had taken to driving slowly past my house off Main Street in Aspen Meadow. He called repeatedly, then hung up. One afternoon his lawyer phoned and threatened a reduction in child support for our eleven-year-old son Arch. That night, John Richard drove more slowly than ever past the house.

Given John Richard's violent temperament, I'd decided that Arch and I should vacate the house for a while. I'd accepted a summer job. General Bo and Adele Farquhar had just moved from the suburbs of Washington, D.C., to the Aspen Meadow Country Club area. They'd built a Victorian-style mansion on land Adele had owned for years. This was where I was now, between sheets I'd only seen in ads, under a comforter I'd only dreamed about. Arch and I occupied two bedrooms on the top level of the enormous (three floors plus basement) gingerbread-trimmed residence. I didn't know why the Farquhars, wealthy, childless, and in their early fifties, needed such a huge place. But that was not my concern. What *was* my concern was that they both hated to cook.

Adele had said they needed someone to take charge of the mammoth kitchen with its state-of-the-art gadgets and appliances. Lucky for me, their kitchen had passed the eagle eye of the county health inspector. So I had jumped at the chance to become a temporary live-in cook in exchange for a haven. During the summer, this was also the center for my business, Goldilocks' Catering, Where Everything Is Just Right! Also lucky for me, the income from the job and the business was enough to send Arch to the summer session at Elk Park Prep, where I was catering this morning.

Best of all, the Farquhars' house had more alarms than the Denver Mint.

I opened my eyes and studied the sloped ceiling of my new bedroom. The gray light of five A.M. seeped through Belgian lace curtains and licked the edges of the room. There was no movement on the floor below; Adele and the general were still asleep.

Outside, a fierce June wind pummeled the house. Branches slapped against the gutters of the other guest room on the third floor, but there was no noise from Arch. When he was little, he would awaken if the doorbell rang. Now he could snore through wind, through hail, through the unfamiliar creaks of this museumlike house.

Arch had not wanted to move. I had promised it was just for two months, while new doors, windows, and a security system were installed in our old house. Insofar as possible, I had tried to put Dr. John Richard Korman—whose initials and behavior had led his other ex-wife and me to dub him The Jerk—out of my mind as well as out of my presence. Unfortunately, I did not know if he would be making an appearance at Elk Park Prep's annual brunch.

My second problem with this highly publicized meal: A man I was seeing *was* going to be there. The renewal of my relationship with Philip Miller, a local shrink, resembled those silver mines they're always reopening in Colorado. The vein may still be strong and the price of silver has just gone up. Philip's large blue eyes and so-happy-to-see-me smile had heated up my social life, no question about it. That's why they called it *old flame,* right? Anyway, I wanted to see Philip, but not at the expense of a confrontation with The Jerk.

The wind slammed against the house, causing it to crack and moan. A stray branch scuttled across the roof. In late spring the Rocky Mountains frequently spin off a chilly whip of air to announce a cold front. Wind screamed through the window jambs. Then it died and the undaunted mating call of a robin pierced the air.

I did a few stretching exercises before checking the thermometer on the windowsill: thirty-four degrees, with ominous clouds to boot. Nice June weather. I slid out onto the floor and eased my body through the yoga positions of Cobra, Morning Star, Locust. My spiritual life is an amalgam of yoga, transcendental meditation, and Episcopalianism. The only ones who would be bothered by this, I thought, were the Episcopalians.

And then I began to think about Philip Miller.

One thing I had learned as a thirty-one-year-old single mother: no matter how your body aged, your feelings did not. At any time of life you could be subject to a high-school-vintage infatuation. Another late-teen aspect to Love in the Thirties: you could feel as if you loved two people at the same time.

For seven months I had been seeing Tom Schulz. He was a policeman who had helped me through a rough time when my fledgling business was threatened with two attempted poisonings. He had the build and appetite of a mountain man. Tom Schulz doted on Arch and me, and he made me feel safe.

But in the last few weeks, perhaps because I was trying to block out the specter of the omnipresent Jerk, Philip Miller had once again stolen into my psyche and my daydreams. Eons ago Philip and I had dated at the University of Colorado. Dated? Listen to me.

In any event, Philip was good-looking, well-off, and intelligent. He looked and dressed like a golf pro. When I talked, he listened with great intentness. Since early May we had been doing crazy things like toting backpacks bulging with exotic foods on long Saturday hikes. One Monday morning Philip had sent me ten bunches of gold Mylar balloons. No reason. Before the move, I had taken my morning cup of espresso out on the wooden deck where the balloons floated, tied to the railing, for two weeks. I would sit and watch them move languidly in the cool morning breeze. I would listen to the silky brushing sound their crinkled surfaces made when they touched. I thought, Somebody loves me.

I had pushed John Richard out of my head. Schulz was on emotional hold. I made up elaborate excuses while off on excursions with Philip. And I felt guilty. But not too much.

Now I reluctantly hauled myself up to do battle with cantaloupe, strawberries, and kiwi. What a mess. The social life, that is; I was used to the fruit. But sometimes the Philip Miller–Tom Schulz problem felt like a nice mess. So much better than worrying about The Jerk. I was taking care of that crisis; I had moved. But the two-man mess . . . that was the mess of a glutton. After dieting for years, the glutton gorges herself on Chocolate Marble Cheesecake and Hot Fudge Sundae. Simultaneously.

I showered, dressed in my caterer's uniform, and reminded myself that gluttony was one of the Seven Deadly Sins. Not to mention lust. I combed out corkscrew-curly blond hair and put makeup over freckles on slightly chubby cheeks. With tap shoes and a big smile, I could have done Shirley Temple. Yes, slightly chubby, yes, occasionally gluttonous. But in the lust department I was pristine in the four years since divorce. Listening to friends' stories had convinced me that casual sex was anything but. Unfortunately, no one was interviewing me on the subject of promiscuity. Interesting topic, though.

I made my way down the back staircase, crept along the second-floor hall past the framed photographs of General Farquhar with Jimmy Carter, Ronald Reagan, and Margaret Thatcher, and tiptoed down the main steps. One of my jobs in this house was to disarm the first-floor security system every morning. I pressed the buttons to deactivate the motion detectors on the first floor and house perimeter. Then I banged open the door to the basketball court–size kitchen.

Well, maybe not that big. But it was gorgeous, the kind you drool over in household magazine centerfolds with captions like *Kitchens That Are Really Built!* Clusters of geraniums brightened deep interior windowsills. Next to the Montague Grizzly stove with its six burners, flat grill, and two ovens, counters patterned in brilliant yellow and green Italian tile glistened in the light of a glass-and-brass chandelier. Burnished copper pans hung from the ceiling, and rows of custom-made oak cabinets glowed pristinely, without a single grubby fingerprint. It was picture-perfect, typical of a home without children.

In the center of this vast culinary sea was an island the size of Antarctica. It was a good bet no kitchen designer ever had to do housework for a living. But the task of washing the expansive tile floor was left to the other staff person, a teenager who had moved into the Farquhars' basement level. For me there were muffins and breads to make, not to mention the stacked fruit on top of Antarctica. I took the smooth lumps of Sally Lunn dough out of the refrigerator for their final rising and then picked up my knife.

"Take that!" I whispered as I whacked my way through juicy green kiwi, fat, ultra-red strawberries, and pineapple so sweet you wondered why they'd let it leave Hawaii. One of the secrets of catering is that you have access to high-quality ingredients unavailable in the grocery store. If you have a good supplier, you can even get delicacies on short notice.

The cantaloupes were luscious, their juicy dark orange centers dense with a caviar of seeds. By half past six I had carved ten of them into centerpiece baskets and used a garnishing tool to give each a scalloped edge. I took the Sally Lunns out of the oven and put them on racks, where they filled the kitchen with the rich scent of baked bread. The last step was to scoop sour cream batter thick with inky blueberries into muffin tins and put them in to bake. The rest of the food was at the school. Once I'd poured the champagne and managed the buffet, the alums could eat while the headmaster made his money pitch.

The kitchen telephone rang. Unfortunately, this was no ordinary ringing but a sustained beeping from a complicated radio contraption boasting three lines, an intercom, and various other functions unknown to me. Two lines in my own house I could handle. But this gadget of General Farquhar's—he had brought it with him from the Pentagon, I was convinced—had been a headache from the time of its installation two days ago. The phone was like the security system. It needed to be disarmed.

I stared at the flashing light and tried to remember how the buttons worked. Between General Farquhar's associates and Adele's various committee people, the phone rang constantly. Who could be calling at this hour? Someone from the East Coast, no doubt. This inconsiderate person would be thinking, Oh, the time change. Well, they're probably already up.

I lifted the receiver and stabbed at what I hoped was the right button.

"Farquhars?" I said hesitantly, and prayed that I was not speaking into the intercom.

"Goldy," said Philip Miller.

I was immediately flooded with relief, desire, and other teenage-type feelings. Why he was calling so early I did not know.

I said, "Are you okay?"

"I have a doctor's appointment before the brunch," he said. "I'll be late."

"We are indeed meeting at your high school, Philip. But I can't give you a tardy excuse."

I could hear his grin when he said, "Not to worry. Listen. May I see you afterwards? There's something about food I need to discuss."

"Sure," I said warily, perusing my appointments calendar on the kitchen bulletin board. For June 3, a hastily penciled *Brunch* was followed by *Prep Harrington Aphrodisiac Dinner*. As good as my supplier was, she had been unable to bring some items for the dinner before she went on vacation. I was going to have to shop for substitutions later in the morning. This afternoon would be given over to cooking for the Harrington affair, which was set for Saturday night.

"No problem," I said, as if to convince myself. Philip did not sound good. There was caution in his voice. I said, "Should we get together before your first appointment? I need to be near your office to shop, anyway. We could have coffee at Aspen Meadow Café." I hesitated as the wind whipped aspen branches against the kitchen windows. "Are you sure you don't want to talk now?"

He said, "Not over the phone."

"Don't get paranoid on me, shrink-man."

"Don't play fast and loose with psychological terms, food-woman."

I said, "Fast and loose?"

But before he could reply, one of the other lines into the Farquhars' house lit up. Through the insistent beeping I told Philip to hold. Then I took a breath and hit a few buttons.

"Farquhars?"

"Miss Goldy," said Tom Schulz.

I looked at my watch: six-forty. What was going on here? I said, "It's a little early, Tom."

"You're hard to reach," he said. I said nothing but felt guilty for the latest creative rash of excuses. He went on, "Besides. As I recall, sometimes you're an early riser."

I could imagine him shifting his big body from side to side on one of the too-small chairs of the Furman County Sheriff's Department. I could see him cocking his head, looking into his coffee as if that dark liquid could give him answers to all his questions.

He said, "You cooking or something?"

"Excuse me, Tom, but yes," I said, irritation masking my conscience as the light for Philip's line continued to blink.

"I won't keep you. It's just that I have today's issue of the *Mountain Journal* in front of me. They deliver it to the Sheriff's Department first, I think."

"So?"

"Well, now, I was thinking this was one issue you might want to skip."

"Is that why you're calling so early?"

"Now, Miss G. Don't get huffy. I just wanted to tell you not to pick up today's paper. Avoid a nasty surprise that way."

"What are you talking about?"

He cleared his throat, then said, "Don't read the paper, Goldy. The guy's crazy." Another pause. "You know *I* think you're a great cook. The best."

"Cut to the chase, Tom. I've got fruit to slice."

He took a deep breath. "Seems our local rag has up and gotten itself a food critic. Name of Pierre; must be French." He took a sip of what I imagined to be coffee. Then he said, "Pierre doesn't like you, Goldy."

Philip's line was still blinking. Sweat sprouted on my forehead. I said, "Read it to me."

"Not a good idea, Miss G. That was what I was trying to avoid."

"Read it to me or I will never fix you my famous Strawberry Super Pie. That would be a shame, it being strawberry season and all."

He groaned, then read, " 'The queen of Aspen Meadow catering cuisine, the unfortunately named Goldy Bear, lays false claim to her throne, we fear.' " He stopped. "You sure you want me to go on?"

I clenched my teeth. "*Yes.*"

"Okey-doke." More throat-clearing. " 'At a recent fête for the Colorado Symphony, we began with heavily sauced eggs for hors d'oeuvres, then plowed onward through avocado cream soup, beef Stroganoff, fettuccine Alfredo, salad with mayonnaise, and finished in a daze with chocolate fondue. Where did this woman learn to cook, the National Cholesterol Institute?' " Schulz stopped. He said, "I've never heard . . . I mean, is there such a thing?"

"Oh, for crying out loud, of course not." I stopped shouting and took a deep breath. I felt as if I'd been punched. My voice was shaking when I said, "And it wasn't Stroganoff, it was London broil. With egg noodles. Is there any more?"

" 'Fraid so, but not much." He read, " 'How many of us came home and threw up? I know I did.' And then it's signed, 'Pierre.' What an idiot."

I pondered the gleaming knife I'd set down near the cantaloupe. I said, "Any more good news?"

"I miss you."

"Really."

"Course. Evenings have been pretty warm lately. Big spring sunsets. I was wondering if you'd like to bring Arch over. You know, we could cook out or something."

"Let me think about it. We could have hamburgers. Direct from the National Cholesterol whatever."

"While you're thinking about it, I got a question—"

The *third* line into the Farquhars' house lit up and began its insistent beep.

"Tom, could you hold—" I said in a panic, and pushed more buttons for what must surely be some dork on the East Coast.

"Farquhars!" I yelled into the phone.

"Need to cut back on the caffeine, Goldy?" The husky voice belonged to my best friend, Marla Korman. Although Marla and I both had been married to John Richard—at different times, this being Colorado and not Utah—we had become allies after the final divorce. It was through Marla that I had landed my present job. Adele Farquhar was her older sister.

I said, "Oh, jeez, Marla, what are you doing calling so early?"

"No time to talk?"

"Not if it's about the newspaper."

"What newspaper? I left two messages for you."

Another pang of guilt; I'd meant to call her back. But I was not a secretary, and I could not juggle three phone lines before seven o'clock in the morning.

"I can't talk," I said breathlessly. "I've got Tom Schulz on line two and Philip Miller on line one—"

"You *slut*."

"Just tell me what you want."

Marla groaned. She said, "You asked, my dear, if I would take Arch to his orientation at that snob school. The one where you're catering this morning. I was merely calling to find out what time you wanted me to come by."

I had forgotten. Not about the summer school, but about the orientation. Arch was probably still asleep, couldn't care less. He was supposed to be at the school—I racked my brain, it wasn't on the calendar—around nine?

"I'm sorry," I said. "Eight-thirty all right?"

Marla agreed, and I tried to get back to Tom Schulz and Philip Miller.

Both lines were dead.

2.

I creaked my way back up to the third floor and gently shook Arch's shoulder. No response. I tried again. A blue sweatshirted arm and balled fist reached out in protest. I sighed. The arm withdrew, pulled back to warm sheets like a turtle head to a shell.

The sweat suit was part of a stage. Arch wore them all day and all night. The parenting trick with this all-purpose wardrobe was occasionally to insist that there be a change—for example, from a gamey green set to a clean gray one. After his swim the previous night in the Farquhars' heated pool, I had convinced him to put on the blue. This was to avoid an argument over clothes the first morning of summer school. Now I just had to get used to the idea of my child spending the day in his pajamas.

I said, "Time to get up, kiddo."

"Oh, why, why, why?" said Arch as he stretched and moaned and burrowed beneath pillows and sheets. "Why do I have to get up?"

I said, "Summer school."

He burrowed deeper. "I'm not going" was the muffled reply.

"Arch."

"No, no, no, I'm never going. I hate that school. This is supposed to be my vacation. Go away."

"You don't even know anything about that school."

He growled.

One problem with living in someone else's house was that you couldn't raise your voice when you needed to. Especially when the other residents were asleep. I leaned in close to where I thought his ear was.

"Arch," I said softly, "you *said* you wanted to go."

A few moments of silence passed. I knew him well enough to recognize when he was reviewing his strategy.

Then his voice was behind me. "Please, Mom," my son said. "Please don't make me."

I whirled around. His actions had been completely noiseless. Now he giggled at my surprise. I said, "I wish you wouldn't do that disappearing act when I'm talking to you."

He squinted at me. His face was all white skin and freckles since he'd had his hair cut in a flattop. This new military-short haircut I put down to General Farquhar's influence. But Arch was so thin and pale he looked like a young prisoner of war. I handed him his glasses.

"You are mean," he said. He pushed his glasses into place and regarded me with magnified brown eyes. "None of those rich kids will like me. They all play tennis and have fancy parties and they never invite kids like me."

"What kind of kid are you?"

He groaned, a deep guttural sound warning against further probing. He looked at the wall and said in a low voice, "Not cool. That's what kind." He turned away from the wall but avoided my eyes. He said, "I had bad dreams again."

Before I could reply, he stumbled past me into the bathroom. I stared at the wall. The lush pink roses on the Farquhars' cheery wallpaper stared back. A few mementos from our house—Arch's new paraphernalia for magic tricks, his sixth-grade class picture, and a glass container of dice for his role-playing games—were propped up on shelves around the room, but they offered scant comfort.

Bad dreams.

I remembered the night three years ago, a year after the divorce was final, when John Richard had slashed my van tires, trashed my mailbox, and kicked in my front door. He was drunk. Arch was asleep and I had rushed into his room, blocked the door with a dresser and a desk, and screamed so loudly that John Richard left. John Richard had never harmed his son. Yet Arch still had faceless nightmares in which I died. Oh yes, the flimsiness of our house, compared with a week at the Farquhars' palace, had shown Arch and me what it was to be not rich and not cool. But we were going to be all right. Safe, once Aspen Meadow Security finished with our old home. And soon the bad dreams would end.

"Listen, Arch—" I began softly when he came out of the bathroom. But words failed. "Look, I have to go over to Elk Park for that brunch. I'm going to meet Philip afterwards—" I stopped to check his face. He was rolling his eyes, a modest indication of his opinion of Philip Miller. I went on, "There are fresh blueberry muffins in the kitchen for you. Marla will be by. In forty minutes."

He glanced at me ever so briefly, then pulled the rumples out of the blue sweat suit. He gave me the full benefit of his large brown eyes, so vulnerable behind the thick glasses. He said, "I'll be okay. Don't worry about me."

Sprinkles of rain blew across the windshield of Adele's Thunderbird just before the turnoff to Elk Park. Her car was the day's transport vehicle because my VW van was undergoing a clutch transplant and would not be out of the shop until Monday. It would take twenty minutes to drive up Colorado Highway 203, which rises to eighty-five hundred feet above sea level, five hundred feet above Aspen Meadow. Blasted out of hillsides, 203's few straight stretches are bordered by sheer drop-offs. I piloted the T-bird carefully around the mountains' curves, then dipped with a little more speed into the high meadowlands. The meadows burgeoned with the gold-green of lush mountain grasses and goldenrod, like green onions melting in a pool of butter. . . .

I clenched my teeth. Melted butter. As is served at the National Cholesterol Institute. How could someone say such a thing? Pierre hadn't even gotten the menu right. For the Symphony dinner I had made deviled eggs. A long way from heavily sauced. The soup had been gazpacho garnished with avocado. The London broil was sliced thin with a variety of accompaniments, one of which was sour cream with horseradish. And he hadn't even mentioned the steamed green beans.

What a simpleton! I braked to slow down around one of the road's lethal curves. I was going to find this Pierre, whoever he was, if I had to picket the office of the *Mountain Journal* for a week.

Think about the scenery, I told myself. Calm down. Look at the mountains. People move here to get away from stress, remember?

The mountains, the meadows, Aspen Meadow, Elk Park—these had been cool summer havens for wealthy Denverites before the advent of interstate highways. This was one of the places I had hiked with Philip only last week. We had made it as far as Elk Park Prep, the stucco and tile-roofed villa that had begun as an elegant hotel early in the century.

How idyllic the school had looked when a brief snow shower ceased that Saturday afternoon. The electrified gate meant to keep out flower-and-shrub-eating deer had been left open. Philip and I trudged silently up the muddy winding driveway. We breathed air that was like milk. Steam from the snow melting on the red tile roof gave the school an ethereal look that reminded me of the southern boarding school I'd attended for five years. Up to last year, Elk Park Prep also offered boarding. Philip asked why I didn't send Arch to Elk Park Prep as a day student, get him out of those large public school classrooms. Great idea, I said, I'd wanted to for years. If only John Richard would foot the bill. But my ex maintained I wanted Arch to go because I was an eastern snob at heart. Private school, I told Philip ruefully, was like money. You only appreciated it when you didn't have it anymore. *But how do you feel about that?* he asked, ever the shrink. I said, *How do you think I feel?*

Now, as I swung the T-bird through the open gate and past the high stone wall with its massive carved sign, *Elk Park Preparatory School,* a shudder went down my back. It was as if an invisible camera were filming my entrance: *Get that woman out of here! She's plummeted from the moneyed class to the servant class!* It was not until I had wound halfway up the long driveway that I realized I had not yet come to the turnoff marked "Deliveries."

The switchboard operator and admissions officer, my ad hoc helpers, were bustling about the school kitchen. With the elimination of the boarding department, the large kitchen crew of previous years was only a memory. In fact, the other staff person at the Farquhars, an eighteen-year-old named Julian Teller, was a casualty of this recent final closing. He had been one of the last boarding students and was now one of Adele's charity projects. Since Arch and I had taken up residence, General Farquhar had kept Julian busy putting together state-of-the-art gardening equipment and doing other odd jobs. Julian had only eaten with us once, although Arch dutifully reported that Julian said my leftovers were the best he had ever tasted. Unfortunately, I had not had the chance to get to know the teenager.

But Arch had. He adored Julian. What Julian did, Arch wanted to do, what Julian wore, Arch thought was cool beyond words. Of course I longed to point out to Arch that Julian was cool but not rich, which was why the teenager had to take a live-in job for his senior year in high school. But I didn't want to appear too preachy. And Julian was giving Arch diving lessons in the Farquhars' pool. In the absence of Arch's old neighborhood pals, Julian could at least be a friend.

I slipped on my apron and returned my concentration to cooking. A local restaurant had canceled out of doing the annual brunch only the day before. The headmaster had called me in a panic. Of course, I never said no to business. I had pulled sausage coffee cakes out of the freezer, then hastily prepared cheese strata and brought the cakes and the strata to the school. I had called Elizabeth Miller, who was not only Philip's sister but also an excellent baker, and asked her to make half a dozen of her heavenly macadamia-nut coffee cakes.

My two ad hoc helpers had remembered to place the strata in the oven. The smooth egg-and-cream layers were beginning to bubble around lakes of melted English cheddar. We laid out thick slabs of bacon, made the coffee, and put the breads and sausage cakes in to heat. I was about to head out with the fruit when the switchboard operator announced that someone was waiting for me in the dining room.

I put the first batch of cantaloupe baskets on a large tray and swung through the doors to the vast space of the formal dining room. The darkness from outside loomed large through tall wavy-glassed windows. Three rows of crystal chandeliers shone brightly on polished cherry tables and cream-colored walls. How unlike Arch's public school cafeteria it was. There, whenever there was going to be a meeting that included a fund-raising pitch, classroom banners with messages like *We Can Do It!* shrieked from every available inch of wall space. Here, all was elegance, with only a hint of what was to come from a slide projector and screen. Elizabeth Miller's head poked out from behind the screen. She gestured at her array of cakes.

"Thanks for coming early," I said to her head of golden hair that was so frizzy it always put me in mind of cartoons dealing with electrical sockets.

Elizabeth greeted me with a sideways smile and a toss of the head of frizz that revealed five-inch-long dangling silver earrings. She walked toward me in the toe-first stride favored by women whose only shoes are ballet slippers. Her casual outfit—black leotard, tights, midcalf-length Danskin skirt—clashed with the formal surroundings. But this was typical. Elizabeth Miller's persona was more along the lines of Tinkerbell hits thirty.

"You can't tell a *soul* I made these." Her smile revealed slightly crooked teeth.

I said, "Your secret's safe with me." Elizabeth owned Aspen Meadow's one remaining health-food store. She didn't even *sell* white flour.

"Will we have a chance to visit before this thing begins? Once the headmaster starts his money pitch I just want to escape."

I said, "I'll bet." The health-food store was not doing very well. The last time I'd been in for dried papaya, Elizabeth had tried to convince me I needed a fifty-pound bag of millet. When I told her she should switch to carrying gourmet items, she looked at me as if I'd suggested sex with an extraterrestrial.

Now she said, "Honestly. I have to pay for this meal, half of which I won't be able to eat. Sorry, Goldy, nothing personal. It's just that I'm into high-performance vegetarianism, and you know champagne kills brain cells." She pointed one of her toes in front of her. "I just come to this thing to see friends. But, God! I hate to listen to six new ways we're supposed to raise money for something the school just has to have. I end up leaving on a guilt trip. Have to unstress with coleus-leaf cocktail and chamomile tea for the next two days."

"You could always give them a bad check," I offered as I placed the last cantaloupe down with a flourish.

She said, "Not a bad idea," and then regarded me with big blue eyes that reminded me of her brother's. "Have you heard from Philip?"

I told her that I had and he would be late. I said, "Anything I can help with?"

She said, "No," without conviction.

"Everything okay?"

She nodded. "Just fine."

Now Elizabeth was pretending to center a cantaloupe. She said, "Did you have to cook a lot for this meal?"

"I made a multitude of goodies. Have the strata. It features high-performance cheddar."

Silence.

I had a lot of work to do and could not visit when the guests' arrival was imminent. Whatever it was Elizabeth wanted, I wished she'd get to it.

"Goldy—" she began. She tilted her pixie face, then pressed her lips together.

Something told me she was not here to talk about the school, or the food, or even to complain about the headmaster. I said, "Why don't we sit down?"

"Oh, no," she said as she bent down close to inspect one of the cantaloupe baskets. From the kitchen came the inviting smells of bacon and coffee. I knew I had to get in there and so did she. She said, "It's just—"

"Just . . ."

"Oh," she said with a grin, "I'm worried about Philip. I think he's getting in over his head with some of his clients. I mean, are you all close enough to talk about this stuff? You know "

People always say, You know, when you don't have a clue. *You know*

... fill in the blank. *You know* ... make this easier for me by not having to say it.

The space of the dining room was intimidating. I leaned toward her in a confidential manner. "You mean," I said, "does he tell me about his clients? Or are we sleeping together? Because the answer is no to both."

She shrugged and said, "Oh no, that's not what I was asking. You know."

I still didn't. I said, "You mean, like are we close enough to be thinking of getting married?"

She was relieved. She closed her eyes and gave a little shrug, as in, You brought it up.

I said, "We aren't. Satisfied?"

"Well, you see ..." she said with more hesitation, then stopped. I thought, Spit it out, Elizabeth.

She went on, "I just need to talk to you, to him I mean ... and I didn't know what his plans were."

I said, "I don't know what Philip's plans are beyond coming here for brunch. If you want to talk about health food with him, he'll be here. If you want to talk about health food with me, I'll be in your store later to shop for this dinner I'm doing tomorrow night. Now be a good vegetarian and come into the kitchen with me to see if the bacon's done."

She wrinkled her nose. "Bacon! I can't even stand the smell—"

But she was interrupted by the first gaggle of aging preppies laughing with forced hilarity as they pushed through the carved doors of the dining room. It was the kind of laugh that said, We're not too old to have fun. Suddenly it was too late to check the bacon or anything else. I lifted the first bottle of champagne from the ice chest and began to open it.

I whispered to Elizabeth, "Do me a favor. Pop into the kitchen and get one of the staff; I'm going to need help here. Then sashay over to your buddies and act sociable so they don't start on the fruit. I'll be around with the champagne."

"Oh, sure," she said, distracted again. She shook her head; the earrings swung like Christmas ornaments. "Just ... please let me talk to Philip myself."

"Elizabeth," I said, "he's your brother. Whatever's bothering you, I think you should talk to him about it yourself. You know?"

3.

"And when we have brought the water line in here," the headmaster was saying with a practiced flick of his pointer at the illuminated screen, "then we will enter into Implementation Stage Two. . . ."

At the headmaster's table, Adele Farquhar touched the undercurl of her severe, dark pageboy. Busy as I had been, I had not seen the general deliver her in his Range Rover. It was almost eleven o'clock. The alums stirred in their seats, checked their Rolexes. Any dummy knew that Implementation Stage Two meant More Money. The alums were exchanging looks—*How much longer could he go on about this?* A perplexed buzz rose from the tables. *Forever.*

My legs ached from standing. The buffet table looked defaced. The food was almost gone, except for what I had saved for Philip. But he had not arrived. If he didn't come soon, he'd be out of luck.

And then he strolled in, acting like he owned the place. His black blazer, white pants, and shock of blond hair gave him the look of a male model. He scanned the room from behind Ray Bans. A hum of admiration rose from the women. I took a deep breath, let it out.

The only time *I* heard a female gurgle of approval was for congealed salad.

"How's my favorite cook?" Philip said in a low voice once he arrived at the serving table. When he leaned his slender body over the table he was so close I could read the engraved words on his gold lapel pin— PROTECT OUR MOUNTAINS! The politically correct shrink gave me an inviting openmouthed smile.

I shook my head and stared at the sunglasses, then spoke to Philip's aristocratic nose. "Fine. How's my favorite psychologist? Hungry?"

"Ravenous." He took a manila envelope out of his briefcase. "Fundraising, I swear," he said under his breath. "They ran out of decals and I had to bring in more." He signaled to the headmaster with the envelope, then asked, "Is this thing almost over? Can we still get together afterwards?"

I nodded to both questions. Philip strode up to the head table and handed the envelope to the headmaster, who betrayed great relief.

Elizabeth caught my eye and waved as if she had a wand in her hand. As Philip wound back through the tables, his sister kept her eyes on him.

The headmaster started to talk about money by trying to make it sound as if he wasn't. He had abandoned the pointer and was droning on about the Phase I Drive for Investments. This year's desperately needed improvement, it appeared, was an Olympic-size heated outdoor pool. For the past month, alumni, parents of students, and friends of the school had been hitting on (okay, he said, "going around to") local businesses, giving them the Pool for the Preps pitch. If they gave, the business got a GET INTO THE SWIM! decal. Parents then patronized the SWIM!-decaled businesses. The headmaster reached into the envelope and proffered one of the decals.

This sounded vaguely illegal, I reflected as Philip turned to me and grinned conspiratorially. I handed him his plate, then quietly emptied pitchers and scraped platters. Philip moved toward the wall to get a better view of the headmaster. I watched as he lifted his plate and then held it close under his chin as he ate.

I put down the platter I had been holding. In that moment, I saw nothing but Philip. I saw him as he had been more than a dozen years before, when we had ditched a sophomore mixer. I had just transferred to the university from an eastern women's college and knew no one. This blond, handsome fellow had come up to me and said, Do you want to get out of here? And I had said, Sure. We had walked through cool evening air redolent with the smell of smoke from wood-burning fires. Philip pointed to birds flitting between the trees: Oregon juncos, he said, returning to their winter nests. He bought us gyro sandwiches. We dripped sandwich juice and minted yogurt on paper napkins as we strolled by Boulder Creek. I remembered Philip holding his napkin carefully under his chin, looking less like a cool sophomore than a well-trained four-year-old.

He had kissed me briefly, a taste of mint. But our dating was haphazard and short-lived. I didn't even remember telling Philip I was leaving school to get married. I just let him go, like a balloon.

Timing, I kept telling myself. That was the wrong time. Here was Philip, holding the plate beneath his chin, wanting to be together again. But I had feelings for Schulz, not to mention ambivalence about relationships in general. I wasn't sure this was the right time either.

Elizabeth was squeezing through occupied chairs to get to the back of the room. When she arrived at the serving table, she whispered, "The food's great and most of my friends are here." She smiled to dismiss her earlier complaint.

I felt like telling her to phone the *Mountain Journal* with a review, but I did not want to interrupt the world's most boring headmaster. I noticed Philip eyeing his sister. I said, "Your brother's here."

She said, "And?"

I smiled.

"No news to report yet," I said. "Can't rush these things. You know," I added.

"I'm depending on you to keep an eye on him," she said in a low voice.

Philip sauntered back. He said, "Want to get out of here?"

I said, "Absolutely."

Elizabeth offered him a bite of sausage cake. "It's not good for you," she said with a sly smile, "but Goldy made it, so it'll taste super. You have time to visit now?"

He chewed, winked at me, then shook his head to her question.

He said, "Call you?" When she nodded, he grinned and gave me a time-to-go look. "If we don't leave, we're going to get caught in the crush."

I glanced at my watch: 11:30. Rain still streaked across the tall windows of the dining room. With some effort, we could load the platters and boxes into the Thunderbird in one trip. The school staff had promised to do the dishes. The headmaster was winding down: he had gone from the fund-raising pitch to a discussion of Elk Park's policies on drugs (they were against them), parties with alcoholic beverages (ditto), and casual sex (ditto ditto). The alums' interest seemed to pick up with this last topic. Philip and I placed the last of the pitchers in a crate and together we carried my supplies through the mud and rain to the Thunderbird's trunk.

Philip gave a short wave before he started his car, a BMW 325 I-X the color of vanilla pudding. For at least the hundredth time, I thought I should have become a shrink instead of a caterer.

Cold spring rain pelted and washed and blew over our cars as we bumped over muddy ruts on our way out of the staff parking lot. We passed the buses and cars that had brought the students for orientation, then came up on the pool construction site. A six-foot-high chain-link fence surrounded the excavated area. The headmaster had just informed us that the plumbing was in and that the concrete would be shot in under pressure in the next few days. The school's board of trustees was forging ahead to build the pool before they actually had the money. Not a luxury, they'd said, but a necessity. Ah, rich folks.

When we drove past the construction-site fence, I waved and flashed my lights at Philip. He did not respond, but signaled to turn onto Highway 203.

As we started down the narrow two-lane, the raindrops turned to white flakes. I sighed; I'd known it was coming. Snow in Colorado on the third of June is not the dry type that powders the ski slopes in winter. Instead, fat wet spring flakes plopped on the car like bits of mashed potatoes. The T-bird's windshield wipers strained against the weight. At our altitude this was—my New Jersey relatives were always appalled to hear—seasonal weather. As we headed downhill I wondered if the Thunderbird had on snow tires.

The BMW belched a cloud of black smoke. I accelerated gently; the five-hundred-foot curved descent to Aspen Meadow would be much more treacherous if the snow began to stick. Behind us the school's red tile roof was already frosted with white. The T-bird's windshield wipers hummed as they swept off thin blankets of snow. I turned on the defroster and for a moment lost sight of Philip whizzing around a curve.

"Machismo," I said with a groan, and pushed Adele's car up to thirty.

Beside the road a red fox, usually a nocturnal animal, darted out from a stand of bushes. I was startled and swung wide. No need: at the sight of the car, the animal scurried back to his lair. Even wildlife knew better than to be out in this mess.

Once around the curve I caught sight of the BMW a quarter mile ahead. My right foot pushed the accelerator.

We had been driving a few minutes when Philip abruptly careened to the right. His tires spewed a wave of mud from the shoulder. The paved part of the road was beginning to ice. I wondered if he had slid or had seen an animal, too.

The snow fell steadily. I accelerated very gently. Philip slowed for a moment and then swerved over the center line to the left. Then he straightened out to straddle the dotted line.

I honked. Was something wrong with his car? Was the snow bothering him? Maybe his windshield wipers weren't working. I honked again, but there was no answer. Surely Philip knew the hazards of this drive. If he was having a steering problem, now was the time to pull over.

Instead, he sped up. We passed a rock wall on the road's left side, then a steep drop-off where a rollover had taken away most of the guardrail. Yellow police ribbons still marked the scene of a fatal accident. Again the BMW swerved to the left. A wave of fear left my hands damp. At the next curve I had to pay close attention. For a moment all that was visible in front of the car was air. My stomach dropped.

After negotiating the turn, I sped up the boatlike Ford to get behind the BMW's square taillights, which shone in the enveloping grayness. My hand groped for the headlights and I flashed them.

No response.

We headed east on the roller-coaster approach to Highway 24, the north-south biway that runs between Interstate 70 and Aspen Meadow. After we rounded another bend, my eyes picked out a trickle of cars heading north out of Aspen Meadow toward I-70.

Cottony clumps of snowflakes clung to the windshield. I strained my eyes and thought I could see Philip shaking his head. My heart beat in time with the windshield wipers. I pressed the accelerator and decided to overtake him. Force him to pull over. But when I pulled up on his left, he sped up. On the right a thin shoulder of ground and a barbed-wire fence were the only things between our lane and a forty-foot drop to whitened meadow. I pressed a button to bring my window down slightly. From Highway 24 the occasional honk and swish of hydroplaning tires punctuated the sifting sound of snow.

Twenty minutes ago Philip had been fine. Now either he was having a heart attack or he was going to give me one.

The last part of eastbound 203 went straight down. Philip again drove between the two lanes. Ahead I could see a tractor-trailer and a grocery-supply truck beginning to chug north on Highway 24, headed back to the interstate.

Near the end of 203, Philip honked wildly. His brake lights flashed as the pale yellow car skidded right. I tried to gauge whether I could pass him again, but he was going too fast.

Through the snowfall, a digital clock's amber squares glowed twelve-oh-oh in the mist. We were only moments from Philip's office, which was near the interstate. Soon this agony would be over. I flicked on the left turn signal as we approached the stop sign at the intersection of the two roads.

"No!" I yelled as the BMW zoomed through the stop sign and screeched to turn right on 24 instead of left toward Philip's office.

I stopped, glanced left, floored the accelerator, and wrenched the steering wheel to the right. The snow was coming down like oatmeal. Philip barreled down the left lane straight into the path of the oncoming trucks. At the last moment he careened out of the lane when the tractor-trailer blasted him with his horn. The big trucks lumbered past. Philip put on his auxiliary lights and appeared to slow down.

I gunned the T-bird forward and pulled up on the BMW's right, on the dirt shoulder of Highway 24. I honked. Through his tinted window glass it was impossible to make out his face. He acted as if he neither saw nor heard me. Again he sped up, as if to get away.

The Thunderbird stalled in the snowy mud.

I leaned on the horn and lowered my window all the way. Cold feathers of snow pricked my face.

"Philip!" I screamed. "Come back!"

Speeding up again, the BMW bumped and rocked southbound down 24. In the right lane I could see a black Porsche passing a silver bus. I took a deep breath and turned the key in the ignition. If I could hit Philip from behind, maybe he would stop.

A Ford is not a BMW. The Thunderbird started with a jolt. I gunned it forward and hit a utility pole with the right front headlight. With all the snow, I hadn't even seen it. A dull pain shot up my spine. When I looked back at the road, Philip was speeding down the left lane on a collision course with the bus. Leaving bells and whistles whining, I unstrapped my seat belt and jumped from the car.

"Stop!" I yelled through the curtains of snow. "Stop!"

But he did not. The Porsche and the bus honked. The Porsche driver careened onto the shoulder. A wall of snow sprayed upward. The Porsche's brakes screamed. Still the BMW raced forward. The bus driver leaned on the horn. Philip heard the honk and braked, then hit the gravel on the left shoulder. The BMW went into a wild skid.

The bus slammed into the BMW on the driver's side. Glass shattered. Tires shrieked. I could hear the bus passengers screaming. The Porsche driver scrambled out. *There's no way,* I thought as I ran, *there's just no way.*

My feet slid through the snow. Ahead the bus and Philip's car stood motionless, smoking. My body whacked the BMW hood. The left front of the car was irreparably smashed. I looked through the broken glass, desperately hoping to see some movement.

The top half of Philip's body was at a skewed angle; he had been thrown back by the impact. His face and chest were splattered with blood and glass. The sunglasses were gone and his eyes were wide, red, empty. The bottom half of his body had disappeared below the BMW's crumpled metal.

"Call an ambulance!" I shrieked at the bus driver.

But I knew. I just couldn't accept it. I couldn't look back at him. I couldn't think of anything, couldn't see or hear anything, only knew one thing.

Philip was dead.

4.

Slow motion, fast motion. Time splintered.

Fast: People moved back and forth. Back and forth. They asked questions and called to me, as if I were at the bottom of a very deep well. A man pulled me back when I tried to tug open the BMW door. I ripped away from him and started to run. A gentle set of hands guided me away and draped a blanket over my hair and shoulders, protection from the snow. A man and a woman put out flares. Directed traffic. Motioned the police car over.

In slow motion: The snow fell. The BMW smoked. Behind the car's dark glass the body did not move.

In the midst of life we are in death . . .

A policeman spoke my name. His voice was far away. I looked at him through eyes that seemed not mine. I cupped my hands and blew into them.

He said, "Just a few questions, if you can manage it."

Thou knowest, Lord, the secrets of our hearts . . .

I nodded and followed him, slowly, slowly. The BMW was behind me now. I was leaving Philip to strangers, foreign men in suits who would make their decree. It was unbearable.

My name again. Yes. I got into the patrol car. I tried to focus on the policeman, but Philip's face invaded my mind. Could you describe what happened? Yes. Even then something inside said: I can describe it. What I can't do is explain it.

Outside the car, snow fell like soft feathers, sticking in some places, melting in others. When I tried to think of what I was going to do with Adele's T-bird, I would see the back of Philip's car, see the black smoke belching, see his forehead and cheeks sprayed with blood.

The ambulance came. Paramedics splashed through the mud. Someone brought me a paper cup of coffee, told the cop the EMS guys had hooked the victim up to a machine to send telemetry down to a Denver hospital. A doctor had confirmed that Philip Miller was dead. Somebody from the coroner's office was on the way.

Now a new policeman, a state patrolman, asked my name, the location of my vehicle, and if I was the one who had witnessed the accident from the other direction. When I made my answers he handed me a notebook and said to write down all I had seen. I wrote and passed it to him. While he was reading, someone rapped on the window of the patrol car. The patrolman, whose name tag said only *Lowry,* stepped out of the car. When he got back in he was grumbling.

My head throbbed. "May I go now?" I asked. I was seized with a surge of panic, as I had been when one of Arch's classmates was killed in a school-bus accident two years before. I needed to see Arch, to be with him, to make sure he was okay. I said, "I need to get home. To my son."

Where exactly was he, Lowry wanted to know, where was home? I dived into the muddle of my brain. Where was Arch now? At the school. He needed to get to the Farquhars. Yes, Lowry said, the police would phone and have Arch call home.

Home. The word brought tears, finally, as if by mentioning one loss there could be grief for all others.

Elizabeth, Elizabeth Miller, my voice was saying, someone needs to find Elizabeth, someone needs to tell her. And through my blubbering Lowry again extracted information and promised follow-up.

I took a deep breath.

Lowry said, "A friend of yours was up in this area and answered the call about the accident. He's from the Sheriff's Department, an investigator by the name of Tom Schulz. . . . He wanted to know if you were all right."

"He answered the call?"

"Didn't know you were in it till he got here. You want to see him or not?"

"Yes," I said as tears stung my eyes again. "Please, I'd like to see Schulz."

"Soon. About this accident . . ." said Lowry.

I looked out the window, but could not see Tom Schulz through the crowd. The snow was coming down now in a slanted rush to the mountain meadow, like millions of tiny arrows shooting to earth.

"Exactly how fast was the victim going," Lowry wanted to know.

"It's on there," I said, and motioned to the pad. "About forty." The speed limit was thirty on that road, but you could do forty on most of the straight stretches if you were careful. Which was not, of course, what Philip Miller had been.

"You see," I said, "it was more the *way* he was driving."

"And the way he was driving was . . ."

"Zigzag. As if he didn't have control of the car."

Lowry narrowed his eyes at me. "So what did you think?"

I shook my head and mumbled something about not knowing. "Maybe car trouble," I said.

"Why didn't he pull over?"

"I don't know. That's what I can't figure out."

Then we had to go back to the beginning, how I had been catering the brunch where Philip had been a guest who had arrived late.

Officer Lowry said, "Why was he late, do you know?"

"He'd just had an appointment. Medical, I think."

"Something wrong with him?"

I shrugged.

"Did he mention his car?"

"No."

"Did he smell like anything?"

I squinted at Lowry.

"Like alcohol, for instance," he said.

"No."

"Did he act at all strange?"

"Well, he . . ." I reflected and moved uncomfortably in the vinyl seat. Had he acted strange? I said, "He hadn't had breakfast . . . he was hungry. And he wanted to see me, that's why I was following him. We were going to have coffee over by his office."

"At this brunch, what did he eat?"

I told him. "Do you know if they reached his sister—"

Lowry said, "The chief deputy coroner's already on the way to the school to find the sister. This won't take too much longer."

I was aware of the policeman's after-shave, of the camphor-scented blanket around my shoulders, of the squeaking noise the front seat made when Lowry turned around to face me. All these made my stomach turn over. I wanted to be where the things and people were familiar. To check on Arch.

Ahead of us, the county coroner's van carrying Philip Miller pulled out slowly onto Highway 24. There were no blinking lights. There was no siren.

"You were telling me what he ate," prodded Lowry. "I need to know what he drank, too."

"I've told you all I saw him eat. He may have had some juice or coffee, I don't know."

"Did he complain of stomach or headache, fever, dizziness, chest pain, anything like that?"

"No."

"Okay," said Lowry. He asked about how to reach me and said someone might call later. I gave him the Farquhars' address on Sam Snead Lane in the Meadowview area of Aspen Meadow Country Club.

I started to get out of the car, then said, "I just don't think I've conveyed to you how weird this accident was. An hour ago he was fine. He drove like a maniac into town and now he's dead. Doesn't that seem odd to you?"

Lowry looked at me. He said, "Sometimes when something's

wrong, or when somebody's drunk, say, they just speed up. They think, I won't stop, I'll just get where I'm going and then everything will be okay."

"But it was so . . . strange."

His jowls trembled when he shook his head. He said, "A lot of car accidents look strange, lady."

Investigator Tom Schulz was talking with a short, big-bellied red-haired man when I walked up.

He gave me a sympathetic look and said, "You okay?"

I nodded. He made an introductory wave with one large hand. "This is one of the coroner's deputies."

"I just got here," the man mumbled to Schulz. "This guy a crispy critter or what?"

I stared at the red-haired man and then lunged for him. Somebody started shrieking, "You bastard, you—"

"Whoa, Goldy, whoa," said Schulz as he deftly grabbed me around the middle. "He didn't mean anything." But the red-haired man looked at Schulz, who must have given him a Get Lost look.

He mumbled, "Catch you later, Schulz," and slunk off.

Tom Schulz gently turned me around and held me against his big body. He arranged the blanket over my head, then held me out to make sure I was all right. Tom Schulz could use his size to threaten those whom he did not trust. He could transform the broad expanses of his handsome face into a scowl, a smirk, or impassive flatness. But now his green eyes were full of worry, now his jaunty sand-colored eyebrows were drawn into an anxious line. He pulled me in for a hug. I closed my eyes and let his warmth envelop me. He said, "I thought you said you were all right."

"Not if I have to listen to some idiot."

"Sorry about that. You work for the coroner, you gotta keep the distance."

We got into his car, a nondescript Chrysler you would expect a cop to drive. I looked down at my shoes. They were soaked, splotched with melting snow and mud. I turned to him and heard my voice waver. "A friend of mine just died."

Schulz turned and looked at me. He offered his hand, which I took and held. It was warm and fleshy and completely enclosed mine.

After a moment, he pulled his hand away and leaned over to fasten my seat belt. "Okay, Miss G., let's get you back to your new place. You'll have to give me directions, seeing as how I've never been there."

I told him to drive to the club area. I did not look at the crumpled BMW as we inched past. We traveled in silence. The snow stopped almost as suddenly as it had begun: June in the high country. The clouds, which were low, began to lift from the ground and part in wisps over the hills of Elk Park and Aspen Meadow. Sunlight made occasional passes across the meadow, turning it to glitter.

"Daylight," said Schulz. "One P.M., 'bout time."

I struggled under the seat belt to untangle my purse, which I had miraculously remembered, then rummaged around for sunglasses. Halfway through my search I forgot what I was looking for. I took a deep breath and threw the purse on the floor.

Tom Schulz said, "You want to talk about this accident?"

I gave him the briefest possible account of what had happened.

"You said Philip Miller was a friend of yours?"

"We'd gone to school together. C.U."

We drove without speaking. Into the silence I said, "I was going out with Philip Miller."

More silence. Then Schulz said, "What's your ex-husband up to these days?"

I sniffed, looked out the window. "Last month he was bugging me, driving by a lot. Making hang-up calls, inventing legal problems. I was afraid he might get drunk, come over, and give me some trouble. That's why I took this job. The Farquhars' house has a lot of alarms."

"Does he still see Arch?"

I nodded and looked at my nails. They looked very strange. I did not want to talk about this subject and said so.

"Just tell me this," Schulz said as he looked over at me. "Did Korman know where you were going this morning?"

I couldn't think. I said, "I don't know. He wasn't at the brunch, although I thought he might put in an appearance."

Silence again filled the car. We passed the stone walls with the wood-carved sign, ASPEN MEADOW COUNTRY CLUB. The phone wires would heat up quickly in the club area, because Philip Miller was, or had been, a resident.

The post-accident daze clung to me like a blanket. Scenes from the last hour intruded on my consciousness: the curves of the road, the feel of the accelerator beneath my foot.

Philip.

"I'm up here because some weird guy phoned," Schulz was saying. With great effort I turned to listen. He mused silently for a moment before he said, "Call comes in and the guy gets out two sentences before he hangs up. He says, You gotta come help me, I live up by Aspen Meadow Country Club. You gotta come help me, my life's in danger. Click."

5.

I sighed. I said, "That's just great. Did you get a number, anything?"

"Anytime you call 911, we've automatically got it. Problem is, the guy called from the clubhouse. It could be any number of extensions. They sent a car over, and nothing suspicious was going on. Anyway. I'm going there to check after I leave you off. Someone at home at this house where we're going, by the way?"

"I don't know. Probably."

"You got a house key?"

I was so out of it I couldn't remember. And then I remembered they were in the Thunderbird. I said, "No keys."

"Guess it's good I turned up, huh?"

I didn't answer. In the distance the golf course was a pastiche of soaked green and ice white. The snow was melting quickly, and golf carts were starting their buglike crawl up the paved path.

For some reason, this struck me as insanity. How could people play golf today? How could they just go on?

I moaned. Schulz reached over, lifted my left hand from my lap, and held it. He said, "Need me to pull over?"

I nodded and he did. I opened the door and was sick.

When I had wiped my mouth with tissues he discreetly handed over, I said, "I'm sorry. I'm so embarrassed."

"Don't worry about it. Let's just get you to this place."

I closed my eyes and mumbled the directions to Sam Snead Lane, a dead end. When I felt a little better I looked out again at the greens, but then changed my mind. Better just to focus on the inside of the car for a while.

"I wonder if they asked these guys if they could use their names," said Schulz. I ventured a glance out. Schulz wrinkled his nose as he started down Arnold Palmer Avenue. I told him in a voice that still did not sound like mine that it had been the developer's idea to make up for the loss of a second eighteen holes by naming the streets after famous golfers. Schulz shook his head. "No second golf course, but a dry sailing club. Houses here look like boats. Great big yachts tied up on the grass."

I looked out at the pale gray and tan mini-mansions sailing past. While the other houses in Aspen Meadow were generally stained dark tones of rustic green and rustic brown, here the palette was light. The magnificent dwellings were indeed like ships made of pale wood and glass; they perched on waves of mountain grass rolling down from the tops of the surrounding hills.

Schulz squinted, rocked the car left onto Sam Snead Lane, then veered right into the Farquhars' cul-de-sac. The tall and expansive pearl-gray Victorian stood on the highest wave of grass. The house's brilliant white trim shimmered in the sudden sunlight.

"Code, Miss G.?" asked Schulz as we arrived at the security gate guarding the fence to the Farquhars' two acres.

I stared at the closed-circuit camera and the panel of buttons. After a moment I remembered the code and told him what buttons to press.

On the porch Schulz pushed the lit doorbell. Inside, the chimes echoed plaintively. General Farquhar's voice boomed *Yes?* over the intercom.

"General," I said, "there's been an accident. I'm here with a police-man. I don't have my keys."

"Just a moment," cracked the voice.

"Nice security system," said Schulz. "You living in a separate part of the house?"

I said, "Sort of. We have two rooms on the third floor, with our own back staircase to the kitchen and pool."

"A pool in this climate? Amazing."

"Heated. Adele has a herniated disc at her fourth lumbar vertebra, as well as degenerative arthritis. She has to swim every day."

"Or ice-skate," said Schulz.

There was a clicking behind the door: General Bo Farquhar was preparing to meet the world.

"Yes?" His sharp features were pinched in puzzlement at the presence of Schulz. "Please," he said again when he recognized me, "please come in," and he pulled the door open.

"I remember this guy from the news," Schulz whispered to me.

I shook my head at him and warned with my eyes, *Not now.*

"Are you all right, Goldy?" the general barked.

I took a deep breath and nodded into the demanding gaze of the general's pale blue eyes. General Bo Farquhar's eyes weren't just light blue, they were almost colorless, like his white skin and cropped-close white-blond hair. He towered over me, holding himself as erect as he had in the West Point class of 1960. General Bo Farquhar was not handsome. His lips were too thin, his chin too prominent, his nose too long. But he had the kind of effortless charisma that people pay thousands of dollars to get from image-development corporations. And don't think he didn't know it.

"Quite a system you've got here," said Schulz after introductions.

"All you need is one ambush," said the general, with a grim smile. "What happened?" he asked.

I motioned toward the living room.

The general started to lead us in that direction, then turned and said, "You all go in and sit down. I'll get some coffee. Brandy, too," he said as an afterthought. Then he pivoted and disappeared across the dining room's Oriental rug, a lilac-and-salmon-colored Kirman.

We settled into the pink and green ocean of a living room adjoining the foyer. I sat on one of the two rose-colored couches; Schulz lowered himself uncomfortably into one of the pale green damask wing chairs. Another Kirman, this one in hues of pink and green, floated beneath us, while on the walls green and pink fans and dried floral wreaths vied with neo-Renoir oils.

Schulz said, "Guy seems awful young for a general. Refresh my memory."

"He was the army's ranking man in studying terrorists. Methods and materials," I said in a low voice. "But nobody told him to share his know-how with the Afghanis. He just did it. He had to retire, sort of a compromise. He still researches and writes about terrorists. My bet is he's trying to regain the respect of the Pentagon crowd. He is a little odd," I added.

"Uh-huh," said Schulz as he gazed at the shelves on either side of the fireplace. "Look at that." He pointed to the Farquhars' stereo. "Motion detector."

I looked, but saw only a small red light on the side of one of the speakers. I knew how to turn off each of the four loops of the security system; that was the extent of my knowledge.

Schulz halted his visual inspection long enough to finger a piece of fudge on the coffee table. "Okay if I have one of these?"

"Sure." The last thing I wanted to think about was food. As an afterthought, I said, "I didn't make them." And then I remembered with sudden pain the golden balloons from Philip, which he'd brought with a box of Ferrero Rocher chocolates.

Schulz eyed the fudge skeptically. "Does that mean they're not very good?"

"It just means I didn't make them. Julian Teller did. Resident teenager whose father owns a candy shop. Julian's one of Mrs. Farquhar's people projects, sort of like Arch and me."

Schulz chewed and said, "Not bad." Then he winked at me. "Not as good as yours, though."

I nodded, uncaring. Fatigue was creeping up my legs like cold water. There was a knot in my stomach. The sight of Philip was coming back.

"I feel light-headed," I whispered to Schulz. He nodded sympathetically.

"Here we go," said General Bo as he strode in with a silver tray. "Brandy and coffee."

"General Farquhar," I said after clearing my throat, "I tried to help the person who was killed. His name was . . . Philip Miller. I'm sorry, I . . . ran the T-bird into a utility pole."

"Philip Miller." The general looked at me with disbelief. "Julian's shrink?"

"Yes," I said, although I had not known this. "And my friend."

The general frowned. "Jesus." He handed me a brandy snifter. "Unbelievable. How did it happen?"

During my retelling of the accident story, the general shook his head just perceptibly with each detail, as if I were a subordinate commanding officer who had let a battle get out of hand. When I came to the part about the Thunderbird, he asked for its location so he could call to have it towed. And where were the keys? He would pick them up later, as they contained a house key.

"Has Arch called?" I asked.

The general lifted one eyebrow above his pale blue gaze. "Yes. He was only told he needed a ride home, he didn't know about any of this . . ." He tilted his head, and I felt myself drawn into the deep furrows of his forehead. "Goldy. Don't worry about anything. I have some work to do here, but I'll pick up those keys and check on the car when I go over to the school later. Adele's volunteered me to work at the pool site." His look turned paternal. "Go upstairs and rest now. One of us will bring your son home."

And then he rose, as if to dismiss us. I drained my brandy, even though I didn't want it. I wanted to sleep.

When no one moved, General Bo said regretfully, "Putting in the garden today," as if he had to leave momentarily for a meeting with the Joint Chiefs. He rocked forward on the balls of his new high-top sneakers and opened his eyes wide at me.

Oh, God! I jumped up. Putting in the garden!

"You have to go, you have to go," I insisted to Schulz.

Schulz did not move. Perched on the absurdly fragile pale green chair, he eyed me and then the general. "Nothing so busy as retirement," he said solicitously.

I grabbed Schulz's hand and tugged. "You don't understand, this is really big, he's doing some—"

"Actually," the general said with great seriousness and a glance at his watch, "what I'm working on is killing two birds with one stone."

"Investigator Schulz," I said in my most pleading voice, "it is imperative that we both leave *immediately*. Like *now*."

Schulz looked at me as if I were crazy. He said nothing and did not move.

"You see," the general was saying blandly, "my field is terrorist technique."

Schulz *mm-hmm*ed as the general glanced at his watch.

"How much time, how much time?" I demanded.

The general frowned. He said, "T minus two, I'm afraid." Then abruptly, to Schulz, he said, "I'm going to have to ask you to leave."

This was not the time for something about the general to attract Schulz's attention. I knew the homicide investigator well enough to see a slight straightening of the spine, a narrowing of the eyes. *Some other time,* I begged mentally to Schulz, *some other time!* My eyes darted around the pink and green living room. White pillows dotted the floral landscape like marshmallows that suddenly swam as I struggled to concentrate. T minus two . . . where should we go?

"Get up," I said sharply to Schulz as I pulled now on both of his big hands. "Get up, you have to go, we have to get out of here."

Finally, Schulz heaved himself out of his chair. I glanced at the general. He was looking anxiously out the window, his forehead again wrinkled, this time in alarm.

An explosion shook the house.

"Damn!" yelled the general as he dashed out.

I lost my balance and fell to my knees. Schulz grabbed his chair. Dust and smoke rose before the living-room windows. A Waterford vase on the mantel teetered and fell. The boom reverberated in my ears.

"What the hell was that?" Schulz shouted.

I straightened up and gazed at him.

I said, "I tried to warn you. You wouldn't listen. That was Putting In The Garden. Terrorist technique."

6.

"Well," Schulz said. He looked around the living room, surveyed the dust rising in front of the windows. Then he eyed me and shook his head. He held out his hand to help me up from the floor.

"Interesting folks you're living with," he said when I was on my feet again. "Almost as good as a problematic ex-husband. Want to tell me about that?"

I rubbed my bruised elbows and muttered a negative. Schulz shrugged and turned. I followed his saunter to the front door. Schulz's presence, his great reservoir of calm, were things I was not yet ready to let go.

As if to reassure myself, I said, "I'll be okay here."

He shook his head again, took a deep breath. "Is there anyone inside this house right now? Or is everyone tending the aftermath of this garden bomb?"

Before I could answer, the phone bleated in the kitchen. I asked Schulz to wait and went to see which neighbor was going to be the first to complain.

But it was not a neighbor. In her role as vivacious volunteer, Adele was helping to coordinate a church music conference that would convene in Aspen Meadow in July. This call was from an Episcopal church organist and choirmaster in Salt Lake City. In a nasal tone, he demanded to know when Adele would return.

To my surprise I was able to put him on hold and press the intercom button to search out the general. He was not in the house. I got back on the line with the choirmaster.

"I don't know when she'll be back," I said, then imprudently added, "I didn't know there were any Episcopal churches in Utah."

The choirmaster yelled, "Listen! I need to know if she got fifty copies of *Songs of Praise*!"

I said, "This is not something I know about." Nor did I know why I expected someone who worked for the church to be civil, if not Christian.

"And who are you?" he asked.

"The cook."

There was a silence, then a groan. Would Adele please call as soon as possible? You bet, I said, and hung up.

Schulz was standing in the hall perusing the panel of buttons that controlled the house security system.

"Neighbor?" he asked without looking at me.

"I wish. It was for Adele. The general's wife."

"Should I have heard of her, too?"

"I don't think so. Remember my friend Marla? Her sister."

Schulz looked up the stairwell, then at the panel of security buttons. "You've got four loops here," he said. "What—fire, perimeter, back door, first-floor motion detector?"

"Very good," I said wearily, then added, "I feel awful."

Schulz put his arm around my shoulders and guided me back out to the kitchen.

"Did I hear you correctly?" he asked as he gave me his patented Santa Claus half-grin. "Do I remember Marla? How could I forget? My ears still haven't recovered. Why don't we get Miss Yakkety-Yak over here to be with you?"

I said something vaguely affirmative and Schulz began to paw through the kitchen desk until a phone book presented itself. Muttering under his breath, he stared at the phone with its many buttons, frowned, and then punched. His voice murmured into the phone, echoed off the surfaces of the shiny pots and pans, and reverberated from the brilliant counter tiles. I looked around the kitchen but then closed my eyes. Everything seemed too bright.

With my eyes shut, I tried to look inward. What was I feeling? Nothing. Absolutely nothing.

"Twenty minutes," said Schulz after he hung up. And then without asking he moved around the kitchen opening more cabinets until he found some tea. He set about boiling water and heating a pot. Eventually he poured steaming amber liquid into thin porcelain cups. The soothing fragrance of Earl Grey tea filled the kitchen. When I thanked Schulz there was a catch in my voice.

He settled onto a barstool and we drank in silence. Only the distant yells of General Bo and Julian punctuated the silence.

"Goldy," Schulz said finally with that half-smile of his, "tell me more about your general."

I *tsk*ed and sighed. "He was in Afghanistan," I said, "role of observer or something. Before that he was a demolitions guy."

Schulz let out a low whistle. "It's coming back. He's the guy, taught the Afghanis how to blow up Soviet tanks with rocket-propelled grenades they'd captured. He was the guy! I knew I'd seen him on TV."

I turned back to my tea. "Nobody could figure out where the Afghanis were getting their recoilless rifles and C4, which is an explosive used by terrorists."

Schulz smiled. "Thanks. I know what C4 is."

I shrugged. "Anyway," I said, "General Bo wasn't talking. Maybe the army didn't *want* him to give specifics. Marla said Bo was supposedly involved with the black market for explosives. Now he's a civilian and he consults. He experiments. If he survives, he writes about it." I stopped talking, exhausted by the effort.

"I don't know if I'd want to be living on the top floor of a house belonging to a former demolitions expert. Emphasis on the former."

"Thanks loads."

"Now tell me about John Richard Korman."

I sipped tea, tried to think of how to put this so it wouldn't seem like such a big deal. I had told neither Philip Miller nor Tom Schulz—until our ride over here today—about The Jerk's behavior last month or how it had frightened me. Why discuss John Richard's behavior? Philip would have tried to explain it and Schulz would have tried to stop it.

Philip. The name brought pain.

I said, "I told you. John Richard was driving by every night. Hassling me about money, about seeing Arch. For about a month."

"Did you report it?"

I shook my head.

Schulz said, "Did you do *anything*?"

I said, more sharply than I meant to, "I divorced him, didn't I? I moved, didn't I? I'm getting a security system for my house, okay?"

"Look," he said, "we've got a weird call and now a death. Someone you knew. You've got a violent ex with a bad family history. I want you to stay in touch with me. You're not safe. Do you understand?"

I nodded, numb.

The security gate buzzed: Marla, thank God. I looked at my watch. 2:30. Hard to believe. Events and conversations were flowing together, out of my control.

Marla arrived at the front door wearing one of her sequined and feathered sweat suits. Here and there jeweled barrettes held her fluffy brown hair. She looked like a plump exotic bird. In her hands were shopping bags. These were undoubtedly filled with ready-to-eat gourmet delicacies hastily purchased to relieve me from cooking. My heart warmed at the sight of her.

"Oh Goldy, God, I don't believe this," she said when she had heaved the bags onto the foyer floor. Her capacious arms circled me. "Are you okay?"

I lifted my chin from her shoulder and said, "No."

"I'll bet. Where's Adele?"

"At a meeting."

From behind us, Schulz said, "I'm off."

I pulled away. "No, wait—"

Marla, sensing discomfort in the air, scooped up the grocery bags and mumbled about getting things into the kitchen. Schulz and I walked out the front door.

Birds squawked and flitted between the pines. The sun was warm. A bird darted into a well of sunlight and flashed a white underbelly. It was getting on to late afternoon. Snow melted noisily all around us as we made our way to the car. Tree branches dripped and the earth sucked and popped in absorbing the wet. Here and there on the lawn and in the general's new flower pots were clods of dirt that had been blown over the roof by the backyard garden-explosion. At Schulz's car, I thanked him for bringing me home. Avoiding his eyes, I said, "You've been kind. Thanks."

He waited for me to say more, to say something about seeing him again or wanting to. But I did not.

He said, "Goldy?"

"Yes?"

"Call me if you want to talk about the accident. Or anything else."

"You need to come home," Marla was saying into the kitchen phone when I returned. She hung up. "Adele," she explained, rolling her eyes. "Wanted to know why I was answering the phone in her house, so I told her about you and Philip and the accident. Talk about stunned. She was speechless."

"Where was she?"

"Still at Elk Park Prep. My sister, the storm-trooper fund-raiser. It's like putting General Bo into one of those paint-pellet games. God help the school." She paused for a moment, then pulled a clear plastic container filled with salad from one of the bags. "Speaking of Bo," she said, "I bought something that sounds like a uniform. Field greens? Think you can get them on the black market, too? Anybody done a study of terrorist food?"

I turned to her with my mouth open. "Field greens?" I didn't get it. Suddenly the absurdity of everything swept over me. I gagged. Marla reached out to hold me.

"It's okay," she said.

Firmly, Marla sat me down. With the efficiency I admired so much in her, she made some espresso. She knew I loved the stuff, and she even remembered not to ruin it with lemon peel or sugar. I liked it better than tea anyway. When she set the tiny cup down, she glanced out back.

"What's the general doing? Putting in a gold mine?"

"No, a garden."

She shook her heavy cheeks. "Too bad he's never gone hand to hand with The Jerk." She giggled and sat down next to me in a flurry of feathers and sequins. She said, "There are a lot of people we should call. About Philip."

I nodded. In Aspen Meadow you had to call people in times of crisis. You had to let them know they'd be needed. She found pencil and paper and asked for numbers, which I read to her from our slender town phone book. At Elizabeth's house she got the answering machine. Next she tried a neighbor of Elizabeth's in the hope that we could get somebody to be with her. There was no answer. Marla then tried Aspen Meadow Health Food. She told the clerk what had happened, asked her to put up a sign closing the place for the next few days, and left our numbers to be called.

When I had finished the coffee we put away the food Marla had purchased: there was enough for several days. She asked me about the evening meal. Chicken salad, in the refrigerator. I could not imagine eating. I looked at my watch.

Where was Arch?

"Goldy." Marla touched my shoulder. "What is it?"

"Find out where Arch is," I said in a whisper.

Marla turned crisply and called the school, was put on hold, fumed and fussed, and eventually had an answer. She held her hand over the receiver. "Adele offered to bring him home when the general comes by later. But she's not authorized to take him, so Arch is still there, and Adele is coming home early with somebody else. Want me to go?"

I shook my head and got on the phone with the minor bureaucrat, said General Farquhar would be by later and he had my authorization to pick up Arch.

Marla asked if I wanted more coffee or what. I shook my head as she took out lace place mats and English china for the evening meal, then searched out the general. I wanted Arch to be home. I wanted this day to be over. When Marla returned, she moved between the kitchen and dining room to set the table. I furiously began to wash the teacups. Work was always the best antidote for frustration.

Also the best antidote for . . .

With a pang I saw Philip's face crinkled with laughter the last time we'd gone out. I'd told him Arch had bought a copy of *The Anarchist's Cookbook* and refused to yield it to me when I'd demanded it. Philip had found this amusing.

"Censorship," he accused. "Even if it is a cookbook."

"For bombs," I said. "I'm not sure the general's influence is good for him."

"You know as well as I do," he said, "that the more upset you get about it, the more he's going to want it. Just talk to him. Don't lose your cool. He's been in therapy; he can always go back. And you've got me."

A teacup slid through my hands and broke to smithereens in the sink. Marla rushed over and ordered me to sit down. She said the general had gone in his Range Rover to check on the T-bird and get Arch. Just relax, she kept telling me, everything is going to be okay.

I looked out the west-facing kitchen window. Gray clouds had again billowed up over the mountains. On the hills below, lodgepole and ponderosa pines absorbed the sudden darkness. Stands of white-skinned aspens stood out like skeletons. The aspens' tiny cupped green leaves held the light and turned a fluorescent lime color as the gloom gathered.

"Goldy!" Adele Farquhar's voice rang down the hall. "Marla? Who's here?" The wooden hall floor echoed her familiar tap-step, tap-step. "Where are you?" Adele appeared at the kitchen doorway. Her thin, made-up face was pinched into lines of dismay. Her strawlike hair, dyed dark to hide the gray and cut into a severe pageboy, set off her navy-blue silk dress. Her hand gripped her cane so tightly her knuckles were white. She swept forward to embrace me; her voice cracked. "Thank God you're alive."

"It was awful," I said, my voice muffled by her shoulder. Adele smelled like floral powder mixed delicately with sweat. Her hair brushed my cheek; her pearls pressed into my neck. I could feel the bones of her thin shoulders under the layer of silk. After a moment I pulled away.

She said, "At the school they told us what happened." She shook her head in disbelief, her hazel eyes filled with questions. "He was a nice man. And a good psychologist. It's unbelievable. Philip was helping Julian so much . . . I don't know. God! This weather's so unpredictable."

I looked at her, a taller, thinner, older version of Marla. She was glancing around the kitchen in a distracted way, as if something contained in the polished, professional space could provide the cure for cold spring weather.

Her eyes found her sister. "Marla!"

"It is I," said Marla as she trundled forward and gave Adele a peck on the cheek. Sequins flashed against navy-blue silk. "I won't be staying long," she added apologetically. "I was just trying to help Goldy."

"No, that's fine, really. Stay. Where's Bo now?"

Marla's and my voices tumbled over each other as we told of the explosion and the general going for Arch.

"For heaven's sake," Adele said, shaking her perfect hair. She pulled herself up stiffly. "Let's go out to the porch. You've had too much of a shock."

"I'll be going," Marla said.

"You don't have to," was Adele's halfhearted protest.

I looked from one to the other of them. This was the first time I had seen the two sisters together since Marla had introduced us a week ago, when I arrived. I had sensed some slight discomfort then, but I had put it down to the move. Where Marla was always full of news and information, a walking radio station in designer sweat suits, Adele was reserved, elegantly groomed, erect in a wardrobe that featured only natural materials: silk, cotton, linen, cashmere. It was more than the ten-year difference in their ages. My emotional antennae picked up on unresolved pain. I would have to ask Marla about it. But not now.

"Bye, everybody," said Marla with a nod to us both. She whipped out the front door so quickly that I had only a moment to remember to press the button for the driveway gate. Her Jaguar revved, then growled down Sam Snead Lane.

"Let's go outside," Adele said. She turned and hobbled efficiently ahead of me to what the general called "the veranda." "Poor Bo, I don't know what he was thinking with that garden. I don't want to know what the neighbors must think . . ." Her voice trailed off.

I whisked back to the kitchen to get a pitcher of water and two glasses, then rummaged through the kitchen desk to get Adele's anti-inflammatory and muscle-relaxant medicine. If I did not bring it with me, she would be asking for it once we sat down. I found them behind a tin of Julian's fudge, which I put along with the pills, water, and glasses on a Florentine painted wood tray. Like the knickknacks and art objects in the living room, the tray was one of the many souvenirs of the Farquhars' travels before Adele's back problems had slowed them down.

On the covered porch it was quite chilly. Storm clouds still threatened to obscure the late afternoon sun. Adele gave me a wan smile and looked off toward the tops of the nearby mountains, where snow glimmered between the deep greens as incongruously as ice in a jungle. Next to the deck, birds—robins, jays, chickadees—were all busy, loud and angry at the weather for disturbing their nest-making. A jewel-winged hummingbird soared past, then swooped back to hover at the long-necked feeder.

"Water?" I asked. Adele nodded gratefully and reached for her pills.

I set the tray on the wicker coffee table, then let myself down into one of the wicker chairs. Again fatigue like a chill crept up from the floor. I sipped water, tried to shake the feeling off.

"Adele," I said, "I need to talk to you about your car. The T-bird. I'm sorry—I was trying to save Philip."

"Don't worry about it," she said. Her cane circumscribed a circle on the tile.

The phone rang. This time Adele motioned me to sit as she painfully rose to answer it. I could hear a one-sided conversation with the choir-master from Utah. Some people never quit.

I pulled a periwinkle-and-white afghan from its matching over-stuffed cushion held snug in a white wicker divan. Adele had decorated the house the way she dressed herself, with elegance and money. The style was traditional, without a rustic wood piece or southwestern accent in sight.

I tucked the afghan around my legs and gazed off into the distance. Fingers of fog snaked down the nearby canyons. In the meadow below, puffs of vapor glided by, ghostlike. Clumps of wild iris stood like clusters of pale-purple flags between hummocks of new green grass. Everything else was a tumult of greens: new green of wet spring grass, black-green of ponderosa pines, pale blue-green of spruce, bright green of new aspen trees. Another hummingbird dropped a twittering ribbon of sound as it shot by us. Adele tap-stepped back out to the porch.

"I put the machine on," she said apologetically. Then she held up a finger as we again heard the phone. After three rings the machine picked up. "Peace," she said as she sat down again. Her eyes found mine.

"I was following him to town," I said to her unasked question, "to pick up a few things for the Harringtons' dinner tomorrow night." I faltered. In my mind's eye the BMW careened down the last hill toward the bus. I looked at Adele, who had screwed up her face at the mention of the Harringtons.

She said, "I don't suppose Weezie will cancel, even though I think she was . . . you know, seeing him." She shook her head. "But you were saying . . ."

"Well. It was awful. I tried to help him, but—"

"You tried to help him? How gruesome. You poor thing." Her voice, like Marla's, was threaded with warmth and sympathy. The muscles in my neck relaxed.

"It all went too fast. And the way he was driving . . . Crazy, just crazy, as if he were drunk."

"Horrid."

I wasn't hungry, but I reached for Julian's fudge anyway. The buttery, rich chocolate melted, warming my mouth.

"Is Julian going to be okay? How close were they?" I asked.

Adele pursed her lips. "Poor Julian, I believe, had just grown to trust Philip Miller. I think this will be extremely hard for him." Her fingers brushed the pearls around her neck; the large diamond in her West Point miniature trapped the sun in a fleeting explosion of light.

I said, "Excuse me, Adele."

I went into the bathroom and buried my face in a towel.

When I came out, Adele assured me she would care for Arch when the general brought him. She convinced me to go up and lie down. The combination of brandy, tea, and espresso had the unusual effect of zonking me out for five hours. I awoke to the gray light of dusk. In my confusion I thought it was the next morning. But the sun slanting through the third-floor dormer windows and playing over the sloped ceiling and walls brought the realization that it was an early-June evening, around eight. I hoped the Farquhars had managed dinner.

In my mind I saw Philip's sightless face. I shook the image away.

Arch was rummaging around next door. I thought with dismay of all the work I would have to do the next day for the Harrington dinner. Usually I organized such affairs well in advance. But the headmaster at Elk Park Prep had pleaded so fervently that I salvage his brunch that my whole schedule had been put in disarray. I remembered that a cop might come out and ask more questions about the accident. Well. Sufficient unto the day. I needed to talk to Arch.

"Arch," I said through his closed door. "Did you hear about Philip Miller?"

"Yeah, I heard," came his muffled voice. "Bummer!" A pause. "Do you know where my suit is? I'm going swimming."

I caught myself making an audible groan and stifled it. Julian was trying to teach Arch how to do the front and back flip, the jackknife, and other dives in the Farquhars' pool. Chronic ear infections and bouts of virally induced asthma when Arch was little had prevented his learning to swim when other kids had. He was still not adept at anything besides the doggie paddle, so the diving gave me fits.

I said, "How'd the first day of summer school go?"

His head appeared at the door. Behind him I could see discarded clothes strewn around in piles. He had found the trunks, expensive blue Jams I had found on sale at a Denver department store. He said, "Huh?"

I repeated my question.

"Okay," he said. "Classes don't start until Monday. Can we talk about this later? I gotta go."

I steeled myself. He hated it when I acted protective, when I told him how much I worried about him, how it was especially bad when there was a loss like this. But. He was okay. That was all that mattered.

I said, "What are you studying?"

Arch pushed past me to get a towel from the linen closet. He said, "We start with Edgar Allan Poe."

"Want to tell me about it?"

He didn't. He backed out of the linen closet with a beach towel. "Not now, Mom. I want to swim." He looked into my eyes hard. "You won't have Philip Miller to go out with now."

"No," I said. Like most children of divorce, Arch held a secret longing for his parents to be reunited. This despite the fact that twice I had been forced to run out our back door carrying Arch to a safe house, to escape the rain of blows from Dr. John Richard Korman. Never for Arch, only for me, but how could I have escaped without my child?

"Oh well," Arch said now, "guess you'll miss him. Philip Miller, I mean."

I returned his look. "Yes," I said. "I will."

7.

I slept fitfully, dreamt of nothing, and lay in bed the next morning, Saturday, as if nailed there. I tried to put the image of Philip Miller out of my mind.

Sunshine and the strains of voices streamed through the east-facing window of my room as I stretched and breathed through my yoga routine. From the direction of the Farquhars' pool and garden, I could hear Julian and General Bo calling amicably back and forth. When I got up to investigate, I could see Julian vacuuming the pool with a long-handled instrument attached to a hose. Over a raked area of what had been the garden-crater, General Bo arranged flowering plants in rows as straight as well-drilled troops.

I had to smile. From here I could see it was the kind of garden an eastern couple with no children but lots of money would put in with great optimism. Lots of money for double-blossom begonias, Johnny-jump-ups, and lilac bushes that bordered rainbows upon rainbows of pansies. No children to worry about poisoning with late-blooming

Christmas rose and cama lilies. And optimism, in thinking the soil would be acidic enough for hydrangeas.

Seeing them labor so diligently made me realize I needed to focus on the day's work. Deadlines for obtaining supplies, cooking, baking, arranging, serving—all these gave caterers their thin and tired look. Alas, the bathroom mirror told me I was not thin, only short and blond and still sporting a field of faded freckles across a nose that even the kinder girls at boarding school had called "snub."

Which reminded me.

I came out of the bathroom and knocked softly on Arch's door. I felt awful because it was Saturday morning, but I needed to remind him that his father would be over later, and that all hell would break loose if he wasn't ready. And I wanted to find out if, on orientation day, he'd been snubbed.

"Arch?" I called through the wood.

To my surprise he opened the door. He was dressed in one of his all-purpose sweat suits and held his bag of magic tricks in one hand. He had his glasses on, a good sign that he had been up for a while.

"Your dad will be by this afternoon," I told him. Then, before he could say anything, I said, "You didn't finish telling me about the first day. Were the kids nice?"

He looked into my face and pulled his mouth into a straight line. "As a matter of fact," he said, "they weren't as bad as I expected." He paused and looked around the room. "Hold on, Mom, I got you something." He reached over to a shelf and solemnly handed me a Russell Stover Mint Dream. My heart warmed. Arch knew I loved chocolate with mint. He was always on the lookout for new combinations of the two ingredients.

"Well, thanks very much," I said as I fingered the silver-green foil. This was Arch's way of saying he was sorry about Philip Miller.

"You going to eat it?"

"Not before eight in the morning. But I will! It's my favorite, you know that."

He was not listening but was again rummaging through his

belongings. "Wait. There's a note here for you from Adele, er, Mrs. Farquhar." He handed me a crumpled index card.

The Nelsons have canceled and Weezie Harrington is beside herself. She called this morning and invited Julian and a date for tonight. I told her you'd already bought the food. I don't think she knows Julian is a vegetarian. Sorry if this causes problems! A.

I looked back at Arch.

"So what about the first day?"

"I told you, the kids weren't too bad. Watch." He turned his back to me, then pivoted and held up one, two, three ropes. He caught my eyes again and gave a tiny, knowing grin. "And now," he said with a flourish, and whipped out a single, long rope.

I clapped.

"I did it for the kids in my class at orientation. They liked it. Okay, Mom," he said by way of dismissal, "anything else?"

"How'd you get the candy?"

"Julian took me to Aspen Meadow Drug in the general's car. I told him my parents were divorced and my mom had lost her boyfriend and I needed to get her something."

"He wasn't my boyfriend."

"Okay, Mom. I need to practice now. Nobody was mean to me at the school. You don't need to worry."

Back in the bathroom, I started water gushing into the Farquhars' claw-footed tub. For myself, I was quite sure I hadn't *snubbed* anyone in years. Poverty will do that to you. But as a former doctor's wife, I had learned all about snub-ers and snub-ees. With the post-divorce reduction in circumstances, my friends, with the exception of Marla and a few others, had evaporated like the steam now rising from the bathwater. Former acquaintances feigned looks of confusion when they encountered me at catered functions, as when I'd seen a surgeon's wife I knew at the Elk Park Prep Brunch. There I was up to my elbows in cheese strata and sausage cake, and Mrs. Frosted Hair Usually Seen in Tennis Clothes had said, "Oh, Goldy!" (as if she'd been trying to reach me for weeks) "How *are* you?" (as if I'd just recovered from a failed suicide attempt) "Are you working now? I mean, besides *this*."

Yes indeed, I thought as I lowered myself into the water. Just this.

I reached for the pad of yellow legal paper I kept on a nearby stool that Arch had piled high with back issues of *Magician* magazine. Well, at least it wasn't *Playboy*. I wrote "Dinner For Six" across the top yellow sheet.

The hostess, Weezie Harrington, had given me an overview of aphrodisiac foods. I had placed a meat and seafood order, but vegetarian Julian and his date would present a problem.

"I have to have six," Weezie had said. "It sets up the right psychological dynamic." For Julian's meal I would have to do additional research. All I remembered at this point was Weezie's raised eyebrow when she'd said, "Chocolate for dessert. At one point, the church banned chocolate because it was believed to be inciteful of lust. So make it decadent."

I wrote "DECADENT" in large letters and wondered why Weezie and Brian Harrington, who had been married six years, needed aphrodisiacs anyway. He was an energetic and fit fifty. She was in her mid-forties, slender and elegant and with the look of an aging Greek goddess. The story around town was that Brian had courted Weezie lavishly to get hold of her gently sloping thousand acres just north of Interstate 70 near the Aspen Meadow exit. Once successful in obtaining Flicker Ridge, the story went, Brian had moved on to other conquests in the world of real women and real estate. And Weezie had recently steeped herself in the lore of desire-producing foods and substances, much to the current amusement of the country club. Whether she would win Brian back by these charms was up to the caterer, apparently.

I stared at the yellow pad. Brian, Weezie, Adele and Bo, Julian Teller and a female friend. I had already asked about food allergies, and managed not to smile when Weezie told me Brian was allergic to nuts. Since Venus was born in the sea, we were starting off with shellfish. Except for Julian. I sighed.

The library did not open until ten, this being Aspen Meadow and suitably provincial. I would have to whip around and finish shopping by eleven to have enough time to cook. Maybe the Farquhars' encyclopedia could yield info. Surely it would carry more than entries for rocket-propelled grenades and C-4.

I pulled the tub's plug. Feel great, I said to myself in the most persuasive way possible. Let the mood fit the food, André, my cooking instructor, had said when he trained me. Act hurried and your clients will feel hassled. Have a great time and your clients will have a great time. How I was supposed to act at an aphrodisiac dinner I did not know.

I reached for one of Adele's plush floral towels. Sudden tears bit the back of my eyes as the water sucked loudly down the drain. Have a great time.

Once dressed, I made my way quickly to the Farquhars' library-cum-study in the back of the house. Outside there was the regular slap-slap of Julian's arms hitting water. Through the window I could see him plowing through his morning laps. He had vacuumed up the dirt clods—remnants of the garden explosion—from the pool floor. But there was still dirt everywhere else, and the water looked somewhat murky. General Bo was sweating over another row of pansies. I turned to the books.

Volume A of the encyclopedia cracked open in my lap to "Aphrodisiacs."

I remembered Weezie tossing her lioness mane of blond and silver hair at our interview.

"Spanish fly," she'd said, "is really dried *cantharides,* a kind of beetle. Deadly as hell, despite its reputation."

The encyclopedia article talked about bark from the yohimbé tree in Africa. No help there; I was pretty sure yohimbé didn't grow in Aspen Meadow. And then there was the warning that ingesting Spanish fly was a highly toxic way of causing inflammation in the lower abdominal and genital regions. Burning pain accompanied the inflammation. If enough was taken, the inflammation was followed by death. Better avoid that one, too; didn't sound as if it would fit the ticket.

What Weezie had told me was that the effect from food was very subtle. She'd said, "You have to *tell* them what's supposed to happen." Tell them *what?* This will work if you *think* it does?

The encyclopedia concurred. The idea of inciting lust rested largely on the powers of suggestion and sympathetic magic. The rhinoceros had been particularly abused, I learned, owing to the unfortunate resemblance its horn bore to the erect male member.

Clearly, I would have to think about the suggestion angle. I closed the book and headed for the kitchen, where I could hear glasses tinkling and jars being moved in the refrigerator.

"Hello, there," I said to Julian's towel-wrapped backside.

He started, surprised, then turned to face me.

His thickly lashed eyes narrowed in appraisal. I didn't know much about Julian except that Adele had volunteered to take him in when the boarding department had closed at the end of this school year at Elk Park. He'd won a science scholarship to the prep school his tenth-grade year. This summer he was taking Advanced Placement Biology. As soon as the schedule was set, he was going to drive Arch to and from his class in American literature. His parents lived in the Four Corners area, where Colorado, New Mexico, Utah, and Arizona all came together. But that was all I knew, except that he made excellent candy.

And that he had been a patient of Philip Miller's.

Julian put his hand on his hip. At eighteen, he already had a swimmer's body, short and tough and muscled. I tried not to eye his bleached hair, which had been shaved in one of those Mohawk cuts with a center ridge. The blond half-inch stood up like a strip of unmowed lawn.

"What are you doing out here?" he demanded. He made no effort to hide his hostility.

"Fixing coffee, okay?" I put espresso makings together and tried to soften the anger I felt rising. What was he so mad at me about? Philip's accident?

"Julian," I said once a fragrant rope of dark liquid was twining out of the Farquhars' Gaggia. "I guess you've heard the bad news—"

"I know. I heard." He sat down at the kitchen desk chair and ran his fingers through what hair he had. "Bo said you were there," he said in a voice I tried not to think of as accusing. He raised thick, dark eyebrows set in a square-jawed, fine-featured face and crossed his arms.

"I was. I was right behind him."

The corners of his mouth turned down. His towel had fallen open over his wet tank suit, but he appeared to take no notice. He said, "What were you doing behind him?"

I took a deep breath, sipped foam off the espresso. "Driving Adele's car, following Philip into town. To have coffee. Then I was going to go buy supplies for Weezie's dinner tonight."

He turned away. Silence filled the kitchen. Then, "I'm a replacement guest," he said contemptuously.

"Lucky you, get to taste the food I make for a catered function. But with the brunch yesterday, I'm swamped. Mrs. Harrington has made specifications about the food. You're a vegetarian, and I need to do a dessert—"

He said, "Why don't you just use some of that fudge with the sun-dried cherries? For dessert, I mean. When I moved in a couple of weeks ago, I made a batch, and Adele took some over to the Harringtons. Brian Harrington loves the stuff. He couldn't believe I made it."

"Well, thanks," I managed to say, "but a client usually likes to have me make something if I'm going to get paid for it." I smiled and ventured, "Cooking is something we have in common." After all, if we were going to share the Farquhars' house and Arch for the next few months, rapprochement seemed in order.

He gave an offhand laugh and said, "I don't think we have anything in common."

Again silence fell between us.

Finally Julian said, "That coffee available or what?"

I nodded, dumped the spent espresso grounds, and started a new cup brewing. He stood up, tucked the towel in, and sat down again. When I had managed not to stare at him putting four teaspoons of sugar and a quarter cup of milk in my perfect espresso, I said, "Would you like to talk about Philip Miller?"

"Not really." He did not look at me, but began sipping somewhat noisily on the coffee. He said, "He was a good guy."

"When was the last time you saw him?"

"I don't remember."

"This week? Last week?"

"I told you," he said loudly. "I don't remember."

I said, "Sorry," and meant it.

Julian pushed back his chair and drained the espresso. "Look," he said, "I need to go change. You want to know about this food stuff, go to the library and ask for Sissy Stone. She, like, helped Mrs. Harrington with her research. She knows who you are. Sissy was a finalist for Colorado Junior Miss, too, how about that? I'm bringing her to the Harringtons' dinner tonight. My date, as Adele calls her." He stopped. "I don't believe aphrodisiacs work," he said defiantly.

"Really?"

"Yeah, really."

"Do you believe other means are more effective for getting the girl?" I asked with what I hoped was a friendly smile.

He whipped off the damp towel, slapped it over his shoulder, and started out of the kitchen. He paused at the door.

He said, "I don't think that's any of your concern."

I couldn't wait to get hold of Sissy Stone, sort of like getting hold of the flu. But when the wooden doors of the Aspen Meadow Public Library swung open at 9:58 A.M., the young woman behind the door gave me a toothpaste-ad smile. She was my height and compactly built, a cross between a gymnast and a cheerleader and probably functional at both. She had pushed up the sleeves on a too-large Elk Park Prep sweatshirt that I suspected was Julian's. Perfect cream beige makeup covered olive-undertoned skin. Her hair fell in thick dark waves that reminded me of the ribbon candy I bought Arch at Christmastime.

"I'm looking for Sissy Stone," I said with what I hoped was an enormous, confidence-winning grin. "Do you know where she is?"

The girl said, "Why?"

"Are you Sissy?" I asked.

"Well. Yeah," she said with another bright smile, as if I had just introduced her on network television.

I gestured into the library so we could go somewhere and talk. "Julian Teller suggested I come talk to you. I'm the owner of Gold-ilocks' Catering. Julian said you knew. . . ." To her unenthusiastic nod I said, "I'm working as a live-in cook with the Farquhars this summer.

You're coming to the dinner I'm doing tonight for Weezie Harrington." Another nod. "I need some help from you, the kind you gave her, if that's okay. In the area of food."

"Weezie Harrington," she repeated. She looked both ways, as if conscious of who might be watching or listening. "I'll have to check."

My hopes for this conversation grew dim. Around us young mothers pulled reluctant toddlers to Saturday morning story time. The front-desk computers whirred and beeped as morning visitors began to check out books, demand paper for the copier, and slap down volumes to be assessed for overdue fines.

I trundled after Sissy. She had a light step and carried herself with confidence. She glanced this way and that on her way to the computer, as if she were looking for someone more important to talk to. Once at the computer, she tapped away. "*Complete Aphrodisia* is out," she announced without looking back at me. "Let's check for articles." She moved efficiently to another machine, where she typed into another keyboard. As the machine whirred efficiently, she said, "I guess you can't wait until Monday?"

I shook my head. "Can we go outside for a few minutes? Please?" Before she could say no, I was on my way to the library garden, a plot lovingly and meticulously tended by the Aspen Meadow Garden Club. Long-stemmed flax, pansies, petunias, and mountain bluebell swayed in the cool morning breeze as I settled on one of the benches and gestured for her to do the same.

"Listen, Sissy," I began, "all I need is a few ideas. Julian is a vegetarian. Can't you remember anything from some of those articles you supplied Mrs. Harrington?"

"Oh, look, a pansy," said Sissy, as if I had not spoken. She gestured to the garden. "Do you know why its juice was used as a love potion in *Midsummer Night's Dream?*"

"Haven't the foggiest."

"Cupid shot one of his love arrows into what was originally a flower of pure color. You see," she said as she bent down to brush the pansy with her fingertips, "it bled."

I looked at my watch: 10:10. Clearly, Miss Priss had no intention of helping me. I would give this conversation five more minutes and then head for the grocery store.

I cleared my throat. "If Cupid were cooking for a vegetarian, Sissy, what would he fix?"

"Mmm," she said, and focused vaguely on a nearby evergreen. "Nothing too heavy. Eggs. Sign of fertility. Can you do that for dinner? Cheese for creaminess and sensuality. Also because it's easy to digest. You don't want to have indigestion at the wrong moment."

I stared at her. She closed her eyes dramatically and shrugged one shoulder. Well, at least we were getting somewhere.

"Cheese," I prompted.

"Something with spice. You know, like garlic or peppers. Onions," she added as an afterthought.

"Got it," I said, and she nodded. I went on, "Now I know chocolate's a must for dessert," another nod, "so I'm just looking at a salad situation here. Give me a tip in the green department and I'll be on my way."

But she was watching someone going into the library. I shook my head along with the flowers bending in the cool June wind.

I said, "What kind of roughage heats up the libido, Sissy?"

No response. My watch said 10:20. I stood up and started to walk toward the car.

She called after me, "Fennel! Endive! Asparagus, carrots, and mushrooms!"

At the grocery store I bought ingredients for Shrimp Dumpling Soup, Chile Relleno Torta, as well as avocados, mushrooms, and baby lettuces for salad. Back at the Farquhars I spread everything out and began to get out pans to grease. My cooking concentration began to rev up, like the adrenaline some athletes claim after the first mile. Then the security gate buzzed.

It buzzed and buzzed. It was apparent that I had gone from live-in cook to phone answerer to butler and general factotum.

"Yes," I said into the speaker. The closed-circuit camera showed two men in a dark sedan.

"Goldy Bear?" asked one of them. "We would like to talk to you."
Police officers.

I said, "I am unbelievably busy."

"Just a few questions."

"May I cook while you ask things?"

"We'd rather you'd take some time out."

"Then you'll have to come tomorrow."

A pause. They looked at each other.

"You can cook," said one.

I buzzed them through. A moment later, I opened the front door
and drew my mouth into what I hoped was a threatening pucker. "My
business isn't in jeopardy, is it?"

"If we can just talk to you, Ms. Bear, we should be able to get some
things straightened out."

"Right," I said as I turned to walk down the hall to the kitchen. "I
can't wait."

8.

The cops introduced themselves and then sat down at Adele's oak kitchen table. I readied my recipe for Chile Relleno Torta. If I made an individual serving, everyone would want a bite, and Julian would have no main dish. Anyway, when serving men a nonmeat entrée, it is essential to serve enormous amounts so as not to offend machismo. Otherwise, after you've cleared the ramekin or quiche or soufflé away, one of the fellows will innocently pipe up, "That was great! Now what's the main course?"

"Ms. Bear?" said the first one, who was named Boyd. He was a barrel-shaped man with a short black crew cut that was not meant to be fashionable. One of his stubby carrotlike fingers held a ballpoint pen poised over a smudged notebook. "Were you the last one to talk to Dr. Miller before he got into his car?"

I removed brown eggs from the Farquhars' side-by-side refrigerator and thought back.

Chile Relleno Torta

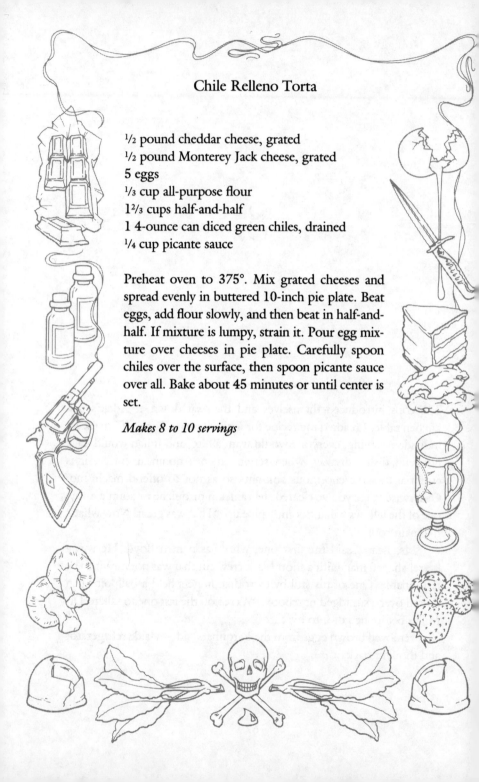

1/2 pound cheddar cheese, grated
1/2 pound Monterey Jack cheese, grated
5 eggs
1/3 cup all-purpose flour
1 2/3 cups half-and-half
1 4-ounce can diced green chiles, drained
1/4 cup picante sauce

Preheat oven to 375°. Mix grated cheeses and
spread evenly in buttered 10-inch pie plate. Beat
eggs, add flour slowly, and then beat in half-and-
half. If mixture is lumpy, strain it. Pour egg mixture over cheeses in pie plate. Carefully spoon
chiles over the surface, then spoon picante sauce
over all. Bake about 45 minutes or until center is
set.

Makes 8 to 10 servings

"I think so," I said. Then, "Yes, I was. He helped me load platters into Mrs. Farquhar's Thunderbird."

"This was at Elk Park," said the other fellow, a stocky fellow named Armstrong who had thin strands of light-brown hair pulled over a shiny bald spot. He had the pasty complexion people get when they've spent too much time inside. I nodded.

"Did he seem to be in any pain to you?" asked Boyd.

I narrowed my eyes at him. "Pain? Like physical pain? Or psychic pain?"

Boyd said, "Philip Miller was late for the breakfast because he had just been to his doctor, according to his sister. Now we still need to talk to the doctor, but we're just asking, how did he seem?"

I thought back to Philip. On such a dark and cold June morning, he had been as smartly dressed as ever in his black and white outfit and Ray Bans. There had been the usual smattering of resentful female glances and whispers as he'd made his way over to me, as if I did not deserve so lovely a man.

Wait a minute. Ray Bans?

"What kind of doctor did he go to?" I asked.

"We're not at liberty—"

"Oh, shut up," I said impatiently. "Was it an eye doctor?"

The two cops exchanged a look.

"Routine checkup," said Boyd. "How'd you know?"

"Sunglasses," I said. But I felt gloom descend again. So? He'd been able to see me across the room, he'd walked over, talked, walked back out to his car . . .

"What did he have to eat at the breakfast?" asked Armstrong.

I ran through that again and added, "His sister gave him some sausage cake. Just a bite, and I saw her do it. Nothing sinister."

"You made the sausage cake?"

I nodded slowly.

"Miller and his sister seem to get along to you?"

"Of course. He helped her out with that health-food store—"

"He helped her out," Boyd repeated.

"So what?" I said.

No response. I said, "Look, I can probably help you more if you tell me more. We're not exactly talking state secrets here. I knew Philip was helping Elizabeth financially, I just don't know how much."

Boyd wrote in his notebook, stopped, then bit the inside of his cheek. He said, "The other two hippie-food stores in this town went out of business over five years ago. Hers was the only one left, because her rich brother had bailed her out with a six-figure business loan."

"Elizabeth was devoted to him. She worried about him," I said. "How many siblings in their thirties can you say that for?"

He sniffed, then said, "She gave him something to eat. Did she have some, too?"

"She's a vegetarian." I left out the high-performance part. "Forensic pathology's not my field. What does the autopsy say about the contents of his stomach?"

"Who prepared the rest of the food?" asked Armstrong, brushing aside my question.

"Except for the nut cakes, I did. But no one—including Philip—got sick." Annoyance bristled in my voice. "Your insinuation is unappreciated."

They ignored me. Then came a barrage of questions: Did Philip have an argument with anyone at the brunch? Was anyone else in the parking lot? Did his car start right away? Was there anything hanging underneath the car? Did the brakes appear to work? I answered as best I could: nothing suspicious with the car or the person.

"You were going out with Philip Miller, weren't you?" asked Armstrong.

For the second time that day unexpected tears stung my eyes. The last thing I wanted to do was fall apart in front of these two.

I cleared my throat and said, "I was very fond of him."

Armstrong pressed on. "Anyone jealous of that relationship? Your ex-husband? Miller's ex-wife lives in Hawaii, but what do you know about any former girlfriends of his?"

"I don't know about his former girlfriends," I said with some sharpness. The only thing I knew about Philip's ex-wife was that she existed. For heaven's sake, we'd only been going out for a month. To my relief the brink of tears passed. I drew myself up and said, "I try to have as little to do with my ex-husband as possible."

"We have several reports on file, Ms. Bear. All from you."

I said evenly, "He wasn't at the brunch."

"Did Philip have anything to drink?" asked Boyd. "Coffee? Juice?" He stared at me. "Champagne?"

I said, "I didn't see him drink anything."

"But twenty minutes later he's driving like he's drunk."

I put my hands flat down on the island, then leaned toward their impassive faces. "Then why wouldn't he pull over?"

Boyd said, "Macho guy, he's not going to pull over and ask a woman for help. Maybe."

I shook my head, then said, "Look, why don't you see what the eye doctor says? Maybe he was on some medication or something—"

"Thank you, Ms. Bear," said Boyd. He nodded to Armstrong to indicate the interview was over. "We need to talk to you, we'll call."

I grated cheddar and jack, beat eggs and swirled in flour and cream, drained chiles, then mounded the cheese into pale hillocks on the pie plates. The cream mixture made a wonderful glug-glug noise as I poured it over the cheese. I spooned the chiles on top and then artfully sloshed picante sauce over each. As I put the pies into the Farquhars' oven the security gate buzzed. Not the police again already. This time I was going to cook whether they liked it or not.

It was not the police.

It was my ex-husband.

He gave me a broad smile in the closed-circuit camera. He lifted up his hands to show he was unarmed.

I let his car through and felt sick. In my state of confusion over the accident and the work for the dinner party, I had forgotten to call up to Arch and make sure he was ready. I stared at the intercom. If I could mince with a Cuisinart, I could master this. I pressed buttons and called hopefully throughout the house. No answer. I made my way out to the front porch. There was no way I was letting him into the house.

"Heard you lost your boyfriend," he said once I came through the door.

I looked around for neighbors, the general, Julian, anybody. The only thing I saw were the little marble and clay pots that the general was supposed to fill with geraniums and impatiens sometime during the weekend.

I said, "News travels fast."

"I need to talk to you."

"I'm listening," I said as I sidled away from him, moved a couple of unpotted plants aside, and tentatively sat.

"I didn't say I wanted to go to bed with you. I just said I wanted to talk."

"I can hear you just fine. And if you want to *talk,* you're going to have to watch your mouth."

He rolled his eyes and shook his head, then smiled at me indulgently.

John Richard Korman's extraordinary handsomeness, his boyish sensitive face, brown hair, and light blue eyes, always made me feel light-headed. He also played his doctor aura to good effect. He did this not just with me but with all manner of women, I came to find out after we were married. It was this type of man Henry Kissinger had been talking about when he said that power was the great aphrodisiac.

This was the man I used to love, the man who had slapped me when he was drunk, the man who did not love me. I knew to guard against his disarming good looks by keeping the conversation short. Kissinger, I reasoned, was probably talking about himself.

I pressed my fingers down into the dirt around one of the geraniums waiting to be planted. It needed water. Then I brought out a paring knife I had slipped into my apron pocket and put it down next to the plant, where John Richard couldn't see it. Just in case.

He said, "A female friend of mine is going to teach Arch a few magic tricks."

I said, "Oh, please. Your last girlfriend tried to teach him geometry and he's gotten D's ever since."

"Maybe that's because someone's too busy catering to help him with his homework."

I closed my eyes. I did not want to get into a fight. When I opened my eyes, John Richard was giving me his toothy innocent smile.

He said, "So where are Marla's sister and her famous husband? What's his name—Rommel?"

"Don't."

He looked at the sky, then said, "Well, let me ask you this. Who're you cooking for tonight?"

"The Harringtons."

He laughed. He guffawed, started to say something, and then snickered and wouldn't quit. I was not going to give him the satisfaction of asking what the joke was. He said, "This is just ironic as hell."

"Why's that?" This conversation was strange, but familiar. One subject, then another, laughing one minute, then . . . my neck snapped up involuntarily. Too late.

John Richard picked up a clay pot and threw it at the front door. The crack of the shatter reverberated in my ears. Then a second pot smashed against the house.

"Stop it, stop it," I squealed and buried my face in my hands. My throat was raw, like in those nightmares when you call for help but have no voice. I looked up in time to see him kick a third pot. Fragments went spinning away from the porch steps.

"Okay! Okay!" My voice begged. I looked helplessly at the knife. What did I think I was going to do with it, anyway? "Whatever it is, you can have it," I cried. "Just stop. Arch is on his way out here."

John Richard glared at me. He spat out each word. "You've ruined my life. My family's gone, my practice has lost business. All your fault, you bitch. So listen up. If I want my son to learn magic, he's going to learn."

"All right! Just calm down, for God's sake! I've got a party to do tonight, and I don't want trouble!"

He picked up another pot and threatened me with it. I could hear my heart beating in my chest. "Don't want trouble?" he mimicked in a high voice. "Don't want trouble?"

Before I could answer, there was General Bo suddenly behind John Richard. The general grabbed The Jerk's neck with both hands. John Richard dropped to his knees like a rag doll. The clay pot fell out of his hands and rolled down the driveway.

"Oh, stop! Stop!" I cried as I jumped to my feet. A ball of nausea collected in my stomach.

General Bo Farquhar took no notice of me. He spoke down to John Richard's head, which he had torqued around to force eye contact.

"Now you listen to me, you little son of a bitch," said the general with such ferocity that my whole body broke out in a sweat. "There's a law in this state called Make My Day. You set foot on this property again, I'll use it. I'll show you how the Special Forces can kill people without making any noise. Is that clear?"

John Richard made the throaty sound of a man about to be strangled. The front door opened. The general released John Richard into the freshly raked dirt at the side of the driveway just as Arch came out. Arch looked soundlessly from person to person, then pushed his glasses high up on his nose.

He said, "Should I go back inside, Mom?"

John Richard was wiping dirt from his nose. I wanted to say, Yes, yes, go back! But I could not. John Richard gave an almost imperceptible nod. I gestured to Arch to go. He plodded toward his father, who was brushing dirt off his polo shirt.

The general moved toward the porch. He said quietly, "Goldy, I'd like to see you inside."

I nodded. But I could not take my eyes off John Richard, who was walking slowly with Arch toward his Jeep. John Richard whirled, and I cringed.

He yelled to me, "Philip Miller was fucking Weezie Harrington!"

9.

I trudged up the steps as the Jeep roared away. The general leaned over broken clay fragments and pressed his lips together. He motioned me inside. Behind us he firmly shut the front door with a no-nonsense, deliberate sound: *chook.*

I thought, At best I'll get a lecture. At worst I'll lose my job.

He gazed at me with those piercing blue eyes.

He said, "Don't ever let that man through my gate again."

I nodded vigorously.

"When he comes to pick up Arch," he spoke the name delicately, as if Arch were his own son, "I will be the one to complete the transfer. Also," he continued as he retrieved a short pole from a closet, "I want to show you this. It's a portable door jam. If that man" (my mind supplied, *the enemy*) "somehow gets through the gate and tries to come through the front door, you expand it like this." He clicked the steel rod open in his powerful hands. I had a sudden vision of Arch doing one of his magic tricks. "Then you wedge it under the doorknob."

The rubber-covered end squeaked across the tile floor like chalk on a board. When the jam was in place, General Bo ordered me to try to open the front door. Of course, it wouldn't budge.

"Thanks for—" I began in a wavering voice. Actually, I didn't know how I felt about his help.

"You're part of the family," he said solemnly. "Just make sure that when you wedge this thing in, it's under a door that opens toward you."

And with that the lesson was over. No sentiment. No sure-you're-all-right? The general took off down the hall with his long loping stride. It was the kind of walk people used to pace off a large distance. How could he get around the side of the house without my seeing him? How can you kill someone without making any noise? How could Philip have been having an affair with Weezie Harrington?

Well. I had cooking to do. I went back to the kitchen and mixed the Dijon vinaigrette and, pretending it was The Jerk's head, shook vigorously. I tried to focus on what Sissy had told me about the lust-inducing properties of onions and garlic and peppers. Concentrate, I told myself.

But I couldn't think. I couldn't catch my breath. Arch would be all right. John Richard had never harmed him.

Arch would be back tomorrow night.

The avocados were impossible to skin without getting my hands slimy. I looked at my green-covered fingers. Would I always be a failure at relationships? Philip's touch on my arm, the earnest look in his eyes, these came back. Had I been so bad a judge of character? Philip had been my age. Weezie was older. Not that an age difference made a difference anymore. Still, it was hard to believe that Philip and Weezie had been sexually intimate, when he and I had not.

The phone rang. After the mess with The Jerk, I did not want to talk to anybody. But the phone rang and rang, and the machine did not pick up. I was grateful that the Farquhars allowed me to use their third line for my business. The theory was that I would answer "Farquhars" to two lines and "Goldilocks' Catering, Where Everything Is Just Right!" to the third. Usually by the time I figured out which line was ringing I forgot to do this last, and just answered "Farquhars" to all three. So far, my regular clients had recognized my voice.

I grabbed a towel and picked up the phone. "Farquhars," I announced, but was met with silence. There was hesitant throat-clearing as somebody checked to make sure this was the right number.

"Is this Goldilocks the caterer?"

"Yes indeed, what can I do for you?"

"Is this Goldy *Bear* the caterer?"

"Well, uh, yes," I said.

My name was not my fault. My first name was Gertrude. Goldy was my nickname from childhood, and I had disliked it. Korman was my last name in adulthood, and I had disliked *it* even more. But the resumption of my maiden last name, along with my nickname, made me sound like an escapee from a children's story.

"This is George Pettigrew from Three Bears Catering in Denver."

Right away, I knew we had trouble. (*Don't want trouble?* I could hear John Richard's mocking voice in my inner ear.) The ensuing conversation proved I was going to get it anyway.

George and his wife had been in business for five years. They were strictly small-time. I mean, *I* had never heard of them. But they had read the article in the *Mountain Journal* and were loaded for bear, no joke. George was screaming about copyright infringement. How dare I use the name Bear? he wanted to know. Because it was *mine,* I said. But my divorce had taken place after George and his wife had started Three Bears. It was *their* name, he insisted. I said, Oh yeah? Then why not call it *Two Pettigrews?*

He said he'd see me in court and hung up.

I stared at the phone for what felt like an eternity. I couldn't face a call to my lawyer, and this being Saturday, he wouldn't be in anyway. I finished the shrimp dumplings and thawed a container of chicken stock I had brought from my house to the Farquhars. Together these two ingredients would make the soup course. Finally, I spent two hours putting together an enormous chocolate mousse cake. I began by making a three-layer chocolate cake. While it was cooling I made a smooth white chocolate mousse for one layer of filling, then a dark chocolate mousse flavored with framboise for the second layer of filling. I built the tower of cake-with-fillings as carefully as any architect, then covered the whole thing with a thin layer of tempered chocolate. I packed everything up.

It was time to visit Weezie Harrington.

The Harringtons lived next door. In New Jersey, living next door meant if you wanted to get from here to there you walked down your sidewalk, down the sidewalk by the street, and then up your neighbors' sidewalk. But this was Colorado, and next door meant a steep driveway down from the Farquhars' fenced property, a slanted stretch of street, and another driveway up to the Harringtons. These were daunting without a vehicle, so I decided to trek the back way, where the security fence had a back gate set to the same code as the front. Hoisting up two heavy-duty boxes, I trudged through the back door of the garage, past the extra-thick walls of the general's magazine, where he kept his explosives. Then I carefully circled the garden-site crater and beat a path through the long field grass between the two houses.

I wished I knew more about birds, I thought, as gaggles of feathered creatures flitted between bushes and trees. Philip had been devoted to the local Audubon Society and had asked if I'd consider catering one of their nature-hike picnics. Would they eat chicken? I wondered.

I sat down to rest on a rock by the gate. In a nearby cluster of aspens, warm afternoon air stirred pale green leaves the size of mussel shells. An iridescent blue-green hummingbird zoomed by overhead. Then a shriek split the calm.

"I don't understand—" cried a high female voice.

I peered through a stand of evergreens. I could just see the Harringtons' enormous deck. It was actually an elaborate cantilevered patio surrounded by a balustrade and filled with delicate white wrought-iron furniture that was all romantic curls and scrolls. The two women on the deck were not sitting down. In fact, from their voices and stances they appeared to be having an argument. I leaned closer to try to make out the words and faces.

"I can't believe you're doing this," came one voice, high, shrill, angry. I moved off the rock and sidled up to a blue spruce. It wasn't that I was eavesdropping or nosy, I told myself. I just didn't want to embarrass the combatants by suddenly arriving with a box of aphrodisiacal dumplings.

"I can't believe you could be so *crass* . . . to ask if he left anything to you—"

"Oh, calm down, for Christ's sake!"

I peered through the sweet-smelling branches of the prickly spruce. Elizabeth Miller had her arms folded across her narrow chest, and had turned away from Weezie Harrington.

I had not seen Elizabeth since the accident. Why was she with Weezie? And what in the world could they be arguing about?

"Please," shouted Weezie. "Listen, will you? We were working on something together. He told me he would leave—"

"*You* listen!" screamed Elizabeth. "He left his body to science, if that's what you want to know."

There was a silence. I felt intrusive, even though I was sure they had not seen me. One of the women was crying; it was hard to tell which one. Returning to the rock, I picked up the boxes, backtracked over the damp ground through the pines and grass and back through the Far-quhars' house. By the time I made it to the front door of the Har-ringtons' place I thought I would start counting the hours until I had my van back Monday morning. The voices became indistinguishable.

The Harringtons' house was a glass and stucco affair with a tile roof, the hybrid of Spanish colonial and French provincial that had been the rage in Aspen Meadow about fifteen years before. That is, insofar as any phenomenon in a town of thirty-five thousand people can be said to have been the rage.

A brass coyote-head door knocker echoed *klok klok klok* through the quiet interior. For a moment the screeching female voices rose again. My chest felt as if it were in a hammerlock.

Sometimes clients start drinking early on the day of a party. To relieve tension. Start the festivities early. Whatever. The problem was that this occasionally resulted in their canceling everything. Then all you got was your deposit, a whole lot of food, and anticipation of going to small-claims court, which I'd had to do from time to time. I fervently hoped that Weezie and Elizabeth had not added booze to their altercation. Just as suddenly as it had begun, the screeching stopped. I knocked again.

No one answered. I leaned against the stucco and peered through one of the double-pane windows, a standard insulating feature in mountain homes. The glass was cloudy, as often happens when the window was getting old. It had been a while since Brian had been king of the hill in Aspen Meadow Country Club, and the people he'd sold land to hadn't yet had the chance to build. The massive rough-hewn door, another hallmark of older club homes, swung open to reveal Brian Harrington.

"Sorry, Mr. Harrington," I said, flustered and apologetic in my clumsy attempt to pull back from the window. "I'm the cate—"

He stopped me with a wave of the hand and closed eyes. Silver chest hairs curled out of the V in his turquoise sport shirt. His shorts, a paler hue of turquoise, revealed muscular legs also covered with curly gray hair. Like everyone else in town, I had seen Brian's elegant self strolling down Main Street in the company of bankers or a Cadillac-load of oil people from Dallas. But I had never seen that chiseled face up close. I took a deep breath. He was gorgeous, the human equivalent of a male silver-backed gorilla. If I were Weezie Harrington I'd get out the aphrodisiacs, too.

My voice wobbled. "I'm the cate—"

"Listen," he interrupted, "there's a bit of a problem out back." He lifted the raised hand and ran it through his wiry hair, then shook his head.

"Problem," I echoed. With some effort I picked up a box. "Mr. Harrington," I said with as much authority as I could muster, "I need to get started in your kitchen if you expect to have a party tonight."

"Oh, yes, sure," he said absentmindedly as he opened the door all the way and I heaved the first of my boxes over the threshold. "Just follow me." He turned away and started down a hallway. Bastard. He could have at least offered to take a box. Good looks, yes. Chivalry, no.

The kitchen was one of those L-shaped affairs that made figuring out where to put and prepare things difficult. Again big Bri was no help. He promptly disappeared around the kitchen's corner. Five minutes later, looking for a platter for the cake, I found him lurking by the back door that led to the patio.

"Unbelievable," he said. "Those women are still arguing." He regarded me, his face pulled into puzzlement. Perhaps this was because his wife was one of those women. He shook his head and turned back to catch the sound of the again-raised voices. He closed the door abruptly and started toward me.

"I wouldn't mind two gals fighting over my body," he said with a wink, "but not if I were dead."

"Do you know where there's a cake plate, Mr. Harrington?"

"No. But you better look busy. They're coming."

With this he started to open cupboard doors and clatter through them as if he were genuinely seeking a plate or a glass or something, which he was not. I was standing holding the cake and feeling stupid when Weezie and Elizabeth came banging into the kitchen.

Elizabeth's voice was loud and still hostile. She said, "You're the one who's vulgar."

Then the two of them stopped, startled to see Brian and me gaping at them. Brian was clutching an upside-down casserole dish and I was balancing the cake. Weezie cocked her slender, evenly tanned face toward Brian. Her silver-blond mane, long, glazed scarlet nails, and crinkled tan pantsuit gave her the aspect of a cougar about to strike.

"What the hell is this?" she demanded.

"Honey, don't—"

"Mrs. Harrington—"

"Don't call me," Elizabeth interrupted Brian's and my protestations in her same furious tone. She cocked her head of wild blond frizz at Weezie. She had that drawn look vegetarians get when they aren't getting enough of something. I wanted to reach out to her, to say something to her about Philip, but her rage with Weezie immobilized me. "*Don't* call," she said to Weezie, her finger stabbing the air, "*don't* write, *don't* get your friends to bug me. Leave me and the memory of my brother alone, do you understand?"

"Why won't you listen to me?" shrieked Weezie, but Elizabeth had whirled and stomped off. While the three of us stood there, Elizabeth's Aspen Meadow Health Food truck whizzed down Sam Snead Lane.

"Honey," said Brian Harrington, "how about a drink?"

"No, thank you," Weezie said crisply. "I have a little surprise for Goldy," she said. One of the glazed nails was pointing at me. "Let me know when you've finished setting up," she ordered before breezing out. She did not look at her husband or me. When she was marching noisily up the hall stairs, Brian eyed me ruefully.

"Do *you* want a drink?"

"No, thanks," I said. I felt sorry for him. But I knew if I had one teensy-weensy drink, with what my ex-husband had told me earlier about Weezie and Philip, and the impending problems with the two Pettigrews, I'd be tempted to drown my grief in an entire fifth. "Maybe later," I added with more sympathy than I intended. "After the party."

"Oh?" He gave me a look. With a half-smile and raised eyebrows, he asked, "Are you staying after the party?"

How had I gotten into this? I had *heard* about Brian Harrington. I had seen him leaning toward my aerobics instructor and asking questions: "Where exactly are the obliques? Trace the muscle out for me when I twist over in this sit-up. Oh," he'd say, "I'm not sure I'm tensing the hamstring muscle when I'm pulling it out in this ski exercise. Put your hand on it."

Was I staying after the party? Ha. I didn't answer, but carefully put the cake down on the countertop. My arms ached. Then I rummaged through a cupboard until I found, miraculously, a crystal serving plate. That feeling of irritation, of being intruded upon, was creeping up. I needed to be alone to work. Never mind that it was *his* kitchen.

I said, "I'm staying to clean up, that's it. Does Mrs. Harrington have a salad bowl she wants me to use tonight? I really need to get to work in here."

"Oh, sure. It's probably around here somewhere." He didn't move but eyed me steadily with a suggestive half-smile.

I pursed my mouth into my best imitation of a displeased school-teacher and put my hands on my hips.

Brian Harrington raised his eyebrows again and said, "Am I being dismissed?"

"Sorry. I need to be alone while I work."

He remained immobile while I began the hunt for a bowl. He said, "You were going out with Philip Miller, weren't you?" I slammed cabinet doors and nodded curtly. He went on, "Did you hear his sister say something about giving his body to science?"

I found a salad bowl on top of the refrigerator and began to line it with paper towels. "He didn't talk to me about being an organ donor. If you don't mind, I'd really rather not talk about it." So saying, I rattled through drawers looking for serving utensils.

"Aah . . ." he began.

What in the world was the matter with the man? I sighed to let him know I was put out and said, "Now what is it?"

He smiled. "Will Sissy Stone be coming tonight?"

"If I tell you, will you let me do my work?"

"Yes, you cute little thing, you."

I picked up the cake and walked quickly toward the refrigerator. I said, "Sissy is coming tonight."

I could feel him moving in my direction. He murmured, "That cake just looks good enough to eat."

I *hrumph*ed and opened the refrigerator with my elbow and knee. If I hadn't been concentrating so hard, I would have realized how close he was. Suddenly there was a small nibble of cool lips on my neck.

He was kissing me.

I dropped the cake.

Crystal shattered with an ear-splitting crash. The mousse fillings splattered wildly, like cream and mud flung all over the floor. Clods of cake skittered in every direction. The tempered chocolate broke like bricks.

"You idiot!" I yelled.

Brian calmly surveyed the mess. "Sorry, dear," he said mildly. "You should have been more careful." He glided out of the kitchen.

I looked around. I think I was looking for a rope. The kind you strangle people with. I shouted after him, "Now what am I supposed to serve for dessert?"

10.

After twenty minutes of mousse, crystal, and cake removal, I traipsed back toward the Farquhars. The last thing I needed was more cooking.

I was so angry I was beside myself. I struggled to focus on André, my mentor in food matters. When I apprenticed with him at his restaurant in Denver, his shelves creaked under their loads of dense Callebaut chocolate and fragrant African vanilla beans. Each of his cooks received a five-pound block of butter at the beginning of the workday. All he would say was, "Use it up." André insisted on making Italian meringue for each batch of fudge. "Essential," he would shout over the roar of the mixer. On our lunch break he would expound. "Let the dieters be responsible for their own willpower. Their health is not your concern; your income is not theirs." He would demand, "Do you know the significance of the last course? It is what will linger in the memory and on the tongue."

What does that best?

Chocolate. In spite of my fury I smiled, remembering. Beneath my feet the ground was cold and spongy. Chilly fingers of grass swished against my heels. I came through the security gate and made a graceless leap onto the Farquhars' driveway, sidestepped rivulets of melting snow, and thought about the most important thing.

Even before Weezie insisted on it, I knew serving clients chocolate nurtured them emotionally. I'd read an article that said people crave chocolate, gorge on it in fact, when they have been let go by a lover, boss, or spouse. Weezie had told me that ingesting the food of the gods, as the Aztecs named it, produces an enzyme that creates sensations similar to sexual pleasure. I couldn't believe that with Brian, something similar was all she got.

I stomped back into the Farquhars' house feeling like one of those cartoon characters with steam issuing from his ears. I wet a clean hand towel and slumped into one of the oak kitchen chairs. Compromises, I told myself as I scrubbed the area on my neck that Brian Harrington had smooched. I threw the towel down, stood up, and tried to think sweet.

Tentatively, I reached into the cabinet where the fudge Julian had offered earlier was stored. I didn't have two hours to make another whole mousse cake. Serving a dessert I had not made was a compromise, but it was one I couldn't help. At least I hadn't compromised *myself.*

And I was thankful for Julian's expertise, if not his temperament. I sampled a piece. Rich semisweet chocolate oozed between sun-dried cherries. The balance between luscious, smooth chocolate and chewy cherries was from heaven. I knew I could make two more desserts simultaneously. The fudge would balance well with brownies, and I could put together something with chocolate chips at the same time.

I banged and searched and groped in the Farquhars' cupboard for ingredients. I jumped sky-high when a cat wove between my legs. As if I didn't have enough problems, I thought uncharitably.

A few weeks before I moved in, good-hearted Adele had heard this feline meowing outside the fence by the pool. She had adopted the scrawny thing, and the general had named him Scout, somewhat prematurely, I thought. Now Scout, whose white, dark-and-light-brown coat meant that his ancestors were from Siam and Burma, jumped up on the counter to see what was up. He was a friendly fellow who had gone unclaimed by ads in the paper and calls to the veterinarian and Mountain Animal Protective League. Still too spooked by the neighborhood dogs to go back outdoors, Scout inspired great sympathy.

Now Scout was determined to figure out what I was doing, and as long as he didn't get any cat hairs in anything, I was willing to let him spectate. I made a crust for what would be a chocolate-chip bar and popped it in the oven. I let Scout be the inspiration for the brownies. I used chocolate in three forms, which was what you needed when times were tough. I wasn't in my proper home. Neither was the cat. I did not have my usual bevy of ingredients. He probably cherished the memory of an old couch pillow he'd never see again. Marching on in the face of adversity, both of us.

I finished the top layer of the chip bars and put them into the other oven. The brownies came out looking like a chocolate lunar surface. I knew I was supposed to let them cool, but who can do that? I cut out a corner and popped it into my mouth. The triple-chocolate concoction I'd come up with under the cat's observation was extraordinarily good. To congratulate us both I dubbed them Scout's Brownies. As the delicious dark stuff sparked the beginning of a heavenly shiver, the phone rang.

"Hmmf?" I said with my mouth full.

"Miss Goldy?" asked Tom Schulz. "You eating something? Must be awfully good if you didn't finish it quick to answer the phone."

"Mmf," I affirmed.

"Let me know when you can talk."

I finished the brownie, but longed for another. To Schulz I said, "I can talk, thank you. What do you want?"

"Uh-oh, she's getting back to her old self."

I said, "Would you prefer to do this in writing?"

"No, no," he said, and I could hear him leaning away from the phone, reaching for something adrift on the sea of paper he called his desk. "Okay," he began again, "you know a Sissy Stone? She's at that Elk Park School, be a senior next year. Has a summer job at the library?" I mm-hmmed noncommittally and he went on, "She was doing an apprenticeship with Philip Miller. Something they do their junior year. Learn about different careers and whatnot." He clucked. "Guy who talked to her said she was pretty flaky."

Scout's Brownies

1 cup (2 sticks) unsalted butter

3½ ounces best-quality unsweetened chocolate (recommended brands: Callebaut or Valrhona—available at Williams-Sonoma)

3 tablespoons dark European-style unsweetened cocoa (recommended brand: Hershey's Premium European-Style)

1½ cups all-purpose flour (high altitude: add 2 tablespoons)

½ teaspoon baking powder

1 teaspoon salt

4 eggs

2 cups sugar

1 teaspoon vanilla extract

1 cup chocolate chips (recommended brand: Mrs. Field's)

Preheat oven to 350° (high altitude: 375°). Melt butter with unsweetened chocolate in top of double boiler, stirring occasionally. Set aside to cool. Sift together cocoa, flour, baking powder, and salt. Beat eggs until creamy, then gradually add sugar, beating constantly. Add vanilla and cooled chocolate-butter mixture. Stir in dry ingredients just until combined. Spread batter in buttered 9-by 13-inch pan. Sprinkle chips over surface. Bake for 30 to 35 minutes, or until center no longer jiggles when shaken. Cool, then cut into 32 pieces.

Makes 32 brownies

"A veritable blizzard. But I think it's an act. She just doesn't want to talk when someone else more important might come along."

"Oh. Well," Schulz went on, "she let on as how she was going out with that young fellow who lives at your place. I mean the Farquhars' place. You might want to see if she knows more about the shrink. You know, in a friendly sort of way."

"I don't get it. Why should I?"

"Now, Goldy, ease up. You were the one who kept insisting Miller's accident looked so strange. Ask a few questions, why don't you? They're doing a drug screen, part of the autopsy, you know . . ."

I shuddered.

". . . but sometimes there's some kind of personal thing going on that you can find out about in other ways. You're not a suspect." He didn't need to add, *this time*. "You're my friend, and I'm talking to you in confidence. Besides, with that 911 call, I'm worried. You know."

As usual, I didn't.

"So what're you cooking?" he asked.

I gave him a brief overview of Brian Harrington's lustful schlep and the cake's demise. Said I had just finished brownies named after the cat and was cooling chip bars.

"Why don't you name something after me?" His voice was so innocent and pleading, I pursed my lips in thought.

He said, "Just nothing about pigs, please."

"Wouldn't hear of it."

"Glad you're feeling better, Miss G."

I smiled, rang off, and christened the chocolate-chip bars Lethal Layers.

When I finished I alternated thick brownies, gold-brown Lethal Layers, and Julian's creamy dark squares in a stunning arrangement, if I do say so myself, atop one of Adele's Italian wood trays.

The dessert issue was under control. What was not settled was what I was going to wear. I hauled the last two boxes of food over to the Harringtons. Weezie had said she had a surprise for me. I hoped it was not her husband.

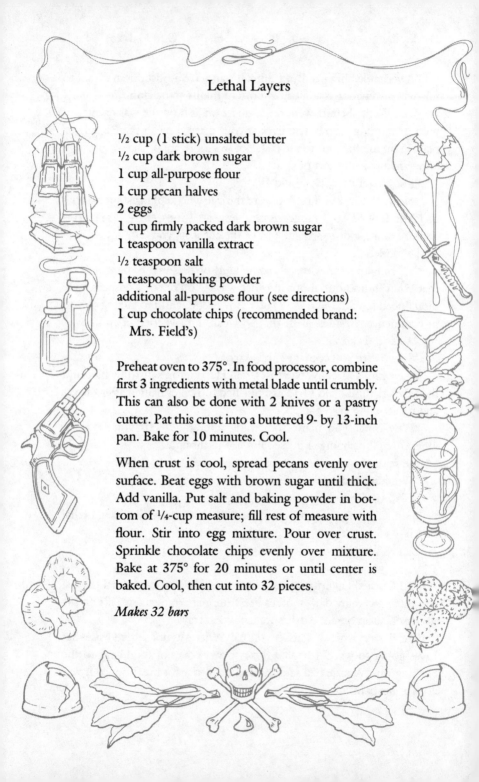

Lethal Layers

½ cup (1 stick) unsalted butter
½ cup dark brown sugar
1 cup all-purpose flour
1 cup pecan halves
2 eggs
1 cup firmly packed dark brown sugar
1 teaspoon vanilla extract
½ teaspoon salt
1 teaspoon baking powder
additional all-purpose flour (see directions)
1 cup chocolate chips (recommended brand:
   Mrs. Field's)

Preheat oven to 375°. In food processor, combine first 3 ingredients with metal blade until crumbly. This can also be done with 2 knives or a pastry cutter. Pat this crust into a buttered 9- by 13-inch pan. Bake for 10 minutes. Cool.

When crust is cool, spread pecans evenly over surface. Beat eggs with brown sugar until thick. Add vanilla. Put salt and baking powder in bottom of ¼-cup measure; fill rest of measure with flour. Stir into egg mixture. Pour over crust. Sprinkle chocolate chips evenly over mixture. Bake at 375° for 20 minutes or until center is baked. Cool, then cut into 32 pieces.

Makes 32 bars

It was not. The short (midthigh) décolleté black and white lace uniform that Weezie proffered left me speechless. It was sort of French maid via Frederick's of Hollywood. If I dared to lean over to serve something, my cups would truly runneth over.

I shook my head and mouthed the word, *No.*

Weezie whined. She pouted. Said, "But I even checked your size!"

"Mrs. Harrington," I said when I finally recovered my breath. "I get paid to cook, serve, and clean up. Period."

She squinted at me. It made her look much older.

"I thought I told you how important *suggestion* was with aphrodisiacs," she said.

"But not with clothing," I said evenly. "When I describe the food, I'll make suggestions that are verbal." I was careful not to say *oral.*

She said, "Oh, all right," and then stalked out of the kitchen. I shook my head in resignation. As I was leaving, Brian Harrington popped out from around the corner. Had he been listening? I didn't know and didn't want to ask. He gave me a broad wink. I did my best imitation of raw egg white and slithered out.

11.

A day given to compromises, I reflected as I heated the broth for the dumplings. No caterer-as-a-centerfold uniform, no response to the Harrington Hustle, and the fee for tonight would pay Arch's tuition for the first two weeks of summer school.

Philip's face floated back before me. Hungry? I had asked. Ravenous, he'd said.

I pushed him out of my mind. I was almost done. The menu was finally set.

Aphrodisiac Dinner for Six

OYSTERS ON THE HALF-SHELL WITH FRESH LEMONS AND LIMES
SHRIMP DUMPLING SOUP
SALAD OF BIBB LETTUCE GARNISHED WITH
YELLOW PEAR-SHAPED TOMATOES, AVOCADOS,
AND GRILLED MUSHROOMS, DIJON VINAIGRETTE

CHILE RELLENO TORTA
SONOMA BABY LAMB CHOPS BAKED WITH HERBS
IN FOIL PACKETS
PURÉE OF ZUCCHINI
ASSORTED BREADS
TRAY OF CHOCOLATE TREATS

Only the flowers remained, I reflected as I stirred the soup. The delicate scent from the bubbling broth threaded through the air. Scent. Yes. On her list Weezie had detailed several flowers that by their smell or shape (I chose not to ask what that meant) would be appropriate for a centerpiece. I only remembered a couple of these, and the last thing I wanted was another harangue from Weezie on the subject of *suggestion*. The library was closed. Not that I was dying to talk to Sissy, despite Schulz's admonition to find out what she knew about Philip. So I called it quits, phoned the florist, and hung up only after I had endured her shower of laughs at my request.

Alone back on the third floor of the Farquhars' house, I bathed and dressed in my stodgy old caterer's white uniform and apron. An uninvited wave of sadness swept through the room as the sunlight faded. Without work to keep my mind occupied, pain flooded in. I lowered myself to the bed and watched as the mountains' shadows lengthened over Denver.

Maybe I never should have started going out with Philip Miller. More even than missing him, I missed the emotional self-sufficiency bred from years of evenings spent in solitude. I had found other things to do: help Arch with homework, talk to Marla, try out new recipes while listening to jazz. In one month, Philip's doting presence, his evocation of memories and hopes I had had fifteen years ago, made all those activities feel less important. Schulz was a question mark, too, retreating as he had behind his cop persona. Now the future span of evenings stretched out the way they had right after the divorce: empty.

I put on my latest necessity for the business, thick-soled walking shoes I used for serving. Then I did a quick step over to the Harringtons. An aphrodisiac banquet was no time to indulge in heartache. *Let the mood fit the food. Buck up, be happy, have fun.*

Brian and Weezie Harrington had left the door open for me. They were nowhere in sight. Upstairs, water was running, closet doors were opening and closing, and there was the occasional hurried call between rooms. I couldn't wait to see what Weezie was going to wear. I preheated the oven for the torta and started the soup simmering. I had been lucky to be able to get the oysters. I could see it all now: the sensual activity of digging, the sound of swallowing, the licking of fingers. Tom Jones, eat your heart out.

Weezie had told me to serve from and clear to a sideboard next to the dining-room table. I assembled trays and ice buckets for the patio and dining room, then got the liquor organized: champagne, chardonnay with the appetizers, Cabernet Sauvignon with the lamb, and Asti Spumanti to go with the dessert tray. I had delicately suggested to Weezie that coffee could help with postprandial love interest for more mature people. Sometimes I'm overwhelmed by my own tact.

The Harringtons' brass knocker echoed through the house—Sissy and Julian. Both teenagers looked exceptionally uncomfortable, their faces reddened by sunburn or anger. The late-day sun caught gold light in Sissy's perfectly waved brown hair. Julian's scalp glistened like a new scrub brush. Perhaps they were put out by having to wear evening clothes. Perhaps I had interrupted an argument. Without getting verbally entangled, I ushered them out to the patio and explained that champagne was going to be the order of business as soon as everyone was assembled. Then I offered them nonalcoholic beer or wine. They were, after all, underage.

They said they were both in athletic training, thank you very much. La de da. The oysters were calling.

When I reemerged with a tray of crudités, the teens appeared to have resolved their differences. Sissy was holding one of the crystal glasses up to the light, as if she were looking for a price tag. I tried to remember what it was I had needed as a teenager, and decided it was more compliments.

"You look lovely," I said as Sissy reached for one of the gold-trimmed crudité plates, then turned it over.

"Buckingham by Minton," I told her. "Very expensive English bone china."

She said, "How about the crystal?"

"What? Are you casing the joint?"

She wasn't amused. "I'm just interested. Those glasses look expensive."

"The pattern is called Star of Edinburgh. Scottish crystal that, to tempt fate, they use on the White House yacht. And no, it's not cheap." I smiled. "That's a becoming dress."

She shrugged. At the library she had been inscrutable. There, perhaps the mention of sexuality had embarrassed her. But if she did not want to encourage interest, she was wearing the wrong outfit tonight. The shirred white bodice of the dress was strapless, showing off superbly tanned shoulders and some cleavage. The above-the-knee black skirt hugged her hips and thighs.

"Thanks," she said.

Julian said nothing. I wondered briefly if you could see someone blushing through a Mohawk.

After a moment Weezie floated out. A diaphanous red chiffon gown billowed around her as she walked. "Oh hello, hello," she sang out. She stopped dead when she saw Sissy. "Nice *dress*," she said sharply.

"This is Miss Stone," I said lamely. "Er, Julian's date. She works at the library and she did an internship with—"

"I know all about her internship," said Weezie.

"How about something nice and cool to drink," I offered in a rush, to fill the silence.

"Why not?" said Weezie in the same frosty voice. "Johnnie Walker Black, no mixer."

So much for her being able to taste the nuances of the dinner. I poured the scotch over lots of ice and handed it to her. From the house came a wave of approaching voices. Brian Harrington was escorting the general and Adele out to the terrace. The general looked spiffy in a navy-blue suit that fit him like a uniform. Seeing me, he broke into his patented wrinkled smile. Behind him, Adele, elegant in a daffodil yellow linen coat-dress, let go of Brian's arm and lightly tap-stepped her way along behind her spouse.

"Now what have we here?" asked General Farquhar as he paced off steps to the bar. He picked up liquor bottles and examined the labels, then took the tops off and gave each a healthy sniff.

"New way to get a buzz, General?" asked Julian.

"You have to be careful, son, you never know when substitutions can be made," he replied seriously. Julian pulled his mouth into a smirk-grin that might or might not have been friendly. Hastily, I started another round with the crudités.

Brian assumed the role of gracious host. He popped the champagne cork and then flitted from person to person like a honeybee attending flowers. Weezie's increasingly loud voice pierced the cool evening air. Once the champagne was dispensed, the host, hostess, and four guests arranged themselves into two groups. Brian appeared engrossed with Sissy and Julian, and Weezie held forth to the Farquhars. At one point Weezie nodded to me, which I took to mean that we should start dinner. I also could not help but notice how she shot several furtive glances in her handsome husband's direction, and how her voice seemed to grow louder each time she noticed Brian moving closer to Sissy.

Inside, I removed the torta from the warming oven and readied the mushrooms for their brief sautéing. I had put the foil packets of lamb chops in the other oven; the guests would open them at table. I lit the candles and called the assembly to dinner with a set of tiny bells Weezie had given me for that purpose.

"*Suggest,*" whispered Weezie as she brushed past me in a cloud of chiffon and sweet perfume.

"Aye aye, Captain," I said clearly.

"Let's avoid navy terms, shall we?" said the general with a wink.

"Sissy, darling," said Weezie, "come and sit down next to me."

No, I wanted to say, that's not the way the seating is supposed to . . . But I let Weezie arrange things in her own way. With a toss of her silver-blond mane she put Sissy on her left and the general on her right. This put Adele on Brian's right and Julian across from her, which was correct enough in the end. But keeping Sissy away from Brian, not etiquette, had been Weezie's top priority.

"What lovely flowers, dear," Adele confided to Weezie. She leaned forward to admire the arrangement of white rosebuds, ruffle-edged pink tulips, and fragrant purple hyacinths. "Utterly, utterly reminiscent of love."

"Why, thank you," said Weezie, without acknowledging the caterer who had ordered them. She did look up and give me another of her withering looks, however, which I figured meant that it was time to start suggesting.

"Food for love," I began, "has a long and illustrious history." All eyes were on me. I picked up the chardonnay and began to circle the table, filling the crystal glasses as I spoke. "In the 1400s the Arab sheikh Nefzawi wrote the first known treatise on the subject. Among other recommendations, he mentioned a number of foods," the wine bottle teetered over Adele's glass as I paused, "to excite passionate desire."

There was an audible collective sigh. I served the oysters to enthusiastic approval from all but Julian, who nibbled unobtrusively on carrots, looking sullen.

"Next is Shrimp Dumpling Soup," I said as I ladled delectable little mouthfuls into each white-and-gold bowl along with the broth. When I had finished passing them around, I said, "The myth surrounding Aphrodite's birth holds that she was borne to dry land on the crest of a wave. The word *aphros* means foam. Traditionally, any product from the sea, Aphrodite's birthplace, has aphrodisiacal properties. In their raw state, seafood such as the oysters contains iodine, reputed to excite the libido."

"Mm," said Weezie after her first spoonful. "Positively sensuous, *n'est-ce pas?*"

Brian did not look at his wife but instead gave Sissy a wink. He tilted his soup plate to catch the last dumpling, then noisily sucked it down. After a moment he said, "I've heard of this Nefzawi. Seems to me he says one of the things that turns a man on is 'various women's faces.' I can buy that."

Sissy said nothing, only turned over an ornate silver fork to see who had made it.

"When a man ages," Julian said flatly, "maybe various women are what he needs to turn him on."

Weezie gave me an icy look.

I wanted to say, This is not my fault.

"Now let me tell you something about oysters," said the general. "Well, actually, it has to do with pearls. Did you know that Mussolini's mistress absolutely refused to wear pearls after she heard about the Nazi experiments to coat the things with poison chemicals? The poison would be absorbed through the skin."

Adele cleared her throat, as in, Shut up.

"I'm serious now!" cried the general. "And Ceausescu wore a new pair of shoes every day because he had heard about how the CIA could introduce poisons through the soles. His wife refused to have her hair bleached because she had heard that peroxide could be used for cheap torture on exposed nerve cells. It's the truth!"

"General Bo," said Julian, "you're great." He reached over and gently braided his fingers through Sissy's limp ones. Brian slid a look across to the teenagers' clasped hands. Weezie visibly stiffened.

I began to clear the plates. I said, "Mussolini and Ceausescu may not have known that the word for love potion in Latin is *venenum*. It also means, ah, poison. So there you are."

But they didn't want to talk about poison. The conversation settled uneasily into local politics while I sliced the torta. A meeting of the county commissioners was coming up, where projects approved by the planning commission would get final approval or denial. Sissy said that Protect Our Mountains would be involved in several of the hearings. Adele beamed at her. I remembered Protect Our Mountains, a conservation group that led various crusades against development, was another of Adele's favorite charities.

Weezie signaled for another glass of wine. "Speaking of Protect Our Mountains, I'm so upset about this accident with Philip Miller. I can't imagine why he would drive like that. He seemed like such a sensible fellow. I wonder if he was having some problems."

I held the pie cutter still. My back was to the guests. They could not know how acutely I was listening.

"Problems?" said Sissy. "Dr. Miller wasn't having any problems. His clients had the problems."

Brian said greedily, "Did he talk to you about his clients?"

This host was definitely weird, I decided as I butchered the last two pieces of torta. What kind of question was that to ask Sissy? At least, I thought he was talking to Sissy. When I turned, all eyes were on me.

Brian said, "Did he tell *you* his clients' secrets?"

I paused and closed my eyes. "If he did," I said, "I can't remember. He was discreet."

"I'm so sorry Goldy had to witness that accident," said General Bo. "Terrible shock."

"Yes," I said curtly. "Who would like a piece of torta?" The steaming slices made their rounds. "Eggs," I began again, "as well as cheese, are reputed to have aphrodisiac properties because of their association with fertility. And chiles are associated with the more southern climes—"

"—where we all know what they do during siesta," finished Brian. There was a silence. Sissy looked wide-eyed around the room. Weezie was pinching the red chiffon of her sleeve into unnecessary pleats.

Julian said, "Why don't you tell us what they do? If you really do know."

Adele reached across the table and patted Julian's free hand. Brian Harrington still eyed Julian's other hand, which lay on Sissy's.

Brian said, "What an interesting haircut, Julian. I imagine it gets a little cold in the winter."

"Oh, Bri," gushed Weezie, "when we met you wore your hair so long. You complained about how it got in your way when you swam."

"Do you still swim, Brian?" asked Adele.

"Yes, of course," said Brian. He watched the teenagers' hands unravel and reknit. He said, "This is wonderful scrambled egg whatever. Should I eat more, or is there an actual main course?"

"Don't tease Goldy." Adele spoke with a slight edge of sharpness. "This is simply delicious."

There were some embarrassed mm's and ah's, and I scurried out to fetch the next course, trusting that Real Realtors Ate Lamb Chops. The guests opened their packets with cautious solemnity. All but the teenagers studiously swilled the Cabernet. But whatever was supposed to be happening was not happening. Sissy finished examining all the costly things within reach while Adele began a long discourse on the fund-raising drive at Elk Park Prep. Julian was quiet. The general, after being shushed by Adele, ate in silence. Weezie fumed. The only noise came from Brian, who continued to direct his syrupy questions and attention to Sissy. Sissy, however, took no more notice of Brian than she had of the food.

Time for the finale.

"And now chocolate," I said with a flourish as I brought out the tray. "Chocolate has the most sinful reputation of all, because the phenylethylamine in it simulates the same feeling we get with, ah, sexual happiness—"

"Simulates or stimulates?" asked the general, bewildered.

"Simulates?" interjected Julian. "How does it do that?"

"You're the scientific person, my dear," said Adele in her most flattering tone. "Why don't you tell us?"

"No, thanks."

"Why don't you tell us?" mimicked Brian Harrington in a high voice.

My heart squeezed for Julian and the embarrassment I knew he must be feeling. It was like the time I had tried to convince the parents of my Sunday-school kids that they should let me take the class down to help at a Denver soup kitchen. The derisive laughter still rang in my ears.

But I knew jumping to Julian's defense would only make things worse. Instead, I concentrated on refilling the platter and glasses with cookies and Asti Spumanti. Weezie held up a piece of fudge and murmured to Julian, "I hope Adele told you Brian's wild about this." Julian ignored her.

When the agony was finally over and they were drinking their demitasse out on the terrace, I washed dishes as quietly as possible. After a very short while I heard rustling in the hall: Sissy and Julian. I scurried out after them.

"Thanks for coming," I said in a low voice once I was behind them at the front door. "It was nice of you—"

But before I could finish, Julian, who had avoided my eyes, slammed the front door with such force that the knocker reverberated, *klok klok.*

"—to come," I said to empty air.

Not much later I ushered the Farquhars out. I told them I would be over in about half an hour. When I came out to get the last cups, I heard Brian Harrington snoring on the living-room sofa.

"Leave him," said Weezie's sour voice behind me. "Let him wake up with a sore back, see if I care. He can swim it off at the club."

"I'm sorry about tonight," I said. "Maybe next time—"

"We'll make it dinner for two," said Weezie through clenched teeth. "And try a more potent *venenum*."

12.

Sunday I tried to put the events of the previous evening out of my head. I missed Philip, and I still did not know when his funeral would be. The Farquhars, sensing my low mood, invited me to go with them to church and then to the country club for the afternoon. I accepted for church but politely declined the afternoon at the club. My calendar indicated I had two big catering events coming up. The first was a western barbecue for forty the following day, Monday the sixth. And then there was the Farquhars' anniversary party, a cookout for thirty, on Tuesday the fourteenth. With all the turmoil in my life, I had neglected to cook for the former and plan for the latter, and so had a load of work to do. Onward and upward.

Before we left for church I started beans simmering, put country-style ribs slathered with homemade barbecue sauce into the oven, then basted chickens before skewering them on the rotisserie for a brief cooking that the grills would complete the next day. When the Farquhars dropped me off after the service, you could have floated into the kitchen on the heady smell of roasting meats.

I kneaded dough for the rolls and wondered why things had gone so wrong the previous night. The dinner had resembled a wedding I'd done once where three-fourths of the family members were not speaking to each other. Elaborate maneuvers to avoid visual or verbal contact took place both on the dance floor and at the buffet table. By the time it was over I'd felt like a wrung-out dishrag.

And the nerve of Brian Harrington to ask me if Philip talked to me about his clients! I pressed hard into the dough as I kneaded out, folded in. Perhaps it was because his attempt at flirtation had ended so badly that he now felt he had to put me down at every opportunity.

When the roll dough was satiny smooth, I buttered a bowl, turned the ball of dough until butter blanketed the top, then put it all aside to rise. I set new red potatoes on to boil for potato salad, then shredded mountains of cabbage, carrots, and onions for coleslaw. When both salads were mixed into perfect creamy mounds, I covered them with wrap and placed them in the refrigerator, before the temptation to indulge became overwhelming. While I was making out a menu for the anniversary party, a sigh welled up. I looked at my watch. Five o'clock.

For most of the world it was cocktail time. The previous evening's bad vibes still clung like depression. I felt as if I had failed in some way. And I missed Philip. I missed Arch. What the heck, I even missed Schulz.

The cooking and menu done, I wandered out to the living room. My eyes fastened on Adele's crystal dish filled with individually wrapped Lindt Lindors, Mozartkugels, and London Mints. I was feeling bad. Adele had told me many times to help myself. Settling on the couch, I reached for the dish.

Opening a wrapped imported chocolate is like a moment from Christmas Eve. Your mouth waters. Each tiny crinkle of paper, each flash of colored foil is agony. You think if you don't get this chocolate into your mouth in the next five seconds, you're going to die.

The first Mozartkugel dropped into my hand like a smooth, dark ball from heaven. I bit into it very slowly. As the chocolate melted I closed my eyes and waited for nirvana.

And oh, it came. When you roll chocolate around on your tongue, the dark creamy sweetness invades all your senses. Delight worms its

New Potato Salad

12 new red potatoes, boiled in their skins just
   until tender (15 to 20 minutes)
about ¾ cup best-quality mayonnaise
   (preferably homemade)
whipping cream
½ teaspoon salt
white pepper to taste
about 2 teaspoons snipped fresh dill
2 garlic cloves, minced

Cool and quarter potatoes. Thin mayonnaise
slightly with cream. Add salt, white pepper, dill,
and garlic. Taste and correct seasoning. Chill.

Makes 4 servings

way down your spine. Your ears tingle. You have to say *Mmmm* because you just can't help it. Some people say the taste of chocolate is second only to sex. I say putting it second is in dispute.

I ate two more Kugels, then a couple of Lindors, and finished off with several London Mints, which are of a cloudy softness that defies description. Well, so much for dinner. Arch and the Farquhars would be home late. Julian was at a rock concert. I cleaned up the pile of wrinkled wrappings and decided to go to bed. I was exhausted, and as I snuggled down between the sheets I consoled myself with the thought that at least chocolate caused no hangover.

Dreams of Mozart's face on the wrapper of the Kugel awoke me at sunup Monday morning. Clouds the color of much-washed pink crinolines skirted the eastern horizon. Out my window, birds sang in a lush concert. Beautiful, but too early. Despite the best efforts of the avian philharmonic, I was able to get back to sleep until seven, when Tom Schulz called.

To my groggy greeting, he said, "Sloth is one of the Seven Deadly Sins."

"Is murder on there? That's what I'm going to do to you if you start up again with these early-morning calls."

"Want me to call you back?"

I told him I could do nothing without coffee and would call him back when I was drinking something very black—within the next five minutes, I hoped. I crept down the stairs and was packing a double measure of espresso into the Gaggia basket when the motion detector began its high shrieking *wheee.*

A quick check revealed that the motion it was detecting was mine. No caffeine, no intellect: I had forgotten to turn off the system. Maybe I was hung over, after all. Once the alarm was off I announced apology to the household over the intercom, called Aspen Meadow Security to interrupt the automatic dial, and turned off the loop. With hands shaking, I sat down at the kitchen desk, sipped the foam from the espresso, and waited for my brain to engage before punching in Schulz's number.

"You doing better?" he wanted to know. His voice sounded farther away than before. Maybe the alarm had done something to my ears.

"No," I said truthfully. "Listen. I catered my first aphrodisiac dinner Saturday night. It was a fiasco. The only thing I could find out about Sissy is that Brian Harrington, who is fiftyish and married, seems unduly attracted to her."

"Whoa," he said, "don't skip the good part! What about the dinner? Did the aphrodisiacs work? I mean, not for you of course, what with your professional involvement in the food and all—"

I sighed and twirled the telephone cord, wondering idly if I could thereby set off another alarm.

I said, "I told them what all the foods were supposed to do. But it didn't happen. In fact, the effect was most definitely the opposite. When I left, Brian Harrington was asleep on a couch."

"Alone, I assume."

"Alone."

"Doesn't sound as if your aphrodisiacs did the trick, Miss G."

"Oh, I never was convinced of the science of the thing. Probably suggestion is all there is to it."

"Sort of like being a psychologist. They suggest a lot except how to agree in court."

I paused, then told him that there had been quite a brouhaha between Weezie and Philip's sister, Elizabeth. I added, "And here's something: Weezie Harrington knew Sissy did her junior-year internship with Philip Miller. And Philip might have been seeing her," I added lamely, "on the side. Seeing Weezie, I mean."

Schulz gasped a little too loudly. "And two-timing the town's caterer? I do know Miller was in contact, but not necessarily amicable contact, with the Harringtons. Something going on in town, still need to get details. I haven't heard anything in particular about Weezie Harrington and Miller, but I'll check on that, too. Did he tell you anything?"

"Who, Philip? Like what?"

"Anything strange. Anything that feels out of place."

I said, "I don't think so."

"Give it some thought, you might know more than you think. Call me later in the week." When he hung up, there was another click, and I wondered briefly if the CIA was checking on General Bo.

I bustled around the kitchen making breakfast. The forty-degree weather demanded a quick bread. I had developed a recipe for Arch's preschool that had become a favorite with clients. Perhaps the idea of eating something called Montessori muffins made people think they were learning something. Food can substitute for so many things.

I got out whole wheat flour and molasses and began to chop prunes. I supposed Schulz had the right to hang up without saying good-bye. After my business nearly collapsed last fall, we had started to date. But not for long.

I broke an egg and swirled it into oil and milk.

Schulz had been attentive, God knew. On my birthday, on Arch's birthday, on Julia Child's birthday, he had sent cards with pictures of mice eating cookies, rabbits downing carrot cakes, French poodles dancing through french fries. Valentine's Day brought the arrival of the most sumptuous box of candy I had ever received. For this gift I had written him a thank-you note. When he called I told him Arch was taking a carefully wrapped piece in his lunch each day.

"What about you?" he had asked. "Did you like it?"

"Of course," I'd said carefully. "It's wonderful." And then I'd begged off with a catering assignment.

Finally he had asked the dreaded question: Do you see our relationship going anywhere? How could I say I didn't know? How could I say stop being so nice? How could I admit to running against stereotype, the first woman afraid to commit?

There are many bad ways that relationships end, I reflected as I mixed together the wet and dry ingredients. Death. Divorce. I knew all about the latter. But I had deliberately let the relationship with Schulz wane until there was little left. We had been like the hot chocolate they sell at the ski resorts. For your buck fifty, a machine first spews dark, thick syrup into a cup. This liquid gradually turns to a mixture of chocolate and hot water. Soon there is just a stream of hot water, and in a moment, drops. You wish the chocolate part would go on gushing forever, but it doesn't.

This was what I should have told Schulz on Valentine's Day. I

Montessori Muffins

2 cups whole wheat flour
2 teaspoons baking powder
½ teaspoon salt
1 cup chopped pitted prunes
1 egg, beaten
¼ cup oil
½ cup molasses
1½ cups milk

Preheat oven to 400°. Combine whole wheat flour, baking powder, salt, and prunes in a bowl. Stir together egg, oil, molasses, and milk in another bowl. Combine the mixtures, mixing just until blended. Spoon into a greased 12-cup muffin tin. Bake for 20 to 25 minutes until a toothpick inserted in the center of a muffin comes out clean.

Makes 12 muffins

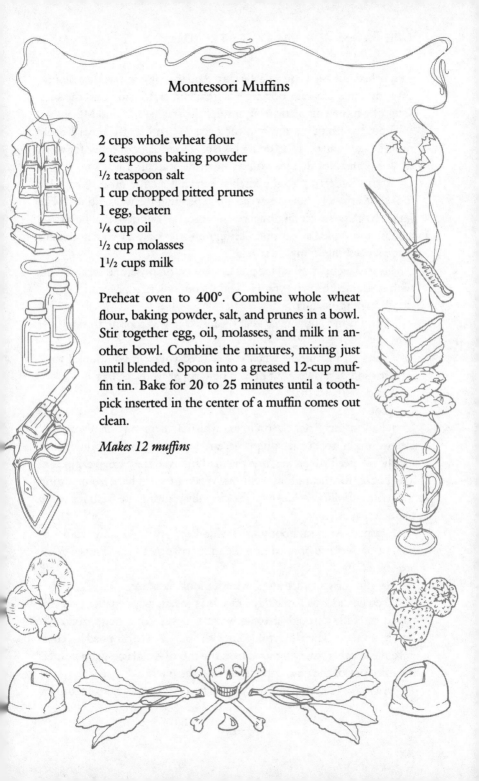

simply had not been equal to the task. And then it was a week, a month, three months: His calls became less frequent, and I had heard the siren song of a more enigmatic relationship, the one with Philip Miller.

I put the tin of muffins into the oven. When I set the timer I could hear the slap-slap of Julian doing his laps. I fixed a pot of coffee for when he was done. Not that he would care or be grateful, I was sure.

Arch wandered into the kitchen carrying a large grocery bag. He looked sleepy, which he often did after spending the weekend with The Jerk. His glasses were far down on his nose, but I noticed that he had on a clean unrumpled sweat suit. Seeing him after only a two-day absence made something in my chest ache.

He looked up, pushed the glasses back on his nose, and regarded me with magnified brown eyes. He said, "You look tired, Mom."

"You're projecting."

"Oh. I don't know what that means." He was rooting through the bag.

"Sorry. It just means when you're tired yourself, you think I am." He did not answer, but drew a newspaper from the bag.

I said, "What's that?"

"You'll see."

I halved fat Valencia oranges, whirred them on the Farquhars' electric juicer to extract pulpy nectar. I poured the thick juice into another Waterford pitcher, one that had survived the garden explosion. The buzzer for the muffins went off. When I turned back from putting them on a cooling rack, Arch was carefully pouring the fresh juice *into* the newspaper.

I gasped. Arch said nothing. Trying hard not to lose my temper as the last of the juice drained into the folded paper, I said, "Please. What are you doing?"

He said, "Experimenting," without looking at me.

Then he did look at me. He unfolded the newspaper with a flourish, paged carefully through it to show that it was just a newspaper. No liquid, no stain. Then he refolded it with aplomb. He dropped his chin, gave me another knowing look over the top of his glasses, and poured the juice out of the newspaper back into the pitcher.

"All *right*!" said Julian from the kitchen doorway, where, unknown to me, he had been standing watching. Julian held on to his towel with one hand and enthusiastically clapped the counter with the other.

I smiled. "Let's drink that juice," I said. "I'll make more for Bo and Adele."

When the two of them had drained their glasses, Julian said to Arch, "You going to show that trick to your girlfriend?"

"She's not my girlfriend!" came Arch's hot protest.

I said, "Excuse me?"

Julian gave Arch a profoundly apologetic look. Then he snitched a muffin and walked quickly out of the kitchen, tossing a comment over his shoulder. Arch, he said, should be ready to go to Elk Park Prep in thirty minutes.

I echoed, "Girlfriend?"

Arch let out a deep breath. He took a bite of muffin. He looked at me and shrugged. Said, "Remember I told you Julian really likes your cooking, Mom? He even told me he wants to, like, take lessons from you."

"Please don't change the subject. You never mentioned a girlfriend."

"She's not my girlfriend! I need to go get dressed."

"You are dressed."

Another sigh.

I tried another tack. "You don't have to tell me about this if you don't want to."

He said, "Good. Because I don't want you asking forty questions."

"How about two?"

He shrugged.

"Was your dad nice to you?"

He nodded.

"How's school?"

His cheeks turned pink. "Fine." Then he pressed the rest of the muffin into his mouth and reached again into the grocery bag. "This is for you," he said with his mouth full. He handed me a thick manila envelope. To my chagrin, it was labeled *Parent Packet—Please read immediately.*

"Apparently paying tuition isn't enough," I said, to no one in particular.

Adele's distant tap-step announced her approach. I slapped down the manila envelope, set her a place at the oak table, and started slicing oranges for more juice.

"Better go get ready," I said quickly to Arch.

"Okay, but I need to ask Adele something."

"What?"

"You'll see."

Smart kid. Arch knew the best way to get what he wanted was to try for it when I was in a rush to prepare food. I nabbed Adele's muscle-relaxant medication from the cabinet and pressed the orange halves into the whirling juicer. Just when I had extracted a new pitcherful of the sweet orange liquid, Adele appeared at the kitchen doorway. Her face was drawn in pain from morning back stiffness.

Arch said, "Good morning, Mrs. Farquhar. That's a really pretty robe."

Unbelievable. Not only was Arch learning tricks, he was taking charm lessons from The Jerk. Even Adele looked at me in surprise. I noticed that the shiny dark blue Chinese silk robe with its red-and-green embroidery was indeed lovely. The astonishing thing was that Arch had noticed it.

"Why thank you," she said with a smile that eased the wrinkles of pain. "The fragrance of those muffins is indescribable." Carefully, Adele lowered herself into her chair.

Arch echoed the movement and sat down in the chair next to her.

"Mrs. Farquhar?" he said when she had taken her pills with dainty sips of juice.

She looked at him with eyebrows raised. When I stepped forward to offer support, Arch shot me a forbidding, dark look. I stood still.

"Mrs. Farquhar," he began again, "I was wondering if you would mind if I had some kids over one of these days."

Again there was a radiant smile from my employer. I pressed my lips together. I didn't want Arch to see me grin.

"A pool party!" said Adele with enthusiasm. "It sounds lovely. Let's have it as part of our anniversary celebration."

"I don't know about a pool party," said Arch. "I don't want them to swim. I want to do an act."

"An act?" I said, incredulous. This from a child who had balked at show-and-tell for six years?

"What kind of act?" asked Adele. "Of course, I mean, it's fine, dear. But what will you be doing?"

Arch stood. He reached into the bag and then walked with great drama to Adele's side. He held up a half-dollar in one hand, showed it to us, and then had it disappear. With his other hand he snapped behind Adele's ear and the coin reappeared. He looked at us both and gave a slight bow. Then he straightened up.

He said, "Archibald the Magnificent's Traveling Magic Show."

13.

"What a precocious child," said Adele as she turned back to her muffins and the pot of Constant Comment tea I had set on the table. I could not read her tone. And as usual, just when you thought you were getting somewhere in this household, the phone rang. Adele slumped her shoulders in defeat: the shackles of noblesse oblige.

I picked it up and said sweetly, "Farquhars."

"Uh, Goldy the caterer?"

"Speaking."

"This is the *Mountain Journal*. There's going to be another review of your cooking in Friday's paper, and the, uh, editor told me to call to say you could, like, do a rebuttal next week, if you want. Okay? Deadline for your copy is Wednesday noon. I need to go."

"Who is this? Put that editor on or I'm never going to advertise in his newspaper again."

The phone clicked off. So much for my consumer vote. I replaced the receiver in the cradle. This was Monday. I had four days to worry about the new review, which was clearly not going to be glowing, and a little over a week to think of something to say. Actually, I didn't even have time to cook, much less worry, because all the phones did in this house was *ring*.

I answered less sweetly this time. "Farquhars."

"I need to speak with Adele Farquhar, please. This is Joan Rasmussen from the Elk Park Prep pool committee. It's extremely important."

"Ah ha," I said, and turned to Adele with raised eyebrows. "Joan Rasmussen from the pool committee." Adele waved her off with half a Montessori muffin.

I said, "Mrs. Farquhar is not available at the moment. She's swimming."

"*Some* people have a pool already," said the uncharitable Ms. Rasmussen. "And with whom am I speaking, may I ask?"

I assumed a businesslike tone. "This is Goldy the caterer, live-in cook for the Farquhars. My son, Arch Korman, is a summer student at Elk Park. Shall I have Adele call you?"

"Yes, you need to do that. But I can talk to you. As the parent of a student, you need to be brought up to date on parents' responsibility for pool fund-raising."

"Oh, no—"

"Have you read the contents of your packet yet?"

"Well, no, Ms. Rasmussen, I just got it a couple of minutes ago—"

"You *need* to read it, then. And when you're done, you need to go around to local businesses, solicit donations, and *then* you need to give them a decal for their window—"

I said, "Look, Joan honey, the only thing I *need* to do right now is get off the telephone." I slammed the receiver down. Honestly, some people.

"Don't tell me," said Adele. "I've just lost Joan Rasmussen as co-chair."

"Trust me," I said, "you're better off." I began to search through the refrigerator for the food I'd prepared yesterday for the western barbecue. When I emerged with the last of the platters, Adele was taking another pill. Reluctantly, it seemed to me.

"Goldy," she said finally, "I know you have a lot on your mind. But I just feel so frustrated trying to raise funds in this town. In Washington we worked hard on it!" She gestured with her teacup. "There were committees for charity balls, fashion shows, luncheons, everything! Everyone worked! The headmaster said the alums would be supportive. They haven't been. Neither have the parents. I'm at a loss."

I put the platters down and sat next to her. "I'm sorry."

She shrugged. "I know you have other things to worry about, dear. I know you're upset about this Miller fellow, and of course there's Arch and your business. It's just that when I set my mind to something, I do it. I know people here have money! But do you think I can get them to work on this committee during June, July, and August? No. The only person who'll do any work is Joan Rasmussen, and she beats people over the head. It's the wrong time of year, the headmaster says. It's hard to get people to work now. But why?" She shook her head and sipped from her cup.

"Oh, my dear Adele," I said with a smile. "It's because the residents have to work on their Colorado Summer Merit Badges."

She choked on the tea. "Their *what*?"

I got a cup, poured myself some of the pale brown liquid, and settled back beside her. "Here's how it works. You've got money and you live in Colorado. Every summer vacation, you're duty-bound to work on your badges. Sometimes they come with a star."

"I beg your pardon? These are actual things?"

I shook my head. "Of course not, although sometimes you get a T-shirt." When she still looked puzzled, I explained: "Coloradans are going to recite their summer achievements to you as soon as they see you in the fall. You say, *How was your summer?* They roll their eyes. *Well! First we hiked ten of the state's fourteeners.* Hiking merit badge. Only earned for hiking repeatedly at fourteen thousand feet above sea level. *Then we climbed the Flatirons, about lost two of the kids when we were rappeling down!* Rock-climbing merit badge. *Then we backpacked into the most remote area of Rocky Mountain National Park.* Camping merit badge. *When we got back we ran a 10K road race over by Vail and did the 60K bike race over the Rockies.* Running and biking badges, the latter with a star."

She grinned. "What about bird-watching? Or . . . or . . . fishing?"

"Well," I said huffily, "I haven't gotten there yet. Of course, the only merit badge you can get in fishing is for fly-fishing. Only a novice uses bait."

"So that's why I can't get anyone to work on a committee. I thought the parents and alums might be on vacation, but then I see them in town."

"Dear Adele. You haven't asked them about their summer! Just listening to them would make you need a muscle relaxant."

Adele smoothed her lips with her finger. Finally she said, "I've got it!" She was beaming. "A bird-watching fund-raiser picnic. Catered by guess who. We set it up for this Saturday, say it was an impromptu sort of affair."

I groaned. "You're not serious."

"Could you work it into your catering schedule? Figure on tripling the cost of your supplies. Then I'll double that and give half to the school. Could you?"

I looked at the yellow kitchen tiles and calculated. I still had to come up with the final payment on my security system. Arch's summer-school costs had put a painful dent in my budget. And this job would be exceptionally profitable. I said, "Sure."

"It's the perfect thing! You'll make money, the school will make money, we can invite Julian and Arch and the Harringtons and all kinds of people! It'll be a smash hit. Oh, Goldy, you're wonderful! I never would have thought of it if you hadn't told me about the badges." She put her finger to her lip again, a bad sign. "And about Joan. She just needs to be coddled."

Right. Rasmussen the Egg. More like hard-boiled, I'd say.

"Brought along, you know." As usual, I didn't. "I suppose I should invite her over for lunch today."

I had been trying to give her comfort. Be a soul friend, the way I was with her sister, Marla. Suddenly, everything was backfiring.

Adele continued, "Could you just do a little soup and salad? Please? I know you need to get your van, but Bo and I can get it for you." Her hazel eyes implored me.

Okay, I'd screwed up with the Rasmussen woman. Here was Adele, new to the community, walking with a cane, trying to make friends, using her time and money to be helpful when she couldn't get people to raise money in the summer, and her employee had just blown off the co-chair. Well, I *needed* to.

I swallowed and said, "Sure. Lunch is no problem. Rolls and fruit salad with Goldilocks' Gourmet Spinach Soup?" She nodded. Good, I'd brought a container of frozen soup from my house. "I can have it done before I leave for the picnic."

Adele smiled in relief. Then she rose like a queen and picked up the phone to call Joan Rasmussen about lunch and the birding expedition. Rasmussen must have thought it was a good idea, because then Adele called Bo on the intercom and asked him to call his golfing friend whose wife was in the Audubon Society. Then with a wink she took the van keys I gave her and tap-stepped her way out of the kitchen.

Adele was like and unlike Marla, I reflected as I stirred molasses into the bubbling pot of baked beans. Like Marla in being used to wealth and the power it confers. Unlike Marla in that Adele never discussed her back problems, she just poured the pain into energy for good deeds. If Marla was in pain, she made sure that it was news for the entire county. And to Marla, good deeds were for the Rockefellers.

Arch reappeared at the kitchen doorway.

"Mom," he announced, "I need two hundred dollars for a silk cape and top hat." He grinned.

"Excuse me?"

"I can ask Dad if it's too much for you."

"Arch, don't. You know he'll say no, that it should come out of the child-support money. Come on, hon. Can't you do without it?"

He looked at me, a child's freckled face wrinkled in adultlike dismay. "Well, I have to have them for the magic show," he insisted. "Maybe Dad will get them since I talked him into paying for the other stuff."

"What other stuff? Like that newspaper?"

Arch ducked into his bag and brought out a pair of handcuffs and a set of Chinese manacles. This latter I recognized as his favorite trick from our visits to magic shows when he was little. He couldn't seem to decide between the two tricks. Finally he held up the handcuffs with his eyebrows raised.

"Lock these behind me, please."

Goldilocks' Gourmet Spinach Soup

5 tablespoons unsalted butter
¼ pound fresh mushrooms, washed, dried, trimmed, and diced
1 scallion, chopped
5 tablespoons all-purpose flour
2 cups chicken broth
2 cups milk
½ teaspoon salt (optional)
black pepper (preferably freshly ground)
ground nutmeg (optional)
¼ pound cream cheese, softened and cut into cubes
1 cup grated Swiss cheese (recommended: Jarlsberg)
¾ pound fresh spinach, washed, trimmed, cooked, and chopped

Melt the butter in a large saucepan. In it slowly sauté the mushrooms and scallion until tender. Add flour and stir just until flour is cooked, a couple of minutes. Whisk in first chicken broth and then milk, stirring until thickened. Add salt if desired, pepper, nutmeg if desired, cream cheese, and Swiss cheese; stir until melted. Then stir in spinach. Heat and stir very gently. Season to taste. Serve hot.

Makes 4 to 6 servings

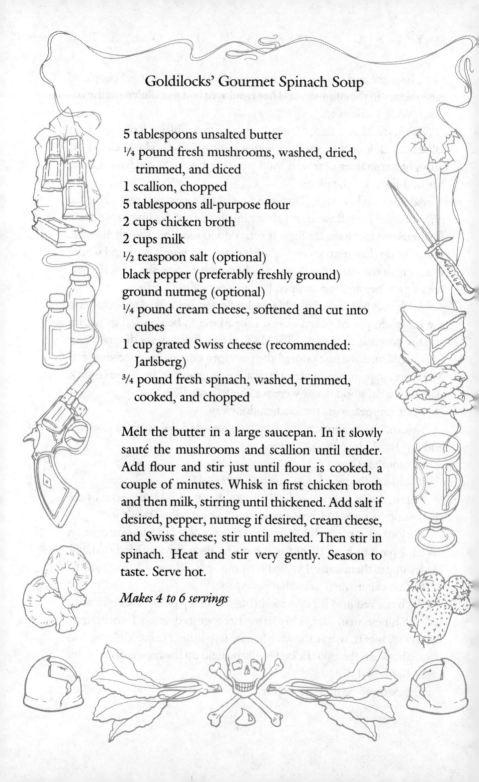

This was turning into a busy morning. But I acquiesced.

There was a pause as he leaned forward slightly. Then he triumphantly brought up his hands and the cuffs.

"How did you do that?"

"A magician never tells, Mom. Anyway, wait until you see me do it under water."

"Under water! You can hardly do the doggie paddle. And remember the doctor said you should be extra careful because of that bronchitis and asthma you had in February—"

Arch turned away. When I opened my mouth to say I was sorry, Julian's honk sounded from outside.

"Gotta go. Oh," he said as he ducked to retrieve something else. "One more thing." It was the tone of voice he used when he knew I wasn't going to like it. These things he always saved until the last moment before his school bus came, so we wouldn't have time to argue. Apparently, summer school was no different.

I said, "I hope this one more thing will mean I can get all my cooking done today."

"Here," he said as he handed me *The Complete Works of Edgar Allan Poe*. "All the parents are supposed to read along so you can help with the final project. There's a note inside," he indicated a mimeographed sheet, "that explains the project. The teacher's really nice, she'll talk to you about the different projects, if you want."

Julian honked again and Arch whipped out the front door. Behind them, Adele and the general waved from the back of the Range Rover. I opened the sheet Arch had given me. It detailed all my Poe homework: *Read two short stories. Discuss them with your child. Develop ideas for projects. You could make a model of a gold bug.* Sure. *You could make a tape of the beating of a telltale heart.* Uh-huh.

I wondered if the teacher would like to be a caterer. What was I paying tuition for, anyway? Oh yes. Arch said she was nice.

The phone was ringing in the kitchen. It was the Audubon Society. Would I please have the general call about an outing? Was it this Saturday, the eleventh, that he wanted? You bet I'd have him call. I wanted to add, *You and General Farquhar have nothing in common,* but refrained. Instead, I stabbed the block of frozen soup so that it would heat more quickly. I had an hour before I had to rush off to do the barbecue for George Rumslinger's ranch hands and staff.

I put the phone recorder on and did a yoga centering exercise. Arch had a girlfriend and wanted two hundred dollars for a magician's costume. Adele needed lunch for two before I did a picnic for forty. There was going to be another rotten review in the *Mountain Journal*. I needed to call my lawyer about the name change. I had a birding expedition and picnic to plan, while Edgar Allan Poe homework awaited me. I chewed the inside of my cheek. How much worse could things get?

The phone rang and I listened to the message as it recorded. It was Marla.

The funeral for Philip Miller was at two P.M. the next day.

Somehow, I finished the cooking and set the table on the Farquhars' covered porch. I banished thoughts about the funeral, went out to the garage and found a small pair of pruning shears next to the camping equipment. The new flowering plants Julian and General Bo had put into the smoothed-over garden crater yielded an acceptable arrangement for the luncheon with the Irascible Rasmussen. Adele and the general arrived in convoy with my van.

My van! The grille seemed to grin at me like an old friend. I started it up, checked the bungee cords that would hold the food on racks, checked to make sure the glove compartment still held my safety kit, with its bandages, sunscreen, instructions for doing the Heimlich maneuver in case someone choked, and my little bottle of ipecac, in case, God forbid, someone ate something he shouldn't.

I tried to think positive thoughts as I drove to the Rumslinger ranch. Sure enough, the barbecue was an enormous success. George Rumslinger was a country-music star who had moved to Aspen Meadow and spent hundreds of thousands of dollars establishing a cattle ranch. The hands loved him not only for the good pay but because they regularly were treated to food and song. They pulled on the pony keg of Coors and dug heartily into the hills of barbecued chicken and ribs, bowls and baskets of salads and rolls, and stacks of Scout's Brownies. Highlight of the day was when Rumslinger serenaded the crowd with his new hit remake of "I'm Just Roadkill on the Highway of Love."

The foreman paid in cash and gave me a fifty-dollar tip. He was feeling so good he even asked if I had a favorite charity. In the spirit of killing two birds with one stone I mentioned the Elk Park Prep Pool project. I pointed out how good the decal would look on the rear window of his pickup truck.

He said, "Pretty ritzy school for the son of a caterer."

I placed the cash in my zip bag and said nothing. If he wanted a decal, he could get it himself.

The black-capped chickadee's plaintive song woke me Tuesday, the morning of Philip's funeral. Adele had given me the day off from cooking and answering the phone. It was wonderful to be free. Part of the message from Marla was that some of us would gather before the service at Elizabeth's house. When I was there Elizabeth said the two of us must get together soon. I nodded. Then we all took off for the Episcopal church. Even a latter-day hippie could revert to the faith of her childhood when facing the burial of a brother.

Into your hands, O Lord, we commend our brother, Philip.

Marla was there; she held my hand. There was a slew of people in country club clothes. The Farquhars came, as did Julian, a very red-eyed Sissy, Weezie Harrington, and Brian Harrington, whose beeper went off during the service.

Do not let the pains of death turn us away from you at our last hour. . . .

Elizabeth Miller had convinced the priest to allow friends of Philip to talk briefly about the good work he had done in the community. So many people depended on him—his clients, his friends, his supporters in the Audubon Society and Protect Our Mountains. There were subdued sobs as acquaintances told anecdotes. Still. In all this, and it was indeed lovely, there was no discussion of the strangeness of the way in which he had died.

Let our faith be our consolation, and eternal life our hope.

Somehow, I felt Philip's presence. Maybe hovering somewhere around, I didn't know. I thought, Did you ever say anything that would help me understand what happened that morning?

There was no response.

After a small gathering at Elizabeth's house I came home and took a long bath. Arch said he was going to work on some of his dives in the pool, and then on some tricks. I asked him about his homework. He said he couldn't do anything until I had done my reading, and had I decided about money for a cape?

No, I said sullenly as I trundled on to bed with the Poe under my arm. I was at the high tide of fatigue; there was no way I would read more than a page or two, I said.

But it was not to be. Splashing, calling, diving sounds from the pool gradually diminished. The floorboards creaked as Arch went to bed. I was glued to the book. The big house became quiet. In a far corner of my brain I could hear the telltale heart, beating its way to discovery. Beating, beating, beat—

"Agh!" I cried when I thought I heard a splash outside. My windows were closed against the cold night air of the mountains. Slowly, I slid the east-facing window open. There was no sound of arms or legs thrashing down the lap lanes. A neighbor's dog began to bark, then stopped abruptly. The pool lights were off. I could not see a thing. I peered into the darkness, thought I heard whispers.

"Who's there?" I called. My whole body shivered.

There was sudden quiet.

14.

In the relationship with John Richard, I had learned I was a physical coward. There was no way I was going outside. If you weren't secure, why call it a security system, anyway? The perimeter motion detector would scream if the house was violated. I crept back to bed and turned out the light.

The next morning, I de-activated the security system and stepped outside to look around and call for Scout the cat. Lime-green aspen leaves clicked in the early breeze, like the sound of tiny hands clapping. It did not sound like a splash.

I had the feeling of being watched. There was no sign of anything or anyone who might have been by the pool after Arch came in. My eye found Scout. He was sitting very still, watching me from inside the French doors leading to the patio.

"Lot of help you are," I said. He looked up with reproachful pale cat eyes. He was still too spooked by the dogs he'd encountered during his tenure of homelessness to have been last night's noisemaker. *Don't venture into the world,* his impassive face said. *It's dangerous out there.*

Adele gleefully announced we had a go for the Audubon Society picnic. Wednesday and Thursday I finished planning and ordering the food for that affair and Adele and Bo's wedding-anniversary party on the fourteenth. Philip's absence was a hole to be filled with work. Keeping busy helped deal with grief.

Bo and Adele were also preoccupied—with phone calls, committee meetings, buying and planting flowers for the garden. The general was one of those rare men who love to shop. Late Thursday afternoon he surprised me with a package of fresh sole fillets. He asked if I could do something with them for dinner the next night. He began a long explanation about becoming an Episcopalian when he married Adele. But there really is no such thing as a *former* Catholic, and could we start having fish on Fridays? In case Vatican II had been wrong.

We eat for different reasons, I said with great seriousness. Fish was no problem.

Friday morning I awoke with a heaviness in my chest. It's not the day of a funeral that's most difficult, or even the next day or the next. I did my yoga routine, turned off the security system, and made my way to the kitchen. No, the first few days you have the memory of the church service, of the casseroles afterward, of the conversations you had with friends when you remembered the person who died. Within a couple of days, though, the reality of the loss hits. The person is gone. Forever.

I set about making Julia Child's Fish Fillets Silvestre for the evening meal. Adele and the general were taking a break from all their activities by making a day trip to Vail. Outside, the rhythmic slap-slap of Julian's arms hitting the water started up.

I poached the fillets and made the sauce—all but its final butter enrichment—and set the whole thing to chill. I looked around the kitchen and tried to figure out what to do next. It was still too early to start breakfast for the household.

I made a double espresso. I put a call in to Schulz. He was not at his desk; I left a message. I hadn't thought of anything, nor did I know anything new, but I missed him.

I sipped the espresso: Lavazza. General Bo had picked some up for me when he bought the sole. However, the caffeine was not doing its perk-up job. My heart felt as if it were in the grip of a vise. I phoned Marla.

"Want to do lunch?" I said.

She said, "It's too early in the morning. I can't believe my ears."

We agreed on Aspen Meadow Café, near Philip's office. Well, I was going to have to go back to that part of town sometime. As soon as I hung up, Schulz called.

"That was quick," I said.

"Are you in a good mood or a bad mood?"

"Good, of course," I said. "Why?"

"Then you haven't seen the paper, I take it."

I had forgotten. "Don't tell me."

He exhaled deeply. In sympathy, I thought. Schulz's voice sounded far away when he said, "I'm not going to read it to you again, Miss G., and risk having my head blown off. Why don't you bring Arch over tonight. We'll cook out."

I reflected. I liked sole, but not that much.

"Sure," I said. "I'd love to."

"I know you feel funny . . . with that fellow you were dating gone—"

"I need to get my mind off the accident. Philip and I had just been seeing each other for about a month. It wasn't that big a deal." Without thinking, I added, "Probably I imagined more than was actually there."

Schulz was quiet. Then he said, "Well. I might need to talk to you about our friend Dr. Miller."

"Talk."

"Confidential, you understand. You were his friend."

"I told you. I'm beginning to think I didn't know that much. What's your question?"

"We found something in his briefcase. Thought it was a drug at first. Had to send it off to be analyzed."

"And?"

"Ever heard of *cantharidin*?"

You bet I'd heard of it. I said, "Spanish fly. Deadly as can be. Did it show up in the autopsy?"

"No, that's the weird thing. You have any idea why he would have something like that?"

Just for the slightest fraction of a moment, I thought I heard someone else on the line. Not the CIA listening in, but someone breathing. My body went cold. Three nights ago it was sounds outside. Now it was eavesdropped conversations. That would teach me to read Edgar Allan Poe.

"None whatsoever," I said, "but let's talk about it tonight." I tried to put some urgency into my voice, something he would read as my having to hang up.

"Before you rush off," he said, "you might like to know that because of finding this substance, they've given me the go-ahead to investigate this as a suspicious death."

I was quiet. Could I hear anything on the line besides Schulz's voice?

After a moment I said, "I can't talk about this any more right now. I'm looking forward to tonight."

I listened on the line after Schulz had hung up. Perhaps there was a very gentle clicking off. It was hard to tell. What had Philip said the last time we'd talked? *Not on the phone.*

Great.

The household separated for school and Vail. I made a nut short crust, folded whipped cream into beaten cream cheese for a mountain of filling that I then dotted with rows of fat strawberries. A final glaze of crushed, cooked fresh strawberries was the finishing touch for the Strawberry Super Pie I was taking to Tom Schulz's. I cleaned the kitchen and headed out to meet Marla. With dismay I noticed that

Strawberry Super Pie

CRUST:
³/₄ cup (1¹/₂ sticks) unsalted butter, melted
1¹/₂ cups all-purpose flour
1 tablespoon confectioners' sugar
³/₄ cup chopped pecans

TOPPING:
2 pounds strawberries, divided
¹/₂ cup water
1 cup sugar
3 tablespoons cornstarch

FILLING:
1¹/₄ cups whipping cream
¹/₄ pound cream cheese, softened
³/₄ teaspoon vanilla extract
¹/₂ cup confectioners' sugar

Preheat oven to 375°. For crust, mix melted butter with flour, confectioners' sugar, and pecans. Press into a buttered 10-inch pie plate. Bake for 25 minutes or until light brown. Allow to cool completely.

Start topping by mashing enough strawberries to make 1 cup. Cut tops off rest of strawberries and set aside. Place mashed berries in a saucepan and add water. Mix sugar and cornstarch into crushed berry mixture and bring to a boil on top of stove, stirring. Boil about one minute or until clear and thickened. Set aside to cool.

For filling, whip cream until stiff. In another bowl, beat cream cheese with vanilla and confectioners' sugar. Carefully fold whipped cream into cream cheese mixture. Spread in cooled crust and refrigerate.

When crushed berry mixture is cool, pie can be assembled. Stand whole (or halved, if you prefer) strawberries on top of cream filling, cut side down. When entire filling is covered with whole berries, carefully spoon cooled crushed berry mixture over all. Cream filling should not be seen between whole berries. Once the crevices have been filled, do not overload the pie with the crushed berry mixture, as it will just drip over the sides. Any leftover crushed berry mixture is delectable on toast or English muffins.

Makes 8 to 10 large servings

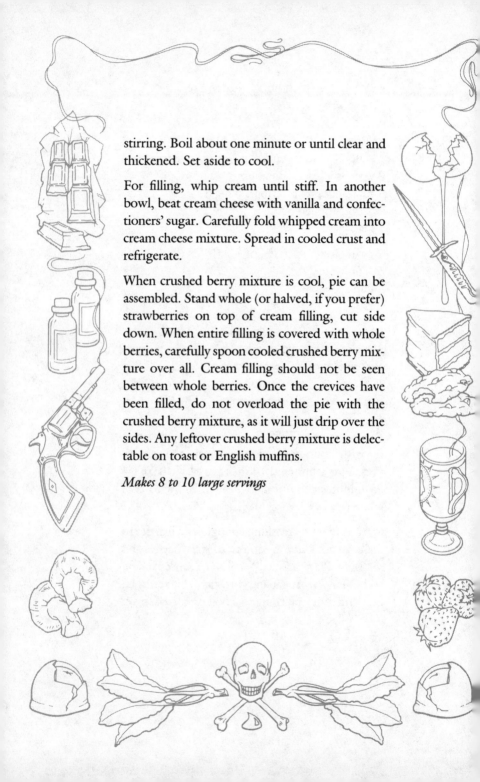

Arch had neglected his one chore: rolling the garbage can to the end of the driveway. Too bad household chores were resistant to his magic.

The Aspen Meadow Café is an attempt to bring continental cuisine to our little portion of the map. Originally a real estate office that had gone under during the 1985 oil slump, it was rumored that the new place had been remodeled à la Nouvelle Bistro. As I waited for Marla, my purse pleasantly stuffed with the tip from Monday's barbecue, the window displays beckoned.

On the inside shelves, baskets filled with every sort of bread crowded the shimmering expanse of plate glass. Braided loaves, round loaves, loaves freckled with poppy and sesame seeds, baguettes, muffins, fragrant nut breads, and oversize whole-wheat loaves crowded over and under each other. Decorously placed in one corner of the window was an Elk Park Prep decal: GET INTO THE SWIM!

The chimes attached to the glass door jingled cheerfully as I pushed through the door to look for Marla. Heady smells of roasting chickens and baking cakes mingled in the air. Above the glass cases filled with carryout items, there was a blackboard with the day's specials chalked in: Red Onion and Basil Tart, Grilled Chicken Santa Fe, Crevettes aux Champignons. Past the glass cases and around a corner there was a seating area. I strolled back. No Marla. She was not at any of the tables, where fresh arrangements of freesias and daisies adorned each white tablecloth. Lunch business was brisk: waitresses bustled about in the dining area. A waitress whispered that she would be out to help me at the counter in a moment and apologized that they were shorthanded today.

I walked unhurriedly around the corner to the counter area and turned my concentration back to the day's specials. I had just decided on the tart when I was whacked from behind.

I did not see who hit me. One minute I was reading the blackboard. The next I was shoved into a pastry case. I felt the glass crack beneath my chest. Shards splintered over tortes and pies. I careened off the glass. My head hit the metal of the bread shelves. I groped wildly for the bread baskets, the shelves, anything to keep from landing on the tile floor. My attacker rammed me again. This time I fell on a small marble table. It clattered to the floor and broke beneath my weight.

Loaves of bread toppled down as I landed on the broken table and tile floor. My body screamed with pain. I couldn't see; I could only hear my voice howling, even as I knew the sound was muffled by loaves of bread.

A husky voice came in close to my ear. It said, "Let Philip Miller rest in peace."

Then I heard abrupt jingling as the door to the café was flung open in haste. My attacker had rushed out.

I began to push loaves of bread away from my face and chest. My head throbbed from the fall; my back and chest ached from the relentless shoves.

"Hey! Hey!" came Marla's voice from far above me. "What happened here?"

Hands groped through the piles of bread to pull me up. I opened my eyes and thought I saw stars. But it was just a pantsuit covered with embroidered galaxies: Marla's sweat suit showing the summer constellations. A waitress and a cook were standing next to her, and they all stared down at me. Their questions tumbled out: What happened? Are you all right? Do you need a doctor?

I laughed at that last one. But that made everything hurt worse. My arm was bleeding. My chest felt as if it had caved in. The rest, luckily or unluckily, would be bruises. I gasped for breath. Something in my chest would not open up.

While Marla fetched clean wet towels for the cut, I told the assembled onlookers that I had been shoved. Had anyone seen anything? I looked into their surprised faces. One waitress said she'd seen someone leave in a hurry, but just assumed I'd lost my balance getting out of that person's way. The most description I could get was dark long hair that could have been a wig, black shirt and pants. She couldn't even say whether it had been a male or female. How tall? Not too tall.

"Should we call your cop friend?" asked Marla.

I shook my head. "Later. Without a description, license plate, or other ID, they're only going to record it anyway."

"Still feel like lunch?" she asked in a low voice.

"Let me pull myself together for a minute." Two of the kitchen staff were cleaning up the bread and marble mess. Broken glass shimmered all across the floor. I clamped the towel around my arm. Several diners eyed me as they left the café. Marla told me I was creating a curiosity slow-down. I said if she would help me around the corner to the seating area, we could get settled.

We limped together slowly through tables of women in tennis clothes and men in fringed leather shirts, jeans, and tooled cowboy boots to a table in the corner.

"I was hoping to avoid the rodeo crowd," Marla mumbled as she lowered me into a chair.

Good old Marla. It was so much easier to smile at her complaint than to think about my own pain. Coming from Connecticut, Marla had a hard time with the male crowd on any given day in any given Colorado eating establishment. Whether they were bankers, real estate agents, surveyors, or petroleum engineers, a large number would be sporting ten-gallon hats, hand-tooled cowboy boots, fringed leather jackets, and turquoise Indian jewelry. Today was no exception, although I somehow couldn't see how western apparel jibed with Belgian endive and peppercress.

"You sure you're okay?" she wanted to know. When I nodded she said, "We need to get Amour Anonymous started up again."

Our version of AA had to do with being addicted to relationships instead of liquor. Unfortunately, Marla and I were the only steady members, and virtually every one of our conversations was devoted to our problems anyway.

I said, "Why?"

"Because otherwise," she hissed, "I don't know what's going on in your life until something like this happens."

"I'll let you know the time and date of my next mugging."

She waved that off and gave me a look of deep concern. "The Jerk been bothering you lately?"

I told her about the clay pots and the general's timely appearance. She said in a low voice, "Think *this* could have been him?"

"Hard to tell. He usually behaves himself in public. Plus I don't know how I could have pissed him off." I felt my spirits sink, as if the adrenaline generated by the attack suddenly had worn off. Had I *ever* known what pissed off The Jerk?

Marla helped herself to a large slice of French bread from the basket on our table and slathered it with butter. She offered it to me and I took it with my free hand. But I wasn't ready to eat yet.

"I have to admit," Marla said, "I mean if you don't mind talking about it, that when I heard Philip had been killed I immediately suspected our ex."

Sweat prickled across my brow and under my arms. I said, "You must be joking."

"No. So I called The Jerk's office Monday morning, got the secretary, gave the name of one of his patients, and said I had a problem with my checkbook. What day had I come in? Said I thought it was last Friday morning. She said no way because the doctor was at the hospital for an induction at eight." She paused. "So I called a nurse I know at Lutheran and got a confirmation."

I took a bite of the sliced baguette. It was warm, moist, and could not have come out of the oven more than twenty minutes before. Minced fresh basil speckled the unsalted butter. Food always made pain recede. I said, "Why did you think John Richard would even care what Philip did?"

She raised her eyebrows. "Oh, don't. You can't possibly be that naive."

"How could he be jealous? We've been divorced for four years!"

Marla spread the soft herbed butter to the edge of another chunk of baguette. She said, "You're joking. You start going out with Miller. The Jerk starts driving by your house, making anonymous phone calls, giving you a hard time. Jealousy, I'm telling you."

"Ready to order, ladies?" said the same waitress who had helped me get up. "Or do you still need a little time? That was a horrible thing out there. Unbelievable." While she was talking, the manager came up to see if I was okay. In a tone I tried not to think of as accusing, he said the rest of the staff was out cleaning up the mess.

Then he swished off and we quickly ordered the tart, greens with vinaigrette, and coffee.

I turned Marla's words over in my mind as the coffee arrived. It tasted like sludge. When the waitress had gone, I said defensively, "I went out with Tom Schulz for four months."

Marla waved off this comment with both hands. "Please. The Jerk is not going to be threatened by a cop who looks as if he belongs in the woods with a camouflage suit, a high-powered rifle, and a six-pack. A gorgeous professional fellow, a wealthy shrink fellow at that, is another thing altogether." She signaled the waitress.

I said, "I never thought dating would cost me the installation of an expensive security system."

The waitress rushed up.

"Darling," Marla said to her. "My friend has just been mugged and she needs better coffee than this. Was it made from ancient beans? Do us all a favor and make a fresh pot. Please," she added with a smile that fooled nobody.

The waitress sniffed. "We serve one hundred percent Colombian coffee."

Marla opened her eyes wide. "Really. Then it must be from the District of Columbia, honey, and I'm not drinking any more of it. Neither is my friend. So either make us some fresh or bring us tea. Your choice."

"I'm sorry," the waitress said, although she didn't sound it. "Things have been crazy. During your . . . accident the people at that table over there," she motioned, "stiffed us for a twenty-two-dollar tab. Comes out of my salary." Before we could say anything, she whisked away.

I said, "Poor woman. Don't be hard on her."

"I swear," said Marla, "I wish that damn food critic would come to this place."

"That reminds me—"

"Don't. You don't want to see it. Have your lunch first."

"Marvelous. Let me get sick on a full stomach."

Marla *tsk*ed. She said, "Before we got sidetracked by coffee, we were going to have a little mini-meeting. Talk about relationships."

"Apart from a strained friendship with Schulz, I don't have any at the moment."

"But you did."

Our salads arrived. I thought of Philip, the balloons and chocolate, the lovely inviting smile. I remembered sitting on the deck of my old house each morning. *Somebody loves me.* I thought of Philip's rumored affair with Weezie Harrington.

I said, "I cared about him. I thought he cared about me."

"But you're not sure." I did not answer. She went on, "You wanted something." She began on her salad. "Did the two of you do things with Arch? Hike, go to a movie?"

I felt a flood of embarrassment. I was unmasked. I said, "I've just been physically attacked, for God's sake." I paused. "No, nothing with Arch. Philip used to say things like, It's nice to have you to myself. Besides, we'd only been seeing each other for a month, and he seemed so interested in knowing all about me. I just was hoping so much for . . ."

She leaned across the table, held my hand snugly in hers.

"Hoped for more than was there? Forget about it, Goldy. Maybe even hold out for the cop."

I pulled my hand away. "Can we change the subject?"

"Tell me how you're getting along with my sister."

I looked at Marla, my best friend. Her probing did not bother me. I knew she cared. Living with an abusive husband all those years had revealed my own skills at denial. Especially when it came to men.

"Are you doing okay with Adele?" she asked again.

I said, "Fine."

"The general?"

I said, "Ditto. He's odd, but nice."

Marla was shaking her head. "I don't understand their attraction. Of course, I really don't know either of them very well."

I said, "Your own sister?"

The red onion tart arrived. The smell of basil was deep and wonderful, and I remembered that, with its high concentration of plant oils, basil was a reputed aphrodisiac. Marla murmured an apology to the waitress, something along the lines of bad coffee making her crazy. The waitress accepted this with a nod and set a pot of tea on the table.

"Take this back pain, for example," Marla said as she dug into the steaming tart. There was bitterness in her voice. She said, "Fifty-year-olds don't walk with a cane."

"The heck they don't."

Marla gestured with her fork. "Repressed emotion, if you ask me."

"What's this, the psychological explanation of illness? Give me a break."

The waitress came up to check if we were okay, and Marla ordered two glasses of chablis. Whatever it was she wanted to talk about, she needed wine to do it: the psychological explanation of alcohol.

Marla waited until the glasses arrived.

"Adele and I were close when we were little," she said after a few sips. "I mean, we fought, you know, and she was so much older. But we cared enough about each other that when she left for college there were lots of tears, hugs, and daily letters. That kind of thing."

"And when you weren't little anymore?"

She lifted one shoulder in a tiny shrug. "You go your separate ways. Her first husband was a doctor." She laughed harshly. "Runs in the family."

"Divorce?"

Marla drank again, shook her head. "He died. Massive heart seizure at a cocktail party. One minute Dr. Marcus Keely was talking to his lovely wife Adele, the next minute he was dead in her arms."

"Good God. How old was she?"

Marla pursed her lips in reflection. "Nineteen years ago. She was thirty-one."

"How old was he?"

"Late thirties. History of heart disease in the family. High blood pressure, type A, all that."

To my surprise, Marla had tears in her eyes.

I said, "I thought you didn't know him."

She shook her head, drank more wine. "I didn't."

"Well?"

She put her glass down and leaned toward me. "Goldy, if you had a sister you'd grown up with, and cried with every time the two of you had to part, and told about the first time you kissed a boy and all that, wouldn't you think that one of you would seek out the other one when her husband died?"

"And she didn't?"

Marla sniffed and delicately wiped her eyes with her napkin. "She came out west to visit when our parents retired here. The doctor left her a lot of money. Her way of dealing with grief was to spend it. She bought a place in Sun Valley and part ownership in a condo in Aspen. That's probably worth a mint. She should sell it. You can't ski Aspen if you walk with a cane."

I nodded. It usually worked the other way around, though. You skied Aspen, you ended up with a cane.

"She spent some time with me, even bought some land here, where their house is now. But did she talk to me about how she felt? Did she cry in my arms? Did she need me? No."

"Well," I said slowly, "maybe she only did that when you were little."

"I wanted to help her," Marla said. Her eyes were red and leaking again.

I remembered the flicker of judgment in Adele's eyes when Marla had appeared at her house last Friday. And then there had been Marla's bent head, her embarrassed acceptance of that judgment. For a moment, I had seen Marla as she must have been afraid her slender, perfectly groomed older sister saw her—as too heavy, too scatter-brained, too frowsy, too frivolous.

I said, "Adele doesn't like others, even Bo, to help her. Well, unless it's for some greater cause, like fund-raising. She doesn't like to seem dependent, I think."

"It's not the same."

I said evenly, "You wanted her to love you—"

"Don't say it." Marla dabbed her eyes, blew her nose.

We had finished our lunch. The heavy conversation was over. Our waitress brought us lemon mousse, on the house, she said, to make up for the coffee.

Marla insisted on paying for lunch. As we began to walk out, I told her I had forgotten something at the table. I hobbled back and left the waitress a twenty-two-dollar tip.

15.

Marla wanted me to leave the van at the café. She would drive me home, she announced. I politely declined. In addition to hating cowboys, Marla could not abide the flood of summer tourists in Aspen Meadow. There you'd be with her behind a car from Kansas, Texas, or Nebraska going ten miles per hour on a mountain road. She'd let down the Jaguar window and yell, "Admit it! You're *lost!*"

So I let her follow me back to the Farquhars. She wanted to make sure I could manage my vehicle. This was no easy task. My arm ached from the makeshift bandage, but I gritted my teeth. Something twisted inside my chest upon seeing the repaired Thunderbird in the garage. I invited Marla in, but she begged off.

"Adele and Bo haven't asked me over once since they've lived here. I'm not going to traipse in uninvited. But the next time your neighbor has an aphrodisiac dinner, why don't you get her to include me? I'll think of some fellow to bring. And believe me, Goldy, I'll make sure the food works."

"How did you know about the dinner?"

She drew her puffy cheeks down into a scowl. "I'd be willing to wager the whole town knows, now." Reluctantly, she reached into her capacious purse and pulled out the new issue of the *Mountain Journal,* then handed it to me with a dour look. "Don't do anything rash," she said before grinding the Jag around in a thirteen-point turn to get out of the driveway.

I tucked the paper under my arm and started up to the house for bandages and an aspirin. The wine had not killed the pain. My aches swelled like a chorus.

Before I reached the house, something caught my attention: the door to the magazine side of the garage was open. Its edge was just visible where the two walls met. Either somebody was in there or somebody had left the door ajar.

I walked through the garage, making as much noise as possible. Peering into the magazine's near-darkness, I could see General Farquhar surveying rows of weapons arrayed over a banquet-size table. He had been alert to my arrival, and nodded to my knock on the open door.

He saw me holding my arm. "Don't tell me that bastard—"

I said, "No, no. At least, I'm not sure."

"What happened?"

"I sort of had an accident."

"Another one?"

I told him about the shove at the café, although I did not tell him what the attacker had said. "It'll be all right. The main damage was to the café, I think. What's all this?" I gestured at the weapons on the table.

"Just doing some cleaning," he said. "After all those flowers and shops in Vail, I needed to do something constructive."

I didn't know how cleaning weapons was constructive, but I let it go.

"May I sit down?" I asked tentatively. "Will I be buzzed by some electronic ray?"

"It's all turned off," he assured me. But he did stop to watch me enter. His blue eyes looked dark in the windowless room. Neon rectangles overhead lit neat piles of cardboard boxes pushed against cement walls. There were No Smoking, No Fires, and No Matches signs, along with an NRA poster. On the far wall was what looked like an antique gun cabinet with a glass front. It was a beautiful piece, probably mahogany. But no way would a gun cupboard fit Adele's traditional decor, hence its placement in the magazine. I shivered and looked for a place to sit.

General Bo came around and helped me to settle on a sturdy wooden box.

"Where in the world did you get all these weapons?"

"Part of my research," he said as he lifted one carefully and I shifted back. "Don't worry, it's not loaded. This is an AK-47, Chinese made. Favorite of terrorists. It's getting hard to get over here. I got this one in Morocco."

"Why?"

His brow furrowed. "I'm one of the few people in this country who knows the dangers of what we're facing. If I can do enough research, maybe someone will start listening."

Instead of treating you like an outcast, I thought.

"But why trek around the world looking for weapons? I mean, it's not like recipes or furniture. You can't swap them or take them to the flea market."

He regarded me patiently, as if I were a dull child. "Because I wanted them, that's why. It's a dangerous world we live in, Goldy, in case you hadn't noticed with that husband of yours. He's the kind of person you want to look out for," he added firmly.

"Ex-husband."

"Like Adele," he said as if he had not heard me. "I love her, too, and I was determined to get her. I thought they'd appreciate us in Washington, but they did not. So I built this house and this storage area. Through my research, the truth will be told."

I resisted the impulse to ask, *Truth about what?* I was fairly sure the general and I did not share a worldview. Still, I liked the man. He was eccentric, but his heart was in the right place. Where his mind was I was not sure. In any event, I was not up to a political discussion. I merely nodded and looked around. Brilliant sunlight from the open door made it hard to see in the neon-lit room. The boxes bore stamps that were meaningless to me. On the open door were numerous admonitions to lock up. Which reminded me.

"Ah, General Bo," I began. What was I supposed to call him,

anyway? We had never quite worked that out. "Ah, I was wondering if I could talk to you about Julian. . . ."

The general squinted at me, continued his cleaning motion with the gun.

He said, "What about him?"

I felt uncomfortable complaining. But maybe he could give me some insights, since he and Julian did seem genuinely friendly.

"Tell me about him," I said. It wasn't just the hostility that bothered me. There was also Julian's distinct discomfort at the dinner Saturday night. And someone had attacked me. Someone strong, perhaps wearing a wig. "He doesn't exactly seem like someone who was raised with . . ." I tried not to say *money or class,* but couldn't seem to find the right words.

"Doesn't seem like someone who knew what all those little forks meant?" The general turned his back to me as he put the pistol back in its cabinet.

"Not just that. He's so hostile."

"To you, maybe," the general replied.

"But why?"

"Because of the food! He helps me with the garden, as you know. Originally he claimed he could handle all the cooking, too. But Adele wanted a professional caterer. Ergo, hostility for the caterer."

"I see. But there's something else. He seems awfully uncomfortable around . . . money."

"Stands to reason, Goldy." General Bo eyed me before turning his gaze on another weapon and carefully picking it up. "Recoilless rifle," he explained. "If it hadn't been for our scholarship for science students, Julian would still be making candy and Navajo fry-bread down in Bluff."

"Meaning?"

He turned the corners of his mouth down, shrugged. "You know how Adele gets a bee in her bonnet. Coordinating the church music conference. Raising money for that pool at Elk Park." He shook his head. "We had sold our house in Washington and were planning this house, when she read a long sad story in the *Post* about a fellow down on one of those reservations who got thrown in jail for theft. Turns out he was a real bright fellow, just poor. She says, That does it, we're going to set up a scholarship for some youngster."

I squirmed on the box. My back and legs were beginning to hurt. I said, "Just like that?"

He nodded. "Of course, I wanted to do an athletic scholarship for a young man to go to military preparatory school and then West Point. But she was having none of it, said she'd like to see the person who won the scholarship. Watch his progress."

I imagined a wealthy client coming out to the kitchen to watch my progress on beef Wellington. I wouldn't allow it. Teenagers were a different ball game, however. Their resistance to control usually manifested itself as rebellion against authority. Or resentment of a more experienced cook. Julian's hostility was beginning to be a lot more understandable.

"So she called her sister," the general was saying, "and asked about this prep school over in Elk Park, since it was near her property. My only request, since it was my money, too, was that the boy be athletic." He grinned. "I didn't want to rule out the possibility of West Point."

I assumed a polite tone. "Of course not."

The general went on, "She called the school and offered the scholarship money. Ha! Took them about ten seconds to decide, although they made a great show out of taking it to their board of trustees and so on." He laughed, remembering. "When Adele told them she was moving out here, they said, Well, we just happen to have a trustee vacancy here, how about it? And it's been all pool fund-raising ever since."

"How can they afford a pool but not afford a boarding department?"

The general moved over to his cabinet and retrieved a large weapon.

I said, "Gosh, General Bo, that looks like something you see in the movies."

"Grenade launcher," he said in a matter-of-fact tone. "You were asking me something about Elk Park . . ."

I said, "The pool. Why have that instead of a boarding department?"

"Attract more locals that way," said the general. "Elk Park has learned it can't compete with the eastern boarding schools for students. So many of those have gone out of business in the last decade anyway.

What's amazing is that Elk Park lasted as long as it did. Although I don't think Adele was bargaining on the boarding department closing as soon as we moved out here."

"Or bargaining on inheriting your scholarship student."

"No," he said thoughtfully, "that either."

A sudden darkness billowed into the room. The general muttered under his breath as he peered outside. I followed his gaze. Dark clouds had swept eastward from the mountains.

"Don't worry," I said to him. "That means it's officially summertime. Every afternoon melting snow in the high country to the west will form clouds, move east, and give us a shower. It's only dangerous if there's lightning and you're out swimming or climbing."

"Beg to differ," he said, his voice crisp. "Lightning is dangerous if you're sitting on hand-held surface-to-air missiles."

I looked cautiously down at the box where I was perched. What exactly *was* under it?

He said, "Not literally, Goldy. It's all over there," and he pointed to a long cabinet built along the wall. In the dimness I had not even noticed it. Now I saw that the cabinet door had a bulky lock. "But," he went on, "I would feel better if you closed that door. The building is grounded. Nevertheless, I don't want to take any chances."

I slid off the box. "I have to be going anyway. Arch forgot to roll the garbage can down."

"I'll do it," he said. "You're in no condition to do chores."

I couldn't exactly argue with that. I waited while he packed up the remaining weapons.

"What was that policeman's name," he asked with his back to me, "the one who helped you the day of the accident?"

I said, "Schulz," and wondered if the general's tone was just a tad too nonchalant.

"Did he mention anything about that explosion? I mean, afterward?"

"No," I said, somewhat tentatively. "He just told me to be careful."

The general drew his bottom lip up over his top teeth and brought his eyebrows together, a studious attitude of reflection. He said, "You didn't tell him about the magazine, did you?"

"No," I said. But I will, I thought. I said, "Why? What you're doing is legal, isn't it?"

He lifted the last of the guns and placed it in the cabinet.

"Oh, of course. It's just that law-enforcement agencies can get so jealous of each other. I wouldn't want the locals poking around here, you know?"

As usual, I did not.

"In any event," the general said when he had locked the cabinet, "when you see him I'd appreciate your not mentioning this room. He'll probably think I'm some kind of wacko instead of a bona fide researcher."

As far as I was concerned, the jury was still out on whether the general was wacko. But I just said, "It's going to start raining. If we're going to do the trash, we need to hustle."

The general locked and armed the entry door.

"Too heavy for a young boy," he observed as he tilted the garbage cart back on its wheels. I tried to help guide it and overcompensated with my good arm. The cart tipped over with a resounding crash. Coffee grounds, orange halves, bills and letters, meat trays and plastic wrap, cans and bottles spilled, rolled, broke, and skittered across the garage floor.

Two catastrophes in one day. I wondered about the Guinness record for mess-making as I gathered up soaked envelopes from Utah, rifle shells, empty bottles of Adele's Estée Lauder cream and Julian's peroxide, as well as bits of cut rope and empty fertilizer bags.

I said, "Why do you suppose Julian dyes his hair?"

"Probably to disguise his upbringing among the Indians," the general said, exasperated. "Although you'd think he'd choose another style." He scooped up mounds of fruit peelings sanded with coffee grounds, old newspapers, and empty chocolate boxes. He lifted one of these and said, "Sometimes you can't believe you ate this stuff in the first place."

Large raindrops had begun to splat down on the driveway when he finally towed the trash wagon to the curb. It was not until we were walking into the house together that it even occurred to me to wonder how the general knew I was going to see Schulz again.

16.

General Bo offered to let me shower first. Since one of the odd things about this luxurious house was that only one person could command the hot-water supply at a time, I told him to go ahead. I would be up after I checked on my culinary domain. I washed my hands in the hall bathroom and went into the kitchen, where Adele was deep into a phone conversation whose bad vibes were readily apparent. A crisis had erupted with a pool fund-raiser set for August, a fifty-dollar-per-seat showing of a film featuring George Rumslinger in a supporting role.

"Doesn't anybody at that school *know* him?" she demanded into the phone. She looked regal in a navy-and-white silk shirtdress and spectator pumps, a dress suited more for a yacht-club luncheon than a day in Vail. With one hand she held the phone; with the other she leaned slightly on the cane, as if she intended momentarily to use it as a weapon. I giggled and devoutly hoped it was Joan Rasmussen who was getting the third degree.

I wrote her a note: "I know the foreman." She nodded, smiled, and held up one finger, as if to say, I'll be off in a minute. I wrote, "Do you have any bandages?" She pulled her mouth into an astonished O, then shook her head. "Do you need help?" she whispered. I shook my head and walked stiffly through the pelting raindrops back out to my van, where my trusty safety kit yielded an Ace bandage. I wrapped up my arm, pulled out Marla's copy of the *Mountain Journal,* and went out to the deck. I decided against taking a painkiller. For the moment.

The headline jumped out at me.

No Love At This First Bite!

In her latest culinary adventure, Ms. Goldy Bear (yes, folks, you read that right), the divorced proprietor of GOLDILOCKS' CATERING, WHERE EVERYTHING IS JUST RIGHT! (no joke there either), has declared herself a goddess of love. Our unmarried Venus claims to reign in the kitchen, where she supposedly prepares aphrodisiac foods.

Contrary to the advertised amorous effects, no outbreak of love was in evidence at a dinner party for six at the elegant home of Brian and Weezie Harrington last Saturday night. Quite the opposite, in fact. The hostilities between the host and hostess began somewhere between the mussels and the quiche, and continued on through the undercooked pork chops and dry chocolate cookies.

How long must Aspen Meadow endure such pain to the palate? Think if Goldy Bear had to cater a peace conference! The U.S. would be nuked before the lemon meringue pie. Since Ms. Bear obviously has no demonstrable skill in the culinary arts and no successful experience in the love department, this reviewer recommends that she try something she's good at. Like carpool.

Until next time, discriminating diners, I am ever your

Pierre

Mussels? Quiche? Pork chops? Carpool?

Why was someone doing this to me? Who could be so cruel? My pain was like that of a fish when he's gutted live. A blade of agony ripped through my psyche. To be skewered so publicly, so unfairly . . . it was beyond belief. The hurt flared into rage. I wondered what my chances would be with a libel suit. Thing was, every time I called my lawyer, it cost me hundreds of dollars to hear that whatever it was I had in mind was not a good idea.

Adele arrived on the deck. The rain had turned to hail, and I had not heard her cane over the rapid-fire thudding on the roof.

She saw the newspaper in my hand. Her eyes clouded sympathetically. "I'm so sorry you saw that."

"So am I. Who could it be? Someone who was there? Someone who heard about it and got the menu wrong?"

Line One began to ring. I rose to get it. Anything to be away from the newspaper.

"Mrs. Farquhar, please. This is the headmaster of Elk Park Preparatory School."

Obviously he did not recognize the voice of the caterer who'd bailed him out of a sixty-plate-brunch problem only the week before. I told him to hang on and brought the portable phone out to Adele.

I closed my eyes, listened to the hail thud on the deck roof. I wished Pierre—whoever he was—were outside.

Naked! Dying! Pummeled by hail and then hit by lightning!

I groaned. The air had turned cold. I felt each thud of hail directly on my heart. You'd think that after being married to an abusive husband you would learn to take abuse. But until you find a way to pull yourself away from the abuser's opinion of you, it still hurts. I was going to find a way to pull myself away. And I was going to find out who had it in for me.

Adele was saying to the headmaster, "I don't understand why nothing goes right in this town . . ."

Tell me about it.

I slipped into the living room for a couple of Lindt Lindors. When I came back out to the porch I picked up the periwinkle-and-white crocheted afghan, moved to a cold but dry wicker chair, and wrapped myself up. I opened a chocolate and popped it in my mouth, then allowed the sinfully dark, soft creaminess to melt on my taste buds and make me feel much better. After a moment I took a deep breath of cool air and opened my eyes to see the hail falling in massive vertical sheets to the meadow. Here and there splashes of white speckled the lush green.

In addition to feeling things will go right in a move to the mountains, people often mistakenly believe that in the midst of such natural beauty, there will be an absence of honking traffic, backstabbing gossip, and cruelty in general. I ate the other chocolate and allowed my eyes to travel around the deck, to Adele shaking her head at the headmaster's distress, to the table with the hateful newspaper review, to the panel of security buttons on the wall. Security, it seemed, from physical intrusions only.

Arch came out to the deck and beckoned. The hail was so loud I had not heard Julian drive up or the two boys come inside. In the kitchen I automatically began to prepare hot chocolate, Arch's favorite drink on snowy days.

"Mom," he said as he looked into the pan of milk, "it's not snowing. Hey!" He pulled back and stared at me. "What happened to you?"

I gazed at him: freckles, eyes full of concern behind glasses, hair damp from being hatless in the hail. I assured him I was okay, just had a little slip in the café and ended up falling. I shrugged it off. With my assurance that things were fine, he pressed his lips together in a grin, opened his eyes wide, and raised his eyebrows.

Something was wrong with the way he looked. I had to keep staring at him for a minute to figure out what it was. This morning he had left without my checking his sweat suit. Now he was wearing baggy black pants and a white oxford cloth shirt, both about four sizes too big for him. While I was contemplating this bizarre turn in personal style, the milk boiled over.

"What are you wearing?" I asked as I reached for a sponge.

He said, "Clothes."

"Whose clothes?"

He glanced down at the pants, then gave me an innocent look. "Julian gave these to me. They were too small for him."

I dumped out the scalded milk and scrubbed the stove. I thought, Let go of it.

"Listen," he said. "Julian and I want to go swimming in the hail. We think it would be really cool."

"Do you want to get pneumonia?"

"No," he said, "I want to show him that I can get out of the handcuffs under water."

"Forget about it. No to all of the above."

"Jeez, Mom!" His voice was furious. "You never let me do *anything*! No money for magic stuff! No swimming, even though the pool is heated, in case you hadn't noticed! You always think I'm going to get hurt! But who's wearing a bandage, huh? Is there anything I *can* do?"

And before I could answer he turned, narrowly avoiding Adele, and stomped out of the kitchen.

Adele was rubbing her forehead with the hand not holding the cane. She said, "The headmaster says we should show another film, since the print with Rumslinger is unavailable. We've already sold the tickets. Of course, he has no film in mind."

I scrubbed scalded milk off the bottom of the pan and made guttural sympathetic noises.

She sighed. "I'm going into the study where I can hear myself think. and call Paramount."

If you have money, I guess you can do anything. I was the last person to try to talk her out of doing battle with Hollywood. I couldn't even make hot chocolate.

She said, "What's wrong with Arch?"

"He wants to swim. Says the pool is heated, so why not? Now he's angry because I said no." I rinsed the pan and dried it. "I hate to have him mad at me. He's all I've got."

"Well," she said in a sympathetic tone, "you know what the psychiatrists say. No matter what you do for your children, they don't appreciate you."

In my many readings on parenting, this was not something I had ever heard.

I said, "What psychiatrist said that?"

"One who had to raise children."

I put down the dish towel and thought for a minute. "Well, actually," I said with my best sarcastic laugh, "I never knew a psychiatrist who had to stay home and raise children."

"That's what I mean, Goldy," she said before she tapped off.

With my arm wrapped, preparations for the Audubon Society picnic the next day proceeded slowly. The hail shower ceased with great suddenness. Piles of silver-tinged clouds dissolved like pulled-apart netting. Sunlight flooded the kitchen around four, as I sliced kiwi, cantaloupe, and strawberry for a fruit salad to go with the Farquhars' Sole Fillets Silvestre. Julian had a date with Sissy and would be gone for dinner. Arch yelled through his door that he did not want to go to Tom Schulz's for dinner and he did not want to eat fish that belonged in the ocean.

"What do you want, then?" I had asked through the wood.

"For you to leave me alone," he said. "I'll fix my own grilled cheese."

"Arch," I pleaded, "don't be angry. I just didn't want you to get sick from swimming in the hail."

"Go away."

"Let me know if you change your mind about going to Tom Schulz's."

"I'm not going to change my mind."

The heck with everybody, I thought as I put the strawberry pie in a container and walked out to the van. I had done the best I could. I strapped the pie container on a shelf with bungee cords, opened the security gate, and walked slowly back up the driveway. With my wrapped arm I could just manage to change the gears in the van. I ground into reverse and closed the gate. Then, pedal to the metal. I couldn't wait to get out of that damn country club, even if I'd already been out for lunch.

It would have been nearly impossible to find surroundings less like the tended lawns of Meadowview than the long dirt road to Tom Schulz's

place. He lived in a spacious three-room log house six miles west of
Aspen Meadow. Of course, since Aspen Meadow was unincorporated
(and proud of it), just about anything past two miles from Main Street
was considered outside of town. In the absence of institutional government, real estate agents set the geographical boundaries.

Light from the setting sun glinted behind wet aspen leaves. The
trees looked as if they were hung with emeralds. Melting hail had made
recent tire tracks shiny ribbons of mud. As the van bumped along,
overhanging trees shed branchloads of ice on the windshield. I turned
on the wipers. When I arrived at his cabin, Tom Schulz was shoveling
hail from the stone walk.

He scooped the last shovelful and heaved it over a gray rock outcropping that looked like a sleeping elephant. I unfastened the pie and
carefully stepped out to avoid deep mud. The cool evening air was
redolent with the sweet scent of chokecherry blossoms.

Schulz leaned against his shovel. "Something wrong? What happened to your arm?"

"Everything is wrong."

He put down the shovel and came over to help me.

"I was attacked at Aspen Meadow Café." I told him briefly about the
mugging, including the admonition to let Philip Miller rest in peace.

"I can't believe you didn't call me." Schulz took the pie from my
hands and laid it on a rock. "I can*not* believe it, Miss G." Schulz hugged
me tenderly, carefully, to avoid inflicting more pain. I loved the rough
feel of his jeans against my legs, the freshly laundered smell of his Izod
shirt that had been yellow once.

When we disengaged, his face took on a puzzled expression. He
said, "Where's Arch?"

"At home. Angry that I wouldn't let him swim in the hail."

Schulz picked up the pie container, made appropriate *mm-mm*
noises, then put his free arm around my shoulders as he led me up the
stone path. "If you would take more care of yourself and less of Arch,
everybody might be a lot better off, Goldy." He looked down at me
with an apologetic smile. "No offense."

I made a gesture toward the pie. I said, "You want to eat that or
wear it?"

"I'll eat it, thanks," he said as he swung it just out of my reach. "Come on in. I need to talk to you before we get into the business of food."

The door to the house sported an elaborate carving of a naked woman involved in some kind of dance. The sculptor who had had this place built had thought of the woman as his muse. The sculptor, long gone, had been caught for back taxes. The house had been sold at one of those IRS auctions for a fraction of its worth, and Schulz had lucked out. I had always been happy that he lived here. After long days working homicide, an investigator needed a remote place with a big fireplace inside and a porch swing that looked out on the mountains. Smoke from the backyard barbecue drifted around front as I pushed through the sculpted door.

It had been a while since my last visit. Stenciled lampshades shed warm light over the handmade cedar paneling and two-story moss-rock fireplace. Schulz knew quite a bit about antiques, and had furnished his house with a spare grouping of expensive pieces, including a cupboard that was called a sink. He had started to tell me about them, but I'd told him I still thought Chippendale were two chipmunks Arch used to watch in cartoons.

While I stood admiring the living room, Schulz called to me from the kitchen. "I figured after all that fancy cooking you've been doing for the Farquhars, you'd be ready for a steak."

"Am I ever," I said. He handed me a bottle of my favorite brand of nonalcoholic beer, then got one for himself. "Did you buy this especially for me?" But I knew he had. "Gee, am I ready for somebody to be nice."

"I take it you saw the paper."

"Change the subject, please. So we're having steak? I thought you *liked* fancy cooking."

"I like so many things, you can hardly imagine." He winked. "Let's go sit."

I went back out to the porch and settled tentatively on the swing. It was one of the old-fashioned kind with slats.

"Wait here a sec," he said as he took my fake-beer bottle and put it on the deck railing. He returned with an alpaca blanket, which he unfolded and carefully tucked around me.

I said, "Thank you, Daddy."

"Shut up and drink this stuff that means I don't have to worry about you driving home." He handed me the bottle and lowered himself to the other side of the swing.

"You really are wonderful, you know," I said without looking at him. The drink was cold and fizzy; my chest warmed in response. The scratchy alpaca felt snug and safe.

"Yeah, aren't I something. Goldy, I want you to report this attack, whether anybody saw the guy or not."

"Will do."

"You can bet we're not going to let any aspect of this thing rest in peace now."

I nodded. Silence enveloped us as the sun sank behind the mountains. The air was gauzy from the melting hail.

He said, "You're still feeling bad about this Philip Miller fellow." It was not a question.

An involuntary tightness gathered in the area where my ribs ached. I said, "Sometimes. It seems like such a waste."

"Oh. I don't think so."

"What do you know about it?" I sipped, looked out at the view.

"Well, Miss G., as hard as it may be for you to believe, I had a girlfriend once. Went to high school together, all that. She was killed in Vietnam."

I was nonplussed. "I thought women weren't—"

"She was a nurse. Hit in an artillery shelling."

"Oh, God," I said. "I'm sorry."

"Thank you. Point is, love is never wasted."

"Really. I wasted it for seven years on The Jerk. And I'm not sure I was in love with Philip Miller."

He let that pass. After a few minutes he said, "Feel like talking about him, then? In an unemotional kind of way? It involves people you know better than I do."

I swished the liquid around in its green bottle until it foamed. I said, "Sure. Go ahead."

"For starters, there's Philip Miller and the people who live next door to you."

I said flatly, "I don't know whether he was having an affair with Weezie."

"That's the rumor I heard from four people. Also, if she's so interested in aphrodisiacs, do you think she'd go so far as to use this Spanish fly? Might explain why Philip had it."

"I told you, I know the rumor about the affair. That's it."

"Actually, I'm wondering if you know anything about the relationship between our good shrink and Brian Harrington."

"Oh, *please*."

"Not that kind of relationship. Business. Rivalry. Philip Miller, the politically correct counselor, active in Protect Our Mountains, president of the local Audubon Society, and an opponent of development of ecologically sensitive Flicker Ridge. Which is owned by Mr. Harrington."

I said, "Show me a part of Colorado, even one rock, that somebody's not insisting is ecologically sensitive." I got up to hunt for another fake beer.

"Okay, okay," he said as he followed me back to his compact kitchen. "Let me do this," he said as he took my bottle and rattled around in the refrigerator for another one. "I'm the host. I just wanted to know if you knew anything about it."

"Audubon Society, I don't know. I'm doing a picnic for them tomorrow with the Farquhars. As to specifics, the only kind of birds I know about are the kind you eat."

"Can't say that I blame you," he said as he handed me another cold bottle. "Bring that out back so we can do the steaks. I need to talk to you about health food, anyway."

"Another one of my favorite topics."

He smiled at me. "The sun's gone down. You need a sweater or something?" He looked questioningly at my thin jacket.

I said I would get the alpaca and meet him around back. When I arrived at the patio, the steaks had begun to sizzle on the grill. The enticing smell of barbecue smoke drifted upward into the darkening sky. I rewrapped myself and sat down on a picnic bench, Indian-style.

"Okay," he said as he tossed a few drops of water on the fire to bring the flames down. The coals hissed. He moved his big body around to face me, and I felt a surge of warmth not associated with the fake beer or the blanket. He said, "The sister. Elizabeth. Having trouble with her health-food-store mortgage payment until Philip's will takes care of everything."

I shook my head. "I just don't think she would do it. She's weird, but not murderous." I reflected. "She and Weezie were having a fight about something, though. Did Philip leave anything for Weezie, that was what the argument was about."

"Leave what, like money?"

"I don't know. Elizabeth wants to get together. Maybe I could talk to her."

"Your mission, Miss G., is to find out what the fight was about. Leave Weezie what?"

"This is kind of gross," I said, "but was he an organ donor or something? I remember Elizabeth yelling he left his body to science. Maybe that's what he was going to leave."

Schulz turned the steaks over. Tantalizing smoke rushed out.

He said, "I checked. He was a donor. Contrary to public perception, a death in a car crash means his heart and kidneys couldn't be donated. Only things that can be, were. Skin and corneas. Both per Miller's instruction." He threw more water droplets on the fire. "No evidence of poison in the autopsy, by the way. I already told you he was negative for drugs. I still can't figure out that cantharidin. He didn't have any of the internal inflammation that would have shown he'd been given some."

"Let's not talk about this anymore."

"I'm sorry," he said. He tucked in the steaks' sides and came over to sit next to me on the bench. He pulled one foot up on his knee. "You doing okay? Need anything? I got a big salad and some baked potatoes inside. Strawberry pie made by my favorite caterer."

I smiled. "Not to mention steaks cooked by a great cop."

He turned, put his arms around the alpaca with me inside, pulled the package close. My inner tightness melted. His facial skin was cool. His sandy hair smelled intensely of steak smoke. I could hear my heart beating.

"I'm worried about you," he said into my ear. "And I miss you."

I unraveled my arms from the alpaca, reached out for his large waist.

"Somebody's driving up," he said, very low.

Just when things were getting good.

"Mom!" came Arch's distant voice. "Mom, I changed my mind!" Tires ground into the mud. A car turned around. "Mom! The general brought me! I even remembered how to get here! Where are you, around back?"

Schulz and I untangled ourselves.

Schulz cocked his head at me. Said, "To be continued."

Arch burst out onto the patio. "Wow, does that smell good! It's okay for me to come this late, isn't it?"

17.

Food always tastes better when it's cooked by someone else. When that someone else was Tom Schulz, you were in good hands. The juicy steaks were redolent of a garlic-Burgundy marinade, the flaky baked potatoes oozed melted butter, and every leaf of the green salad was unabashedly coated with thick guacamole dressing. Schulz confessed to having called Arch to find out how I liked chocolate best. Arch had said, With mint. Therefore, alongside our strawberry pie we had Schulz's famous chocolate-mint cheesecake. So much for the National Cholesterol Institute.

Arch was happy in Tom Schulz's company. He felt accepted and it showed; he even called Schulz by his first name. After some initial hesitation, Arch dug in and ate voraciously. Toward the end of our visit he became downright chatty. Did Tom know how to call the wizard to tell him what card was in his hand? He did not. Arch took out a deck of cards and had Tom pick one. Then he called a friend of his, and the wizard announced the card to Tom, who was amazed.

"It's a code," said Arch. "Like Mom and I used to have when I was

Schulz's Guacamole Salad

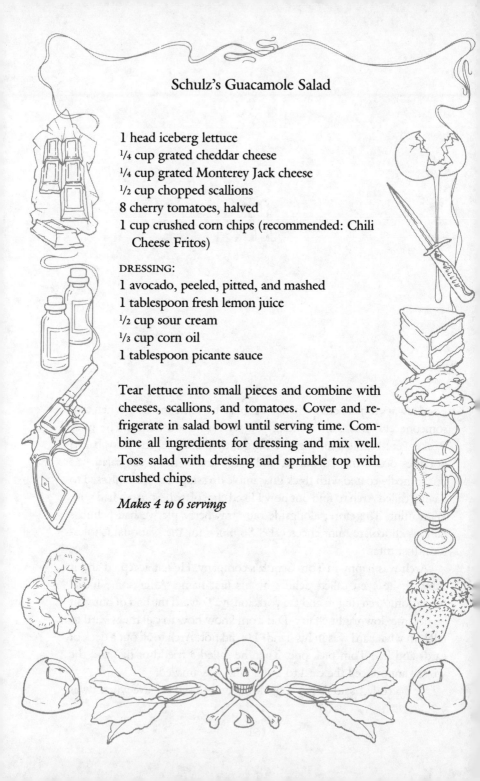

1 head iceberg lettuce
1/4 cup grated cheddar cheese
1/4 cup grated Monterey Jack cheese
1/2 cup chopped scallions
8 cherry tomatoes, halved
1 cup crushed corn chips (recommended: Chili Cheese Fritos)

DRESSING:
1 avocado, peeled, pitted, and mashed
1 tablespoon fresh lemon juice
1/2 cup sour cream
1/3 cup corn oil
1 tablespoon picante sauce

Tear lettuce into small pieces and combine with cheeses, scallions, and tomatoes. Cover and refrigerate in salad bowl until serving time. Combine all ingredients for dressing and mix well. Toss salad with dressing and sprinkle top with crushed chips.

Makes 4 to 6 servings

little. If I wanted her to come pick me up at a friend's house, or if I was having some kind of problem at school or something? I would just call her up and say, 'The seven of spades.' She knew to come right away, and I wouldn't be embarrassed trying to explain things. Calling the wizard," Arch went on, "is a code that a lot of magicians use. The caller knows the card. The wizard is just any one of your friends who knows the trick." He gave me a wide grin, the first I'd seen in a while. "Even Mom knows it."

"Would you teach me?" asked Tom Schulz. "Please?"

Arch hesitated, then said he could use another wizard, anyway. He told Schulz that if someone called and asked for the wizard, to run slowly through the suits, until the caller interrupted him. Then the wizard ran downward from the ace until the caller interrupted him again.

Schulz was impressed. "Will you call me sometime? Not at the Sheriff's Department, but here at home? That is, if you can tear yourself away from that fancy summer school of yours."

Arch said he would, then confessed he didn't really like summer school except for his mini-course in French. This he was taking to avoid an hour of sports (*tennis,* he said with disgust, in the same tone of voice that one might use upon discovering *ants*). Had Tom read Poe, Arch wanted to know. Yes, a million years ago. Arch said, Imagine, we even have ravens in Aspen Meadow.

Tom asked if Poe was a good dresser. Arch said he wasn't sure. Well, Arch's taste in clothes showed some new influence. Arch said, Just a guy named Julian. I could not remember the last time I had seen Arch so happy. He even hummed along with Schulz playing his guitar and singing "Love Is a Rose" after the cheesecake. When the three of us did the dishes, Schulz taught him "Mama, Don't Let Your Babies Grow Up to Be Cowboys." Arch alternated humming the two tunes all the way home.

As I drove up to the Farquhars' house with its numerous floodlights, I realized I had forgotten to tell Schulz about the general's private magazine. Before I went through the security gate I picked up the Farquhars' mail and made a mental note to tell him about it when I thanked him for the evening.

There were letters for General Bo from the Center for Poison Research and from the Department of the Army, for Julian from some government agency, and a note to me from Elizabeth. I opened it. She thanked me for flowers I had sent after the funeral. The Farquhars had invited her to be their guest at the Audubon picnic. She would see me there and we could arrange getting together soon.

Another missive awaited me in the kitchen. It was from Adele, written in her cramped, arthritic hand. We were going to leave at eight-thirty in the morning for the birding expedition to Flicker Ridge. The Audubon Society had helped with the calls soliciting attendees, and we had twenty people coming at sixty dollars a pop. It was a good thing I'd cooked for about thirty. Adele went on to say that a woman who worked in the bird house at the Denver Zoo would be our guide. Julian was going to assist. He knew so much about biology in general and birds in particular! I felt a pang. Why was everyone enthusiastic about Julian except me? Arch was welcome to come along. Thank you for making the picnic vegetarian, hope this didn't cause too much trouble, but you know how Julian and Elizabeth Miller are about eating flesh.

When you put it that way, I thought, who wouldn't be?

She closed saying the sole was stupendous, and that whoever wrote that article for the paper was a simpleton, wouldn't know pâté from a can of peas. Or, I added mentally, pork chops from lamb chops. But I would have my chance in the rebuttal.

I set the alarm system, got into bed, and read "The Murders in the Rue Morgue." Perhaps sensing that the last time I had done nighttime reading it had not ended well, Scout slipped into my room and eyed me askance. Then he did a soft cat-leap and plopped himself on the end of my bed, perhaps to keep me from trundling off in the middle of the night. But sleep came with ease, and I dreamt of chocolate-mint cheesecake.

The next morning brought one of those magnificent sunrises that make a soul glad to live in Colorado. Radiant feathers of cloud along the eastern horizon went from brilliant pink to burnished gold as the sun climbed. A mild breeze swished through the pines and aspens around the house. I watched a dark rope of espresso unwind from the Farquhars' Gaggia and realized I felt happy for the first time in a week. Before packing the lunch for the Audubon Society, I allowed myself the luxury of sipping my coffee out on the Farquhars' porch. Golden banner and dandelions speckled the deep greens of the mountain meadow. Birds of every ilk vied in chorus.

The Audubon Society would be appalled to hear that our feathered friends were no obsession of mine. I loved western flowers and tried to learn their names and seasons. Birds were more difficult. For one thing, they kept moving while you tried to figure out what you were seeing. I couldn't tell a finch from a flicker. Despite twelve years of living in the state, I had never been birding and was glad of it. For many Coloradans, keeping their life lists, participating in yearly counts, and searching for new species were activities undertaken with religious fervor. I felt the same way about any given bird that I did about modern art. I could appreciate it without knowing too much.

But who was I to worry? All I had to do was cater. I packed containers of vichyssoise, croissants filled with Jarlsberg and curly endive, chilled cooked angel-hair pasta with tomatoes and pesto, green salad with balsamic vinaigrette in a separate container, sour cream chocolate cupcakes, chardonnay, beer, and thermoses of iced tea and hot coffee. If they had no success in the birding arena, the guests could still eat to their hearts' content.

Our party of twenty consisted of Elizabeth Miller, Julian Teller, the Harringtons, the Farquhars, Arch and myself and the young woman from the zoo, plus eleven hardy naturalists with graying hair, sun hats, sensible boots, and plenty of heavy binoculars to go around. My van, the general's Range Rover, and several other four-wheel-drive vehicles were scheduled to rendezvous just inside Flicker Ridge around nine o'clock. Julian helped pack the picnic boxes onto the van shelves. He was in a foul temper. My efforts to lighten his mood backfired. He had followed up the latest bleach job on his hair with a close shave on both sides of his head, and a trim on the Mohawk.

I said, "Julian, you don't look like a Navajo."

He squinted in my direction. "No kidding. You don't look like a bear."

Give up. The kid had no sense of humor. But when we all bumped and rocked over the ridge road that was more of a trail, I realized he was nervous. Although I could see that the nervousness might be causing the hostility, I was getting tired of always making excuses for him.

When we got to the tables I blissfully began to unpack checkered tablecloths and to place rocks on them to keep the breeze from wafting them off. The birders settled around on the benches and opened—yes!—notebooks. Lord, I was glad not to be a part of it.

"Goldy," said General Farquhar, "what do you think you're doing?"

I looked up at him in surprise. "Why," I said, gesturing to the tablecloths, "getting ready for the picnic. What else?"

"You're a part of the family," he said firmly. "I want you to come on this expedition with us. No need for anyone to be left out."

"But I really, really, really want to get ready for the picnic," I said earnestly. I leaned in toward his ear and smelled Dial soap. In a confidential tone, I added, "I think birds are dumb."

When he shook his head his translucent cheeks glowed with authority. "This is going to be fun! I want you to enjoy this along with everyone else. No excuses."

Arch breathed a singsong *You'll be sor-ry,* but I did not know whether this was intended for the general or me. Giving up, I cursed the resourcefulness of the Audubon Society when a notebook and pen were provided for me.

"The eagle population is down on the Front Range," the zoo-lady began after a brief look at her notes. She stared at us. I picked up my pen and wrote, "Eagle pop. down," then looked up at her expectantly.

She said, "This is because of the drought. There are fewer prairie dogs and voles for the birds of prey to feed on."

She had lost me. I didn't want to risk another reprimand from the general, so I scribbled, "What's a vole?" Must be some kind of bird, I figured. What was that Domenico Modugno song about flying? "Volare."

I smiled at everybody and got up to pour coffee. Listen, look, lift—these were the rules for hunting birds with the binoculars. It sounded like an explanation of working with hand weights. In any event, within ten minutes the zoo-lady had outlined the list of birds we would probably see that day, beginning with a redheaded woodpecker.

Redheaded woodpecker? What was the big deal about that? In New Jersey you saw them all the time.

But we were off and running, or at least the general was. He knew the site of the woodpecker's nest and was forging ahead to set up the tripod and the scope. In the absence of actual military operations, the r.h.w. was the enemy.

Adele hobbled along the dirt path behind the gaggle of old-time birders. Weezie, elegant in designer jeans and an Indian leather jacket, chatted vivaciously alongside her. Next was Elizabeth Miller in a black leotard and peasant skirt. Weezie studiously ignored her. Arch walked quickly to keep up with Julian. Behind them were Brian and the zoo-lady. She had kind of a beak nose and a profusion of plumage on the top of her head, so I didn't know how the birds would be able to distinguish her from one of their own. How about if we just set up the scope and looked at her?

"There it is," the general whispered as he sighted the woodpecker. "Check it out," he added in the tone you'd associate with spotting a MIG-29. We took turns peeking through the scope. It was a wood-pecker, all right.

When we had all had a look I glanced anxiously around at the group. I said, "Are we done?"

There was a sigh of disgust from Julian. He turned back toward the path. The zoo-lady announced we were headed to a slightly higher elevation to look for the dusky flycatcher.

General Bo shouldered the equipment. We hiked along the trail until we came to the new site. We fanned out, walked for a ways, and listened. Listened *intently*. For what, I wanted to know.

"Gray-headed junco, first pine straight ahead, two o'clock," said Julian.

To my dismay, everyone in the party, even Arch, knew what Julian was talking about. They all whipped up their binoculars to view the tree in question. I sidled over to Arch and said, "What's going on?"

He put his finger to his lips and then passed his binoculars over. I tried to look through them. I tried to focus. I saw a bird. It flew away. Then everyone in the group lowered their binoculars and looked around like they'd just had great sex.

"Wow," said the zoo-lady. "That was really something."

We all listened again. Julian whirled and spied through his binocs. "Blue-green vireo, third ponderosa pine, eleven o'clock."

"Sounds like an air raid," I said under my breath. But I pulled up my borrowed binoculars, then had to put them down to count one, two, three ponderosa pines, then put them back up and tried to figure if the tree was a clock, which branch would be right before noon? While I was doing all this, I did catch a glimpse of turquoise flitting away from the tree. Branch eleven was empty.

By the time I took my binoculars down, everybody was giving me patronizing looks.

I said, "Maybe next time."

The zoo-lady announced that since we had not spotted the fly-catcher, we were going to look at the nest of a Brewer's blackbird that Julian said he had found the previous week. We started down a path leading to Flicker Creek. Cottonwoods profuse with new leaves crowded the crumbling shores on both sides. The sun glided out from behind a cloud and turned the cottonwood leaves to silver. A flick of breeze whispered through the trees. Clouds and wind moving in meant our afternoon shower was not too far off. Thank God.

"Just look through those bushes at the cowbird," Adele said to me when we came to the creek.

I looked where she indicated, and actually saw a dark bird sitting on the branch of a bush. Another bird, unseen but not far off, was squawking frantically. Yet the cowbird sat calm and quiet.

I whispered to Adele, "What's going on?" Before she could respond, Julian held up his hand to stop the group, and pointed to the bush where the cowbird perched. The group looked. The loud bird began to circle overhead, and then we looked at that.

The zoo-lady turned to the group, which had huddled around her. "The cowbird," she said, "has no nest of its own but will lay her eggs in the nests of other birds. That's what's upsetting the Brewer's black-bird."

Well, I was glad we had gotten *that* straightened out. We waited and eventually the cowbird took off. Then we started across the creek. The general was so chivalrous it touched my heart. He put all his equipment down and gently lifted Adele as if he were carrying her across the threshold. When he put her down on the other side of the water, he kissed her cheek. Instead of looking happy, Adele lowered her head as if she were embarrassed. She glanced at the Harringtons to see if they had noticed. When she saw that they had, she closed her eyes and turned down the sides of her mouth. She veered and started up the bank with such suddenness that she wobbled on her cane.

I couldn't wait for lunch.

We strode through a batch of spearmint that I would have liked to pick and take back with me, only by doing so I would have broken at least sixteen state laws about leaving things in the wild.

"We're getting close to the Brewer's blackbird nest," Julian whispered.

He needn't have whispered, as the bird in question began to throw another fit. She circled us, pretty low it seemed to me, and squawked to wake the dead.

I asked timidly, "Are we in any danger here?"

Julian looked at me crossly. "The blackbird might peck at our heads when we approach the nest. That's all."

I said, "Will it hurt?"

Julian scowled. "It shouldn't."

I put both of my hands over my head, walked back through the spearmint to Arch, and told him to do the same.

He said, "No, it looks stupid."

On we stumbled through the meadow toward the nest, with the mother bird shrieking louder and louder, until finally Julian stopped us in a small circle. He opened his mouth to say something, but Arch interrupted him.

"Oh, look! A nest of voles!"

I craned my neck back to see what new flock of flying creatures we were now going to encounter. I felt a slight tickling around my feet, but I was determined to see the birds in question this time.

I said, "I don't see any voles."

"Well, Mom," said Arch, "you're standing on them."

Everyone else was looking down. I looked down. *Rodents*. They were jumping over my feet. I screamed bloody murder.

"That's just great," I heard Julian saying. My shriek faded from the air. I stopped hopping around and thanked God I had survived.

The zoo-lady said, "There isn't a bird left within two miles." I hadn't noticed before how beady her little black eyes were.

"Let's eat," said Brian Harrington. It was the first time he had spoken since the outing had begun, but I thanked him for the magic words.

We recrossed the creek and marched in silence back to our picnic tables. I opened the van and took everything out of the coolers. No one volunteered to help. Once the adults got going on the chardonnay, however, the mood started to lift. While I was setting out the stuffed croissants, the general disappeared behind a rock outcropping with some of his equipment.

He strode back to the table without telling us what he was up to, and we all enjoyed a pleasant lunch. After the chocolate sour cream cupcakes were reduced to a platter of crumbs, General Bo got to his feet.

He cleared his throat. "I want to demonstrate something to you all."

Adele gave him a fearful look. Apparently, he had not cleared his plans with her.

"Now don't worry," he said to mollify us. "I just want to demonstrate to you how a terrorist can detonate a briefcase from a thousand feet."

He pointed. Obediently, we all turned our attention to the rock outcropping. A brown briefcase perched on the humps of gray. I scuttled around to the edge of the picnic bench where Arch sat and put my arm across his shoulder.

"My Lord," murmured Weezie.

"The environment will not respond well . . ." said Elizabeth Miller.

"Bo. Stop this immediately," said Adele in a low hiss. She glared at him, her mouth set.

"You can't do this," said the zoo-lady. "You'll upset every—"

But her words were swallowed in the explosion.

When I opened my eyes, I checked to make sure Arch was all right. He was fine, and he was gazing up in admiration at an exultant General Bo.

Arch said, "That guy is so cool."

18.

We packed up to go home, a human pastiche of solemn and joyful silence. Since it had started to rain right after the explosion, I was one of the happy ones. General Farquhar's experiment had awakened the thunder to its job. Flashes of lightning, celestial booms, and fat cold raindrops sent us all scattering toward the vehicles. No more birding! My relief was inexpressible.

General Bo, Arch, and Brian Harrington were quietly exultant as they heaved baskets onto the van shelves. The general and Arch were flushed with excitement about the success of the briefcase-detonation. I was reminded of the silent incredulity of the fans when the Broncos pull one out in the fourth quarter.

And then there was Brian Harrington. He was smiling to himself. This was a little harder to figure. Then I remembered. Flicker Ridge belonged to Weezie—or it had until they got married. Their very public exchange of wedding gifts had been trumpeted in that paragon of journalistic reliability, the *Mountain Journal:* He had given her a house in Vail; she had deeded him the ridge. Now Brian had slated the land for development, and had mysteriously managed—at least according to the *Mountain Journal*—to obtain preliminary approval from the county planning commission for planned unit development. An outing emphasizing Flicker Ridge's ecology, soon to be disrupted by development, would make him look bad. At least, that was my guess for his jolly demeanor. On the other hand, maybe he had made a date with the zoo-lady.

Adele, Weezie, Elizabeth, and the zoo-lady scooped up silverware and gathered up defiant, wind-whipped tablecloths. The women were sullen and preoccupied. The notion of studying our feathered friends obviously had enthralled them. I tried to swallow my grin but could not.

When the advance guard of our convoy returned to Sam Snead Lane, a white VW Rabbit I did not recognize was parked outside the gate of the Farquhars' driveway. General Bo, Adele, and Julian had dropped off the zoo-lady at the bus stop, and would be coming along soon. As long as it wasn't The Jerk's car, I felt safe going into the house alone. But no need to worry: the Farquhars' Range Rover chugged up alongside the Rabbit as I was entering the gate code. Windows were lowered; heated discussion followed. It was Sissy.

Eventually we all ground up the Farquhars' driveway. Once inside the garage I busied myself emptying the picnic debris. Whatever the latest conflict was, I didn't want any part of it. Relationships were like small picnics, I decided as I emptied out croissant crumbs and strings of endive. You always thought they were going to be so great—look at those happy people in ads, relating and picnicking!—but were so inevitably disappointed. Whoever said, Life is no picnic, obviously had never been on one.

I carried in the baskets. Adele, impeccably attired in a beige cashmere sweater and perfectly creased matching slacks, limped slowly behind me. Her slouched shoulders and downcast face tugged at my heart. I asked her if she was pleased about the amount of money she had made for the pool project. She shrugged, then said in a weary, trembling voice that the trip had fatigued her. She went to lie down while the general headed for his study. It was my great hope that he would tie up all the phone lines while I prepared dinner. Arch came out to the kitchen with me.

"Mind if I work on my magic while you cook?" he asked.

"Of course not."

I scanned the refrigerator. I had all the ingredients for Chinese-style cod. I set to work on it while trying to rid myself of the image of Pilgrims eating with chopsticks.

"Not fish again," said Arch when he saw the ingredients. He was setting his supplies out on the kitchen island.

"But you didn't even have it last time," I reminded him, then changed my tone. "Shall I order you a pizza?" I was trying to stay charitable. After all, this was the child whom I had never allowed to have a mouse, gerbil, hamster, guinea pig, or other rodent for a pet. And I had ruined his one interaction with voles.

He pulled some cups out of his bag and said, "Let's ask Julian."

At that moment the menu arbiter himself appeared at the kitchen door, as he was so prone to do, just when his name was mentioned. He had Sissy with him. She was dressed all in white—crisp white halter top, white shorts, white socks and shoes. A white bow held her spill of brown curls off to one side of her pretty face, now set in petulance. As usual, Julian didn't look too happy either.

"Doing magic?" he asked Arch.

"Just practicing."

Without further explanation Julian and Sissy moved off toward the deck, where he ceremoniously shut the French doors. Even when you don't want to appear nosy, people will assume that you are.

"Okay, Mom, watch the cotton ball."

I turned my attention to the island. Arch had a cotton ball and three red cups. He deftly placed one over the cotton and then began to shift them around. When I incorrectly guessed which one had the cotton under it, he piled the other two on top of the final cup, gave them all a tap, and triumphantly lifted the stacked cups. There was the cotton ball.

"Great," I admitted. "Simply marvelous. When are we having this show? Before or after I serve the food at the barbecue?"

Before he could answer we could hear raised voices coming from the deck. A moment later there were shouts.

Arch pulled his mouth into a wry, knowing knot. Over the shouts, he said, "Guess they're having a fight."

Poor Arch. His only model for male/female relationships was one of continual conflict. A moment later, Julian stalked by the kitchen door. He did not look in.

"Hey, Julian!" Arch called. He ran after him. "Wait up!" Wanted or unwanted, Arch tromped down the steps to the lower level and Julian's lair. I did not know whether an eleven-year-old would be welcome after a teenagers' quarrel. But I went back to the cod and resolved to stay out of it.

"Goldy?" Sissy's voice startled me. I turned around. Her smile was tight, forced; her tense posture distinctly at odds with the portrait-of-innocence outfit. She said, "Are you working?"

No, I wash fish for fun. I said, "I'm about done."

"What're you making?"

"Baked cod with Chinese seasonings. Low calorie, low fat, and full of virtue." I looked at her drawn face briefly, finished chopping the scallions, rolled out and cut squares of foil, placed the fillets and seasonings on top, and rolled each into individual packets. I put them in the refrigerator and took out two soft drinks.

"Want to go out on the porch?"

She gave a facial gesture as if to say, Might as well, and turned. I followed her. The smell of pines moist from the shower was as lovely as it had been on the drive to Schulz's. I inhaled deeply and tried to bring the feeling back. Sissy's voice, honed to sharpness, interrupted my reverie.

"Where were all of you this morning?" Sissy demanded. She thrust her face toward mine and sent the jaunty hair bow askew.

"I, um, we went to look for birds at Flicker Ridge." Her tone was so aggressive that it was a moment before I wondered what business it was of hers where we were. I said, "Why do you ask?"

She did not answer, only took a sip of her drink, then pressed her lips together and gave me an accusing look. "And last night? Where were you then?"

"Well, excuse me, Sissy, not that it's any concern of yours, but Arch and I went out. For dinner and the evening. Now, what's going on?"

"Was Julian with you?"

"Is this what you two were arguing about?" I thought back. Julian had said he had a date. I'd just assumed it was with Sissy. I said, "You're not married to him, you know." I tried to make my tone soft. "Men don't like possessive women." It didn't come out sounding soft.

She closed her eyes and leaned her head against the back of the wicker chair. She had the deflated look of a week-old carnation.

I said, "You want to tell me about it?"

With her eyes closed, she said, "When I found Julian, I thought he was the smartest kid I'd ever met."

"How'd you find . . . meet him?"

"During the Elk Park shadow program for careers. You know, when you follow someone around for a semester to see what it's really like to be a lawyer or whatever." She flipped her hair over her shoulder. "Oh sure, I'd been in the same classes with him. But he shadowed Dr. O'Neil from the country club. Dr. O'Neil said Julian was the most gifted student he'd ever met. Wanted to write him a recommendation for Columbia."

"Well," I said, "that's nice." Not meaning to sound judgmental, but I had seen this phenomenon before: Young woman seeks husband. Only premeds need apply.

"I'm just trying to help him," Sissy said fiercely. "He's so smart, and he won't do anything with it."

"What do you mean?"

She looked at me and spat out the words. "He wants to *cook*. He said he should have done his internship at Aspen Meadow Café."

My, my. I wanted to ask Sissy why *she* didn't become a doctor. I sipped slowly on my soft drink and decided to leave the career counseling to someone else. I said, "So what does that have to do with last night and this morning?"

"The only reason I wanted to know where he was is that he said he was going to be here. Writing off for catalogs, he said. So I called and called, but just got the machine."

I looked out at the bowled meadow, where thick fog had settled like cream. Here and there pine trees poked through the white, like aberrant cornflakes.

I said, "You're not his mother, you know."

There was a long silence. Sissy turned her face to the meadow.

"Yeah," she said softly, "maybe that's the problem."

I tried to sound lighthearted. She had, after all, sought me out. I said, "Now don't go getting Oedipal on me." Another long silence ensued, in which Sissy chewed the inside of her cheek. I said, "It's hard to lose your counselor. It sounds as if Philip Miller was like a support system for Julian. Maybe you're expecting too much."

She grunted. "I'm still not his mother."

"So *what*?"

She said nothing for a few minutes. "It's what came out in his sessions with Dr. Miller," she said. Hearing Philip addressed by the medical first name, Doctor, still fell strangely on my ears. Sissy went on, "Julian's adopted. Now he says he can't go on and make plans for the rest of his life without trying to track down his biological parents first."

I said, "Oh, Sissy, for heaven's sake. Let him. People do it all the time now. It's the quest of the decade."

She leaned toward me. Her curls shook as she spoke. "If you ask me, it's a grossly misguided quest. A waste of time. So you find out your father is an insurance salesman down in Dallas and your mother is teaching elementary school in Oregon. These are the people who didn't want you in the first place, remember? Now they've married other people and you have half-siblings who resent your appearance on the scene all of a sudden. Getting on with your life is more important."

"Well, that's your opinion."

She grunted. Maybe she didn't want to share him with as-yet-unknown relatives. I didn't know. She did seem awfully angry and bossy all of a sudden. But then at the dinner she had seemed to be studying the Harringtons and their wealth. At the library she had looked around for someone more important to deal with than me. Teenagers. I was dreading Arch becoming one.

She said, "So what do you think? Should he be able to lie to me? Not tell me where he's going so I'll worry?"

I looked at her, her earnest dark-brown eyes, her long curly brown hair, her good-looking but anxiously determined face. Here was a girl who had gone through all the hard work of beauty pageants to get to the finals of Colorado Junior Miss, who had decided on her psychology interest and shadowed Philip Miller, who was working at the library to get her college money, the way she got everything else. Foiled in her attempts to have Julian, despite her strong ambition in that area, she was asking me for advice. Me. It was too much.

I said, "I don't give advice to the lovelorn. You're going to do what you want to do anyway. I'll just tell you one thing."

She waited.

I said, "People don't change. You can try all you want to make him do what you want, but it is not going to happen."

She took a deep breath, blew it hard out of both nostrils. "I guess I'll be going," she said, and abruptly stood up. "Thanks for trying to be helpful," she said over her shoulder as she left the deck.

I felt sad and amused. It was like trying to tell someone about childbirth. You just had to go through it, and no amount of advice or description was going to make it any easier. Out on the meadow the fog had lifted. The sun blazed out once again before it began to set. I went back to the kitchen, made a rice pilaf, then washed and trimmed asparagus stalks.

"She gone?"

It was Julian.

I nodded. "Where's Arch?"

"Down by the pool. Don't worry, Adele's watching him. He's practicing his front flip. He's getting pretty good," he added.

I leaned against the counter and crossed my arms. Julian had never once sought my company. He looked around the kitchen.

"You fixing dessert tonight?" he asked.

"Sherbet."

"Let me fix something, then," he said. He reached for a cookbook, a fancy one on chocolate. The recipes were fairly complicated, I had noted on a recent reading, and pretty iffy at high altitude.

He read, " 'Filbertines, good with ice cream.' " He stuck out his chin. "Want me to?"

"Up to you. Why don't you just tell me why you came up?"

He began to open cupboards, got out French chocolate and superfine sugar and flour.

"Did she tell you we were having problems?"

I said, "She did." *Can this relationship be saved?*

Julian backed out of the refrigerator with unsalted butter and eggs. "Who taught you to make filbertines?"

"My—" He hesitated, swiveled his head to eye me. "You've been talking to Sissy."

"More like, I've been listening to Sissy."

"Yeah, well, it's my business."

I poured myself another soft drink. "Fine," I said, and sipped. "Sure."

"That's really not the problem with our relationship, anyway."

"What isn't the problem?"

"What I'm trying to do."

"You mean like looking for parents, learning to be a doctor or a cook, what?"

"No, none of that. The problem with our relationship is just . . . that you don't learn to be cool down in Navajoland."

"Learn to be cool," I echoed.

"I mean, you know, sex appeal and all that dumb stuff." He began to whisk eggs in a copper bowl.

I reflected on his words. *You know, sex appeal?* No, I really did not.

"I'll tell you what I do know, Julian." I refilled my glass and watched the foam fizzle up the sides. "Sissy likes you a lot, cares about you."

He snorted.

I said, "It's like with Arch and me. Or even Arch with his father. Some people have strange ways of showing they care."

He gave me his defiant look. He said, "You should know."

As if in answer to his comment, the security gate buzzed. I flipped on the closed-circuit camera. Oh yes, Saturday afternoon, how could I have forgotten who would be arriving?

The Jerk.

19.

I called the general over the intercom. He made one of his silent appearances in the kitchen and about scared me to death. How could he get around so quietly? Of course, that immediately made me think of what else he'd said he could do without making any noise.

I said, "He's here."

"Right. Call Arch. Meet me in the front hall."

I obeyed orders, alternating between feeling cold waves of fear and a sense of silliness. Were these elaborate troop movements really necessary? Five minutes later we all reconnoitered in the foyer. The general was wearing a shoulder holster.

Arch said, "Wow! Is that cool!"

"Oh please," I said, "not a gun."

The general narrowed his eyes. He said, "Deterrent."

"This is Aspen Meadow!" I cried. "Not Beirut, for crying out loud."

The Jerk's Jeep horn blew. *Braat! Braat!*

The general leaned into my face. "Let me tell you something," he said. "They thought I was crazy in Washington. They may think I'm crazy here. But. It's all the same, Goldy. All over the world. You have to be ready."

Arch said, "Can we go? *I'm* ready."

And so the three of us walked slowly to the end of the driveway. Seeing John Richard made my heart involuntarily twist. He wore a white shirt, white shorts, white socks with his Nikes. His long fingers threaded through the bars of the fence. Sunlight caught gold glints in his brown hair. A tennis racket lay across the back seat of the Jeep. We used to play tennis quite a bit. Was he going to play with someone now? Was that what he had done this morning? Why did this still hurt so much?

"Is the show of force really necessary?" he called through the gate.

I did not answer and neither did the general, who gazed stonily forward once we had let Arch through. When Arch was in the Jeep, John Richard paused before getting in. Always the parting shot.

He said to me, "I was nowhere near that damn café, you bitch. Just think of how many patients I lose when your cop buddies come around, and what that does to my ability to make money, and how that can affect you and Arch, and maybe you'll be a little less eager to bug me."

"Say nothing," the general instructed me under his breath. "Walk slowly back to the house. I'll stay here until he's gone."

This I did. So Schulz had not waited for me to report the incident in the café. Somehow this did not make me feel better, and my shoulders felt terribly heavy as I walked. Worse, the aches in my arm and chest began to pound, as if they had been awakened by the menace in John Richard's voice. Not Beirut, I reminded myself.

When I came back into the house the phone was ringing. To my surprise it was Elizabeth Miller, who asked if I wanted to have lunch on Monday. I said that I would love to, which was true. People who are grieving need to be with other people. Unfortunately, an unwanted skepticism crept into my voice. Why go out for lunch? This was a new activity for me, and it was fraught with problems. Did the person who asked intend to pay? Marla had paid for mine at the Aspen Meadow Café, but I had been under duress. Besides, she had money. I felt as if I should treat Elizabeth.

Elizabeth must have thought my silence meant I was meditating. She jumped in with, "Let's picnic out by the Aspen Meadow."

Another picnic. I said, "I don't want to look at any birds."

"Oh! Philip was the bird expert. Not me. Listen. I'll bring tabbouleh and Tassajara bread. You bring whatever you feel moved to bring."

The next morning after the early church service I felt moved to make tomatoes vinaigrette and a pound cake. As I beat the butter for the latter, the phone's twang cut through the morning air. My spirits plunged. For heaven's sake, it was Sunday! The day of the week did not matter to some people, apparently. I was the designated answerer. The general and Julian were out getting equipment for the next experiment. Adele was in the pool and had just started her slow, slow laps that were supposed to help strengthen her back. She would not be available for phone duty for a long while. For Adele, *crawl* was the perfectly named stroke.

"Farquhars," I said brightly.

"This is Joan Rasmussen."

Without actually willing it, I looked over at the eggs on the counter. What had Adele said? This woman needed to be coddled.

"Yes," I replied, still bright, "how are you? This is Goldy the caterer."

Silence. *She* was not meditating, I felt sure.

Eventually she said, "I understand your son is having some kind of party."

"Yes. We were thinking about this Tuesday evening, the fourteenth. He wants to demonstrate his tricks." I cleared my throat. "Er, magic tricks, uh—" Did I call her Joan, since we were both parents of students, or did I call her Mrs. Rasmussen, since I was the Farquhars' cook?

"He's invited my daughter."

"Wonderful," I said without feeling it.

"The last time I talked to you," she went on, apparently unsure by what name *I* should be addressed, "you did not indicate enthusiasm for our pool fund-raising efforts."

"Ah—"

"Although I understand that your son is indeed learning to dive," she said as if this concluded her thought. She sniffed. "Our daughter has been on the country-club swim team for three years."

These subjects were related. Joan had passed Manipulative Behavior

101. Arch was learning to dive. Joan's daughter was an excellent swimmer. The school needed a pool. If I helped with the fund-raiser, Arch would learn to swim, save the school, and get the girl. I bit the inside of my cheek. How Arch wooed his female friends was up to him. And I had no money.

I said, "I'm glad your daughter is a good swimmer."

Joan Rasmussen *tsk*ed with impatience. "Would it be possible for you to pick up your fund-raising decals at the school tomorrow? You're one of the very few parents who has not participated in any way."

A shrink would have a field day with this woman. Or with me, as I succumbed to a crushing wave of guilt.

I said, "I'd be happy to pick up my decals tomorrow. Did you need to speak with Adele?"

"Is she swimming this time, too?"

"Well, yes, actually, but she'll be at the school tomorrow for a fund-raising meeting—"

Joan Rasmussen hung up on me. I replaced the receiver with the comforting thought that type A behavior usually had its own reward.

Monday morning after I had done my yoga routine and seen everyone off for the day's activities, I set out for Aspen Meadow, namesake for our little burg. Nothing like driving out in the unsullied Colorado high country to rid the mind of peevish folks like Ms. Rasmussen.

As I drove, I was thankful that the preservers of Aspen Meadow's environment had held their own during the state's boom-and-bust periods. In our town, a shaky alliance between the old-time naturalists and new-age Greenpeace and Audubon Society types had kept the lid on rampant development. Philip Miller was definitely in the latter category, although he had never talked to me at any length about his involvement. To our age group, environmental activism was as natural an activity as bridge club and Republican women's club had been for my mother and her set in New Jersey.

Meadows and forest refulgent with growth bordered upper Cottonwood Creek on the way to the meadow. My environment-preserving friends had worked unceasingly to scuttle the state's plan for a bypass through here about ten years ago. Before that, the do-gooders had moved heaven and earth to keep Aspen Meadow from being a site for the winter Olympics. Most towns would kill to *get* the Olympics. Not folks in Aspen Meadow. Imagine our meager hills being torn up for ski runs! No thank you! One of their posters had become a collector's item: *Save trees from skis.*

Out my window the wildflowers of mid-June seemed to wave in appreciation. Near the road, stands of chokecherry bobbed long, sweet shoots of white blossoms. Arrows of crimson fireweed dotted a dirt embankment, while the creeksides burgeoned with golden banner. Through the meadows, brilliant Indian paintbrush splashed orange amid the green.

At the entrance to the wildlife preserve the van thudded from pavement to dirt. If I could ever get ahead in the financial arena, I was considering getting one of those new four-wheel-drive vans. Then I could ferry comestibles through any manner of blizzard and road conditions. But for now I would coax the old VW along, even on cratered dirt roads like this, and not ask too much of it.

Elizabeth and I had agreed to meet around ten to have time in case the rain made its habitual appearance in the early afternoon. Elizabeth had not felt moved to be on time. I staked out our spot, an old picnic table by the stream. Close by I could see the boarded-up cabin of a beekeeper friend of mine. But the beekeeper was long gone. Standing on one of the picnic benches, I could just see one of his hives. Would the bees still be there, I wondered, and did they miss him?

"What do you suppose happens to you after you die?" asked Elizabeth, who had appeared next to me. Her black ballet slippers had made no noise in the grass.

"Gosh," I said, startled. "I don't know." I was willing to bet my pound cake that Elizabeth subscribed to some esoteric theory of reincarnation. And at that moment I was not prepared to hear about Philip as a butterfly alighting on a nearby wild iris.

"I've been reflecting on it. What did Philip think about life? What was important to him? I know how he felt about vitamins B, E, and C, and how he felt about our parents. But I haven't a clue about his view of the afterlife."

"Let's sit," I said. She followed me to the table. Cottonwood Creek, muddied by the spring snowmelt, gurgled over a bed of rocks. I fluffed out a green-and-white-checked tablecloth and we both put down our baskets.

I ladled out thick slices of tomatoes vinaigrette onto two paper plates. "What I think," I said, "is that you have a clue about what was important to a person in life when you look at how he spent his time."

Elizabeth peered into her bowls and said, "Uh-huh." She scooped spoonfuls of tabbouleh out for the two of us. Her offering looked like a cross between birdseed and the mixture they give in the cat cage at the Denver Zoo. I took a bite of tabbouleh, to be polite.

"So," I went on, "what was important to him was his practice and his activities like Audubon." I took a deep breath. "And giving his body to science?"

She looked away. A bee buzzed around the frizz of her hair.

"Yes," she said delicately. "He was an organ donor."

"I heard you arguing with Weezie about it."

Elizabeth squinched up her pixie nose. "That first-class bitch."

"Oh," I said to keep her talking, "I don't know if I'd go that far."

"You want to know what she wanted that day? The day after my brother died. You're not going to believe this." Elizabeth mimicked Weezie in a clever, accurate high pitch. " 'Did he leave anything to me?' Of course, I thought she meant money. But the day of the Audubon Society picnic she pulls me aside. She says, 'Don't you think this ridge is beautiful?' When I say of course, she says, 'Well, where's Philip's ecological strategy plan? Last Thursday he told me he had it ready to present to the county commissioners!' "

I shook my head. Last Thursday. The day before he died.

I said, "A friend of mine is a police officer down at the Sheriff's Department. Mind if I tell him this? He might be interested."

She shrugged. "I don't care. I think Weezie's out of her mind. I don't know whether she and my brother were . . . having an affair, the way everyone thinks. But I doubt it. Besides, she used to *own* the damn ridge. If she doesn't want Brian to develop it, why'd they go to the planning commission and say they did? You know the county commissioners aren't going to veto a development once the planners have given the okay."

I said, "I don't know. Maybe she just got carried away because she knew it was important to him."

Elizabeth studied the creek.

She said, "You were important to him."

I shrugged. "Yeah. I know."

She sighed. "I didn't know much about his practice. You know, couldn't tell tales. But the two of you seemed to be happy."

"Yeah, well."

Her brow furrowed. "Remember the morning of the brunch? I never really had the whole picture of what was going on in his life, you know. He just didn't *share*. But I did want to talk to him, because this time I knew he was stressed out."

"About what?"

"A couple of clients, I think."

"Really?"

"Yeah. One was homicidal, can you imagine? That's all he told me. He said, Guess there are crazies everywhere."

I was stunned. "That's all he told you?" Schulz had found no notes, nothing indicating this, I was sure.

"Yeah, it was something that had just come up. He was getting some research done on it. The other was some woman who had been abused."

"Excuse me?"

"I don't know who it was. He'd been seeing her for about a month."

About a month? I felt as if I'd been punched in the solar plexus. Elizabeth, I was quite sure, did not know why my marriage had broken up. I said, "Really?"

"Yeah, he said he hadn't broken through to the abuse yet, but that it was a puzzling case because he'd known her a long time ago. She was a strong woman, or so he thought, but she ended up staying with this abusive guy for seven years. His question was, how could somebody who was so competent in other areas be that self-destructive?"

"That was his question, huh? So she was a client?"

"Well, I just assumed she was," said Elizabeth as she helped herself

to more tabbouleh. "She must have been important to him. Oh, I don't
want to make you jealous or anything. I think he really wanted to study
her. Wanted to help her, you know?"

"No," I said carefully, "I guess I don't."

Elizabeth and I parted when the raindrops began to fall. I was a good
actress. I let my words fall as lightly as the pinpricks of water coming
down. "Can't wait to get together again." "Everything you brought was
so delicious." "Call me anytime."

There was a ringing in my ears. I was not aware of crying, only
aware of wetness on my cheeks. I batted it away. Crying was a volitional
act. Therefore, I was not crying.

Didn't know how someone could flunk relationships, but be so
competent in other areas? Hadn't they taught him anything in Shrink
School?

It felt strange to have been betrayed by someone who was now dead.
If indeed that was what had happened—although it was hard to believe
one of his clients had exactly the same history as mine, or presented the
same psychological puzzle to be solved. I had been an idiot. It was like
someone had shot an entire round of ammunition at me a month ago.
The bullets were just now reaching their mark.

And here I thought he'd liked me.

*I stayed for seven years with an abusive spouse because I was afraid I would
lose Arch. I stayed for seven years because I was afraid I would not be able to
make a living. But let me ask you about our relationship, Philip, yours and
mine. In that relationship, who abused whom?*

Within half an hour I had driven back to Aspen Meadow and renegoti-
ated the road to Elk Park Prep. Of all people, I knew the dangers of
Highway 203, especially when it was wet. And yet I found myself
whipping around its curves as if defying death.

About a hundred feet past the school's entrance I vaulted my first
speed bump. The van caught a foot of air and landed hard. I down-

shifted. The engine whined in protest. No question about it, I was not driving the way a good prep-school parent should. But I was furious.

I pulled alongside a man-made clump of perfectly planted wild-flowers. These mounds, like mock ruins landscaped into nineteenth-century gardens, were placed at irregular intervals along the split-rail fence that ran the length of the drive. This was why they had put up the electrified gate to keep out flower-eating deer. Profusions of asters, daisies, columbines, and poppies spilled every which way. My guess was that the desired impression ran something like, We can tame the wild! This was undoubtedly similar to what they wanted to do with teenage prep students. But our state's annual rainfall averaged only fifteen inches. Even Mother Nature could never grow flowers that densely. As if in answer, a hidden sprinkler erupted with a tent of mist.

To my right, past the fence and the border of old blue spruce trees planted during the hotel days, more sprinklers gushed over closely shaved, too-green hockey and soccer fields. The *shush* sound of the water filled the air. I shook my head. If Philip had truly been concerned with the state's ecology, he should have started with his alma mater's depletion of the water table.

I began driving again, slowly, up toward the pool construction site. Warning signs—Building in Progress. Keep Out!—were enough to make me swing wide of the chain-link extravaganza. No more speed bumps, I thought with glee, as I pressed the accelerator.

"Jeez, look out, Mom," Arch yelled as I roared into the dirt between the pool construction site and the school parking lot.

I stepped out of the van and slammed the door behind me, scanned the parking lot with angry eyes, and ended up looking at my son. He was regarding me with some puzzlement. He pushed his glasses back up on his nose.

He said, "What are you doing here?"

What was I doing here, anyway? I stared back at Arch, as if his face could prompt my memory. Oh yes, *decals*.

"I'm not here to get you," I told him.

He announced in his grown-up, greater-knowledge voice, "I'm

waiting for Julian. He's going to take me back when he finishes in the lab."

At that moment I noticed two girls about Arch's age lolling on top of a hill of dirt behind the pool site. They were watching us.

"Arch, who are those girls?" I asked. I pointed.

He said, "Never mind, Mom. Let me just take you into the office."

"Great."

We started to walk toward the stucco building. Behind us female voices called, "Hey! You're cute!"

I whirled around. "Arch! Are they yelling at you?"

His cheeks were crimson. He was staring at the sidewalk. He said, "Just keep walking, Mom."

The switchboard operator chirped, "Elk Park Prep! Please hold!" into five lines in quick succession while I waited to ask for my dreaded decals. Arch disappeared. I sat on an imitation-leather bench and allowed blankness to fill my mind. I was just getting started on my mantra when Joan Rasmussen caught sight of me and, like a human Amtrak, chugged purposefully in my direction. I groaned. Loudly, I'm afraid.

"Excuse me, Goldy the caterer, right?" she said with her best imperious tone. "Surely that wasn't a *groan* I just heard from you? I am working very hard on this pool project, a lot harder than most parents, I might add, and to think that you—"

"It wasn't a groan," I said as I rose to my feet. My face only reached her matronly bosom, which I tried to avoid looking at. "I was doing an *om* . . . it's a guttural sound issuing from the soul."

"I realize that you are in the service industry, Ms. Bear, but we really must ask that you go door to door—"

"Doctors and lawyers are in the service industry," I replied evenly. "Do they go around pitching the pool and handing out decals?"

"Of course not," she huffed. "But that is because they can afford to give—"

"Oh, I get it!" I cried. "If you can give a certain amount, you get out of grunt-work! Tell me, Joan, how do I apply for an exemption?"

At that moment, the headmaster appeared from behind the switchboard operator. I had never seen him up close. He was a baby-faced fellow whose round-rimmed glasses gave him the look of a young owl. Despite the fact that we were halfway through June, he was wearing tweeds. *Mister Rogers goes to Yale.* He peered at us and frowned. *Trouble in the neighborhood.*

"Here are your decals," said Joan Rasmussen as she handed me a packet. *"Thank you* for volunteering your time so generously."

A noise arose from deep in my throat. "Ommmmmmmm."

There was a simultaneous sharp intake of breath from Joan and the headmaster as the two of them fixed their eyes at a point beyond my shoulder. Glancing backward, I saw a senior member of the Coors family coming through the doors of the school lobby. Too late I realized that the only thing between the headmaster and all those brewery millions was me.

"Gah!" I yelled as the headmaster mowed me down. I teetered backward and then fell over the imitation-leather bench. The fund-raising packet flew up out of my hand. My back hit the wall and I landed ungracefully on the floor. Decals floated down like confetti.

Joan Rasmussen marched off to use one of the phones. The switchboard operator continued to sing her greeting to callers. As I gathered up the decals from the floor, I watched the headmaster do a slithery Uriah Heep routine with the politely attentive Mr. Coors.

"What happened here?" said Sissy Stone from far above me.

I looked up and tried to give her a big smile. When we had last parted, she had not been in a terrific mood.

"I'm cleaning up my decals, what else?"

She craned her neck around to see if anyone more important was in the vicinity. "My, my, look who's here," she said under her breath.

"I don't suppose you'd be interested in gathering some of these up?"

She sighed with great drama. "Sorry. I'm waiting for Julian, and I can't get my pants dirty on the floor."

I grunted, and stuffed the last of the decals into the envelope. When I had heaved myself back up on the bench I thought again about what Elizabeth had told me about Philip's problematic clients. I gave Sissy a long look. Perfect makeup, perfect hair, perfect rounded and polished nails, perfect pink-on-blue printed blouse coordinated with blue-on-pink printed pants. Miss Perfect had worked for Philip Miller. I wondered if he had been interested in her psychological makeup as well.

I said, "Let's go have a Coke. I've lost Arch. I'm parched, and I want to talk to you about something. Does this school have a lounge?"

Her pretty face clouded. "We used to have vending machines in the basement. But the parents protested against chips and cookies and soft drinks. Now you can get juice and granola bars and stuff they sell at Elizabeth Miller's store. They still call it the snack corner. Should be the birdseed corner, if you ask me."

I forced a smile. "Let's go anyway. Get healthy."

I gave a sidelong glance back at the headmaster and his wealthy prisoner before Sissy and I headed down to the snack corner. Maybe having money wasn't such a good thing after all. We successfully avoided another encounter with Joan Rasmussen and within a few minutes were happily munching on peanut butter–coconut bars and drinking strawberry-guava juice. It's hard to think of how to frame questions with several tablespoons of peanut butter cemented to the roof of your mouth, but I tried.

"I miss Philip Miller," I said finally, after taking a long pull on the grotesquely sweet juice.

"Yeah, he was a good guy."

"I understand you shadowed him during the school year." I tried to sound wistful.

She pulled down the corners of her mouth. "Nothing sensitive, you know. Nothing confidential."

"Right," I said, shaking my head, "absolutely not. I know how he was about ethics and all that." To avoid grinding my teeth, I took a tiny bite of granola bar. "So what were you doing for him, then?"

"Oh, he used to talk to me about his schedule, the kind of problems he saw, what kind of training you had to have. Sometimes he would give me research projects. I hadn't heard from him in a while. Then the last week he was"—she hesitated and cleared her throat—"you know, alive, he asked me to work on something. He was kind of in a panic about it, it seemed to me. He knew about the case, but needed specifics. He didn't have time to get all the details from the research." She finished her juice and set it down on the linoleum floor, then gazed at the wall. "Tarasoff versus California," she said in a far-off voice.

"Excuse me?"

She puckered her lips in thought. "It was a court case. I was running it through InfoTrac at the library, trying to find articles to help him see how it applied to him."

"I don't get it."

"Tarasoff was the last name of a woman in California. She was dating this guy, and he was in therapy. There at the psychiatric clinic at one of the University of California schools. I forget which. Anyway. The Tarasoff woman dumped the guy. The guy went in to see his therapist. He was a mess. Said he wanted to kill this woman who just dumped him. The shrink recognized that the guy was unbalanced. You know?"

For once, I did.

She went on, "So the shrink tried to get the guy institutionalized. He realized the guy was losing it. But the guy terminated his therapy instead. The shrink called the campus police. He was worried about protecting the confidentiality of his client, but he was also worried for the woman named Tarasoff. Without telling the cops why, he asked them to beef up their security around the house where the Tarasoff woman lived." She paused.

"And did they?"

"Yeah, they did. But it wasn't enough." Sissy's voice caught. "The guy killed her."

"Sheesh." I thought for a minute. "But who brought suit?"

Sissy pushed her pink-and-blue striped Pappagallos out in front of her and crossed her legs. "Her relatives did. They sued the University Regents, since the guy, the killer, had been going to a shrink connected with the school. The court maintained that the shrink had a greater obligation to keep the Tarasoff woman alive than to protect the confidentiality of his client."

"What do you mean?"

Sissy gave me a long look. "The idea was that the mental-health counselor had a duty to *warn* the person whose life was in danger."

"Who won?"

"The Tarasoffs. That's what I told Philip the day before he died. If he knew that somebody wanted to kill somebody, he had to warn the would-be victim. That was his legal duty."

"Holy cow. Do you know if he did?"

She shook her head. "I think he was going to do something, tell whoever it was that there was danger. Have the person call the cops or something, but I can't be sure."

I stared at her, transfixed. The call Schulz had received just before the accident. From the Aspen Meadow Country Club.

You gotta come help me, my life's in danger.

20.

At that moment, Julian came shuffling down the stairs to the so-called snack bar. How long had he been listening? I did not know.

"Hey, what's happening," he said. I said nothing. He scanned Sissy's face and then mine. He was looking for a mood.

"Are you done with your lab work yet?" Sissy demanded.

"Yeah, I'm done, are you upset?"

She assumed a light tone. "I'd hate to think what would happen if you actually had to be responsible, Julian. Now you have to drive back to the club, and I'm going to be late for the library. If you were me, would you be upset?"

I took a deep breath and said, "Now, now." Almost immediately, I regretted opening my mouth. Both teenagers turned mind-your-own-beeswax looks in my direction. I said, "I'll take Arch home if it will speed things up. There's really no need for a conflict here."

Sissy said, "Since when are you the expert at patching things up?"

I itched to say something bitchy, but remembered my words to Arch regarding taunting on the playground. I'd say, *Don't get down on their level, sweetheart, just walk away.* For once, I took my own advice.

"Hey, wait up!" Julian hollered after me when I had reached the landing.

"I'll be looking for Arch," I called over my shoulder.

Outside the weather obliged by rolling a cool breeze off the mountains. More dark clouds threatened. Where had Arch gotten to, anyway?

"Look, hey, I'm sorry about that," said Julian when he reached me. He cast his eyes down, embarrassed. I leaned against a dusty Acura Legend. It was an expensive car; probably belonged to a seventeen-year-old.

I said, "You're not responsible for the way she acts, you know. Even if you were married to her, you wouldn't be responsible for her. And by the way, I would strongly advise against further interest in this girl."

He pulled his mouth over in a half-smile.

"The caterer with the advice."

"Oh," I said, "spare me." I called Arch's name.

Droplets of rain splatted into the dust as I began to traipse toward the pool site. Julian was close on my heels. I found myself worrying about the water dripping through the pinpoints of Julian's bleached hair. His scalp would become drenched. He would come down with bronchitis. Not responsible, I reminded myself, not responsible! In fact, I would serve Hostess Twinkies in hell before I would tell him to cover his head.

"Look!" Julian raised his voice over the hissing of the rain. "Sissy's just—"

"You don't need to make excuses."

We came up on the pool site. Fat lot of good a six-foot fence would do if someone left the gate open. In the pool, Arch, splashing around as if he were blind, yelled, "Marco!"

I called again. The two friends who had been answering "Polo!" leaped out of the pool and disappeared. I thought, Aren't there any regulations around here? I howled for Arch and glared at Julian.

He went on talking as if it were not raining and I was not trying to get Arch out of the pool. He said, "Sissy's sort of, like, possessive."

"Ah. Explains everything." I crossed my arms and tried to ignore the rain. Once Arch realized his friends were gone, he opened his eyes, saw me, and propelled himself up the side of the pool. He yelled that he would be there in a minute.

"Really," Julian said. He craned his neck back and shook his head the way a wet dog would. "She worries about me."

"I think you had it right the first time."

"Thing is, I'm not sure she . . . wants me." He shifted his weight and looked around. I wanted to say something about perhaps trying another hairdo when without warning he leaned close to me.

"What is it?" I blustered, and thought immediately of Brian Harrington. Why were males suddenly attracted to me? Maybe I was losing weight.

"What's the secret?" he said in a low tone.

"What secret?"

"About aphrodisiacs."

I said, "You're a child, for God's sake!"

A throat cleared behind us. I turned around.

It was Tom Schulz. His head was cocked, his eyebrows lifted. Arch, wearing flip-flops, clopped up to join us. He shivered underneath his towel.

"What were you doing?" I demanded of him.

Arch *tsk*ed, as if I were terribly overbearing.

Tom Schulz murmured, "Might want to ask the same thing of you, Miss G."

At that moment Sissy strode up; she and Julian wordlessly withdrew.

"Hey!" Arch called after them. "I thought you guys were taking me!"

"Things have changed," I announced. "I'm taking you. After I get an explanation."

His lips were blue, but he managed to say, "It's not official, but they've filled the pool with water. We were just having some fun. But then it started raining."

I said, "No kidding." I brushed raindrops from my face and arms. "Would you please get into the van?" I handed him the keys. He knew how to start it and warm it up. He also knew better than to launch a verbal defense at that moment.

Schulz said, "Want to get into my car for a minute? I can tell when you're not in one of your better moods, Miss Goldy."

"Should I be in a good mood?" The raindrops turned to heavy mist. The road to Aspen Meadow was shrouded in fog and rain, just as it had been after the brunch. The pool water reflected the dark sky. "I'm worried about Arch," I said. "I want to stay where I can see him."

Schulz said, "By the way, I do think Julian Teller is a little young for you."

I gasped sharply.

His large, moist face beamed when he laughed.

"Didn't you see what he—" I began.

"Yeah, yeah, yeah." Behind us my van started up. I hoped Arch turned the heat to high. "Listen, the general said you'd be out here doing fund-raising for someone other than yourself."

"Excuse me? How'd he know that? I was the only one who talked to the fund-raising lady."

"Look, Goldy, you live with a former member of the intelligence community, you gotta figure he's going to do what he does best."

"Great." If he was going to listen in, why didn't he just answer the phone himself?

"Anyway," Schulz was saying, "something's come up with the Philip Miller case." He paused and looked around. "Something you said about the way he was driving made me call back the coroner's office. They just checked Miller's eyes briefly because he was a cornea donor. You know, that procedure has to be done within a few hours or it's no good. So I called the cornea bank. You're not going to believe this." He took a deep breath, his green eyes suddenly solemn. "Miller's corneas were rejected."

"What?"

"The coroner's office doesn't remove contact lenses, which Miller had on. Remember, he had gone to the eye doctor that morning?" I nodded and he continued, "Miller's contacts, according to the ophthalmologist at the cornea bank, were embedded with peroxide. The tainted contacts burned off the epithelium, or top layer of the cornea. He couldn't see."

I was incredulous. "Couldn't see? He could see me at the brunch. He drove fine on the road for a while. How could this happen?"

"Goldy. I do not know. I called the eye doctor. He said Philip Miller was fine when he left his office. And obviously he could see well enough to get to the brunch. Another thing. The doctor said peroxide on your lenses would cause intense pain. And right away. It's not possible anyone could stand the pain for more than a few seconds."

I ran my fingers through my damp hair and shook my head.

"I gotta go," said Schulz. "Lot of work to do. Mind if I peek in at Arch?" He eyed the van.

"Sure."

He opened the door and said a few words to Arch that I could not hear. They both laughed, then Schulz slammed the door and swaggered over to give me a hug. Into my ear, he said, "There's just one thing I want."

"What's that?"

"Whatever it was Julian Teller wanted."

Arch explained on the way back to the Farquhars that he was so sick of doing his schoolwork that he just needed a break in the pool.

I said, "That's not the point. It's too dangerous to go into a pool that's not completely built."

"*Mais la piscine est finie!*"

Well, I was impressed that he knew how to say in French that the pool was finished. But I was not going to let him off the hook that easily.

"Then why have a security fence around it?"

"Oh, Mom! They just filled it with really, really chlorinated water yesterday. It's supposed to, like, shock the bacteria out of the pool. The gym teacher said the water would be clear in a couple of days." He drew some rope and a piece of bamboo out of his magic bag, then dangled them by my face. "Just wait, Mom," he said. "You're going to be amazed. Check out these Chinese manacles."

I smiled. This was no time to argue about dangerous tricks. The potentially treacherous road to Aspen Meadow demanded my attention. "You always amaze me," I told him evenly. "If we're going to have a magic party, we need to call your pals pretty quickly. Have you talked to Adele?"

"Yes, didn't she tell you?" He tilted his head from side to side in front of the dashboard heater. His hair was a mass of dried fluff and wet streaks. "You were supposed to invite my friends to the anniversary barbecue tomorrow night. I left you a list of friends in your Edgar Allan Poe book. Also, hate to tell you, but I still need to get a top hat and cape."

"Arch! I haven't called anybody!"

"Mom!"

I sighed. "I'll do it when we get home. Find out how much the cape and hat cost when they're not made of silk."

"Gee, Mom, thanks."

"I didn't say I'd get them!"

"Yeah, but whenever you tell me to check on the price I know you're going to do it."

I dropped Arch at the Farquhars and drove toward Philip's office. Between Interstate 70 and downtown Aspen Meadow there was a business complex done all in dark horizontal wood paneling with pale turquoise deck railings and trim. This mountain style–meets–Santa Fe commercial space, known as Aspen Meadow North, housed Philip's office, Aspen Meadow Café, Elizabeth's store—To Your Health!—and assorted real estate and medical centers. Aspen Meadow had more chiropractors per square foot than any area outside of northern California. Two new ones had set up shop in this complex, which had originally been developed by Harrington and Associates. There was also, I noticed as I drove in, an optometrist.

I parked and picked up the packet of decals. My cover, I would tell Schulz later.

Elizabeth was not back in her store yet. To my surprise, there was no GET INTO THE SWIM! decal in her window. The clerk did not feel a donation from the cash register was possible in the owner's absence. No problem, I said, and bought some dried pineapple. Neither of the chiropractors wanted to give to the school. I asked if there was anything I could do to adjust their opinion, but they just looked at me blankly and said no. Aspen Meadow Café already had a decal. The curtained windows of Philip's office had no decal. I moved on to my true quarry.

Doggone. The optometrist's window had a decal. I went in anyway.

"I'm interested in contact lenses," I told the receptionist.

We discussed an eye exam. When was my last one? I couldn't remember. There had been a cancellation for that afternoon; she thought she could schedule me. She'd have to ask the doctor. I entreated. She disappeared and I quickly turned the appointment book back to Friday, June 3.

There it was. *9:30. Philip Miller.* I flipped back to the current date.

The receptionist returned, triumphant. "He can see you in half an hour," she announced.

I said I'd take it. While filling out the necessary forms, I felt the attention of the receptionist on me.

She said, "Don't I know you?"

I felt so proud when people recognized me. It made all the work on publicizing the business worthwhile.

"I'm Aspen Meadow's only caterer."

"No," she said, shaking her head, "that's not it." There was a flash of recognition. "You're the one who was married to Dr. John Richard Korman."

"One of the ones."

"God," she said as she rolled her eyes and giggled. "He is *so* good-looking!"

The nurse appeared at the doorway and called me.

Within five minutes, I wished I had taken extra-strength pain reliever before starting the exam. I couldn't read the bottom row of letters, tried too hard, felt like a failure. If my eyes were good enough for the driver's license test, why weren't they good enough here? Then on to the big circles of lenses. Which looks better, number one or number two?

Neither.

The optometrist was named H. D. Cartwheel. He had more freckles than I would have believed possible for a single human being. He had tamed his mass of red hair over to one side with a sweet-smelling cream. I had to bite my lip to keep from asking if the H. D. stood for Howdy Doody. Actually, I should have been asking questions about contact lenses. But I couldn't think of anything except how soon the pain would be over. Cartwheel pulled my eyelid to one side and put a drop in, then repeated this with the other eye. It was anesthetic for the glaucoma test, he explained. Then he dimmed the lights again. My head felt as if a toddler was banging on it with a wooden hammer.

"Please stop," I said finally.

"Now don't be frightened," he said in a patronizing tone.

I said, "I can't take any more."

"Sure you can."

"Please! Turn the lights on!"

He did. Then he wrinkled his forehead and blinked at me. He said, "I'm not finished with the glaucoma test. We need to—"

"I'm sorry," I said. "I can't deal with any more in one day."

Cartwheel was taken aback. The nurse came scurrying in.

"What's the problem?" she asked.

"The problem," I said quietly, "is that I am only interested in contact lenses."

They both said, "Excuse me?"

Cartwheel said, "You have to let me finish the glaucoma test."

"I don't have to let you do anything," I said. "If I had contact lenses," I said to the nurse, "where would they be right now? In my eyes?"

Cartwheel stood up and walked out.

"Doctor's very upset," said the nurse.

"That's too bad," I said. "Where would the contacts be?"

She shook her head. "Not in your eyes," she said. "We usually remove the enzyme buildup in the ultrasound machine while the patient is in the exam."

"This machine disinfects?"

"No, that's to get rid of bacteria. But there's another kind of—" She looked at me sympathetically. Didn't want to use too many big words, apparently. "Another kind of—stuff—that grows on the lenses and can make them foggy and uncomfortable. Patients use a separate procedure to remove that buildup weekly, but when they come in for their exam we do an extra-good job with the machine." She smiled weakly. "Shall I call Doctor back?"

"No, thanks. I'd like to see the machine. I can't manage any more exam today."

She said, "Well, Doctor was almost done," but led me down the hall to the machine anyway. "This is it," she said, and pointed to a metal box on a shelf.

"What's in it?" I asked. "I mean besides ultrasound."

"A peroxide solution."

I looked at her. "A peroxide solution dissolves the buildup?"

"Yes, kind of burns it off, you'd say. But, don't worry, we rinse that solution off before we give the patients back their lenses."

"Rinse it off with what?"

She picked up a bottle of saline solution and handed it to me. "Believe me," she said, "if even a trace of the peroxide is left on the lenses, the patient will scream bloody murder because of the pain. Most of them wear prescription sunglasses out of here, because when people actually *finish* the eye exam," here she gave me a stern look, "their pupils are dilated and they don't want to wear their contacts anyway."

I thought for several minutes. She asked me if I wanted to finish the exam. I said no.

"Then do you want to leave? We do have other patients coming in."

I closed the door to the room with the ultrasound machine.

"Please," I said, "I need your help."

"If you want contacts, you have to finish the exam."

"I don't want contacts," I said slowly. "I just need to ask you about a contact-lens patient of yours." I gave her my most beseeching look. "His name was Philip Miller."

21.

She shook her head. "You must know I can't talk to you about patients. Especially," here she paused for effect, as if I were a criminal, "since the *police* have already been in."

"I know, I know," I said. "But please listen. Philip Miller was a friend of mine. A good friend," I added earnestly. "And you don't have to tell me anything about him personally or his medical history. I just want to know a couple of things about his visit."

She hesitated. Her experience with odd patients was clearly limited.

"You see," I went on in a rush, "I was behind him when he crashed. I'm trying to help the police." Sort of, I added mentally.

She was mellowing. "So what do you want to know?"

I picked up the saline-solution bottle. "This—" I said after a minute. "Do you remember this from his appointment?"

"I told the policeman all about it. Miller was the first appointment of the morning."

In good Rogerian fashion, I said, "The first appointment."

She took the bottle and shook it. "I always do that before I rinse off the lenses. There was just a little bit left in the bottle when he came in. I used it to rinse off his lenses, and then I threw it away. That's all. That's it."

"And did he put the lenses in?"

She nodded. "I watched him do it."

Whatever happened, I thought on the way home to the Farquhars, must have been something of a delayed reaction. Philip had not excused himself from the brunch, had not left me for more than a moment. I didn't believe he could have done anything to his lenses—or had anything done—without my noticing. Still, though, figuring on an hour for the appointment, how could you account for that half hour from leaving the optometrist's office, coming to Elk Park Prep, and then driving back to Aspen Meadow? Why didn't Philip feel any pain? Why did he suddenly go blind?

As usual, cooking was the cure for distress. The rain had cleared and the air was filled with a sweet, moist smell. I turned off the security system that guarded the first-floor windows and opened them all. Out back, Arch and Julian were splashing and yelling in the pool.

With Julian in for dinner I decided on a crustless quiche made with Jarlsberg and two other cheeses, a salad of lovely greens the general had picked up on one of his shopping expeditions, and some cloverleaf rolls I had brought frozen from my old house. I grated the Jarlsberg into a golden mountain of creamy strands. To my surprise the phone only rang once. It was my lawyer telling me Three Bears Catering had a legitimate case and it would not cost too much to have my name changed. Of course, to him nothing cost too much. I told him I would think about it.

After plugging in the recorder I let my mind wander back to what it was Elizabeth had said about Philip studying an abused woman. One thing I had noticed about making a marital mistake: you compounded the error by spending even more emotional energy ruminating on why you made the mistake, even if you corrected it by divorce. Furthermore, if Philip was so interested in why I had stayed with John Richard for so long, why hadn't he asked me himself?

Crustless Jarlsberg Quiche

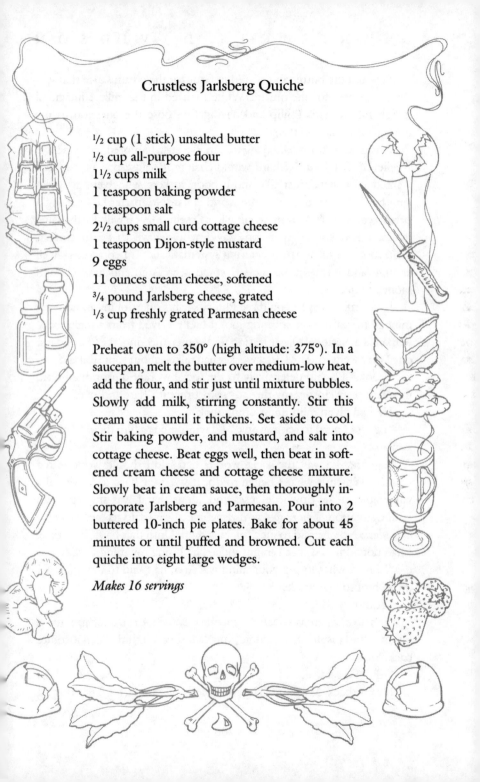

½ cup (1 stick) unsalted butter
½ cup all-purpose flour
1½ cups milk
1 teaspoon baking powder
1 teaspoon salt
2½ cups small curd cottage cheese
1 teaspoon Dijon-style mustard
9 eggs
11 ounces cream cheese, softened
¾ pound Jarlsberg cheese, grated
⅓ cup freshly grated Parmesan cheese

Preheat oven to 350° (high altitude: 375°). In a saucepan, melt the butter over medium-low heat, add the flour, and stir just until mixture bubbles. Slowly add milk, stirring constantly. Stir this cream sauce until it thickens. Set aside to cool. Stir baking powder, and mustard, and salt into cottage cheese. Beat eggs well, then beat in softened cream cheese and cottage cheese mixture. Slowly beat in cream sauce, then thoroughly incorporate Jarlsberg and Parmesan. Pour into 2 buttered 10-inch pie plates. Bake for about 45 minutes or until puffed and browned. Cut each quiche into eight large wedges.

Makes 16 servings

I melted the butter and stirred in flour for the cream sauce that was the actual base for the quiche. While I stirred in the milk, I imagined myself hiking with Philip and having him pose the question to me himself. *Why did you stay?*

Because, I saw myself saying to him. Because I ignored the evidence. I believed that John Richard would change. Because that was what I wanted to believe, just like those poor suckers who went to great lengths to demonstrate that the world is flat. No matter how strong a person you are, if you want to cling to a falsehood, you will. By the same token, I had known that someday I would have to get out. That realization led me to study catering systematically. If I could cook well enough and learn the business, I could keep Arch and have enough money to live on.

In my mind's eye I could see Philip, see his questioning look. It reminded me of the questioning look I had received from a male social worker at a National Organization for Women meeting, the first and last one I ever went to. The social worker had talked about spouse abuse.

"Look," I'd said defensively to the social worker during the break, incipient tears closing my throat, "sometimes it's hard to leave."

He had given me a questioning look.

"I guess I need to see a shrink," I'd whispered to him then. "Are you available?"

Sage that he was, the social worker had said I should work with a woman. Which is what I began to do. It was very hard to be verbally vulnerable, to let down defenses and admit that I was staying in an insane situation. *You're so together,* people always said to me. *You're so articulate.* No one said to me, *You're so crazy.* Until that NOW meeting, I had not admitted that I might indeed be losing my mind.

"I know what losing your mind is," Arch had said to me once as I drove him to first grade.

"You do?"

"It's like when you can't remember someone's name, just for a minute. And just for that minute, you've lost your mind! Then it comes back."

"Ah," I'd said.

It came back. My mind. The counselor was wonderful. The cooking was salvation. André, who trained me in catering, was a friend. In his big Denver kitchen the activity swirled all around me as I tried to keep tears from falling into the bread dough I was mixing.

"You know salt slows down the action of the yeast," he had said once over my shoulder. He saw me crying but never asked about it, just handed me gifts of food to take home to Arch. He would ask me, How did that dinner for Mrs. Sweeney go? Those chile rellenos stay hot? André offered his presence and his faith in me. It sped up the healing process.

Cooking helped, both before and after I told John Richard I was divorcing him. That was what I would have told Philip, I decided as I scooped the egg, cheese, and sauce mixture into two pie plates. Cooking anesthetized my feelings. I could throw myself into a complicated recipe and within an hour I would feel better.

Wait a minute.

By the time I was done, I would feel better.

The cooking took the pain away.

Anesthetic. That was it.

Philip Miller. He had not felt any pain in his eyes for thirty minutes *because he had had anesthetic in his eyes from the glaucoma test.* He could see. He just couldn't feel the damage that was being done to his eyes until it was too late.

I reached for the phone.

Tom Schulz was not at his desk. I left a message and finished preparing the dinner. The quiches puffed up to golden-brown perfection. Arch had two slices, Julian four. When we finished, General Farquhar surprised us with a new jar of macadamia-nut sauce for our pound cake.

Later, I tucked Arch in over his protestations that he was getting too old to be tucked in. I asked him if he remembered when he was six, telling me that losing your mind was when you forgot something.

He said, "Why? Did you forget to call the people for the magic party?" I had promised to do it as soon as I got home.

I apologized. I promised to get the list from the Poe book and make the calls first thing in the morning. Kids could do things on the spur of the moment, couldn't they?

He said, "I guess," and gave me a brief hug.

I went into my room and waited for the house to get quiet. I was going to sneak out. I didn't want anyone in the household to know my intentions.

Ten o'clock: Adele tap-stepped her way up to the master bedroom, ran water for twenty minutes, and then settled in after a therapeutic soak.

Eleven: The general's muffled telephone voice stopped and the door to his study gently opened and closed. Then there was the sound of more water, then quiet.

Midnight: The faint boom-boom and twang of Julian's rock music stopped wafting up from the ground floor.

Finally there were no sounds except the breeze sighing in the pines. I had left my van on the street. Now all I had to do was get out of the house without making a catastrophic amount of noise.

General Farquhar had closed the windows and reset the security system. If I set it off and no one interrupted the automatic dial, an armed representative of Aspen Meadow Security would arrive in a pickup truck at the bottom of the driveway. He would then wait for someone to come out and give the secret password, signaling the all-clear. If no one came, the security man would call the police. Julian had provided the password: CHOCOLATE.

But I should have problems with none of that, I reflected as I tiptoed down the staircase, pressed buttons, and slid through the front door. An ocean of summer stars glittered overhead. As on most moonless nights in the high country, the Milky Way shone like a wide ribbon across the inky sky. At the end of the driveway, the security gate yielded to the code my fingers punched in, and I was off.

I had broken into an office once before. It had been the ob-gyn office of my ex-father-in-law, Fritz Korman. Alarms had gone off instantaneously. But that time, I had known what I was looking for. This time I was not so sure. I ground the gears into third and started up toward Philip's office at Aspen Meadow North. This is crazy, I thought. It's not as if I'm being paid to figure out what happened to Philip Miller. It had been an accident. Involving peroxide. An accident with the man whom I thought had loved me. He had not loved me; he had been studying me. I felt betrayed. I wondered if he had betrayed anyone else.

If someone had decided to kill Philip Miller, how would that some-one have gone about it? What would you need?

In addition to having a motive, and I was still unclear on what that was, you would have to know his schedule. Know when he was going to the eye doctor. You would have to plan. And, I thought regretfully, you would have to have some way of killing a psychologist so that it looked like an accident.

You would have to be smart.

The parking lot at Aspen Meadow North was empty. Neon security lights glowed like fluorescent plants in the asphalt. Not wanting to look conspicuous, I pulled into a far corner of the lot under the shade of an ancient pine. The wide branches swaying in the breeze made a pocket of darkness. The office building's angles and corners, so innocuous during the day, cast long geometric shadows. I got out and was startled by a buzzing sound. But it was only a neon bulb. I tried not to think of it as warning me off.

One thing I had learned from the general about security: Most bur-glars will try to make it look as if they had not broken in. That delayed any action being taken against them. I climbed up the wooden stairs to Philip Miller's office wondering how I would do that. A step creaked loudly. Immediately there was a brushing sound in the trees. I froze and stared at the place where the noise had come from. Without a moon, it was hard to make anything out. My eyes adjusted slowly. After a few minutes a bull elk stepped gingerly from behind the trees and then trotted toward the brush behind the building. Welcome to the mountains.

I made my way quickly down to Philip's office door and wondered if I could slide a charge card into the area between the lock and the door frame, the way they did on television. My charge cards were of limited use in charging things, anyway.

No luck. Finally I just kicked hard. Two, three, four times. The door opened. No alarms. You should have been more careful, Philip.

Schulz had told me that the Sheriff's Department had taken the files to look through them regarding the clients. Had Elizabeth told Schulz that Philip thought one of them was homicidal? I did not know. The schedule, I told myself. Who saw him that last week?

I looked for a calendar on the secretary's desk and on Philip's. Nothing. Then I opened a closet in his office and turned on the light. *Voilà:* a large paper month-to-month calendar was tacked on the back of the closet door.

The last week he was alive, Philip Miller had appointments with General Bo Farquhar, Adele Farquhar, and Julian Teller. On the day before he died, he had lunch with Weezie Harrington.

22.

I couldn't sleep. As I had so many times before, I ran a mental film of Philip's BMW's terrifying swerves and then sickening smash. I added to the film the new knowledge that he had been blinded. It explained everything.

Well, almost everything. Blinded by what? By unrinsed contact lenses embedded with peroxide. You couldn't drive that road if you couldn't see that road. Could the lack of rinse have been an accident? Reason said no. So did the existence of a murderous patient. Or perhaps it was not a patient at all, but Elizabeth had just *thought* it was.

Blinded by whom? Julian had problems that erupted in hostility. In meeting with Philip Miller, General Bo and Adele were probably trying to help the troubled teen. Weezie had her own agenda: to protect her land and win back her errant spouse. And of course there was Brian himself—ace developer and, perhaps, jealous husband.

I did not know if there was a way to figure this out. Psychologists keep notes on their patients and Schulz had Philip's. Their content remained a mystery. Arch had gone to a counselor after he became addicted to escaping from reality in fantasy role-playing games. That fellow had referred to notes during our three-way monthly discussions. But what *kind* of notes did they teach you to take in Shrink School? Moreover, as academics love to say, there were other ramifications. Sure, I had kicked in Philip's door. I had looked for and found a schedule for his appointments and activities. I presumed the police had seen his schedule, too. But Schulz would never let me see the files. I was his friend and confidante, but there were limits.

Images of Philip with Adele, Philip with Elizabeth, Philip with Julian, Philip with Weezie floated up as I tossed fitfully in the guest-room bed. Philip with Weezie. Mapping out a game plan for dealing with county commissioners? Or playing some other kind of game? I didn't want to think about it.

Against all transcendental teaching, I started to repeat my mantra just to get to sleep. That plus the early sunrise had their usual soporific effect. I fell into a deep cloud of slumber that was only dispersed when my radio alarm blasted me at seven o'clock with the Beatles' version of "Twist and Shout."

I pressed all the wrong buttons and finally got it off. Arch was still asleep so I turned off the motion detector, stumbled to the phone in the kitchen, and wondered if you could free-base caffeine.

I punched the buttons and got Schulz, the early bird. I said, "Finally!"

There was a pause. "Well," he said, "I didn't want to wake you up returning your call."

"Sorry, had a bad night. Any chance we could get together today?"

"Let's see. Later in the morning? 'Bout ten?"

At that moment I was sure I heard someone pick up the phone. Paranoia or no, I did not answer Schulz.

"Hello?" said Tom Schulz and General Farquhar at the same moment.

"I'm on the other extension, Goldy," said the general.

I said, "Do you need me to get off?" Although I didn't see why he would, with two other lines in the house.

"No, no," he said, "sorry to have bothered you, it's just that I want to talk to you about a special dessert for our anniversary party tonight."

I told him to come on down and heard the distinct click of him getting off the line. I asked Schulz if he would meet me at the Aspen Meadow grocery store.

He said, "At the grocery store? Hold on, I have to check my calendar. . . . I have to be in court this afternoon. I can come up there, but not for long. The supermarket's not where I usually interview people. You've been reading too many spy stories."

I said, "My life is a frigging spy story."

General Farquhar slipped into the kitchen and began pacing like Napoleon. I rang off, fixed espresso, and took out some cookbooks. I sipped the velvety dark stuff, felt my brain coming to life as the general began to grunt over photographs of million-calorie desserts.

He looked up at me with a puzzled expression. "What exactly are you fixing for the party?"

I tried to rid the word *interrogation* from my mind. Instead of my name, rank, and serial number, I said, "Grilled shrimp, French hamburgers, something vegetarian for Julian, rotini salad with a creamy Dijon dressing, cold cooked asparagus with lemon, and whatever you want for dessert."

"Great, great," he said with some impatience. He flipped a cookbook shut, paced, paused by the counter. "Listen, I have a surprise for Adele, a piece of jewelry that I never thought I'd get my hands on, something she admired once in Florence. So I'd like a real special dessert."

I said, "Fourteen Carrot Cake?"

He craned his neck back to gaze at the ceiling. "She admired this ring in a shop on a bridge over the Arno. Later we had those hard Italian cookies that have nuts in them. Sometimes they have chocolate on top. Know what I mean?" He gave me his characteristic squint.

I said, "Biscotti?"

He smacked his hands together. "That's it. Could you make some for tonight? Instead of a cake? She would understand. Hell, she'd love it."

I told him it would be no problem. The fifteenth anniversary was crystal, I wanted to say, and Adele might want you to replace the Waterford vase destroyed in the garden-explosion, but never mind. The

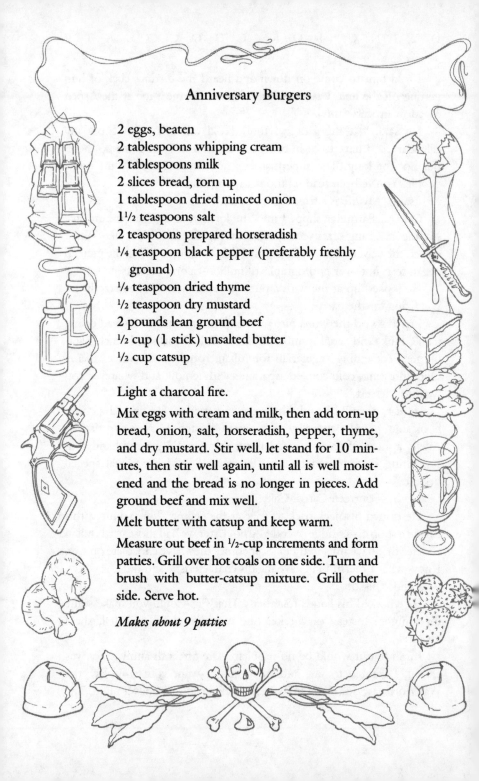

Anniversary Burgers

2 eggs, beaten
2 tablespoons whipping cream
2 tablespoons milk
2 slices bread, torn up
1 tablespoon dried minced onion
1½ teaspoons salt
2 teaspoons prepared horseradish
¼ teaspoon black pepper (preferably freshly ground)
¼ teaspoon dried thyme
½ teaspoon dry mustard
2 pounds lean ground beef
½ cup (1 stick) unsalted butter
½ cup catsup

Light a charcoal fire.

Mix eggs with cream and milk, then add torn-up bread, onion, salt, horseradish, pepper, thyme, and dry mustard. Stir well, let stand for 10 minutes, then stir well again, until all is well moistened and the bread is no longer in pieces. Add ground beef and mix well.

Melt butter with catsup and keep warm.

Measure out beef in ½-cup increments and form patties. Grill over hot coals on one side. Turn and brush with butter-catsup mixture. Grill other side. Serve hot.

Makes about 9 patties

Dijon Pasta Salad

1 pound tricolored fusilli or rotini pasta
$^2/_3$ cup corn oil
2 tablespoons cider vinegar
2 teaspoons Dijon-style mustard
$^2/_3$ cup mayonnaise
2 large celery ribs, chopped
6 thick bacon slices, cooked and chopped
2 hard-cooked eggs, chopped
2 scallions, chopped
$^1/_2$ to 1 teaspoon salt
paprika (optional)

Cook pasta in boiling water just until done, usually 11 to 13 minutes. Drain. Run cold water over pasta until it is completely cool.

In a large bowl, whisk together oil, vinegar, mustard, and mayonnaise. Add pasta and all other ingredients to dressing, mix carefully, and taste for seasoning. Chill thoroughly before serving.

Makes 8 to 10 servings

Farquhars had managed to keep a good relationship, a married one, too, for fifteen years. Maybe they could give me some pointers.

The general was rattling on about the fact that he had ordered all the flowers and for me not to worry about that. I patted him on the back and told him he was just a huge help, then managed to shoo him out of the kitchen so I could check recipes and make a list. There would be thirty of us this time, all the same people who were at the Harrington aphrodisiac dinner, friends from the school, the club, and various committees, plus Arch and me.

Plus Arch's friends! Oh Lord, I thought on the way to the grocery store, I had forgotten to make the calls as I'd promised. I would have to call the kids' parents the moment I got home from seeing Schulz. Could Arch have given up and be inviting them while he was at summer school today? There were too many things to worry about, I reflected as I swung my van in next to Schulz's car in the parking lot. When I found him, he was picking out artichokes.

I leaned into him, spylike, and said under my breath, "You need to stop calling me on the Farquhars' phone. It's dangerous."

"Yeah, 007? Why's that?"

"Get serious. I've discovered the perfect crime."

He said, "Artie Chokes Two for a Dollar."

"Are you done?"

"No, I'm waiting by the vegetables for the town caterer to tell me how to do my job."

I told him my theory about the peroxide on the unrinsed lenses. About the anesthetic delaying the burning of the corneas. I finished with, "All the killer would have to do is sneak into the doctor's office somehow, do a trade with the saline solution, and then just wait for things to self-destruct. But you'd have to know Philip's schedule beforehand." I handed him two firm artichokes.

"No offense, Miss G., but it sounds a little thin. If you've got a real homicidal person on your hands, there are easier ways." He put down the artichokes, picked up some celery, put it down. "Like guns."

"But this way it looks like an accident," I said.

"If the guy dies."

"He'd die driving blind on that twisting road," I insisted. "Listen.

Do me a favor. I'm going to see Weezie Harrington tonight, and I want to try to find out more about her. But when I found the calendar—"

He leaned against the celery bin and closed his eyes. "I'm afraid to ask."

"Well . . ." I said slowly, "don't get mad, okay?" He let his shoulders go slack. I went on, "I got into Philip's office and looked at his schedule."

"We saw his schedule, too, Miss G."

"Yes, but you didn't know at that time that Julian Teller used peroxide for his hair! He saw Julian for his regular appointment and also the Farquhars, probably something to do with Julian's behavior, I'd say. I had to go in to see Arch's counselor monthly about the fantasy role-playing games. Don't you think it's strange that he saw the three of them, all in the few days before he died? Then on the day before he died, he had lunch with Weezie Harrington?"

"This is great. You broke into and entered Miller's office. You rifled his desk. You found his schedule. You figure, they don't license private investigators in this state, you're home free?"

I pressed my lips together.

"B and E is still a crime."

"Julian bleaches his hair," I said. "That's like new evidence, or whatever you call it. Can't you just run a background check on him?"

"I gotta go," Schulz said. He patted me on the shoulder.

"Do you even care about this?"

"Do you?"

I was taken aback. "Yes," I said after a minute, "I guess I do."

"I have a big caseload, Miss G. But I'll do what I can to find out about Julian."

I made a face at him.

"Mainly because," he said before wheeling off with his empty cart, "you aren't going to be able to get this Philip fellow out of your mind until I do." He paused to look at me. "Am I right?"

I looked away.

After half an hour my cart bulged with packages of fresh rotini, bunches of dark slender asparagus, a feathery dill plant and shiny lemon,

almonds, as well as anise seed, and unsalted butter. Finally, I stopped
to pick up what I had ordered the previous week: pounds upon
pounds of jumbo shrimp and ground chuck that the grocery had
meticulously wrapped in butcher paper. I loved spending other
people's money.

The van gave me a little bit of trouble when I turned the key.

I whispered to it. I coaxed. I shrieked. The engine finally turned over
and I started toward Aspen Meadow Country Club. I would have made
it in ten minutes, too, if I hadn't seen Arch walking along the dirt
shoulder at a very determined pace. When I pulled over, the van sputtered and died.

"Arch! Where are you going? Why aren't you in school? This road is
too dangerous for you to walk along, what's—"

"Go away! Leave me alone! You don't care anyway!"

I put my head on the steering wheel. This was why women could
never get ahead. Just when you thought you were getting somewhere,
your child was going to have a crisis. I put on the emergency flashers
and got out.

"Arch," I said as I pursued him along the narrow path of dust and
weeds, "please stop and talk to me. I do care. Come on and get in the
van and we'll go back to the Farquhars and we can talk while I cook—"

He whirled and glared at me. "I'm going into town to get some
magic stuff and then I'm going to walk over to my friends' houses and
ask their parents if they can come tonight."

"I'm sorry. Why don't you just call them?"

"*You* were supposed to call them."

"I didn't see the list—"

"It's in your Poe book! You always tell me not to invite friends
myself! That it's the mom's job!"

I felt my body slouch. "I'm sorry, hon, but I haven't had time to
read . . ."

He turned his back to me and resumed walking.

"Okay, look!" I called. "Just get into the van and we'll go home and
make the calls together. It'll be much faster!"

He stopped and turned again. "I still need a hat and cape."

"Okay, okay, I can probably manage a cape," I said. "The top hat will have to wait until the next trip to Denver."

Arch walked toward me, apparently satisfied with the compromise.

"Where are you going to get a cape?" he asked once we had settled into the van.

I turned the key. Nothing happened. I looked at him. "I was thinking the church might have one."

Arch reached for the door handle, as if I had double-crossed him and he was going to get out of the car as quickly as possible.

He said, "I don't want a *chasuble*."

How he could remember the names of all the priestly garments when that same vocabulary eluded me was another of Arch's amazing traits. But in this particular context, when the van again refused to turn over, it just made me angry. Why couldn't Arch know about cars, say, instead of magic and fantasy role-playing games and ecclesiastical trappings?

I said, "We'll go to Aspen Meadow Drug, then. They have everything." The van, as if in agreement, finally turned over.

We pawed through the drugstore racks. Nothing. I told Arch to let me have one more look, and while I did he saw one of his friends from the list. The kid had just come from the doctor where he'd had an ear check. I invited him to the party. While they were chatting ("Bring a swimsuit," Arch was saying, while the mother gave me a startled look. How can *you* afford a pool?) I trundled off to find a clerk, a teenage girl who was so fat my heart went out to her. Still, I was not above promising her a dozen Scout's Brownies if she would check the upstairs storeroom for a cape left unsold at Halloween. Her eyes brightened, and after disappearing for five minutes she handed me a black satin adult cape still in its plastic wrapper. Fifty dollars. I thanked her profusely and got her name so I could leave her the brownies.

"We're in business, kid," I called to Arch as I held the package aloft, headed for the checkout, and prayed that my groceries had survived this half-hour delay.

But the van would not start. Arch gave me an impatient look.

I screamed, "This is not my fault!"

To my complete amazement, he said quietly, "Why don't you just get out the jumper cables?"

I nodded in dumbfounded silence and began to extract the jumper cables from old newspapers and cans and other things I had been meaning to recycle. Arch climbed out of the van and found his friend's mother, who agreed to give us a jump. Problem was, she couldn't remember which wire went where, and I was so frazzled I couldn't either, so it was something of a relief when Arch took the wires out of my hands and commanded the woman to start her car.

"Do you really not know how to do this, Mom?"

"I do, I just forget. It's like changing a tire. You have to figure it out, just like when you have a flat tire. Only when you get a flat tire you're so frustrated it takes fifteen minutes to calm down enough to think."

"You have to pretend you're an electrical circuit," Arch said as he pinched open the toothed cable-claws and attached them to the batteries. "The cables just complete the circuit." After a few moments he said triumphantly, "Now try it."

It started like a charm. Arch disconnected the cables and threw them in on top of the shrimp. I was awash in guilt for thinking he did not know about cars. I yelled thanks to the woman and her son.

Back at the Farquhars, though, things did not go so smoothly. The phone began its incessant ringing. Aspen Meadow Florist called. Did General Farquhar really want three rare orchids on the corsage, at fifteen dollars each? Yes, I said. What could it hurt? Then Brian Harrington called. Was sweet Sissy going to be at the anniversary party? What business was it of his, I wanted to know, but only said yes. Then I heard a click and couldn't get a dial tone. Either the Farquhars were having trouble with their phone or the person who kept picking up the line was doing it again.

"Damn, damn, damn," I said as I slammed the phone repeatedly into its cradle. Whoever it was, I thought savagely, that shouldn't feel too pleasant on the ear.

"Now what's wrong?" Arch demanded.

"I can't get the phone to work," I said crossly. After a few more receiver-slams the dial tone finally popped back, and I tried four of the names on Arch's list. Three no-answers and one busy signal.

"I'm sorry, Arch, I'll keep trying once I get the pasta going for the salad. Nobody's home, so it's really not my—"

"Nothing is ever your fault! Whose fault is it?" He stomped out of the kitchen. When he got into the hall, he yelled, "Sometimes I just want to go and live with *Dad*!"

I let cold water gush into deep pots, then set them on to boil. I gritted my teeth. All my motherly work for nothing. Go and live with your father, I wanted to yell back. But I would not. I dumped the almonds into the food processor. The blade made a huge noise, as if it were grinding gravel. It was strangely comforting. I was not going to get angry. I was not going to say what I knew to be true.

Your father doesn't want you.

23.

Adele and the general entered the kitchen. They were together, they were quiet, they avoided my eyes. I figured I was either going to get sympathy or get fired.

To my surprise, it was the former.

"Let's go out on the veranda, shall we?" said General Bo in a time-for-the-staff-meeting tone. "We couldn't help but overhear."

I mumbled in the affirmative. Before we could move in that direction, though, Julian padded across the kitchen tiles. Ignoring the Farquhars, he lightly touched the fudge he had made that morning before he left for school. *Left without Arch,* I added mentally, but was in no mood for another hostile encounter. The candy appeared to be cool. Then he peered into the blender with the almonds. Satisfied, he moved to the refrigerator, opened the door, and clanked jars around. He emerged grasping soft drinks under each arm. He said, "Could you send Sissy down when she comes? I'm helping Arch build his stand."

"You're home early," I observed coolly.

"Yeah, I skipped my lab because I thought Arch might need some help."

I said I would indeed send Sissy down when she arrived. Pressing my temples with my fingers, I followed the Farquhars out to the porch. I welcomed anyone's willingness to help Arch.

"Goldy," said the general once he was seated and had fixed me with his ice-blue gaze, "you're under a lot of fire. Let us give you a hand."

I explained to them that I was just trying to get Arch's party set up, the party that was going to be at the same time as their anniversary soirée. I turned to Adele. Which was your stupid idea, I almost said to her, but did not.

Adele clucked. "Oh, and I was so hoping it would make him happy." She paused. "I think children go through ungrateful periods. Marla had tough teenage years, I remember."

I looked out at the sky. It was a liquid blue that permeated the air and brought the hills, the trees, the lumps of mountain grass into sharp focus.

I said, "I don't want Arch to go off the deep end. You can't imagine what a shock it was to see him walking into town today. I thought he was running away. I ended up doing a money-binge at Aspen Meadow Drug on something extravagant that he doesn't even need."

The general cleared his throat. "If you really don't want him to be going AWOL on you," he said in a conspiratorial tone, "I can just set the perimeter alarm whenever he's in the house. If he tries to run away, we'll know."

"No. I would never . . . but thanks very much. Really." I regarded them both, a pair of tilted heads, two pairs of empathetic eyes. "Keeping him prisoner won't work. I'll call his friends while I'm cooking. Maybe you two could invite him out now for a swim."

They beamed. They were so willing to be supportive.

Adele sat outside on a lounge chair while the general and Arch splashed about and screeched "Marco!" and "Polo!" to each other. I began to fix the anniversary meal in earnest. The tricolored rotini bubbled merrily, a riotous, bleached version of the Italian flag. That was probably what the pasta makers had in mind. I ran cold water over it and remembered André's admonition never to add dressing to hot pasta if your ultimate objective was to serve it cold. Hot pasta acted like sponges, sopping up the sauce and turning a light noodley texture into a sodden mass.

"Not at this soirée," I muttered as I drained the asparagus and ran cold water over it to set the color.

I had just begun to mix the biscotti dough when Adele appeared with her cane. She was wearing a blue bathing suit and a smile frozen with pain.

"Pills," she said. "I should know better than to attempt the frog kick. It always throws my back out. I would have sent Bo up, but he had to check something in his precious magazine."

"Oh my," I murmured. "Just sit down and I'll look for them."

But I did not have a chance, because at that moment the general appeared, fierce as a warrior in one of the heavy bathrobes given to him at his retirement by his West Point classmates. Embroidered across the back of this one were the words SUPPORT THE ACLU—CUSS IN PUBLIC.

"I'm missing a detonator," he boomed as he began to pull out canisters from the kitchen shelves.

"I don't think it would be out here," I said in a low voice, but they both ignored me. Adele still hadn't found her pills. The two of them began to sort through the gadgets, foodstuffs, flowerpots, and knick-knacks on the counters. When no pills and no detonator turned up, they started through the kitchen desk drawers.

"Where's Julian?" the general demanded finally.

"Downstairs, I think. Have you looked in the garage?"

"What's this?" said Adele as she leaned over the biscotti dough.

The general and I exchanged panicked expressions. Adele looked up at me when I didn't answer.

"Dessert," we said in unison.

"I'm going upstairs to find my pills," she announced, and limped out.

"Did you really lose a detonator?" I asked. "Or have you misplaced the Italian ring?"

"I haven't misplaced anything." The general's voice was gritty as sand. "I have the ring. I do not have the detonator." He stalked out.

"Alone at last," I said under my breath. I finished rolling the biscotti dough into loaves and put them into the oven. While I whisked together the salad dressing, I called the rest of Arch's friends.

First name on the list was female. Arch had put an asterisk beside her name: Andrea Coburn. She lived on Arnold Palmer Avenue. Coburn père was extremely nice.

"Oh yes, Arch! He's been over here. We love his magic tricks. He made my wife's diamond earrings disappear!" At this he began to laugh uproariously. Clearly Arch also had made the diamond earrings reappear. The father agreed to bring Andrea over that night for dinner and to pick her up. One down, five to go.

I got lucky: all but one of the kids were available. The others were all eager to come. So much for advance notice.

The sun had begun its slow descent over the mountains and I had refrigerated the orchid corsage and set out the six bouquets from Aspen Meadow Florist when Sissy buzzed the front gate. Since I never knew what kind of mood she was going to be in, I put on a happy face in hopes that she would mirror it. Miraculously, she did, and after watching me work in the kitchen for a while, she clopped down the stairs to see Julian. I had not seen Arch since . . . when? I reviewed the cooking: two salads for the adults plus a molded lime concoction with pineapple and marshmallows for the kids, asparagus, biscotti, hamburgers . . . yes, I distinctly remembered my hands immersed in ground beef the last time I had seen Arch. When he came up for more soft drinks, I had told him his friends were coming and he could do his magic tricks after all.

"Oh no!" he'd squealed. "I have to go get ready!" And I had not seen him since.

The doorbell rang: the Harringtons. To my chagrin I realized that Weezie had bourbon on her breath. I sneaked a glance at my watch: five-thirty. It was going to be a long evening. I hadn't even started the fire; I asked Brian to do it.

He leaned in close to me. "Starting fires is one of my favorite pastimes."

I thrust the lighter fluid at him. "I'm so glad. Men can't resist starting a charcoal fire. It brings out their caveman persona."

Between the arrivals of the Rasmussens, other Elk Park friends, golf partners, and Arch's pals, I squawked over the intercom to the general and Adele the news of the guests' arrival. The general reported that Adele had awakened from a nap. Would I please entertain their guests?

And cook, too? Arch was the magician, not me. But I told him it would be no problem.

Brian Harrington was fanning smoke madly when I stepped onto the brick patio. Weezie had helped herself to a drink from the outside bar. I tried not to think of how drunk she would be by the time the shrimp and burgers were ready. Arch and his friends milled about the pool self-consciously. All except for Andrea, that is. She was serious-looking, with straight brown hair and bangs that fell to her nose. She was giving Brian Harrington cheerful, unwelcome advice on how to start the fire.

I hopped back up to the kitchen and made a tray of soft drinks and popcorn for the young set. Since some of them had mistakenly thought this was Arch's birthday, there were presents to open. We occupied ourselves with this enterprise until the Farquhars made their appearance and we all sang "Happy Anniversary." It was a good moment, marred only by the concluding hyena laugh from Weezie as the fire once more went out.

General Farquhar offered to work on the charcoal. I rushed back to the kitchen to start the parade of food. I put the burgers and shrimp on a large tray, and prayed for balance.

When I came back out, Sissy and Julian had appeared on the patio. Bo, Adele, Weezie, and most of the other adults were sitting on white Adirondack chairs, chatting amiably. Julian sat apart, alone. Weezie cast occasional smoldering glances in the direction of Brian and Sissy. Julian was more direct: he glared. I followed his line of vision in time to see big Bri lean forward, ostensibly to tell Sissy something important, but really just to glance down her dress.

"Brian!" screeched Weezie. "Come over here! We're talking about Philip Miller!"

My heart ached. I wanted to hear what they were going to say, but I had to get the salads and asparagus. When I was almost to the sliding glass door General Farquhar trotted up behind me and caught me lightly by the arm.

"This is a party," he said forcefully. "I want you to enjoy it."

"Yes, sir! Just like the bird-watching!"

He said, "You're part of the family." Behind us the hostile voices of Weezie and Brian careened into shrieking.

I said, "You bet. Just let me go get the rest of the food." I smiled in what I hoped was a familial manner. "Did you ever find your detonator?"

"No. The biscotti come out?"

"Beautifully," I said, and turned to go back to the house.

In the kitchen I had the sudden hollow feeling that dusk often brings. I tried to put the feeling aside as I balanced covered bowls on a large tray. I wished Schulz were here. Arch had his friends. Among the adults I was odd woman out. Why hadn't I invited him? You should be used to solitude by now, I told myself. I had seen him just this morning, and he had said he would be in court all afternoon. Could he possibly have some other engagement on a Tuesday night? I put down the tray and punched in Schulz's office number.

"Speak!" he answered gruffly. His voice flooded me with warmth.

"Hi, it's me, the Farquhars are having a dinner party and I was wondering if you'd like to join us, sorry about the late notice." I ended out of breath.

"You getting lonely or something?"

I bristled but held it in. "Just trying to be nice."

"You are nice. And I miss you, too." Wonderful words. Why should I be upset if he could read my mind? John Richard had always said I *expected* him to read my mind. Schulz said, "No can do, sorry to say. I'm waiting for a couple of calls back on that background check."

We promised to see each other the next day and rang off. I felt much better until I hoisted my tray and reemerged onto the patio. Brian and Weezie were still arguing. Let the mood fit the food. I tried to think festive. But the squabble had become so heated that even Arch and his friends were watching from beside a stand of shrubs.

"*My* family owned Flicker Ridge," Weezie was saying. "*I* was the one who brought it to the," she spat out the last word, "*marriage.*"

"Salad, anybody?" I said brightly. I proffered the tray. "I'm just about to put them out here on the buffet—"

Weezie interrupted me, her voice still scathing. "Philip Miller and his Protect Our Mountains group got in the way, didn't he, Bri? He had an ecological strategy for the ridge; he even talked to me about it right before he died. But he doesn't seem to have left it to anybody. What luck for Brian Harrington Associates."

Adele turned a miserable face to me. Some party.

"Let's eat!" I cried. Grateful for a diversion, the group rushed toward the buffet. I concentrated on the grill, and shortly the shrimp and burgers threw off luscious barbecue smoke. The hostilities ceased while people ate.

When I brought around a second tray of the mixed grill, Arch murmured to me, "Thanks, Mom, this is really great." I told him to be ready to do tricks when the food was gone.

When the guests had revisited the buffet for thirds and begun to look around expectantly for dessert, I said, "Who's ready for a magic show?"

All the faces turned to me. I looked at Arch. After a moment's hesitation, he assumed a businesslike manner. He asked a cohort to help him carry out the stand he and Julian had made from plywood. On its front was painted ARCHIBALD THE MAGNIFICENT. Julian put a tape into his recorder and a whiny horn fanfare crackled through the air. Deck chairs scraped and screeched over brick as the guests turned their attention to Arch. I looked around nervously. Arch had never performed in public before, and I didn't want any interruptions. Weezie was still casting murderous glances at Brian, while he in turn winked at Sissy. It was as if he were trying to say, I'm still in control of this situation. But he did look shaken.

Arch bowed to light applause. He tossed the satin cape over his shoulders and flourished a baton, one John Richard had bought him in Denver. He began with some of the tricks I already knew: the liquid in the newspaper, the string through the neck, the disappearing/ reappearing cotton balls under plastic cups. There was polite clapping after each. I was enjoying myself so much that I almost forgot about dessert. I had dipped the biscotti in Valrhona *couverture,* a dense, silky chocolate that wrapped itself around cookies like a luxurious blanket. Then I had used meringue to attach them to three large Styrofoam cones. I had put a sparkler on top of each. Showmanship demanded appearing with the cones at the conclusion of Arch's routine. Accordingly, I gave the magic show a wide berth and scuttled back up to the kitchen.

What I did not know was that Brian Harrington was right behind me.

While I was assembling the plates for ice cream to have with the biscotti, he cleared his throat to let me know of his presence. I whirled and gave him my meanest stare.

I said, "Don't come near me. Don't try anything. If you make me ruin another dessert, I'll call 911."

He said, "Calling 911 won't do you any good."

I intentionally raised my voice. "No funny stuff, Mr. Harrington. I'm not kidding. Keep your distance. I'm busy."

"Lower your voice this instant," he hissed. "I want to talk to you about Philip Miller."

"Make it fast," I said as I searched for the almond fudge ice cream.

"Just look at me, will you? Goldy? Please? I have this feeling you're the only one who will understand."

I slapped the ice-cream boxes down on the kitchen island, pressed my lips together, and gave him the benefit of my attention. "You have two minutes."

"Look," he said, "I haven't always done the right thing. I mean, I admit it."

"Do I look like a priest?"

"What I'm trying to tell you is that . . . sure, I didn't like the guy. He was a pain with his do-gooder liberalism trying to put hardworking builders and developers on the unemployment rolls."

"Hey! Spare me the Right Wing Economics lecture, okay?"

"Okay, okay," he went on, "and I heard the rumors about him with my wife. I'm not sure those are true. Are you?" His eyes questioned me.

"I don't know," I said truthfully. "I didn't know him all that well myself." I moved the ice-cream boxes around on the island. I added, "Although I thought I did."

"Right. Well." He sensed the end of the two-minute warning. "Here's the thing. Okay, I didn't like him. He could have undermined my project. He could have been involved with my wife. But . . . twelve days ago, he called me. Very mysterious. He said my life was in danger. I said, Is this some kind of threat, you Greenpeace of shit?"

"Your two minutes are up," I announced loudly.

Brian Harrington regarded me earnestly. "I hung up on him. Tossed and turned all night. Next day I drove over to the club, I don't know why, thought I might run into somebody I knew, have a Bloody Mary. I was sneaking around though; didn't want anybody to know I was there. Thought I was losing my mind! I saw a phone and panicked. Dialed 911. Told them they had to come help me, my life was in danger."

I stared at him.

"I chickened out," he said. "You know, I was just so paranoid, I thought the cops might be in on it, too. So I left. Next thing I knew, Philip Miller was dead."

24.

The anonymous phone call.

I said, "Have you told the police?"

"I tried that once and I couldn't go through with it. With Miller gone, what could they do now?"

"A lot more than I can. Look, I'm in the middle of a job." His head and shoulders slumped in defeat. Well, what did he expect me to do? I found a pen and then reached for a paper cocktail napkin. "Here's the number of a friend of mine at the Sheriff's Department." I jotted down Schulz's number. "Call him and tell him what happened. He's an investigator looking into Philip's death."

Brian gave me his earnest look again. "I just didn't want you to think that I had something to do with your boyfriend's accident."

"Why do you care what I think?"

"Well, the implication of what my wife was saying . . . the innuendos . . . it's a small town. You know, with all my real estate developments, everyone always thinks I'm such a son of a bitch." He lifted his eyebrows.

"With all the money you make, it can't bother you that much."

"Oh, but it does, you cute little thing! If only you knew! Sometimes I wonder, how long must I endure such pain to the psyche?"

"Such pain to the . . . ?" The Styrofoam cones scraped against my fingers like chalk going the wrong way on a blackboard. "How long must you endure . . . ?"

He closed his eyes and shrugged.

How long must Aspen Meadow endure such pain to the palate?

"You son of a bitch!" I yelled.

Brian Harrington opened his eyes wide and jumped back. "*Now* what? I told you I didn't have anything to do with your boyfriend's . . . Oh! Don't tell me you're still mad about that cake!"

"I suppose your middle name is Peter, eh, Pierre?"

"I don't know what you've been drinking while you've been catering, but you must have me confused—"

Julian poked his mowed blond head into the kitchen. "Hello in here! The general sent me up. Can the two of you chill out so we can have dessert?"

I said, "Chill out yourself, Julian. I've just found my anonymous food critic."

Julian glanced from one of us to the other. He said, "Who? Him?" He sucked air into his cheeks, blew it out at Brian Harrington, then set his mouth in a frown. "What have you got against Goldy?"

"Nothing! Nothing! Why are people always accusing me of things I didn't do?" Brian Harrington turned on his heel and marched out of the kitchen.

Julian said, "Whoops. Guess you won't be doing any more catering for the Harringtons."

I slammed the Styrofoam cones on the tray. "Nothing would give me more pleasure. Now, Julian, if you really want to be helpful, would you please take these matches and try to do a better job with the sparklers than Brian Harrington did with the charcoal?"

When we arrived at the sliding glass and screen doors that opened onto the patio, a drumroll was issuing from the tape recorder. The guests had turned their attention to the pool. Arch was standing on the diving board. I almost dropped the tray. His hands were cuffed behind him.

"Open this door, open this damn door," I demanded of a startled Julian.

"I haven't lit the—"

"Just do it!"

Julian scraped the screen in its tracks. I wiggled through, hurried across the concrete, and slapped the tray down on the buffet table. I sent Arch vibes: *Don't dive off that board with your hands cuffed, don't dive, don't* . . .

His body lifted and flipped. There was a splash. I counted. *One, two, three, four, five, six, seven* . . .

No Arch.

I did what any mother would do. I ran to the pool and jumped in. Water drenched my clothes, pulling me down. I kicked off my shoes, took a deep breath, and went under. Arch was standing on the bottom of the pool, thrashing about with the cuffs. I swam and kicked fiercely until I got to him. I grabbed him under the armpits just as the cuffs came off. Lunging from the bottom of the pool, I tugged him upward as hard as I could.

"Braaugh!" he gargled when we splashed through the surface. He coughed and choked on the water. "Stop!" he shouted. "Stop! What are you doing? Mom! Jeez! You've ruined everything!" He broke away from me and doggie-paddled to the side of the pool.

"I was trying to help you," I sputtered, to no avail.

Effusive clapping greeted us when we climbed up the ladder. Arch gave me his most hateful look.

"You screwed everything up! Why do you always have to embarrass me?"

"I'm sorry. I'm sorry." When I could bear his angry eyes no longer, I stared down. My clothes were soaked. Puddles were forming around my feet.

"Did you plan it that way?" cried Weezie. Her voice was shrill with delight. "That was quite a performance!"

Arch slunk into the house. I went after him and plodded upstairs to change. When I got to the third floor there was a tightness in my throat. Next door Arch crashed about, looking, I assumed, for dry clothes. I found tissues, wiped my face, and coughed.

All I had ever wanted was to be a good mother. I hadn't thought it would be that difficult. I read the books. I took my child to the pediatrician, the park, and the playground. I read to him and spent time with him and helped with the schoolwork. I'd never even had a regular job until it was a financial necessity. I just wanted to take care of Arch. I thought all I had to do was love him, keep him safe and well, and do the best I could. In turn, he would turn out well-adjusted, happy, and appreciative.

Right.

The sun finished its slide into the mountains. The air was suddenly chilly. When I was putting on a sweat suit and dry sneakers, there was a knock at my door.

"Mom, it's me."

I wrapped a towel around my wet head and opened the door.

He avoided my eyes. His voice was shaky. He said, "Mom, I know you want to help. But it's just not working."

"Honey, please. I thought you were drowning."

"Well. I just wanted to tell you. I'm definitely going to ask Dad if I can go live with him for a while."

Somebody had told me once, In times of crisis, do nothing. I wished I had remembered that before The Poseidon Adventure.

Now I said, "Let's talk about this tomorrow. You've got guests downstairs."

The show went on. The biscotti-cum-sparklers were a hit. Now that the excitement was over, both adults and children conversed quietly. I felt low. I didn't know whether I wanted to eat a dozen biscotti or none at all, so I settled on three. They were heavenly: the thin coating of dark chocolate blended exquisitely with the breath of anise and crunch of almonds, and melded perfectly with the hazelnut-flavored French roast coffee. The planet Venus floated in a dazzle of brightness just above the western horizon. The perfumed evening breeze brought the guests' voices down to hushed tones. The guests discovered the delights of dipping biscotti into their demitasse before eating them, and there was much exclamation over the result.

That afternoon the general had placed torches at the edges of the concrete. Around nine o'clock, he lit them. He sat down next to Adele and drew a small jewelry box out of his pocket.

He said, "For my bride," and smiled with such adoration that something closed in my throat. Adele unwrapped the ring and held it up. Sapphires and diamonds glittered in the torchlight.

But Adele's smile was forced. After the gift she avoided Bo's eyes. Maybe her back was bothering her. Perhaps she felt bad that she didn't have something for him. Maybe it just wasn't a very good party.

I could sympathize with that assessment; I wasn't very happy either. I didn't want to think about Arch, about his living with John Richard, about how John Richard would ignore him. The guests filtered out. Their voices full of gratitude rose into the night air. I did the dishes and crawled upstairs, exhausted.

Scout the cat sensed sadness. He followed me up to my room and gathered himself into a ball in one corner of the bed. I thanked him for his company, treated myself to an emergency chocolate in the form of a Toblerone bar, and reflected on the rest of the evening. The interchange with Brian Harrington had been bizarre. I guess I hoped he would call Schulz, although I didn't really care. The implications of Harrington's political and social conflict with Philip Miller could lead to a maelstrom of gossip in our little town. Good, that would serve Brian Harrington right, if he was indeed Pierre.

I closed my eyes, let the chocolate melt slowly in my mouth, and tried not to think about the *Mountain Journal*. This same group of people (minus kids and extraneous adults) had been at Weezie's aphrodisiac banquet, subject of the last derisive review. Had I once again entertained Pierre the critic? Alias Brian Harrington? He would probably interpret the pool incident as my trying to save Arch from an earthquake.

People will tell you chocolate is a relaxant, but I don't believe it. The soothing power evaporated once the Toblerone was no more. I couldn't sleep. I remembered my rebuttal for the *Mountain Journal* was due the next day. If Brian Harrington was not the critic, who could it be? Julian and Sissy were both in high school, which was a little young to be so venomous. The general and Adele seemed sympathetic. Weezie. Maybe she had indeed been sleeping with Philip Miller. The criticism could be her revenge against me. But that didn't feel right either. You never know who your enemies are. I turned on the light and got out pen and paper.

To my anonymous, misspoken critic, the infamous Pierre,

Perhaps I should not say he misspoke himself, like someone working for Richard Nixon. This was someone who really did not like me. His taste buds had deteriorated. After his lobotomy.

Dear misguided son of a bitch,

No, that wouldn't do either. I put down my pen and tried to think positive thoughts. Let go of it. For all the time I had denied, stuffed, repressed, and done other unhealthy things with anger during my marriage to John Richard, I had paid for it with rage during the divorce. Ventilate first. I went into the bathroom, twisted a towel into a rope, bit on it, and screamed. Okay. I splashed cold water on my face and opened the bathroom window.

Again I thought I heard splashing noises out by the pool. It was probably Julian. Whoever it was, I'd be damned before I would try to save two people from drowning in one night.

I plopped down on the bed and frowned at the paper. What was my real worry with this cruel person? Did I really care about him or his silly ideas? I did not. I only cared about preserving my business. This dolt would not get the satisfaction of a response from me.

Dear supportive clients and friends,

Thanks to all of you who have called, visited, or written in response to the spiteful reviews my culinary work has received in the pages of this newspaper.

Thanks to all those who have pointed out the wild inac-
curacies of the menus reported and the cowardliness of the critic
who refuses to sign his name. And thanks especially to all the
clients who have remained loyal and enthusiastic in giving me
your business.

I remain,
Goldy the Caterer

I still had not resolved the name issue, but that was the least of my
problems at the moment. It felt good to get my feelings on paper. I
looked around my room to see if there was any other unfinished business. What the heck, I was on a roll.

The Poe book sat—reproachfully, it seemed to me—on the bureau.
The thought of starting the school project made me immediately sleepy.
But as I snuggled under the covers, I remembered Arch saying that
three other kids in the class were making tapes of telltale heartbeats.
One kid's father, he had earnestly informed me, was even a cardiologist,
and *his* tape was coming with a murmur! It made me wish Edgar Allan
had written something along the lines of "Brutalized in a Baltimore
Bakery," but you can't have everything.

I got up and flipped open to "The Purloined Letter."

Within a paragraph Poe had me by the cerebrum, if not by the
throat. His narrative wove around the insight that the way to thwart a
villain was to think the way he did, and follow those paths of thought
until villainy was undone. This without a major in psychology, no less.
The story was mesmerizing. I went to sleep satisfied that by having read
it, I was on the road to reclaiming good-mother status. Now all we
needed was a school project to go with the story. This, too, I would
have to point out to Arch, would be an undertaking for which his father
would have no interest.

When you have read Poe just before sleep, your dreams are full of
persons identified only as D— and G—, with events happening in
18—. Nevertheless, I awoke refreshed and ready to tackle the custody
crisis.

Scout meowed to go out. I tiptoed down the first set of stairs, disarmed the security system, slipped silently down more stairs, and let Scout out on the patio. The door to Julian's room was closed. Rather than risk having him emerge suddenly and see me standing foolishly by the door, I followed Scout out onto the cold ground.

The early-morning sun cast dark pools of shadow across the landscape. Tops of the far mountains were hazily lit. The near mountains were immersed in dark green, like still, silent hills at the bottom of a lagoon.

I crossed my arms and breathed the cool, piney air. Arch just didn't appreciate me, I thought for the thousandth time. This time of day reminded me, for example, of one of my volunteer jobs at his Montessori school. My job was to go in early and replenish paper, mix new batches of tempera paints, and set up the special projects of the day. The teachers asked all the Morning Moms, as we were called, to check the animal cages first thing, in case any member of the rodent-and-bird menagerie had died during the night. Given my hatred of rodents, I had done this job with some trepidation. Luckily I had avoided the job of animal undertaker. A Morning Mom in my car pool had been confronted with the corpse of a baby gerbil, and it had not been pleasant.

I shivered. Scout had not returned. Perhaps if he had, I would not have experienced the unwelcome and ghastly return of my worst fears as Morning Mom. For there, floating face down in the Farquhars' pool, was Brian Harrington.

25.

I knew it was Harrington from the gray hair floating serenely, like the tendrils of a flower, around his head. I knew him from his clothes. I knew he was dead. What I did not know was who was screaming. The general appeared on the patio in his West Point bathrobe. He grabbed me and shook me, saying, *What is it, what is it?* The screaming voice was mine.

I shouted at the general to call 911 and then Schulz directly. I ran up to check on Arch. He wasn't in his room. I panicked and stumbled back down to the main floor. Arch was in the kitchen, leaning over a bowl of Rice Krispies to check for sound.

"Don't go outside," I said, my voice choking. "Something awful has happened."

He looked up and straightened his glasses to regard me more clearly.

"You look awful, Mom," he said. "What's wrong?"

Before I could answer, one of the phone lines rang. Police, Weezie, who? What would I say? Another of the lines was lit; perhaps General Bo was already talking to the authorities.

"This is George Pettigrew from Three Bears Catering in Denver—"
he began.

"Call later," I said abruptly. "We've got a crisis here."

"Young lady, trademark infringement is a crisis for some of us—"

I hung up. The phone immediately bleated.

"What?" I screamed.

"Stay calm," said Tom Schulz. "General Farquhar just called here
and said you found Harrington. Listen, don't talk to anybody. I want
you to make some excuse this afternoon and come down to the department. I need to talk to you about these people you're living with."

I said I would have to find someone to take care of Arch. But I
would be there, I promised.

"Mom! What is going on?"

But before I could answer, I heard sirens. The fastest thing about
this town was the fire department. I remembered that they always came
when there was a suspected drowning. Unfortunately, I was certain it
was too late for them to help. There was the buzz for the front gate. A
groggy-looking Julian came into the kitchen.

"I overslept. When I went out to do my laps, the general said not to
come out on the patio. What's—"

"Just let me open the gate," I said to both of them. "Then I'll get
back with an explanation."

Julian and Arch exchanged looks. I pressed the button that would
allow admittance to the fire department. How had this happened? I
knew in some corner of my brain that I would have to give a statement,
to tell again, as I had with Philip Miller, what I had seen.

But I had not seen anything. I had come outside and there he was. I
didn't even know why he had tried to swim with his clothes on.

"I want to take you out for breakfast," I announced to Arch. He and
Julian traded another look.

Arch assumed his serious tone. "I'm finishing my breakfast, Mom."

"I want you to come with me into town."

"Whatever."

I went on, "It looks as if Brian Harrington might have drowned in
the Farquhars' pool last night." I looked at Julian. "You can come with
us if you want," I added lamely.

Julian knew I didn't really want him along. He mumbled a regret. Without eating, he left the kitchen.

Arch finished his cereal. As he spooned mouthfuls in, he swung his feet under the table. Was he sympathetic? Sad? I tried to think how I would feel if a neighbor had drowned when I was eleven. Arch's eyes made an arc around the room and settled on me. He was afraid.

"I'm going to go talk to the police," I said, "while you get dressed." My watch said that it was eight o'clock. It was hard to think. What time did the school office open?

"I'll call Elk Park Prep and tell them I'm not coming today either," he said to my unasked question. "But you'll have to write a note tomorrow." He got up, rinsed his cereal bowl, then walked over to me. His large brown eyes held mine. To my surprise he hugged me.

"I'm sorry about Mr. Harrington, Mom. I'm sorry about Dr. Miller, too. And I'm sorry I haven't been doing very well lately."

I held him close, momentarily wishing he was little again so I could rock him. "Arch," I said, "you're doing fine. If you want to go live with your father, that's okay with me." That last part was a lie, but I wanted to give him his freedom.

His voice cracked. "I love you, Mom."

I said, "I know."

After the police questioned me, I couldn't stay in that house. But I didn't know where to go. Finally I left a note saying I was taking Arch to church. I felt awful about Brian Harrington. Seeing a dead body is not something you recover from quickly. Arch and I sat in a back pew and whispered.

I said, "I want to tell you again that I'm sorry I hauled you out of the pool. The thought of you down there in the handcuffs was more than I could take."

"It was just so embarrassing." His voice wavered. We were on dangerous ground. "And right before that we could all hear you fighting with Brian Harrington."

"I wasn't fighting with him!" I whispered fiercely.

"It sure sounded like it."

My spirits took a dive. The last thing I needed was to be a suspect in a murder. I forced myself to think about something else.

I said, "I finished one of those Poe stories last night." I started to tell him about "The Purloined Letter" as a dozen or so people began to straggle into the pews for Wednesday's service of Morning Prayer.

"But what's a project with a letter?" Arch whispered. "It's not cool like a heartbeat or a gold bug."

"We'll think of something," I promised as I opened a prayer book and pointed to where the service began. After what had happened to Philip and now Brian, I was frightened and needed comfort. It seemed like the right thing to do.

I had quit going to church when my ex-husband began making beautiful music with a choirlady. Interestingly, our Episcopal priest had seen nothing wrong with The Jerk's liaison with Miss Vocal Cords. My cynical thought was that The Jerk could afford to give a lot more money to the parish than I could. But that priest eventually had left for greener pastures, and the liaison with the choirwoman had given way to a failed engagement to a high school geometry teacher. John Richard's new girlfriend, Arch had told me, was Presbyterian or nothing. So I had started going back to my old parish. The new priest had welcomed me, and to my relief, had not asked me—as had his predecessor—to cater free luncheons for clergy meetings.

When the service was over and everyone was gone, Arch and I walked quietly down the nave to the intercession table. We knelt and lit a candle for Brian Harrington.

I called Marla from the church office. No answer. I called two of Arch's friends who were not going to summer school. I got recordings saying the kids were at camp. Finally, I called The Jerk and asked the receptionist if Arch could stay with his father for the afternoon. Through the receptionist John Richard relayed the firm message that he was leaving the office at lunchtime. Take Arch back to the Farquhars, I was instructed, and Doctor would be over within the hour.

Reluctantly, I took Arch back. Sam Snead Lane was crammed with cars, both official and unofficial. The policeman in charge told me to go on down to the department to see Investigator Schulz. I left Arch in his room with strict instructions to go with nobody but his father.

Then I zipped over to the *Mountain Journal* office and left off my letter before hightailing it down Interstate 70 to the Sheriff's Department. The van spewed dust when I skidded into the municipal parking lot. With great relief I saw Schulz sitting in the front seat of his Chrysler.

When I climbed out of the van, he got out of his car. He said, "You find someone to take care of Arch?"

"He's at the Farquhars with all kinds of cops around. His father's going to pick him up shortly."

"Goldy, I know I've said this before, but I don't know how I feel about you living in that house."

"Brian Harrington lived next door."

"Uh-huh. Crime lab's already turned up a note in his pocket with my name and number. You wouldn't know how he got that, would you?"

"Brian bared his soul to me last night," I replied, and gave him the details of the party: Weezie's rage, Brian's defensiveness, Philip's cryptic message to Brian before his death, Brian's 911 call. And, I added lamely, my suspicion and anger that Brian had been my anonymous critic in the *Mountain Journal*.

When I had finished talking, Schulz said, "We already have a handful of people who've told us the two of you had a loud argument in the kitchen."

"We did. Before he told me about Philip's warning, I thought he was trying to hit on me."

"Where were you between midnight and five this morning?"

"In bed. Reading, writing, and sleeping."

"Gotta ask, you know. Did you push Brian Harrington into the pool?"

"No, I did not."

He put his arm around me. "You look awfully tired, Miss G. Have you had anything to eat today?"

I laughed. What a question, after the other ones! No, I had not eaten. I couldn't. He asked if he could get me something from the department vending machines. Chips, crackers? I told him I would have a drink of water.

We walked inside the department in silence. The fountain water tasted metallic. But a distant part of my brain cleared. When we sat down on the one couch in the reception area, Schulz asked if I felt better. I replied in the affirmative and looked out the ground-floor window. A clinging haze had turned the sky powder blue.

After a long silence, Schulz said, "I want to talk to you about Julian Teller." More silence. "Real name Julian Harrington."

My heart felt as if it had stopped beating.

"Philip Miller," Schulz began, "was a very interesting fellow. Well-off. Cautious. Hardworking. Wanted to unlock human behavior. Poor guy." He sighed, raised his bushy eyebrows, and puckered his mouth. "The files said Julian turned eighteen this year."

"So?"

"Julian was adopted."

"This isn't news, Tom."

"Miss G. Give me a chance. In some states, if you're adopted, you can find out who your biological parents are when you turn twenty-one. Other states, like Utah, it's eighteen. According to Philip's records, Julian's issue in therapy was finding out who his biological parents were."

"I know this," I said. "Sissy told me."

But I felt distracted, confused. Brian Harrington had shown no interest in Julian, and Julian had been openly hostile to the erstwhile real estate agent on more than one occasion. I said, "But Julian's adoptive parents are in Utah."

"According to Philip Miller's records, they were opposed to him going on this quest."

"So—"

Schulz lifted his jacket flap and took out a folded slip of paper. He said, "Take a look at this. I got them to fax it up to me."

I opened the slippery, shiny sheet of paper. It was from the Bureau of Vital Records, State of Utah. The words and numbers swam before my eyes.

I said, "Who else knows about this?"

Schulz said, "Don't know who does. Don't know who does not."

The paper said that Baby Boy Harrington had been born eighteen years before in Salt Lake City. Parents listed were Brian Harrington and Adele Louise Keely, her name before she married General Farquhar.

26.

Call it intuition. Call it projection.

Call it fear.

I had to see Arch. I felt like a fool leaving him in that house. Too much was happening; too much was coming to light. Someone he trusted could hurt him before John Richard got there. He could be in terrible danger from people who had been around him—Julian, Weezie, Adele, the general. Or whoever had murdered Brian Harrington.

I said to Schulz, "I need to go get Arch."

"But I thought you said your ex had him. I don't want you alone with John Richard Korman."

I thought for a moment. What had John Richard said? Lunchtime. I checked my watch: two o'clock. All the warning signals about John Richard's unreliability went off at once. I bolted for the van.

Schulz trotted to his car and then to the van. He handed me a can of Mace and a house key. He said, "Get Arch and go to my place. Then call me on the mobile line."

I stashed the key and the Mace, then revved the van. I said, "What are you going to do?"

"Call the coroner. See if he has any idea yet how Brian Harrington died."

I waved and spun the van through a corona of dust. Terror gripped my heart so acutely that when I took the Aspen Meadow exit off I-70 I could not remember where I was headed. After our divorce, John Richard had moved into a house in the older section of the country club area. I set the van in that direction and broke speed limits.

The new girlfriend answered the door. She pulled the collar of her bathrobe around her neck and gave me an impassive face.

"What do *you* want?"

"My son. Arch. Is he here?"

She let out an impatient breath.

"I don't know where he is. Or John Richard, either. His secretary told me he left the office twenty minutes ago to get his son. What's going on?"

I did not stay to answer.

When I pulled up at the end of Sam Snead Lane, John Richard's Jeep was sitting outside the Farquhars' security gate. There were no cars in the Farquhars' driveway. There was no sign of Arch. I hated to think what kind of mood my ex-husband would be in if he had been here waiting even for ten minutes. The driver-side door of the Jeep flew open. I gripped the Mace.

I knew better than to get out of the van. I rolled up my window and locked the doors.

"Get out of that damn car!" he shrieked at me. He pounded on the glass. His face was livid, contorted with rage that I knew only too well.

"What do you want?" I screamed back.

"Arch isn't here! Nobody's answering. I've been here for fifteen minutes. If somebody was here, don't you think they'd open the gate? You bitch! You didn't give me *the damn code*! Do you want me to take Arch or not? Because I have better things to do—"

I let go of the Mace and waved him off, then started the van and eased it slowly from the curb. I took care to wait until John Richard had stepped away from my window. Much as I would have liked to run over his feet, that only would have made matters worse.

My fingers trembled when they pressed the correct buttons to get through the gate. John Richard said he had rung the buzzer, to no avail. Where everyone was I did not know.

I took comfort in one thing. Arch knew I worried about him; he knew it only too well. There was one admonition I had drilled into him since the time he could write. It was: Always leave Mom a note. Even if you're just going to play, going to the convenience store, circling the block on your bike. Let Mom know what's up.

I prayed that he had.

The gates opened with their smooth buzz. Talk about magic. John Richard trotted up beside the van. I cautiously rolled down my window.

"Do you want me to stay or not?" he demanded. Heat and anger had made his face shiny with sweat.

"*Not,* thank you," I sang out, and accelerated up the driveway. I don't know why I had called him in the first place. In any given situation The Jerk was more liability than asset.

When I opened the doors to the garage I saw only the general's Range Rover. I eased the van in alongside. When I alighted I noticed something was missing from the walls. I looked around. The snow shovels were in place; ditto the garbage cans, tool shelves, and all the attendant tools. The mulcher, fertilizer, gardening equipment—all were where they belonged. But there was a gap, an empty space usually occupied by . . . I looked around carefully, closed my eyes, and tried to imagine the garage as it usually was.

The camping equipment. I reopened my eyes and scanned the left wall. No tent, no cooker, no backpack. I let out a sigh. Even if running away was his objective, he never would have taken all that paraphernalia. Arch hated to camp.

I pulled the Mace out of the van and went through the door to the kitchen. With my free, trembling hand I used the intercom and heard my voice crackle throughout the house—*Anybody here?*

Sometimes you just feel someone is there. In the meantime, I began a room-to-room search.

I found General Farquhar sitting on the covered porch. He was gazing out at the mountains. In front of him was a bottle of scotch. A half-full glass of whiskey shook ever so slightly in his hand, like a bell that had only just stopped ringing. I put the can of Mace on the table.

"General Bo!" I said, and shook his shoulder. "Are you all right? Where is everybody?"

He shook his head slowly from side to side.

"Gone," he said in a low voice. "All gone."

I came around in front of him and got down on my knees. I wanted to get some visual contact. His face looked terrible. The circles under his eyes were darker than usual, and his air of dejection made him seem older.

"Where's Arch?"

"Gone!"

"Gone where?"

He closed his eyes, whether to get me out of his sight or search his mind I knew not.

"Where is Arch?" I demanded, more loudly this time. I put my hands on his free one. "Where is Julian? Where is Adele?"

He winced. My heart said, *Talk, talk. Please.*

He opened his eyes. Liquid brimmed out.

"Gone, gone, gone," he said.

"Gone *where?*"

He sighed, reached for the scotch, shakily poured some. "The camping equipment is gone." He sipped, then slugged it down. "They didn't leave any written indication of where they were going. There's nothing on the tape. Your ex-husband came, but I didn't let him in. I could see with the scope he didn't have Arch."

I got up. My knees cracked. I was having a hard time not losing my temper.

"Could you please tell me," I said evenly, "what has happened since the police left? Is everyone out shopping?"

"They're not out shopping. Adele said her back was bothering her and she was going to lie down. I went out to look for that damned detonator in the storage area. When the garage door opened I saw Julian headed out with all the camping equipment. I called after him.

He ignored me, started running down the driveway." His forehead was a mass of wrinkles; he shook his head. "It was almost as if he couldn't hear me or he was ignoring me. I kept hunting for the detonator, between the boxes—" He broke off and emptied his glass. "Later I heard the car starting. I looked out and there were Adele and Sissy. They were getting into the Thunderbird."

"Did you see Arch?"

He wrinkled his brow, his eyes unfocused in my direction. "No. Did I call? Yes. Did I ask where they were going, when they would be back? Yes. Did they answer? No. It was the same hurry routine."

"I don't get it."

The general refilled his glass, sipped the scotch, and looked out at the mountains.

"Snap out of it," I ordered. "Did you and Adele have a fight, or what? Where would she go with Sissy?"

He tipped up the glass and drained it. He asked softly, "Where's the detonator?"

"I don't know," I said firmly. I picked up the bottle of scotch and walked out to the kitchen. I tried the intercom again. *Arch? Arch?* My voice echoed through the whole house. There was no note on the desk, the refrigerator, or anywhere else that I could see.

I ran up the stairs. Up, up to the third floor, my heart thudding in my chest the whole time. Arch's room was a wreck. Nothing unusual about that; he had been a neat child until this past year. I went into the bathroom. No note. But his bathing suit was not hanging on the shower curtain rod where he usually left it.

I called Andrea's house. Was Arch over there, had he called, had they seen him? No to all of the above. What was I getting upset about? He went places all the time without telling me. But not the day of a drowning, and especially not when I had told him specifically to stick around. Where would he have gone?

I looked around my room. No note on the mirror. No note on the bed. I allowed myself to collapse on the comforter. I looked at my watch. It had been three hours since I had left him here.

I tried to focus on a mental image of him. My heart said, *Where are you?*

It was then that I looked down at the rug, a warm speckled mix of Easter egg hues—purple, pink, green. The pattern swam before my eyes.

Near the edge of my bed was a playing card. I bent over to look at it. I had not brought a deck of cards when I moved into the Farquhars. Where had it come from? I stared at it in disbelief.

Someone had been with Arch. Someone had been watching him. Someone had prevented him from leaving a note. But like a magician, he had used sleight of hand, distracting his watcher so that he could surreptitiously drop a card, a careless act, apparently unnoticed.

A note. A card. A signal of distress. I lifted the seven of spades from the floor.

27.

I called Schulz. "Arch is gone," I heard my disembodied voice saying. "I can't find him. I'm losing my mind."

He said, "Back up. Begin with when you left the parking lot."

"John Richard couldn't get Arch because the security gate was locked and the general wouldn't let him in. He said he could see through his scope that Arch wasn't with him. Which was true. Tom. I know Arch is in trouble. He left our old danger code."

Schulz was calm. He asked questions: about the card, about Bo, about when everyone had disappeared, about where Julian could go, about Sissy.

He said, "I'll call the girl's parents. If we haven't found him by tonight I'll put out an APB. You call Arch's friends, Adele's friends, see if you can come up with anything." He hesitated. "Something you should know. It's been six hours since they got Harrington's body out of the pool. I had the coroner make a preliminary check for what I suspected, and it looks as if it was there."

I struggled to focus back on the floating body of Brian Harrington. "What?"

"He didn't drown. There wasn't any water in his lungs. But his insides were burned up. My guess would be by cantharidin."

I was numb. I said, "I'll make those calls and drive around to look for Arch. Think I should go talk to Weezie Harrington?"

"We already did. She said Brian was restless last night, told her he was going out for a walk to look at the stars."

"And?"

"That was the last time she saw him. She says. The guys believed her."

"What do you think?"

"I think, Miss Goldy, that you should be careful."

I phoned Weezie. One of the women who had come to be with her answered. Weezie would be grateful for my sympathy. At my request she asked the assembled group about Arch. No, nobody knew where he was, no one had seen him on the street. I said I would be coming over to talk to Weezie myself, if that was okay. It was.

I called Marla. Adele wasn't there and she didn't know where she could be. Marla said, "Should I be worried about my sister? She never worries about me."

"I don't know why she would be with Sissy, who can be pretty hostile sometimes. I really don't even know what's going on," I said truthfully. "If you want to worry about somebody, worry about Arch."

Marla said she would call Arch's friends. I gave her a list of numbers and asked her to drive over by our old house and check to see if any of the neighbors had seen him.

"I know he loves you, Goldy. He wouldn't run away."

A rock formed in my throat. I whispered, "Sure," and signed off.

I steeled myself and called John Richard.

He said, "*Now* what?"

I said, "Arch is missing. I need you to get a new attitude and help out."

He said, "Whose fault is this?"

I hung up.

The general responded with a nod when I said I was going to ask Weezie some questions and look for Arch. I asked him again if he had any idea where everyone had gone. He shook his head. I picked up the Mace. He said, "An ambush."

The van whined all the way down the driveway. I decided to do a street-by-street search for Arch in Meadowview before showing up at the Harrington house. Even if I did not find him, at least it would make me feel that I was working on it.

The sky, covered with pearly haze most of the day, now boiled with dark clouds. Here and there gray wisps of moisture hung over the mountains. If Arch was with Julian, they both would soon be soaked. If Arch was with Sissy . . . but why would he be with Sissy?

I rolled down my window. As if on cue, raindrops pelted the windshield. Thunder rolled like gunfire in the distance. I called Arch's name as I chugged in first gear along Sam Snead Lane, Arnold Palmer Avenue, Gary Player Parkway.

Nothing. There were not even any playing children I could ask; they'd all been driven in by the rain. I headed back to Weezie's.

I parked the van behind the Audis, Buick Rivieras, and Lincoln Continentals lining the Harrington driveway. The cars belonged to women, I discovered when I went inside, who knew the Harringtons from the athletic club and the country club. They cooed, hugged, and whispered to Weezie and each other. They were happy to see me, but puzzled. One woman asked, "Are you a friend of Weezie's?"

I swallowed an angry response. A svelte brunette who had been sitting across from Weezie on a leather recliner asked us if we wanted anything. I said, "Coffee," to be rid of her, plopped into her empty spot, and mumbled my condolences.

Weezie raised bloodshot eyes. Her mane of silver-blond hair was wildly askew. She said, "Thanks. Did you find Arch?"

"No, but people are looking, and I'm going to keep searching when I leave here. Are you sure you never saw him this afternoon?"

"Not once. This has been a nightmare. I have to believe . . ." Her voice broke. "I have to believe there was a reason for his life. He was a good person." Her eyes searched mine. "Wasn't he?"

"He was," I said without hesitation. "He did lots of good things in the community. And I know he adored you. Very much."

I didn't know if she knew I was lying, but she started crying anyway. A startled face appeared at the kitchen door: What had I said to cause such an outburst? I waved the person off and left the recliner to sit next to Weezie.

I said, "It's okay," and patted her back.

"He didn't love me," she sobbed.

"Sure he did, yes he did, he told me so himself."

"He did?" She sniffed and opened the red eyes wide at me. "When?"

I stalled. I said, "Let's see, let me think. When did he tell me he loved you. Why, uh, during that party last night, when he helped me with the dessert."

"I thought I heard you two arguing up there."

"Oh no, it was just something about the dessert. You know." As white lies went, it didn't sound too bad.

Weezie snorted and said, "Did he tell you where he was going after we went to bed? Did he say he was going to meet somebody?"

"Gee, no, I don't think so. No, definitely not. Probably he had insomnia, Weezie. I have it myself."

"And do you go swimming to get rid of it?"

"Well, no, that never occurred to me. . . ."

She burst out crying again.

"He was jealous," she said between sobs. Her eyes narrowed in a glare of accusation. "He thought I was seeing Philip Miller," here she lowered her voice, "that I was sleeping with him. That was a lie, a grotesque rumor."

"It's a small town," I said, again trying to sound consoling. "You know how people talk."

She was not listening to me. Her head was in her hands. "I just wanted him to love me," she said fiercely. "That was all I wanted."

I felt the molecules in my hand draw back, draw away from Weezie as my mind began to spin. I had learned something from "The Purloined

Letter." The narrowed possibilities had been before me all along. I murmured something about needing to go look for Arch and made my exit.

Philip had known Brian's life had been in danger. He had started to tell me about it. He had wanted my help, and that was why he had called me before the Elk Park Prep brunch. It was this that someone had heard on the phone. This that had prompted the incident in the Aspen Meadow Café.

I want to talk to you about food, Philip had said to me.

But why? Because I was the one who was researching the question, *Can you make someone love you?*

They had found Spanish fly in Philip's briefcase after the accident. The accident that was not an accident.

I rushed back to the Farquhars and took the Mace inside with me. There was something I had to find, something I had seen only once. I came through the security gate and crept around the house. The general had fallen asleep on the deck with his mouth open. His loud, drunken snore reverberated through air cooled by the late shower. I put one of the crocheted afghans over him and tiptoed into the study.

Where would it be? I searched through drawers. The clock in the study clicked the minutes away. I hauled out a pile of papers and sifted through them. Nothing. The general's file cabinet was next. The first drawer held everything from *Army* to *Explosives: Conventional, History of, New,* through *Intelligence, Domestic, Foreign.* The first file in the next drawer was given over to *IRA* and the last was half an inch of papers on *Qaddafi, Muammar.* The last drawer started off *Radicals* and ended with *War.* Now that was a cheerful thought. I slammed the drawers shut, then had an idea. *Intelligence, Domestic.* The file nearly fell through my hands. Within a minute I held the piece of mail I had been hunting. I put it on top of the pile from the desk and sat down.

The envelope had been addressed to Julian. That was what had thrown me off.

Inside was his birth certificate.

Why was it in the study, concealed in a file? I put the certificate back in the envelope and tapped it with my finger. Because. Because unknown to the Bureau of Vital Records, and unknown to Julian, someone else had been the first one to do the seeking.

I heard a small noise behind me. I looked up. My hands covered the address on the envelope. The ink seemed to burn through my fingertips.

Adele gave me a polite, inquiring look. She said, "Did you find what you were looking for?"

28.

I bluffed. "Actually, no," I said with a smile I hoped was both apologetic and casual. I had to get information from her, had to find out about Julian's past and her own. And how much other people knew, like the general. I had to stall until Bo woke up. I also knew that in a potentially dangerous situation like this, I had to call Schulz.

I said, "Arch is missing. Have you seen him?"

She shook her head and pulled her mouth into an O of surprise. "No . . . where could he be?"

"I've looked all over the neighborhood, and Marla is calling his friends. Did you see him go out with Julian? The general doesn't seem to know anything."

"Well, neither do I. I didn't see him go out with Julian, but I do need to talk to you about that. Do you know *when* Arch left? Was it after the police finally drove off? I went to lie down for a while, it was all so trying." She opened her eyes wide. "The police had quite a few questions about your argument with Brian Harrington last night."

I said, "I didn't kill him." I took a deep breath. "My main concern is the whereabouts of Arch."

"What in Bo's study would tell you where Arch is?"

I thought wildly. "Well . . . I'm looking for some cards. They were Arch's. Sometimes he tricks me . . . you know how he is. So if this is a trick, I need to play along. You know?" As I got up I pushed a box of pencils onto the floor with my left hand. With my right I moved some papers from the bottom of the pile to the top before setting the whole pile down. I leaned over to gather the pencils.

"Cards?" said Adele. "I don't know. Perhaps he left them in the kitchen. Shall we look?"

I stood up. "Sure." I felt in my right pocket and fingered the seven of spades. This would be my only chance to call Schulz undetected. I had to think of a way to pull this one out. What made it all worse was that I wasn't quite sure what was going on. Or who the enemy was.

"No cards here, I'm afraid," Adele said. She patted through the piles of bills, gardening catalogs, and manila envelopes in the kitchen desk drawers.

I slipped the card from my pocket into the knife drawer. "Oh, my goodness, look here," I said. "He wanted to leave it where I would find it. Now we need to call the wizard."

"I beg your pardon?" She stared at the card in my palm.

"Indulge me, Adele, maybe this is it. I promised Arch I would practice, and maybe this will help out," I said as I punched in the buttons for Schulz's number and prayed that he would be at his desk.

"Schulz." His voice.

Adele said, "May I ask *whom* you are calling? Are you calling Weezie? Please give me the phone."

I held up one finger and said, "Is the wizard there, please?"

"Oh, jeez, Goldy, don't make me do this, what the hell is going on? Did you find Arch?"

I said again, more merrily, "Is the wizard there, please?"

He sighed. He began, "Clubs, diamonds, spades—"

"May I speak to him, please?"

"Okay," said Schulz, "so spades? Now what? Let's see, ace, king, queen, jack, ten, nine, eight, seven—"

"Hold the line, please."

Before I could do anything, Adele took the phone from my hand and listened. She looked at the receiver and then at the card. She said, "No, thank you." Then she shrugged. She tap-stepped across the kitchen floor and hung up the phone.

"Well?" I demanded. "Did he know it was the seven of spades?"

"I have no idea," she said. "It was a man, and he said, 'Do you want me to come over?' so I said I didn't and that was that."

Adele straightened up. She flicked one piece of lint off the beige cashmere sweater and another off the matching slacks. "I'm so tired, let's sit down," she said as she tap-stepped over the yellow Italian tile toward the living room. "I need to talk to you about Julian. He's taken the camping equipment and gone off somewhere." She paused by the pink sofa and looked around, apparently confused. She said, "Where's Bo?"

This is what quicksand feels like, I thought. Nothing to hold on to and sinking deeper by the minute. But I had to keep Adele talking, no matter what.

I said, "Asleep on the porch. Had a bit too much to drink, I think."

She shook her head and leaned awkwardly against the back of the sofa. "God! What's happening? Brian drowned, and now, God knows." She eyed me. I had come up beside her. We stood in silence, both unwilling to commit to speaking freely, much less to sitting down.

"You look exhausted," she said. "Have you had anything to eat today?"

Schulz's question. I said, "No."

"Oh, Goldy. You of all people. You should have something to keep you going."

A swell of fatigue made me shiver. I realized I had even missed my daily injection of espresso. All normal patterns of living had been disrupted by the discovery of Brian Harrington's corpse.

I had to keep her talking. Had to make her feel I knew something, but perhaps not everything. I said, "Want coffee?" She shook her head. "I'll be right back." I made myself a double espresso and came back out to the living room, where Adele had settled into one of the lime-green damask chairs. I sat on the pink sofa, sipped, and waited. From the porch came the undulating noise of the general's snores.

Finally Adele said, "Sissy and I went looking for Julian. He was so upset when the police were here. He talked to Arch for a long time. I just assumed they had gone off together." She took a deep breath. "I'm afraid Julian may have found some very distressing correspondence and asked Weezie Harrington about it. This may have had the most dire consequences."

I said, "Where do you think Julian could have gone after reading this correspondence?"

"To the Harringtons, perhaps. Oh, it's such a long story—"

"Why to the Harringtons?"

We both stopped talking at once. There was a long silence while we looked at each other.

I said, "Do you want to talk?"

Someone buzzed the security gate.

"Julian!" I said with false enthusiasm and leaped up to check the camera, press the admittance button, and open the front door. Schulz's car ascended the driveway. I darted back to the study to make sure the general was still asleep. He was. But the Mace was gone.

"You okay?" Schulz asked when he came through the door. "The seven of spades a trick or not?"

"Just chatting with Adele. We think the general is asleep," I said with a false sprightliness that hopefully warned him, *Be careful*. Then I introduced him to Adele.

She pulled herself up into a regal stance, limped over to take his hand, and said, "Can we get you something?"

Schulz regarded me: *Is this some kind of game?* I said, "Go on in and sit down with Adele. I'll bring you some coffee." I made him a double espresso. It was fast and I wanted him awake so he could help me look for Arch. Also, I did not trust anything else one might eat in this house.

When I handed him his cup, I said, "Adele was just telling me she thinks Julian might have seen correspondence that put Brian Harrington in danger."

Schulz's eyes looped around the room. "Oh yeah?" he said. "What was that?"

Adele looked from one to the other of us.

She said, "You can never go back. You think you can, but you can't. That's what the general thought with all his experimenting, but Philip Miller just thought he was crazy. I knew he had it in for him, and he wanted so badly to go back. . . ."

Schulz raised his coppery eyebrows at Adele. He said, "Go back where?"

She said nothing, only glared at him, as if she were waiting for his own response to the question. But all he did was sip the coffee. I could hear the clock ticking the minutes away. My hands itched with anxiety for Arch. If the general had harmed Philip Miller, then why had Philip warned *Brian Harrington*? The coffee was not clarifying my mind.

Finally I said, "Perhaps you are as concerned about your son as I am about mine."

Her eyelids flickered in appraising me.

She said, "You can't imagine what I've been through."

I nodded. Schulz's gaze traveled from one to the other of us.

He said, "Why don't you tell us? We're especially interested in the last couple of weeks."

Adele ignored him. "You know," she said to me, "a death is like a divorce in many ways. You are left alone, whether you like it or not. When you're divorced, you can't express your sadness. When you're widowed, it's not considered proper to express . . . anger. And in either case, the financial burdens are tremendous."

I said, "You seem to have weathered the financial part okay."

"Oh, you think so?" Adele raised her thin eyebrows at me, then flicked more invisible lint from the beige sweater. "I've seen the way men eye Sissy for her body. Imagine being sized up for your dollars." She cleared her throat. "At least in Sissy's case, when men tell her she's beautiful, they're not lying."

"Did Brian Harrington say you were beautiful?"

She paused. She said, "Many times."

I looked over at Schulz. His face had gone pale and was filmy with sweat. He excused himself quietly. Adele dismissed him with a wave.

I said, "Was this before or after he was married to Weezie?"

She looked at me, the corners of her mouth turned down. Water was running in the hall bathroom.

She said, "Both."

I said, "Did he know Julian was his son?"

Her face and composure crumpled. She shuddered, rubbed her cheeks and pulled herself together.

She said, "He knew so little. There were things he chose not to know. He had a single purpose. To get the woman with the money or land to fall in love with him. He did it with Weezie and he did it with me." As tears leaked from the edges of her eyes, she wiped them off with her index finger.

"You don't need to talk," I said. In fact, I wondered why she was talking about this to me at all. Where was Schulz? Was he in danger from the general?

"Yes I do," Adele was saying. "It was a terrible rejection. Rejection! My God, that sounds like the way we used to talk in adolescence. I was thirty-one when I was with Brian. I felt all my anger, all my grief dissipate in that time with him. You hear about affairs. You think, oh, illicit sex." She regarded me with disgust. "Sex is incidental." She looked wistfully at the mantelpiece that had held the Waterford vase destroyed in the garden-explosion. "It's being loved that we all want." She sighed with a kind of moan. "Brian loved me. He wrapped me in love. All my anger, my grief over losing my first husband dissipated. And do you know what? I didn't even feel guilty. I even thought Marcus Keely had had his heart attack so I could find Brian. My true love. Ha!" She cackled.

My gastrointestinal tract was doing flip-flops. I put it down to caffeine on an empty stomach. I wanted to get this over with, to untangle the past and find out what was going on in the present.

I said, "You got pregnant."

Her eyes wandered back to me. "Yes. After I'd invested in the Meadowview area of Aspen Meadow Country Club. I was the first one to buy a two-acre homesite, and Brian was the second, buying the parcel right next to mine. Forever together, he'd said. He also said he wanted to get the ball rolling for the business. He wanted to be able to say,

We've had some sales but there are a few parcels left. I kept thinking he would ask me to marry him. . . . He said he wasn't ready.

"When I was four months along and unable to hide the pregnancy any longer, I left and went down to Utah. To collect pottery and whatnot," she said with another hideous laugh and wave. "But really it was to have a baby and arrange a private adoption in Bluff. I found out about a Navajo woman who had married an Anglo. The Anglo was opening a candy store. They had been unable to have children. When you have money," she said with a sniff, "you can arrange adoptions any way you want."

I nodded and looked around. I had not seen Schulz for a while and was worried. Perhaps the general was awake. But Schulz could take care of himself; I couldn't risk Adele shutting down on me. I stayed put.

"If you arranged to have the adoption done," I said, still preoccupied with thoughts of Schulz, "why did you arrange to have it undone?"

"It fell into place. I thought, again foolishly, that it was for a reason. Bo's adoration embarrassed me terribly. I hated Washington and was all too glad to move out here once the Pentagon forced Bo's retirement. I had the land; I'd never sold it. And then I felt such a strong pull, to see Brian again, to live next door . . . and I thought maybe if I could get Julian here, that we could—" She broke off, lost in reverie.

"You were the one who said you can't go back."

"I know," she said, her voice shrill, "don't I? So much work, so many preparations. Arranging the scholarship for Julian when I found out that the boarding department at Elk Park Prep was about to close down. Building this house next to Brian and that inane woman, Weezie!" She spat out the name, then softened. "And Julian. God, Julian." She broke off then and stared at the fireplace in a way that seemed to signal the end of the conversation.

I remembered her words: *Whatever you do for your children, they don't appreciate you.*

And then it all fell into place. A wave of cold fear swept over me. She was the one. I thought I'd needed her information to finger Weezie or the general or even Sissy. I was wrong.

I said, "You tried to seduce Brian again, didn't you? By the pool. I heard you splashing around. But he showed an unhealthy sexual attraction for Sissy instead. That must have made you furious. The general loved you, but it wasn't enough. And . . . you're the one who started the rumor about Weezie sleeping with Philip Miller. Yes?"

She sucked in a sob and pursed her lips, then opened reddened eyes and nodded. Proudly, I thought. And then the full force of what she could have done struck me. I thought of the calendar in Philip's office. She had had one of the last appointments with him.

I said, "You went to see Philip Miller. Because Julian was living with you and having problems, Philip had called you. He must have wanted to see you and the general together." She did not move. I wasn't even sure she was listening. "But you went alone, because of what you were afraid would come out. Philip told you Julian wanted to research who his biological parents were. You must have told him the truth."

Her eyes blazed. "Yes, I told Philip Miller the truth," she said fiercely. "I didn't want to, but he just kept egging me on with all his questions, just like you are now. How did we come to have Julian in our house? he wanted to know. How were we relating to him? How did he *think* I was going to relate to my own son whom I hadn't seen since birth?" Her face contorted. "And I said the biological father, Brian Harrington, had shown no interest in his son. I said I wanted to kill Brian Harrington. I had learned about getting things on the black market from Bo. I'd gotten Spanish fly and I was going to use it, because so many women had wanted Brian to love them. It would serve him right."

"But Philip took it from you—"

"Yes, he took it! He threatened to call the police right away if I didn't give it to him. Said I needed help, and that he was going to have to notify Brian that his life was in danger." She smiled. "But he didn't get my whole supply of Spanish fly. And the black market wasn't the only thing I'd learned from Bo. After I'd seen Philip Miller, later that afternoon, I created a distraction. Pretended I'd left my cane in his office. The receptionist went to look for it and I memorized Miller's calendar. I knew I'd have to act quickly before he turned me in. The eye doctor appointment was perfect."

The abdominal pains in my stomach had turned to cramps. I felt hot. How I wanted this conversation to be over. How I wanted Schulz to come back. And most of all, how I wanted to know where Arch was, to be assured that he was all right.

Adele was talking. I struggled to focus on her voice.

"I'd just had the glaucoma test myself, so I knew they used anesthetic. And Bo had told me all about peroxide torture when he was researching sabotage. There are more nerve endings in the eye than anywhere else in the body. The more nerve endings, the more pain. Put peroxide on those nerve endings, and you're going to do a lot of damage. Very quickly."

I whispered, "How'd you do it?"

"I went into the eye doctor right after I saw Philip's calendar. Pretended I was there to raise money for the pool, while I took the saline rinse bottle from beside the ultrasound machine. Right under their noses! Then I came home and emptied the saline rinse bottle and put in Julian's peroxide. I called the headmaster and insisted that Philip be the one to bring more decals, that no one else could do it but Philip Miller, especially if they wanted me to give the last twenty thousand for the pool." She cackled. "So right after his eye appointment, he'd have to drive out to the school, then drive back to town. I thought with any luck he would die on that road. I couldn't afford for him to talk to anybody, least of all Brian Harrington or you. You see, he wanted to warn you about living here. That's why he called so early that morning. He thought he was being so careful, saying to you, Not on the phone!"

I said, "So you were the one listening in on my calls. Then you told the general what was going on in my life." She didn't respond. I said, "You never gave up on Brian."

She sniffed and moved her hands in a nervous motion. Then she looked at me, as if she were searching for something. She said, "Oh, yes I did. At that anniversary party, when he kept on and on with Sissy, I knew it was over."

"How did you get him to take Spanish fly?"

She sighed, fluttered her hands again. "I told him to come back after the party. I wanted to invest in Flicker Ridge. I smoothed cantharidin on top of his fudge. He died for chocolate!" She laughed. A wave of nausea swept over me. "Your son saw us the last time we were together. That's why I'm sorry to say that he's going to drown, too."

I screamed, "Where's Arch?"

"Where you won't be able to save him this time."

I was going to throw up. I bolted for the hall bathroom. But I could hear Schulz in there. He was sick. I couldn't listen to it. I held my stomach and lurched back to the living room.

"What have you done?" I yelled at her.

She said calmly, "The only thing I could be sure you would ever eat or drink was that damn espresso. So I put Spanish fly in your coffee can. I'm sorry, Goldy. You and the policeman should be dead in an hour."

29.

I lunged toward her. "You bitch!" I screamed. "Where's my son?"

Just before my hands reached Adele's neck she grabbed her cane and whacked me across the stomach. I doubled over with pain. My stomach heaved. The cane lashed my back. The living room blurred as I crash-landed on the floor. Pain surged through my body. I vomited on the Oriental rug.

Adele stood over me and caned my arm. She screeched, "Get up!"

It was so hard. Everything hurt: my stomach, my back, my innards.

"Move!" she yelled. She flailed at my legs with the cane. "Get down to that bathroom!"

I moved. "Tom!" I cried as I limped, furious at my physical weakness. "Tom! Bo! Help me!"

"Shut up!" said Adele as she prodded my calves. "Bo can't hear you. I put Valium in his scotch. And your policeman friend may be dead. One hopes."

Desperately, I whirled to attack her. But she caught me across the shoulders with the cane. Pain shot through my body. I fell against the wall outside the bathroom. She poked the bathroom door open.

I peered in. Tom was on the floor. His big body was curled tightly in the fetal position. Prods from Adele elicited a few moans. He rolled over and lifted his face. It was pallid, an awful yellow. His eyes beseeched me.

"Get in there!" howled Adele as she cracked me across the ankles. The woman was strong. I lost my balance and put my hands out to avoid hitting my head on the tile floor.

Adele hovered overhead, a fuzzy-faced helicopter. "You just don't understand," she said as she closed the door. I heard her wedge something under the knob and then tap-step away.

I turned to Schulz. His eyes were glazed with pain.

He whispered, "I think I'm going to die."

"You're not," I told him with as much firmness as I could muster. Fire consumed my insides. The poison had to be diluted with water immediately, I knew that. I cupped my hand under the faucet and brought handful after handful of water to Schulz's mouth, then to mine. Ten, twenty, thirty handfuls of water. My body burned with pain. In some distant part of my brain I heard Adele slam a door. She was leaving the house. Leaving us to die. Who would be blamed? The general? Me? Pierre the critic would have a field day with this one.

I swallowed more water, squeezed my eyes shut, and summoned a mental picture of Arch. I had to find him. I had to. Find, find, find. I repeated this mantra while I got down on my hands and knees and peered under the bathroom door.

Bathroom doors can't be locked from the outside. To keep us in, Adele had anchored the general's portable door jam under the knob. I could just see the rubber end of the extended pole on the wooden hallway floor. It was no comfort to think her fingerprints might be on the top of the jam.

I closed my eyes and saw Arch. I tried to think about what the general had told me about the door jam. The wedged pole made it impossible for an intruder to push a door open. The trick, the general had said, was to put the jam under a door that opened toward you.

I rolled over. I was not going to try to push the bathroom door out.

It was constructed to open inward, so it would not swing out to hit anyone passing in the hall.

"I just wouldn't understand, huh?" I said weakly as I delicately turned the knob, pulled on the door, and heard the jam clatter on the hall floor. "I don't think so."

I hauled up on my elbows, whispered a prayer that Schulz, who was groaning weakly, would understand why I was abandoning him, and dragged myself down the hallway. Spasms of nausea tore through my body. I crawled toward the garage. Twice on my way I had to stop to be sick.

I had thought Adele was my friend. I had wanted it. I had imagined we were confidantes. And now I was paying the price of my own self-deception, with the poisonous drug mistakenly taken when you tried to make people love you.

I kept my head up as I crawled. I visualized ice, coolness, anything to get my mind off of what was really happening inside my abdomen. I visualized Arch.

The garage door was open. I dragged my body across the gritty floor. Each movement was a struggle, getting into the van, hauling myself up, opening the glove compartment. My hand closed around my trusty safety kit. I prayed thanks and swallowed some ipecac.

When I had made my torturous way back to the bathroom I asked Schulz to try to get up on his elbows. I cradled his head under my elbow. His face was awash in sweat.

Before he would take the ipecac, he murmured, "If I die, I want you to know how I feel about you."

"I know how you feel about me. Swallow."

He did. I was sick into the toilet and then I held him around the torso while he was sick. It didn't take long, but it was horrible. If Schulz and I could go through this together, we could weather anything. I stood up shakily, then helped him to his feet.

"I'm going to look for Arch," I said once I had rinsed my mouth out with tap water.

"The heck you say," he said feebly. He grasped the side of the marble basin and tried to steady himself. "I'm calling the department. Get help to track down Adele Farquhar. Get a medic here for you, me, and the general."

I didn't say anything. I was shaky but okay, and there was no time to wait for the Furman County Sheriff's Department to muster itself up to Aspen Meadow. I needed more water, and then I was going to look for Arch, whether Tom Schulz liked it or not.

I limped shakily out to the porch. Bo's face was extremely pale. His snores sounded like a small propeller-plane engine. I shook his shoulder. Nothing. The automatic timer flicked on the pool lights. It was 9:00 P.M. The murky, phosphorescent half-spheres on the walls of the empty pool cast an eerie pall across the patio. I heard Schulz wobble to the kitchen, then murmur into the phone. I moved slowly to the living room and picked up a bottle of Perrier from the bar. I didn't have any weapons, so I threw the general's toolbox into the van. Wrenches and Perrier: yuppie defense. I roared down the driveway.

Where could Arch be? Why had Adele seemed so sure he would die tonight? *Where you won't be able to save him this time.*

The pool.

I peeled off in the direction of Elk Park Prep.

I was so used to that road I could whip around its curves and drink bottled water at the same time. The Perrier was a necessity to help dissipate whatever poison lingered in my system. I knew from reading about Spanish fly that some people became much sicker than others, and it didn't necessarily depend on the dose. This would explain why Schulz had been sick before me. I shook my head from side to side. My brain felt woozy. I ordered myself to sharpen up. My sensibilities might be the only thing to save Arch.

Luckily, some vestige of mental sharpness kicked in just when the van careened around the last curve and came up on the school entrance. I had to slam on the brakes to avoid smashing into the electrified gate.

I cursed mightily and stepped gingerly out of the van. The gate was armed and the stone wall was too high to scale. I wished every flower behind Elk Park Prep's deer-proof gate would burn in hell or be eaten by a marauding herd of wild animals.

I stared at the electrified wires. I couldn't risk touching it: I had heard too many stories of electric shock throwing unsuspecting humans for first-and-ten yardage. But I had to get through. Short of breaking the power circuit . . . But why break it? Why not keep it? I walked back to the van and got the general's wire cutters and my jumper cables.

I hustled back to the gate and began to attach the jumper cables to the wire. I thought that I would have given a year's supply of unsalted butter for the presence of a rocket scientist. Ten years' worth for an electrical engineer.

I clipped the wire and didn't die. Hallelujah. I cut savagely at the fence, tore out the hole I'd made, and began to run up to the school. I didn't want them—whoever they were—to hear me coming.

There were no infrared security lights here to detect human approach. Why should there be? They had electricity to keep Bambi out. Still, the shadows of trees cast long, fingered shadows across the road and made my heart pound in my chest. Voices carried through the night air from the pool site. Every fifteen yards up the driveway, short lanterns on poles shed disks of yellow light. Poppies and bluebells waved in the night breeze like fairy-sentries on their mounds. I focused straight ahead and walked fast until I was at the wire fence surrounding the construction area.

Another damn fence.

I knew it was six feet exactly, and that it was required by building code when a pool was under construction. If you wanted to get in easily, you had to go through the gate, now closed and locked. Adele had somehow weaseled the code out of the construction workers, because I could see Arch. I could hear him splashing and calling to someone who was holding a flashlight and either reading or writing in a notebook next to the gate. But who was it? There was no car in the parking lot. The voice I could hear was female. If Adele was around, she was not visible. I listened and then recognized the voice: Sissy.

Arch had known something was wrong. Why was he playing? Or was he?

On the far side of the pool area behind the newly installed diving board, a small mountain of dirt bordered the concrete deck. The chain-link fence ran behind the dirt pile. On that side, the area behind the fence fell away sharply. I could hide behind that ridge, but what good would it do me? I had to get through the chain-link fence. Arch had signaled he was in trouble. Maybe Sissy had some kind of weapon. I didn't want to find out by feeling it against my skull.

I scanned the school grounds. The dark silhouette of the old hotel building rose ominously over the parking lots. Here and there in the darkness, floodlights shed tents of light. The tall evergreens that peppered the campus whooshed in the night wind.

I crouched like an Indian and stumbled over to behind the fence. From where I was hidden, I could not see Arch. I gripped the wire cutters and began to clip. Arch must have been over by Sissy. Their voices were somewhat distant. They began to argue. "You . . . you . . ." Arch was saying. I couldn't make the rest of it out.

Then she said sharply, loudly, the way you do when you want to change the subject, "Forget about it! You *have* to do this thing with the manacles! Adele doesn't want another messed-up magic trick in her pool!"

Arch shrieked, "I don't want to! My mom wouldn't want me—"

"Shut up, scaredy-cat. Besides, if you don't do it, Adele's going to fire your mother! Is that what you want?"

I ran through the soft dirt to where I could see them. Dim light from a distant floodlamp cast long, thin shadows across the concrete deck. Sissy leaned over and appeared to be rummaging in a bag. Her notebook was on the ground, papers askew. Did she have a weapon? I couldn't tell. Arch had his back to her. He put his hands behind him. Sissy took out a stick and two pieces of rope. My heart stopped.

The Chinese manacles. Arch's favorite trick. The magician appears to be shackled at the wrists with the ropes, which are threaded back through the tube and drawn tight by one or more assistants. The trick is that a tiny piece of string attaches the ropes. When the trick is done right, the assistant who puts the magician into the shackle breaks the string by appearing to pull the ropes taut. Sissy accompanied the cuffed Arch over to the diving board.

I clawed madly at the dirt to get back around to the fence. Blood beat in my ears. I sent clods of soil flying. *God, help me,* I begged as I cut as fast as I could. I could not imagine what Adele had used to replace the string inside the manacles.

"I think you need to be over here next to me while I'm doing this," came Arch's voice, much closer now. He must have been on the diving board. Sissy said something indistinguishable. "Okay!" cried Arch. "You pull it tight and then I'll go off the board. Then it'll look like I get out of them underwater."

"Oh, all right," came Sissy's voice.

I clipped the last two wires and ripped out the hunk of fence just as a splash erupted from the pool. Seconds ticked off in my head—*one, two, three, four, five*—as I tore up the dirt mound behind the diving board. Sissy, fully clothed, was still standing on the board. I leaped up on the board and pushed her into the water. She shrieked before splashing in.

Arch's head emerged from the water. He sputtered and coughed. Yelled, "I can't seem to get them off!" His voice was full of panic.

The water was like ink. I jumped away from the board and Arch's voice. The cold was a shock. Once in the water, I couldn't see a thing. Fear seized my body. Arch was thrashing nearby. Sissy was yelling, "Who is it?" but I had no intention of answering. I swam to where I thought Arch was. With my arms rigid in front of me, I dove. I was hoping to reach Arch, but only nicked the bottom of the pool. I brought my legs to the pool floor and pushed upward. Sissy had scrambled out of the pool. I heard her voice but could not see her. A few feet behind me, Arch surfaced and yelped. I lunged for him.

"It's me, it's me, it's me!" I screamed when I had hold of one of his arms.

He was screaming and thrashing in a complete panic. "Mom!" he sobbed. "Mom! I can't get out of these things!"

I put my arm across his chest. Treading water madly, I pushed up on his head and shoulders so they were above the water. With his arms locked in the handcuffs, Arch's body was heavy, hard to grip. He thrashed against the constraints and gagged helplessly on the water.

"Hold still! Stop moving!" I yelled. The water raged with his kicking and jerking. I couldn't hold on to him. My hair fell like cold seaweed over my eyes and I was blinded. A sudden unwanted memory of being caught by the undertow on the Jersey shore rolled over me. The dark water had sucked me down like a muscled giant, and I had had the very clear thought, at age eleven, that I was about to die.

My lungs burned as I heaved up again and caught Arch under his armpits. *Come on, honey, come on,* I sent my thoughts to him the way I had prayed in childbirth. *If we can just get through the next five minutes,* I thought, *if we can just get through . . .*

His slippery body quieted. His cough was still ragged, but he had stopped fighting the water so hard. I began a one-armed crawl to the side. Slowly, slowly, I kicked and pulled and fought off sheer panic. My eyes burned. I swallowed the heavily chlorinated water. I couldn't see the pool's edge, but in a minute my head cracked the cement.

"Okay, carefully, carefully," I said to Arch. He shook loose from me, his hands still bound, and walked soddenly up the submerged concrete steps.

"Goldy, it's you!" said an astonished, shivering Sissy. "What happened in there? Did you push me in? What happened to Arch?"

I glanced around at my son. Despite the burn from the chlorine, my eyes were growing accustomed to the darkness. He had crouched down to bring his hands close to his feet. Savagely, he tromped on the bamboo pole with its ropes that pinned his wrists. Within a moment the bamboo broke and he wriggled his arms free.

Sissy's hands were empty. No weapon. "Get a towel," I ordered her, unwilling for the moment to accuse her of attempted murder or being an accessory thereto. Her face puzzled, she silently handed me a couple of small towels. I wrapped both of them around Arch, who was sniffling hard and coughing.

"Mom, I was trying to get away from her! I thought if I could get out of the manacles quickly, I'd be able to run away!"

"It's okay, Arch, it's okay." I grabbed a tarpaulin that was covering some pipes, then picked up one of the pipes. I looked around to where Sissy had been sitting. No weapon there, either—nothing but the bag, her flashlight, and her school notebook.

"Let's all get back to the van," I said. I reached the long-handled flashlight before Sissy could get it. "I don't want to be here if Adele comes back. And don't touch me or Arch," I warned Sissy fiercely as I brandished the pipe and the flashlight. She gaped at me.

Arch said, "But, Mom, you have to look at her notebook! You have to—"

"What we have to do is get out of here," I said curtly. Sissy marched sulkily in front of us. When we were all in the van I turned the heat to high and handed Arch the pipe and flashlight. He knew what to do with them if he needed to. Greeted by a rush of cool air from a cold engine, I turned to Sissy as we lurched forward.

"You want to tell me why you're here?"

"I was taking care of Arch," she whined. "Just until Adele got back with you. I don't know what happened to her." She added, "She was paying me to keep him there."

"Did that include drowning him?"

"No!" she exclaimed. "Of course not! Adele gave me the bag with the tricks and just told me to make sure he practiced with the Chinese manacles tonight. That's all."

"And what about pushing me into the glass case at the café? Did she pay you for that, too, you little bitch?"

Sissy snorted. "I wasn't trying to hurt you!" she protested. "I was just supposed to warn you off. She's Julian's mother! She told me! She could do so much for him financially, for his future and everything. She said you were screwing it up!"

I heard Arch gasp and cough upon hearing about Julian's parentage.

"And yes," Sissy was saying, "she paid me to push you. She said it would save you from being hurt."

I was so angry I didn't even want to talk to her. I said, "Arch? Did you see Adele with Brian Harrington out by the pool last night?"

Sissy caught her breath. Arch snuffled mightily, then coughed again. He said, "Yeah, I guess. So what? I thought she'd tell on me for turning off the security system and sneaking in late from the pool. When she didn't, I didn't tell on her, either."

Ah, playground morality. I said, "You know she fixed your manacles not to work? You should have told me you saw her!" I could hear the scolding in my voice so I stopped. I was so happy to see Arch alive, I couldn't imagine bawling him out.

Arch coughed and tried to clear his throat repeatedly as we jounced and swerved along the road to Aspen Meadow. Whenever he stopped coughing, he sniveled and shivered. Where was I supposed to take him? I felt bad about Schulz. I knew I had to go back and check on him at the Farquhars. Arch's clean, dry clothes would be there, too. But I would only go in if the entire Furman County Sheriff's Department assured me it was safe.

"*Maman,*" said Arch with a loud sniff. "*Comment s'appelle t'elle?*"

"Oh, Arch," I said, "I'm in no mood—"

Sissy said, "This isn't fair. My father's the only one in my family who speaks French."

Arch coughed. He insisted, "*Comment s'appelle t'elle?*"

What was Sissy's name? What kind of question was that? I took a deep breath.

I said, "*Elle s'appelle Sissy.*"

"*Et le surnom?*" Arch persisted. "*En français, s'il vous plaît.*"

I shook my head. Too much stuff going on in one evening. I was not in the mood, not in the mood . . .

Slowly, my mind shifted French gears. I pulled the car over onto a narrow slice of shoulder. I turned with great deliberateness to Sissy. What was the word for stone in French?

I glared at the teenager sitting next to me.

I said, "*Pierre.*"

30.

"Tell me," I said, "was the pseudonym your father's idea?"

She sulked. Said, "No, I got it from a dictionary."

I could feel my voice rising out of control. "Now tell me," I shrieked, "what did I ever do to you?"

Sissy's nostrils flared in indignation. "Julian said he wanted to be a *chef*! He wanted to ask if he could apprentice with you! He was going to do that instead of be a doctor! Of course I had to make you look bad!"

I should have known. The *unfortunately named Goldy Bear*. Julian's *grossly misguided quest*. The undeniably pedantic use of language.

I said, "Sissy, if you are worth anything, which I doubt, I'm going to sue you for it. Now shut up until we get to the Farquhars."

When we got to the end of Sam Snead Lane, lights from police cars flashed importantly at the top of the driveway. The place looked like a carnival. I drove up to the police line and asked for Schulz.

After some conferring between officers, Schulz came walking slowly down the driveway.

"Where did you go?" he demanded. His color was still awful, but his eyes were furious.

"To the school," I said. "To get Arch."

His face softened. "Thank God. Where is he?"

"In the van. He's still pretty cold, and he has an awful cough. Did you find Adele?"

He rubbed his forehead. His tone was weary. "Yes and no. She got out on I-70, turned off her lights, made a U-turn on the median. Hightailed it back here. She's in that damn storage area screaming about a detonator. They're trying to talk to her."

My heart quaked with fear for Bo. "What about the general—"

"He's okay, on his way to Denver in an ambulance. Soon as he recovers we're going to book him."

"Oh, that's nice. For what?"

"For breaking every explosives-storage law on the books, thank you very much."

There was some shouting from the top of the driveway. A wave of police officers came running out toward their vehicles, shouting about clearing the area.

Suddenly there was a flash and a boom. We were all thrown to the cement. Booms, hisses, more booms. I covered my head and hoped that the van had not been hit by a rocket-propelled grenade. Light erupted and then abruptly went out. The booms wouldn't stop.

There was a great roar. The garage was on fire. Debris showered around us: the remains of the magazine. There was one final, terrible explosion, then a silence, broken only by the crackle of the fire and my ragged breathing.

"Arch!" I cried. Schulz grabbed for me, but missed. I ran back to the van. It had survived the explosion. As I was about to open the door I heard a loud meow and felt a wad of fur dash between my legs. I looked down at Scout. I scooped up the cat and climbed into the van.

Sissy looked at me wide-eyed. Her wet hair was disheveled, her face white with fear. "Adele?"

"I'm sorry," I said. I handed her the cat. Wordlessly, she opened the van door and climbed out holding Scout.

Arch was coughing, choking. His chest heaved. He was having trouble breathing. *Why, why, why?* I asked myself.

"Breathe for me, Arch. Take deep breaths," I ordered. He wheezed and coughed. His history of virally induced asthma made this doubly frightening. He must have aspirated pool water. I gave myself a mental kick. This happened all the time to river rafters. The raft would capsize in rapids and rafters would aspirate river water. After initial coughing and gagging, they would appear to be fine. But water could get trapped in the air side of the lung wall, and an hour after being pulled out of the water, they drowned.

Arch wheezed and could not get his breath. He gasped wildly before he went unconscious. I catapulted backward out of the van and went shrieking up to Schulz for help.

After some initial confusion, a medic pulled Arch out and began to work on him in the driveway. He cleared out the airway while a second medic put in a call to Lutheran Hospital for permission to intubate. Once the medic got the permission, he checked with a laryngoscope and put down an endotracheal tube. *Breathe, breathe,* I prayed. The EMS team hooked Arch up to oxygen from their truck, then shooed me away.

I told somebody to call Dr. John Richard Korman. I knelt down on the side of the driveway, aware for the first time in the last hour that cold wet clothes clung to my skin. There were people all around; I ignored them. All of them except for Schulz, who sat down heavily beside me and put two clean sweat suits in my hands.

I said, "I'm a terrible mother."

Schulz said, "You are a wonderful mother. Now I risked my life getting these dry clothes for you and Arch, why don't you find some place to put them on?"

My arms reached for Schulz's large body. While my head was buried in his shoulder he murmured, "Well, look who's here."

I jerked back and whirled to face a very disheveled Julian Teller dressed in camouflage gear. He flopped down beside us. After a moment he said, "I was on my way back here when I saw the explosions."

I could think of nothing to say. I was aware that I was shivering. At that moment a member of the EMS team trotted up. He looked very serious. I braced myself.

He said, "Your son has gained consciousness. He pulled the tube out! He's breathing okay now, but we've got to take him down to Lutheran for twenty-four hours' observation." I nodded and handed him the kid-size sweat suit.

Schulz said, "Let's go."

I pulled myself together enough to ask the cop in charge to call Marla Korman with the bad news about her sister. Then I asked Schulz if he was feeling well enough to drive. He smiled and muttered a macho response I was glad not to catch. I climbed into the back to change. With Sissy gone, Julian sat in the passenger seat, and the three of us took off in the van behind the EMS ambulance.

There was the usual flurry at the hospital. Despite the dry clothes, Arch kept shivering, so I asked for heated blankets from the warming cabinet and got them. The EMS guys had started him on an IV, in case the hospital needed to give him antibiotics, antiwheezing meds, or vasoconstrictors if he dropped into shock. I knew I had to call John Richard, but I couldn't leave Arch's side just yet. After chest X-rays and blood-gas tests, they finally settled him into a private room in the Pediatric Observation area. I would let John Richard pick up the tab.

Despite much protestation from Arch, Julian and I tucked a cocoon of blankets around him. Tom Schulz moved chairs in for us all and then went in search of a vending machine. Within ten minutes he was back with a cardboard tray with four cups: one filled with water and three with steaming hot chocolate. Schulz mumbled an apology to Arch that the nurse had said clear liquids only. Arch smiled and said Schulz could buy him a milkshake when he got out of this place. Then he tossed off the pile of blankets and sat up to receive the water from Schulz's big hands.

"You should be down in the ER being treated with activated charcoal to get out the rest of that cantharidin," I chided Schulz.

He raised those wonderful tentlike bushy eyebrows at me, reached into his pocket, and pulled out some aspirin-shaped tablets. "Speaking of which," he said, "a nurse in the ER gave me some when I identified myself and told her what happened. We can take it together."

I groaned, but took my medicine. Anything tastes good when you wash it down with chocolate.

Then Schulz handed Julian a cup and demanded, "What happened to you?"

Julian sipped. He said, "When I was doing some filing for the general, I found that letter from the Utah Bureau of Vital Records. It was a shock. I ran away . . . to think." He told us briefly that he had seen the magazine erupt on his way back from Flicker Ridge, where he was going to practice camping skills the general had taught him the night he was supposed to have a date with Sissy. "I didn't want anybody to know I might take off," he said. "But I decided to come back. When I saw the explosions I knew there was only one place . . ."

I told him Adele was gone. I said, "I'm sorry about Adele and Brian. Your . . . parents—"

He said, "My parents are in Utah." He paused. Dirt crusted along his hairline; he looked haggard. Arch gave Julian his adoring attention. Julian said, "Where's Bo?"

I told him. He sighed wearily. He said, "I really liked the general. I'd like to help him. You know, like be his support person when he's going through his trial. That's what Dr. Miller was always telling me. Everybody needs support."

I said nothing. I had tried to be supportive of Julian, but it had never worked out. And maybe Philip Miller had tried to be supportive of me. That had not worked out either, despite what may have been his intent. I conjured up Philip's face. With some effort, I willed forgiveness.

After a moment Julian turned to me. He said, "My scholarship at Elk Park runs through next year. I'd like to finish there. But I need a place to live and a part-time job." He eyed me. His scalp under the bleached, clipped hair was covered with dried mud, like soil between parched rows of corn. There were dark smudges under his eyes. He put his cup down. I looked at Schulz, who raised his eyebrows.

Julian went on, "You had a boarder once, Sissy told me. I know I'm not real . . . sophisticated."

"Julian—"

"Let me finish. I'm asking if you would hire me to help cater. Teach me, like. Let me rent a room in your house. Please?" Before I could answer, he looked up at Arch and grinned. "I could help you with Arch, too. He likes me."

We were all silent.

After a while Schulz said, "If she says no, you can come live with me."

I said, "She's not going to say no."

Arch indicated he needed help getting into the bathroom, and Julian jumped to his aid. I looked at my watch. Time to phone John Richard.

I was almost as surprised to reach John Richard at his house as he was to hear I was at the hospital. I told him Arch was fine, but that the Farquhars' house had exploded. He demanded to know what the hell was going on, why the hysterical phone calls saying Arch was missing, unconscious, why the devil couldn't I—

I said, "You owe me."

He was stunned into silence. "Owe you what?"

"Listen. Why did I have to go to the Farquhars in the first place? Because of you. You were jealous of Philip Miller. You tried to intimidate me."

The Jerk began to say, "Excuse me—"

"You owe me," I pressed on, "and you can either make it up to me now in terms of dollars and cents or you can wait for me to haul your stupid ass into court for breaking a bunch of flowerpots. That ought to be great publicity for your precious medical practice."

The Jerk hesitated. I could feel his rage through the telephone wire. He said, "What do you want?"

Well, it didn't take a corporate accountant to figure that one. I said, "I need money for two things. Number one, I've already started to put in a security system. You can pay for it. Number two, I need to change my name."

He said, "Again?"

I told him briefly about George Pettigrew and Three Bears Catering, and that I needed money for legal fees.

"How much?"

I said, "I'll send you the bill," and hung up.

Arch came out of the bathroom. Julian helped him back into bed and resettled the IV. Then they silently toasted each other with their cups of cocoa and water. Schulz took my hand and held it determinedly. I asked him if he was feeling all right and he said he was.

He said, "Just tell me this. How come your ex-husband isn't jealous of me?"

I couldn't help it. I burst out laughing.

Schulz said, "So what are you going to change your name to? Would you consider Schulz?"

Oh my God. Julian gagged on his hot chocolate. I looked at Arch, who tilted his head and gave me a serene smile. I was utterly flabbergasted. Speechless, for once.

Finally I said, "I can't answer that one right now. Let me think about it. Thanks. Sheesh! I don't know what to say."

"Well then," Schulz went on, "for now, how about B-a-e-r? Sounds the same without the grizzly connotation. Of course, you could make it B-a-r-e, but people might get the wrong idea. Schulz has a better ring to it."

I smiled.

"Well," he said, "I'm not going to force the issue."

We were all quiet for a few minutes. I reflected on the people who had come to inhabit my life in the last month. That was what everyone wanted: to force love's issue. Adele and Weezie adored Brian and had tried to make the adoration mutual. I had cherished the illusion that Adele was my friend and confidante. Julian was enamored of Sissy. Sissy in turn had great affection for the idea of being married to a doctor. And I wanted to make Arch love me, so that he would choose to live with me instead of his father.

"Mom," Arch said, as if he were reading my mind. He put down his cup. "I'm sorry I said that about going to live with Dad. I'd like to stay with you. I mean, if you want me to." I got up to hug him. Schulz joined us. Julian held back, but after a moment he put a hand on my shoulder and a hand on Arch's back.

When we were all hugging, Arch said, "Can Julian share my room?"

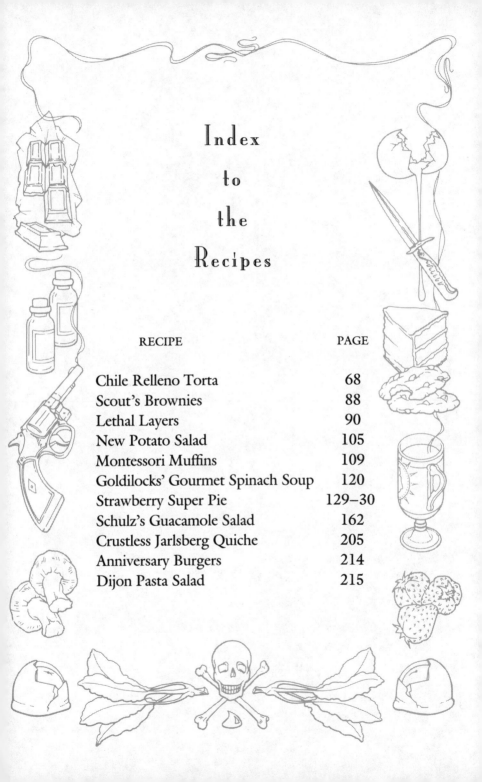

Index
to
the
Recipes